The *Arabian Nights* Reader

Series in Fairy-Tale Studies

General Editor
DONALD HAASE, Wayne State University

Advisory Editors
CRISTINA BACCHILEGA, University of Hawai'i, Mānoa
RUTH B. BOTTIGHEIMER, State University of New York, Stony Brook
NANCY L. CANEPA, Dartmouth College
ISABEL CARDIGOS, University of Algarve
ANNE E. DUGGAN, Wayne State University
JANET LANGLOIS, Wayne State University
ULRICH MARZOLPH, University of Göttingen
CAROLINA FERNÁNDEZ RODRÍGUEZ, University of Oviedo
JOHN STEPHENS, Macquarie University
MARIA TATAR, Harvard University
HOLLY TUCKER, Vanderbilt University
JACK ZIPES, University of Minnesota

A complete listing of the books in this series can be found online at
http://wsupress.wayne.edu

The *Arabian Nights* Reader

Edited by Ulrich Marzolph

WAYNE STATE UNIVERSITY PRESS DETROIT

Manufactured in the United States of America.
10 09 08 07 06 5 4 3 2 1
Library of Congress Cataloging-in-Publication Data
The Arabian Nights reader / edited by Ulrich Marzolph.
p. cm. — (Series in fairy-tale studies)
Includes bibliographical references and index.
ISBN 0-8143-3259-5 (pbk. : alk. paper)
1. Arabian nights. I. Marzolph, Ulrich. II. Series: Fairy-tale studies.
PJ7737.A735 2006
398.22—dc22
2006001977

∞ The paper used in this publication meets the minimum requirements
of the American National Standard for Information Sciences—
Permanence of Paper for Printed Library Materials, ANSI Z39.48-1984.

Contents

Introduction

No work of fiction of "Oriental" provenance has ever had a greater impact on world literature than the collection of tales that in English was initially labeled *The Arabian Nights' Entertainments* and that later came to be known as *The Arabian Nights* or, shorter even, simply *The Nights*. While the collection's long history of origin, transmission, and growth incorporates above all Indian, Iranian, and Arabic tradition, the work was shaped into its presently visible form by European demand and influence after its introduction to the West at the beginning of the eighteenth century. Since then, it has exercised an unprecedented influence in literature as well as in theater, opera, music, painting, and even architecture. In this manner, it has not only shaped the West's perception of the "Orient" as the quintessential "Other" but has also contributed decisively to developing and channeling creative imagination in virtually all areas of human activity. Today, the broad tradition generated by the *Nights* represents a multifarious tapestry peacefully incorporating both a phenomenon of "Oriental" origin and a vibrant and dynamic constituent of Western culture.

General and detailed information about the *Nights* in English is available in a number of surveys, such as, most recently, Robert Irwin's *The Arabian Nights: A Companion* (London: Allen Lane, 1994; reprinted London: I. B. Tauris, 2004) and *The Arabian Nights Encyclopedia* published by Ulrich Marzolph and Richard van Leeuwen (Santa Barbara, CA: ABC-CLIO, 2004). While those works have transformed the results of two centuries of previous research into readable concise information, many of the numerous studies that have been prepared about the *Nights* still deserve to be read in their own right. The present reader, then, offers a limited selection of essay studies aiming to introduce a number of the most relevant items of previous research. Even though research on the *Nights* started early in the nineteenth century, some of the most puzzling aspects of the collection's complex history and character were solved only quite recently, while others remain to be studied in detail. The majority of earlier studies, even though at times presenting groundbreaking contributions, has been superseded by more complete research. In consequence, the present selection focuses on valid findings mostly published during the latter half of the twentieth century. Following an introductory essay on the history of the *Arabian Nights'* reception in research from the nineteenth century onward (Ali 1980), the approaches covered here include studies about the collection's history (Abbott 1949; Goitein 1958; Grotzfeld 1985 and 1996–97; Mahdi 1993), surveys of generical concern (Grunebaum 1942; Heath 1987–88; Todorov 1977), various case studies of single stories (Allen 1984; Bencheikh 1997; Cooperson 1994; Hamori 1974; Mahdi 1984; Molan 1987) and, finally, an essay on the repercussion of the *Nights* in modern Arabic literature (Malti-Douglas 1997).

Muhsin Jassim Ali's 1980 essay takes us back in time to the reception of the *Nights* in research from the nineteenth century onward. The publication of Edward William Lane's translation (1838–40) fueled a lively discussion in contemporary English journals that both contained and initiated scholarly interest in the *Nights.* Already the (anonymous) critic who published his views in the journal *Athenaeum* developed a significant documentation that must be considered "basic to the foundations upon which subsequent Orientalists have built." Also largely forgotten, but significant in their contemporary context, are John Payne's (1879) early attempt to classify the genres in the *Nights,* and the investigations into the Arabian origin of several European folktales by William Alexander Clouston (1843–96), foreshadowing the nascent discipline of comparative folk narrative research. As Ali rightfully claims, the contributions he surveys "must be numbered among the factors that have exerted a marked influence on modern literary taste for the *Nights.*" In terms of more recent research, Ali proceeds to critique Mia Gerhardt's groundbreaking "literary study of the Thousand and One Nights," *The Art of Story-Telling* (Leiden: Brill, 1963), a work that "has brought to the reader's mind the artistic and literary wealth" of the *Nights* tales. Furthermore, he discusses the views of such famous literary critics as Tzvetan Todorov and John Barth, all of which contributed to creating "a greater awareness of the aesthetic richness of the tales and the complexity of their socio-cultural milieu." Consequently, the significance of his contribution lies in pointing out the close relation between the scholarly interest on the one hand and the ensuing creative activity on the other, an aspect that continues to be relevant to the *Nights* up to the present day.

Nabia Abbot's 1949 essay about a ninth-century fragment of the "Thousand Nights" presents the exhaustive study of a document acquired by the Oriental Institute of the University of Chicago in 1947. Incredible as it may seem, regarding the rarity of early paper documents from the Arab world, the fragmentary document (besides other written items) yields the title page and the first page of the text of a ninth-century version of the *Nights.* Following her diligent reading and translation, Abbot discusses the item's contribution to Arabic paleography and to the history of paper and paper books in early Islam and, most significantly, the relevance of the manuscript for the early history of the *Nights.* Abbot convincingly argues that the document is more than a century older than the earliest reference to the *Nights* previously known and thus constitutes the earliest known factual evidence of the collection's material existence. She then proceeds to posit her finding in the general context of previous knowledge about the early history of the *Nights* and eventually proposes a chronology of the collection's development that has, more or less, remained valid up to the present day.

Solomon D. Goitein's brief communication about "The Oldest Documentary Evidence for the Title *Alf Laila wa-Laila*" (1958) presents a similarly important finding for the history of the *Nights* prior to the oldest preserved manuscript. A manuscript from the Cairo Geniza now preserved at the Bodleian Library in Oxford contains the notebook of a Jewish physician who also sold, bought, and lent out books. The short notice that this man lent out the book *The Thousand and One Nights* to a certain person can be dated to a period ranging from 1155 to 1162. Besides constituting evidence of the collection's elaborate title (which previously supposedly had been *The Thousand Nights*), it thus documents the fact that the book could be borrowed from a bookseller in Cairo around the middle of the twelfth century.

Heinz Grotzfeld (1985) draws attention to the fact that the conclusion of the *Nights* as presented in the "vulgate" version of the printed editions constitutes but one out of a multiplicity of choices. Drawing upon an admirably broad access to various manuscripts of the *Nights*, he argues that the particular recension that later came to be known as ZER (Zotenberg's Egyptian recension) was given "the status of a *canonical text* while other recensions were degraded to the rank of *apocrypha.*" In the neglected conclusions Grotzfeld discusses, Shahrazād either presents varying numbers of children to the king or none at all. In doing so, the redactors of different recensions of the *Nights* varied the weight and characteristics of the ruse employed by Shahrazād the storyteller to save her life. Above all, Grotzfeld's contribution convincingly demonstrates that mainstream solutions to Shahrazād's dilemma only started to dominate with the introduction of the printed editions that reached a much wider circulation than the previously known manuscripts.

The age of the Galland manuscript has constituted one of the most controversially argued points in scholarship since Muhsin Mahdi's edition. While Mahdi himself was convinced that the manuscript dates back to the fourteenth century, Heinz Grotzfeld in his 1996–97 essay presents a detailed discussion of the main point of dissension. This point consists in the dating of a particular coin, the so-called *ashrafī*, that is mentioned in the story told by the Jewish physician in the Hunchback cycle. Drawing on a variety of historical sources in Arabic, Grotzfeld argues this coin to be the *dīnār* minted by al-Ashraf Sayf al-Dīn Barsbāy (1422–37) that met with such a success as to make the name of this coin *ashrafī* (literally: relating to al-Ashraf) synonymous with the respective generic name of *dīnār*. In consequence, the Galland manuscript could not have been copied before the coin gained its popularity some five to ten years after its introduction and was most probably not prepared before the second half of the fifteenth century.

Mahdi's edition of the Galland manuscript of the *Nights* (Leiden: Brill, 1984) constitutes a lasting achievement and an invaluable source of research. For the first time, it makes available the main source text employed by the French scholar for his adapted translation that introduced the *Nights* to world literature. In his study on Galland's sources, Mahdi dutifully criticizes both Galland and some of his successors for mystifying their sources. While Galland never made it clear how many volumes the manuscript in his possession actually had, later scholars even went so far as to compile Arabic manuscripts on their own. Yet, given the fragmentary nature of his original manuscript, Galland also took recourse to fabricating not only missing passages but also complete stories, besides adapting the text to his needs in numerous ways. Presenting his view as an Arab philologist, Mahdi agrees to regard Galland's translation as an "important contribution to the evolution of narrative prose in the West and the Middle East." At the same time, he makes it a point to criticize Western scholars for their uncritical perception of Galland's work as a literary masterpiece, whereas his own research has convinced him that Galland did not "improve the material he borrowed but rather degraded it."

Gustave Edmund von Grunebaum's essay "Greek Form Elements in the Arabian Nights" (1942) is an enlightening contribution to the study of possible relations between Greek literature and the *Nights*. While it is generally accepted that direct translations of Greek fiction into Arabic did not exist (in contrast to the numerous translations in the field of philosophical and scientific texts), Grunebaum argues that the *Nights*, besides the survival of single motifs, owe to classical literature patterns of style and of presentation as well as emotional conventions. This is most evident in the genre of the Greek novel or romance that treats "the fate of two lovers as an organic unit of dramatic composition." While the Near East in its own right has contributed to the formation of the Greek romance above all in terms of "scenery and ethnographical lore," according to Grunebaum style and form patterns in the *Nights* derive from the Greek. Relying on a number of specific tales, Grunebaum specifically points to the convergence of such characteristics as the supreme rule of Fate, sentimental love, and beauty. He concludes his study by listing short references to various other close similarities between Arabic and Greek literature, such as the topos of "Ubi sunt," the elegy for animals, and the obvious importance of rhetoric.

In his highly detailed presentation, Peter Heath (1987–88) deals with romance as one of the most important single genres in the *Nights*. By relying on Tzvetan Todorov's method of literary analysis in three levels (the semantic, the syntactic, and the verbal), Heath discusses a large variety of tales from the *Nights* whose common denomination (on the semantic level) is defined as investigating "the concerns of honor as balanced between the demands of love and social propriety, within the context of Fate." Heath sensitively explores the universe of romantic tales in the *Nights* by constantly referring to the relation between the backdrop of social reality and the image of love conveyed in these tales. While "almost anything is allowed to those who love deep and true," Fate is identified as the "overseer of poetic justice." Protagonists of romances in the *Nights* are often adolescents who tend to suffer a loss or blurring of social status before eventually returning to security. Heath also draws attention to the didactic and entertaining intent of the "narrative voice" in the *Nights*, while in conclusion he refers to the fundamental subliminal function of romances in the *Nights:* they reassure and comfort.

Tzvetan Todorov's essay on "Narrative-Men" (1977; first published in French in 1971), points out a simple yet all the more essential characteristic of the *Nights:* characters are actions, and vice versa—they are both at once, forming an inseparable unity. It has long been acknowledged that narrating in the *Nights* equals survival. This is demonstrated from Shahrazād's basic ruse of storytelling in order to evade execution in the frame story through numerous other tales that altogether constitute the so-called group of ransom-tales. Todorov, in addition, argues that narrating equals living and, in consequence, the absence of narrative signifies death. As the characters are "merely narrative" who must narrate in order to be able to live, their action generates the overwhelming abundance of embedding and embedded tales in the *Nights.* Newly introduced characters in the tales would never be able to confine themselves to a short introduction, *who* they are, but by necessity would delve into a lengthy first-person narrative as the ultimate justification for their being *what* (and *how*) they are. This ingenious device, as Todorov rightly claims, generates "the incessant proliferation of narratives in this marvelous story-machine, the *Arabian Nights.*"

The section of case studies on single stories contained in the *Nights* presents a selection of different approaches. In his discussion of *The Tale of the Three Apples,* Roger Allen (1984) analyses the function of the framing technique that "illustrates clearly the interconnections between the different situations in the story and points towards certain moral conclusions which might be drawn," above all the "none too subtle commentary by Shahrazād herself on the very situation in which she finds herself."

As a sample item of French research available in English translation, Jamel Eddine Bencheikh's diligent interpretation of the tale of ʿAlī b. Bakkār and Shams al-Nahār focuses on the relation between historical and mythical Baghdad as depicted in that tale. While situated in a historical setting, the tale is seen as a social fantasy proving that "climbing the social ladder is perfectly possible in this society." Once more, a story is proven to demonstrate a pivotal moral of the *Nights:* "What could have happened is not less true than what did happen, and vice versa."

The "monstrous births" of the tale of *Aladdin* and, more specifically, its Disneyfied version (1992) as an animated cartoon, are discussed by Michael Cooperson (1994). By relating the Disney feature film to two "classic Arabian fantasy films, Douglas Fairbanks Sr.'s *The Thief of Bagdad* (1924) and Alexander Korda's 1940 film of the same title," Cooperson brilliantly demonstrates not only the various sources of inspiration but also the continuities as well as the shifts in interpretation. What once was a tale about the "effortless acquisition of wealth" in the wake of the Gulf War became a "fantasy of escape from the terrors of apprenticeship" situated in a magic never-never land alienated from its historical implications so as to serve as a playground for Western imagination.

Andras Hamori's 1974 essay interprets the "gloomiest of travelogues," the story of *The City of Brass* as an allegory acting out the "idea of the world as mirage." Incidentally this particular story besides the "orphan tales" of *Aladdin* and *Ali Baba* belongs to the relatively small group of tales from the *Nights* continuing to inspire numerous interpretations up to the present day.

Muhsin Mahdi's 1984 treatment of *The Tale Told by the King's Steward* discusses the creative impact of the compilers of the *Nights* who refashioned a historical tale already contained in the book *al-Faraj ba'd al-shidda* by al-Muhassin al-Tanûkhî (died 994). By shifting its historical setting and systematically removing "from the historical report all details about the historical topography of Baghdad," they transformed "history as something that actually took place" into "fiction as something that could possibly take place but may not have in fact happened."

Peter Molan (1984) studies the tales told by Sinbad the Sailor from a structuralist point of view. He interprets these tales as a "commentary on the ethics of violence" that turns them into a "parable for the instruction of King Shahriyar in self-deception and injustice thus integrating the episodes of the sailor's voyages" within the general frame story of the *Nights.* The underlying moral—or rather "amoral"—message can be read as justifying Sinbad's unjustifiable criminal deeds by the protagonist's ultimate success as demonstrated by his attaining political power as well as commercial success and material wealth.

The last essay to be introduced is Fedwa Malti-Douglas's study of the literary transformation of Shahrazād in modern Arabic literature. Taking as a point of start the fact that "for many a modern critic, Shahrazād becomes the prototypical woman whose existence permits Arab women to speak," Malti-Douglas discusses two feminist reworkings of Shahrazād's tales, by Ethel Johnston Phelps and Nawal El Saadawi. In Phelps's narrative, the "positive female Shahrazād is opposed to the negative ruler" and the ruler's death permits the narrator to become independent: Her ending "glorifies the solitary woman." In contrast, El Saadawi's project recasts the "patriarchal system that pervades the Islamic and Judeo-Christian religious traditions, as it does the Middle East and the West." El Saadawi's complicated metafictional postmodern narrative portrays Shahriyār as a "universal male figure," while Shahrazād is "transformed into a mysterious shadowy figure." The ultimate message of her reworking of Shahrazād's tales is that "politics may vary, places may vary, but sexual politics, we learn, do not." While both revisions of Shahrazād "join forces in their feminist project" by undercutting "the medieval male scribe's agenda," both writers thus offer radically different solutions.

The idea for the present Reader originated in the framework of the *Arabian Nights Encyclopedia*, and my former collaborator Richard van Leeuwen is to be credited with a first suggestion as for which essays to include. The final selection had to consider various arguments, above all the language of publication, as a budget for the translation into English of important contributions toward the study of the *Nights* originally published in languages other than English was not available. As a scholar I strongly advise serious students of the humanities to command a certain range of "old world" languages, including at least German and French, some of whose contributions are truly indispensable for an adequate understanding of the subject concerned. Nevertheless, I am confident that the present selection of English language essays meets the requirements of representing some of the most important contributions to the study of the *Nights* that will be useful for classroom reading as well as satisfying the interest of a general public. As the chronological range of the present selection includes essays published over a period of several decades, some of the opinions voiced might have been modified or even outdated by subsequent research. In that respect, updating some of the minor details mentioned in the various contributions to the present state of the art would have meant writing a new book, a task the present editor has committed himself to by compiling the above mentioned encyclopedia. Readers interested in checking those details are advised to verify the statements of the historical research presented here by referring themselves to the most recent studies. A Web site containing a continuously updated bibliography of modern studies on the *Nights* is soon to be published at the editor's Web site at the *Enzyklopädie des Märchens.* Both the general validity and the inspiring quality of the published statements are not questioned by those minor flaws.

Selections such as the present one may only offer a glimpse of the universe of studies compiled about such a highly influential collection as the *Nights.* It is only natural that other choices than those decided by the present editor might be argued for. Besides incorporating a large variety of tales from a multitude of sources in myriad different ways, the collection has inspired research for the past two centuries. Moreover, it continues to remain an invaluable point of reference for studies in world literature and, more specifically, for the apprehension and appreciation of the "Orient" in its relation to the "West" in a globalized world that at times risks to neglect the inspiring communal forces of transnational narrative.

It is my pleasant duty to acknowledge the help of various individuals and institutions toward the publication of the present Reader. First and foremost, I am grateful to the authors and their respective publishers for their permission to republish their original work. Some of the authors have even generously contributed financially by abstaining from their fees or by pointing out additional sources of funding. Without this assistance, the present Reader would not have materialized. Second, I thank Don Haase as the general editor for consenting to integrate this volume into his series and for his valuable suggestions in making the selection readily accessible. In addition, the involvement of various people at Wayne State University Press is gratefully acknowledged, including above all Kathryn Wildfong. The final manuscript has greatly profited from the meticulous proofreading it was submitted to by Dawn Hall, resulting in a certain amount of adaptation to modern usage or linguistic preferences. Taken together, the collective effort of preparing *The* Arabian Nights *Reader* is certainly much less than the effort of the compilers of the various manuscripts and translations of the original Arabian Nights. Still, it proves—if such a proof was needed—the integrating quality of one of the greatest narrative collections humanity has ever produced.

1 The Growth of Scholarly Interest in the *Arabian Nights*

Muhsin Jassim Ali

Even a casual survey of late nineteenth- and early twentieth-century criticism of Scheherazade's tales will indicate a heavy bias in favor of textual and literary-historical research. Numerous essays have appeared dealing with the literary genesis of the tales and their place in fictional literature. At the close of the century the investigations of August Müller, Nöldeke, Oestrup, and others into the typological, generic, and genetic characteristics of the various layers of the work were widely known.[1] The immediate impact of these researches is manifested not so much in the subsequent critical concern with specific tales and motifs as in the relative disappearance of sweeping generalizations about the composition of the *Nights*, a point that will become obvious in due course. No less influential, but more comprehensive and thorough, is Victor Chauvin's *Bibliographie des ouvrages Arabes*, especially volumes IV–VII.[2] Besides the excellent listing of numerous European editions and imitations, Chauvin supplies exhaustive bibliographic references to Western criticism of the major translations. Soon after its publication, interested scholars embarked on studying the early history of the *Nights* and assessing its impact on world fictional and legendary lore.[3] William E. A. Axon admits, in a review of Lane's version,[4] that "Prof. Victor Chauvin's 'Bibliographie Arabe' is a perfect storehouse of information about the literary history of the 'Thousand and One Nights,' and of the analogues of the tales of which it is composed. It is in this direction we must look

Reprinted from Muhsin Jassim Ali, "The Growth of Scholary Interest in the *Arabian Nights*," *The Muslim World* 70 (1980): 196–212. Reprinted by permission of Blackwell Publishing, Ltd.

for the scientific value of the 'Arabian Nights.'" No less indicative of Chauvin's influence was Macdonald's address of September 23, 1904, to the International Congress of Arts and Sciences at St. Louis. Obviously provoked by Chauvin's meticulous listing of analoguous tales and conventions, Macdonald invoked researchers to inquire more thoroughly into the impact of Arabic fiction on such romances as "Aucassin et Nicolette."[5] Whether seen as part of the rise of academic scholarship or as a manifestation of the evolving taste for the freshness and vitality of folklore and romance, this rather specialized pursuit is a marked advance in the criticism of the *Nights*.

Unlike early nineteenth-century philologists, late eighteenth-century European scholars first embarked on examining and classifying individual stories before attempting to tackle the genealogical implications of the whole work. Their achievement in this respect is significant, for rather than adducing sporadic evidence from one exclusive portion, they wisely began establishing the different layers that form the collection, classifying each according to its prevailing topographical detail and generic characteristics. This endeavor quite legitimately entailed extensive search not only for internal circumstantial or stylistic peculiarities but also for external evidence. Besides Arabic literary histories, Indo-Persian, Babylonian, and Greek documents were investigated to decide the milieu, origin, and possible transmission or migration of specific motifs and story elements. But before sketching the bearings of these efforts on subsequent undertakings, it is worth stressing that late nineteenth-century and modern Oriental scholarship owes more to early and mid-Victorian writings than is readily acknowledged in current bibliographic surveys. It is only proper, therefore, to assess in the following sections the real significance of some Victorian contributions that are developed but not invalidated by later researches.

Insofar as the textual and literary-historical study of the *Nights* is concerned, it is fair to say that landmarks had already been laid down in the first decades of the nineteenth century. Aside from his enduring contribution to the sociological interest in the tales, Edward William Lane's endeavor to establish a sound text still elicits admiration and respect.[6] No less pertinent is the periodical criticism of the years 1838–41, which was mainly provoked by the latter's significant achievement.[7] Within the limits of this overview, it is enough to refer to the *Athenaeum* effort to eludicate the involved history of the *Nights.* Although taking into account the then current views of de Sacy, von Hammer, Schlegel, and Lane, the *Athenaeum* critic was fully aware of the pitfalls of basing final judgments regarding the date of composition on scattered references to historical events.[8] No great value must be set on these allusions in a book that passed into many redactions and underwent a number of omissions, changes, and interpolations. A "careful and critical exmination of the tales," he postulated, "would convince the reader that they were chiefly composed by illiterate persons, unacquainted with the history of their country; and it is unfair, therefore, to assume the accuracy of some particular date referred to, considering the numberless anachronisms contained in the work, and urge it as an argument either in favour or against opinions respecting the authorship, or age when written."[9] Disapproving of Lane's conclusion that the social and cultural setting points to Egyptian origin, the reviewer observed that Islam regulates and models manners and customs in the whole Muslim East, establishing social conformity to which the *Nights* plainly attests. As for the very distinctive Egyptian traits, the reviewer urged that they ought to be seen in the light of the tendency of copyists and compilers to impose their regional predilections on the text.[10]

No less articulate is the critic's discussion of the genealogy of the work. Well acquainted with the Arab's taste for the marvelous and his appetite for storytelling, the *Athenaeum* reviewer acknowledged the existence of some historical romances anterior to the ʿAbbāsid reign. These he distinguished from the *Nights* not only because they depict a chivalrous and warlike atmosphere but also because they make hardly any reference to domestic practices.[11] He regarded these romances as true to the spirit of the pre-Islamic Arabian society. But following on the urban expansion in Iraq, Syria, and Egypt, such tales gave way to a new narrative art that drew quite heavily on bourgeois manners and aspirations. Rather than developing a sociological interpretation of the evolution of the *Nights,* the *Athenaeum* reviewer was, however, bent on proving that the increasing urban demand for entertainment drove storytellers not only to invent or record accounts of adventure and roguery but also to ransack the light literature of neighboring nations. Like contemporary scientists and philologists, Arab storytellers, he argued, must have appropriated a portion of this literature during a period of commercial and cultural expansion. Thus, although largely Arabian and Muslim in spirit and temper, the *Nights* contains some sporadic foreign elements. To round off his genetic criticism of the tales, the reviewer partly sided with von Hammer, concluding that the Indo-Persian *Hezār Afsāneh* (which the Arab historian al-Masᶜūdī had mentioned in *The Golden Meadows*) was "either in whole or in part translated into Arabic, and served as a ground work to the various collections of tales circulated in the East."[12]

Beyond these insights into the early history of the *Nights*, the *Athenaeum* critic came across some external evidence to corroborate the existence in the twelfth century of a work called the *Thousand and One Nights.* His citation from al-Maqqarī's, "History of Spain Under the Moslems"[13] is still included, although without due acknowledgment, among the pertinent documentary findings of von Hammer, Torrey, Ritter, and, lastly, Nabia Abbott.[14] Taken together this significant documentation as well as the reviewer's effort to reconstruct the historical growth of the *Nights* must be considered basic to the foundations upon which subsequent Orientalists have built. Aside from minor disagreements regarding the history and volume of some cycles, such twentieth-century scholars as Littmann, Macdonald, and Nabia Abbott have reached conclusions that are not basically different from those of the *Athenaeum* reviewer. From the Islamized *Hezār Afsāneh*, they conclude, was borrowed the framing tale, around which clustered a few Arabized and numerous genuine Arabian tales that continued to accumulate until the early sixteenth century. The reviewer's method is no less rewarding than the substance of his argument. Rather than confusing the general with the particular and treating the collection as homogeneous, he demonstrated some awareness of the component parts and genres that comprise the whole. By pointing to the need for separating possible interpolations from essential detail, he touched on a topic that has engaged the attention of a number of scholars, ranging from August Müller and Oestrup to Horovitz and Elisséeff.

Another Victorian contribution to modern academic scholarship of the *Nights* is John Payne's classification of the genres that make up its colorful and highly entertaining body. In his study of the history and character of the work, Payne divides the tales into four main categories: histories and romances partly founded on historical data, anecdotes and short accounts concerned with historical figures and daily adventures, romances and romantic fictions of different proportions, and didactic stories. In the section dealing with romantic fiction, Payne distinguishes between three cycles. Apart from the romantic stories that make a free use of the supernatural agency, there are narratives in which the fictional blends with the realistic. More entertaining, however, are the "nouvelles" and tales of roguery to which Payne traced back many medieval European romances.[15] In these classifications, Payne has worked out a basic pattern that later scholars have continued to appropriate in their descriptive critiques of the generic richness of the *Nights*.[16]

A survey of Victorian contributions to modern Oriental scholarship would not be complete, however, without due mention of a number of nineteenth-century attempts to assess not only the impact of the *Nights* on medieval romance but also its probable, although meager, indebtedness to Greek, ancient Egyptian, and Babylonian sources. A few late eighteenth- and early nineteenth-century writers advanced some ideas regarding possible Greek elements in the *Nights.* A century and a half later, the late Gustave von Grunebaum attempted to track down classical conventions in Scheherazade's intricate web. Well-acquainted with Arabic and Greek literatures, von Grunebaum has come to some interesting conclusions concerning the process of borrowing and adapting literary patterns.[17] Similarly, Biblical and Sanskrit scholars have continued to search for relevant echoes in the *Nights* to substantiate their respective views of the transmission and diffusion of folk literature.[18] But whether engendered by late eighteenth-century apologetic admirers of the *Nights* or the Biblical and Orient scholars, this search for foreign elements represents a mere eddy when set beside the more solid tendency to trace Arabian motifs and details in European literature.[19]

Although mainly provoked by Huet's and, later, Warton's speculations on the origin of romance, late eighteenth- and early nineteenth-century attempts to tackle the involved genesis and growth of popular fiction evolved into two different schools. The first accepted the theory of Benfey, Goedeke, Köhler, Nöldeke, and Liebrecht respecting the Oriental origin of a great body of European legendary and fictional lore, whereas the second followed Cox, Dasent, and Max Müller in stressing direct Aryan descent.[20] As far as the present topic is concerned, it is worth mentioning that the most obvious medieval borrowings from Arabic romantic fiction were noticed by such scholars as Henry Weber, Dunlop, Charles Swan, Francis Douce, Keightley, B. E. Pote, and, later, John Payne.[21] But no matter how valuable these writings might be, they were done at a time when comprehensive surveys of the Arab impact on Sicilian and Spanish popular literatures were inaccessible and when the study of folklore was as yet undeveloped. In fact, as late as July 1876, T. F. Crane complained that it was too soon to decide upon matters of transmission and diffusion of popular tales, for the science of folklore had not yet advanced beyond the primary stage of collecting and arranging materials.[22]

In the closing decades of the nineteenth century and with the publication of sound surveys of South European and Asian popular fictions and the appearance of some detailed researches into the typology and semantics of the *Nights*, there has been established a solid foundation for thorough analysis of single themes and motifs. Clouston's investigations into the Arabian origin of several European folk tales must be cited among the prominent developments in the study of the *Nights*.[23] No less rewarding are the writings of Edward Yardley, E. Rehatsek, Henry Charles Coote, W. F. Kirby, Sidney Hartland, and, later, John W. Mackail.[24] Whether tracing the Arabian origin of some motifs, modes, and thematic conventions or examining the process of their migration and diffusion into European literatures, these and other writers have demonstrated keen awareness of the impact of Arabic fiction on European literature. But although many penetrating remarks and sharp insights into the nature of this impact could be gathered from the foregoing surveys to be synthesized and developed into a brillant chapter in comparative literature, modern scholarship has left this field virtually untouched. With this sad situation in mind, Joseph Campbell criticized those occidental literary historians who, while collaborating in "a curious fiction of the virtual nonexistence of our debt beyond the boundaries of Europe," have continued to "rehearse the outdated schoolbook story about the Greeks and the Renaissance."[25]

The foregoing contributions must be numbered among the

factors that have exerted a marked influence on modern literary taste for the *Nights*. Whether substantiating critical inquiries into the amalgam of the tales, stimulating creative use of their thematic and structural properties, or provoking a reaction against the increasing preoccupation with factual detail, academic scholarship has left noticeable traces on some twentieth-century creative and critical writings. While recognizing this influence, we must, however, not assume that modern criticism of the *Nights* has not benefited greatly from relevant Victorian insights. In fact, the main body of twentieth-century criticism builds on and, at times, echoes the patterns of response that I have already discussed. Another point that needs elucidation before sketching some current appraisals of the *Nights* is the cosmopolitan nature of modern criticism. With the collapse of cultural frontiers, it is no longer tenable to speak of a particular English or American response. With such qualifications in mind, we can briefly assess the modern literary reputation of the *Nights*. But within the limitations of this essay, I shall dwell only on some salient features of this interest, focusing at first on literary studies that have drawn directly on academic research before considering the more theoretic appraisals of the work.

Since the publication of late nineteenth-century academic studies of the *Nights*, several literary critics have embarked on making good use of these achievements to develop psychoanalytic, sociological, or general literary critiques. Numerous articles and book-length essays have appeared dealing with individual themes in the *Nights* and pursuing a variety of topics, ranging from its "teachings" and pictures of social conditions to its subtle Freudian implications.[26] As it is beyond the scope of this article to cover these twentieth-century studies, I shall consider only Moffitt Cecil's and Mia Gerhardt's critical estimates of the major generic and literary features of the *Nights*.[27]

In a brief but very penetrating survey of the generic characteristics that distinguish the *Nights* as a work of fiction, Moffitt Cecil has stressed the elemental aspects for which we must look when evaluating the impact of the tales on Western writers. In his analysis of this impact on Edgar Allan Poe, the critic has first established these features before embarking on tracing patterns of borrowing and assimilation in Poe's writings. As it is not part of my concern to appraise Cecil's estimate of Poe's indebtedness, I shall limit my review to his analysis of the inherent richness of the *Nights.* Echoing Leigh Hunt and, among twentieth-century writers, Walter de la Mare, Cecil rightly explains that the narrated event is the center of attraction.[28] Whether exciting wonder and terror or titillating one's desire for wealth and adulation, the story is appealing enough to arouse the listener's curiosity and sustain his interest. A second aspect on which he has dwelt is the casually identified narrator. A fisherman, a trader, or a barber may step in at the most unexpected moments to narrate his own life story, which must always prove more fascinating than the preceding. No less notable is the absolute faith in God. The medieval Arab storyteller draws no lines of demarcation between the natural and the supernatural in a universe that merely stands as one manifestation of God's sovereignty. Hence in Scheherazade's world, the "supernatural, ordinarily hidden from us, might at any moment crowd miraculously over into the sphere of the senses."[29] But although dominating the whole atmosphere, this faith in Providence is not incompatible with ingenuity, cunning, and perseverance. As Sindbad and Morgiana (Ali Baba's female slave) demonstrate, one should benefit to the utmost from these human attributes to avert impending disasters and to turn events to one's own gain.

As far as the main generic aspects of the *Nights* are concerned, it is fair to say that Moffitt Cecil shows acute understanding. When set against the whole discussion of Poe's "Arabesque," his estimate, however, is not comprehensive enough. In justifying Poe's use of the term to describe his own tales, Cecil draws the reader's attention to Poe's acquaintance with medieval Arabic fiction and Islamic theology in general, as well as to his familiarity with the graphic implications of the term. But like all other critics of the *Nights,* Victorian or modern, Cecil fails to stress the applicability of the term "Arabesque" to medieval Arabic fiction. The ʿAbbāsid or medieval storyteller was no less susceptible to the prevailing religious teachings and traditions than his contemporary, the graphic designer. Although the term is still exclusively applied to Islamic geometric, vegetal, calligraphic, and (only occasionally) figural ornaments and designs, its early genesis coincided with the origin and growth of the *Nights.* Its very form (a denaturalized vegetal ornament with leaves spreading from a spiral, interlaced, or undulating main stalk) is also similar to the involuted structure of the *Nights.*[30] Finally, the principles of "Arabesque," such as reciprocal repetition and density, are identical with the stereotyped formulas that begin and end each tale as well as with the abundant detail with which each story abounds.

A more impressive testimony to the value of academic research for the literary critic is Mia Gerhardt's *Art of Storytelling*, mentioned above. Using Littmann's sound edition of the *Nights* and drawing profitably on the outstanding scholarship of Chauvin, Elisséeff, Horovitz, Macdonald, and Oestrup, she has produced the first thorough literary appraisal of the work. Aside from her fair evaluation of the major translations, she has demonstrated a sharp insight and a great deal of meticulousness when analyzing the form and content of the work. She divides the thematic contents into stories of love, crime and travel, fairy tales, and tales of piety and learning. In so doing, Gerhardt supplies a comprehensive survey of the thematic diversity of the *Nights.* As the Haroun cycle forms a major portion in the collection, she has treated it in a separate section, where she dwells with particular care on the caliph's character as well as on the bourgeois substance and the narrative skill displayed in the whole cycle. No less rewarding is her description of the structure of the *Nights.* By pointing to the oblique and witnessing narrative systems employed in the work and classifying the thematic nature of the framing tales, she has brought to the reader's mind the artistic richness and literary wealth of Scheherazade's peerless *Nights.*

While Mia Gerhardt is primarily interested in describing the thematic and technical richness of the work, more theoretic critics have probed into the aesthetics of storytelling. Foremost among these is Tzvetan Todorov. Whether seen as a pure expression of the modernist concern with the intrinsic and total value of the work or as an indirect flowering of late nineteenth-century researches into the generic and typological features of the tales, Tzvetan Todorov's formalist approach to their marvelous element represents a prominent current in modern literary criticism of the *Nights.*[31] His analysis is worth considering at some length because it deals with the aesthetic totality of the *Nights*, its musical blend of form and content.[32]

According to Todorov, the supernatural in the *Nights* is of the "marvelous" rather than the "uncanny" type, for it transcends the laws of reality and plunges into a world of totally different obligations. Todorov classifies the marvellous into three categories: the hyperbolic, the exotic, and the instrumental. Under the first heading, the hyperbolic, he places Sindbad's descriptions of enormous fish, huge birds, and serpents. In such accounts the sailor reports about beings that are "supernatural" only by virtue of their superiority to the commonplace and the familiar. Whether occuring as mere rhetoric or as an observation of strange lands, this element does no excessive violence to reason. From Sindbad's voyages, too, are cited examples to describe the "exotic marvelous." In this case, the listener is supposed to be ignorant of the remote regions that the sailor describes. He has no reason, therefore, to doubt things he is unfamiliar with. The "instrumental marvelous," however, denotes a different genre. As a term, it is applicable to such devices of magical nature as the enchanted carpet and the healing apple in Prince Ahmed's story or the revolving stone in "Ali Baba" (p. 54).

In analyzing the literary function of the "supernatural," Todorov explains that this element involves the collapse of the limits between matter and mind, between the physical and the spiritual. It claims its own conditioning laws that transcend our commonplace explanations of coincidence and chance. He cites the story of the second calender to elaborate on the semantic function of the supernatural. In this tale the realistic theme is sustained as long as the protagonist complies with certain taboos. Soon after violating these, the "supernatural" intervenes in the shape of a wicked genie who is bent on punishing the princess and her amorous companion. According to Todorov, the intrusion of the supernatural is a salient constant in the literature of the fantastic. Rather than merely symbolizing dreams of power, the existence of beings superior to ourselves compensate for "a deficient causality." While most events in our daily life are explained by logical reasoning, many are inexplicable and as such are usually passed off as mere coincidence. Coincidence or chance, however, have no place in the realm of the fantastic, for although we tend to consider the intrusion of the genie upon the amorous frolic a sign of the calender's bad luck, we have to realize that the protagonist himself as well as his listeners consider this intrusion inevitable. To them a conditioning and determining cause is no less so for being of a supernatural order (pp. 107–10).

Todorov assigns another function to the supernatural in imaginative writings. Apart from its literary significance, the supernatural is introduced as a cover to transgress institutionalized censorship or to escape self-imposed taboos. But as the nature of taboos varies from one society to another, the "social" function of the supernatural must be viewed in relation to the moral and religious standards of a given milieu. Thus, when considering the function of the supernatural in the Gothic romance or in the *Nights*, we need to understand that the former was the product of a milieu that was puritanic in its attitude toward sexual love. It should not be surprising, therefore, that in the Gothic romance the supernatural is usually used to elude such inhibitions and taboos. On the other hand, medieval Arabic fiction depicts a society that cherishes rather than condemns sexual love. Hence, the supernatural assumes another function. It is mainly introduced to transgress class distinctions and, thereby, to fulfill the protagonist's wish to marry the princess. In "Aladdin and the Wonderful Lamp," for example, Aladdin's love for the Sultan's daughter "would have remained a dream forever without the intervention of the supernatural forces" (pp. 138, 158–59, 166).

No less engaging is Todorov's discussion of the syntactial function of the supernatural, in which he cites a number of stories where the supernatural intrudes to mobilize the action and to accelerate the narrative. In the story of Kamaralzaman, for instance, the imprisonment of the protagonist in the tower represents a static situation. But as soon as the "jinniya" Maymūna intervenes, "the median disequilibrium" gives way to rapid action (pp. 164–65). The same explanation applies to the second calender's tale, for as long as the prince retains his sobriety and refrains from touching the talisman, he can live happily with the imprisoned princess. Such immobility means, however, the termination of the story, a thing that runs counter to the storyteller's design. To work out a good story, the reciter explains how a glass of wine provokes the prince to violate the ban and touch the genie's talisman, a move that brings about the intrusion of the genie to break the established equilibrium. In this, as in many other tales, the supernatural agency becomes identical with the artist's knack for storytelling. With this fact in mind, Todorov concludes that "every test in which the supernatural occurs is a narrative, for the supernatural event first of all modifies a previous equilibrium" (p. 166).

Different from Todorov's structural approach, but indicative nonetheless of the increasing interest in the elemental charm of Scheherazade's art, are the writings of such critics as Laura Spencer Portor, E. M. Forster, G. K. Chesterton, and P. H. Newby.[33] In his estimate of the irresistible appeal of this art, Newby elaborates on the most obvious thematic dimensions of the tales, stressing the obsession with luck, the belief in the supernatural, and the seeming indulgence in love and money fantasies. In these explications as in his preference for the more realistic tales, Newby repeats what nineteenth-century critics have already said. What is new in his appraisal, however, is the awareness of the storyteller's extreme cynicism and raillery. Rather than mere willful fantasies, Newby traces in the *Nights* thematic patterns that are heavily charged with irony. According to the writer, the storyteller figures throughout as the "keenest mocker" of self-deceptions despite his seeming indulgence in agreeable illusions.

Both Portor and Chesterton were more attracted to the meaning of Scheherazade's experience as a storyteller. Early in the century, Portor regarded Scheherazade's involuted storytelling as no mere narrative thread. It is synonymous with the very magic that permeates the whole work. As magic transforms the commonplace into lovely and majestic forms, so does Scheherazade's imagination recreate enchanting narratives from familiar themes, thereby engaging the Sultan's attention and simultaneously transforming him into a perceptive admirer of literature. Portor's conclusion is not very different from Chesterton's estimate of Scheherazade's aesthetics. In "The Everlasting Nights," Chesterton looks upon the scenes of splendor in the *Nights* as symbols of the richness of life itself: "The richness of gold, silver and jewels is a mere figure and representation of that which is the essential idea, the deep and enduring richness of life." Expounding on this point, he further explains that the "preciousness of emerald and amethyst and sandal-wood is only the parable and expression of the preciousness of stones, dust, and dogs running in the streets." The length of the tales is, therefore, essential to the meaning of the collection, for it signifies the devouring desire for life. As long as Scheherazade can engage the tyrant's attention and arouse his curiosity, she will continue to live:

> The tyrant can sway kingdoms, and command multitudes, but he cannot discover exactly what happened to a fabulous prince or princess unless he asks for it. He has to wait, almost to fawn upon a wretched slave for the fag-end of an old-tale. Never in any other book, perhaps, has such a splendid tribute been offered to the pride and omnipotence of art.

Chesterton was not the only one who dwelt on the aesthetic dimension of Scheherazade's experience. E. M. Forster has already elaborated in his *Aspects of the Novel* on Scheherazade's capacity "to wield the weapon of suspense" in order to avoid her fate.[34] Although recognizing her other qualifications as an accomplished novelist (exquisite descriptions, tolerant judgments, ingenious incidents, advanced morality, vivid delineations of character, and expert knowledge of three Oriental capitals), Forster argues that Scheherazade "only survived because she managed to keep the king wondering what would happen next." Thus, in line with the general drift of his thesis, Forster cites her experience as conclusive testimony to the importance of a well-sustained narrative in novel writing.

No less varied than the preceding theoretic and critical approaches are twentieth-century literary efforts to assimilate and appropriate some Arabic themes and techniques. As it is not part of my intention to cover even the most significant of these, I shall devote the remaining pages to a survey of a number of creative writings that reveal a pattern of relation and reaction to some academic and critical investigations that I have already studied. In such a consummate exercise in Oriental exoticism as Flecker's *Hassan*, for instance, the reader will notice that the author's picture of the caliph is inspired by a late nineteenth-century view of al-Rashīd as less just and wise than Tennyson's idealized hero.[35] Impressed perhaps by Payne's analysis of al-Rashīd's character, Flecker has willfully manipulated his source (the tale of Aladdin Abū 'l-Shāmāt) to present the caliph in a very unfavorable light.[36] An entirely different literary recreation of the Orient is Chesterton's deliberate use in "Lepanto" of a medieval image of the Muslim faith. In reaction against the accumulation of the factual and historical information about Islam and the Arabs, Chesterton in this poem seizes upon an obsolete convention to retain a clerical picture of the Muslim East.[37]

In line with these early literary recreations, but more closely related to their authors' everyday experiences, are the attempts on the part of some modern storytellers to emulate Scheherazade's hypnotic art. Although no less dissatisfied with his reading than was Poe,[38] William Sidney Porter (O. Henry) continued to derive inspiration from the *Nights.* Mainly fascinated by the caliph's role in this collection, Porter reads in the former's nocturnal adventures an expression of the Arabian storyteller's search for subject matter in the streets of Baghdad. These same adventures have suggested to Porter the idea of roaming his own "Bagdad-on-the-Subway" (as he used to call New York), looking for incidents and detail:

> You may be familiar with the history of that glorious and immortal ruler, the caliph Harun Al Rashid, whose wise and beneficent excursions among his people in the city of Bagdad secured him the privilege of relieving so much of their distress. In my humble way I walk in his footsteps. I seek for romance and aventure in city streets—not in ruined castles or in crumbling palaces.[39]

No less attached to Scheherazade's art is John Barth. In his "Dunyazadiad," the genie of storytelling poses throughout as the author's surrogate who draws on Scheherazade's mine of fictional devices.[40] To Barth, setting his surrogate in a remote and alien culture is inevitable, for to escape standardized and stereotyped modes and genres he has to go back to the vital sources of the literary forms.[41] Barth admires the convoluted structure of the *Nights* as a symbol of the very richness of Arabian fiction and a testimony to the creator's fecund imaginativeness.[42] By hypnotizing the reader without letting him into the secret of this seductive art, the storyteller demonstrates a superb narrative skill that must be drawn upon to escape the dry conventions of modern writing.

Although it is too early to attempt an adequate assessment of the main currents in twentieth-century English criticism of the *Nights,* it is hardly too much to suggest that the preceding selections indicate a greater awareness of the aesthetic richness of the tales and the complexity of their socio-cultural milieu. Compared to Victorian literary journalism, a considerable portion of twentieth-century treatment of the tales recognizes their composite nature, a recognition that is manifested at its best in the more or less specialized analyses of specific modes, thematic cycles, and artistic patterns. Along with other reasons, this specialized pursuit informs current impersonal researches and indicates therefore a drastic break from the nineteenth-century reception of the *Arabian Nights.* Although its countless simplified versions still entertain children all over the world, its complete texts attract only the specialist. Thus, for the ethnologist, the sociologist, and the student of aesthetics, the *Nights* is a rich storehouse of information and modes that invites investigation and research.

Notes

1. For a brief bibliographic survey of these, see Enno Littmann, "Alf Layla wa-Layla," E. I., new ed. I, 361; C. Brockelmann, *Geschichte der Arabischen Litteratur*, 2nd ed. (Leiden: E. J. Brill, 1938), II, pp. 72–74; *Suppl.*, II (Leiden: E. J. Brill, 1938), pp. 59–63; and Mia Gerhardt, *The Art of Story Telling* (Leiden: E. J. Brill, 1963), pp. 475–87.

2. Liège: H. Vaillant-Carmanne; Leipzig: O. Harrassowitz, 1900–3.

3. As far as Anglo-American studies are concerned, Duncan Black Macdonald's writings stand among the best scholarly researches in the history of the collection, while the literary accounts of Martha Pike Conant, R. C. Whitford, and William Axon represent early twentieth-century interest in the impact of the *Nights* on English (mainly eighteenth-century) literature. A comparison between Macdonald's output with the latter's brief and hardly exhaustive surveys will tell much about the bias in favor of philological, editorial, and ethnographic research. For Macdonald's writings, see *The Macdonald Presentation Volume*, Essay Index Reprint Ser. (1933; rpt. New York: Books for Libraries Press, 1968), pp. 473–86; and John Jermain Bodine, "The Romanticism of Duncan Black Macdonald," (Ph.D. dissertation, Hartford Seminary Foundation, 1973), pp. 232–44.

4. Bookman, XXXI (March 1907), p. 258.

5. Duncan Black Macdonald, "The Problems of Muhammadanism," *Hartford Seminary Record* XV (Nov. 1904–Aug. 1905), p. 82.

6. See, for example, Gerhardt's comments, *Art of Story Telling*, pp. 62, 252–53.

7. The reviewer for the *Asiatic Journal* n. ser. XXX, no. 117 (Sept.–Dec. 1839), p. 84, was impressed by the growing academic interest in the *Nights*, noticing that it "is becoming more than ever an object of grave attention and research." The reviewer might be C. Forbes Falconer as Burton guessed (see the "Terminal Essay" in the *Burton Club Edition* [no date], X, 87) for he, at times, could hardly be distinguished in style and substance from the *Athenaeum* reviewer of the *Nights* in the late 1830s. The latter was identified

as Falconer by Chauvin, *Bibliographie*, IV, 116. Although Chauvin's reference was to the authorship of the Sept. 28, 1939, item, the reviewer himself made cross-references to his other writings: nos. 572–74 (Oct. 13, 20, 27, 1838), pp. 737–39, 759–60, 773–75, and nos. 622, 624 (Sept. 28, 1839, Oct. 12, 1839), pp. 741–42 and 773–75 respectively.

It is quite possible, however, that Chauvin was mistaken in this identification, for in the late thirties the outstanding Spanish Orientalist Don Pascual de Gayangos (later Minister of Public Education and Senator in Spain) worked as a reviewer of Oriental works for the *Athenaeum*. His citations from manuscript material accessible at the British Museum testify to his authorship of the aforesaid contribution, for during his residence in England the British Museum put him in charge of cataloguing Spanish manuscripts.

8. The views of these philologists and literary historians were widely known at that time. Aside from their original appearance in French and in German, the writings of de Sacy and von Hammer were available in English. De Sacy's discussion of the Syrian origin of the *Nights* appeared in the *Asiatic Journal* XXVIII (July 1829), whereas von Hammer's documentary evidence respecting the genesis of the framing tale appeared in his article, "On Arabian Poetry," *New Monthly Magazine* XIII (Jan. 1820), pp. 15–16, and in the introduction to his version of the *Nights*. Lane's survey of the question of origin and date of composition formed a large portion of the introduction and concluding "Review" to his translation. All these views were discussed by Leigh Hunt, "New Translations of the Arabian Nights," *Westm. Rev.* XXXIII (Oct. 1839), pp. 132–33; B. E. Pote in "Arabian Nights," *Foreign Quarterly Review* XXIV (Oct. 1839), esp. pp. 143–45; and by John Payne, "The Thousand and One Nights," pt. 1, *New Quarterly Magazine* II (Jan. 1879), pp. 154–61. For Schlegel's observations and Henry Torrens's rejoinder, see the latter's "Remarks on M. Schlegel's Objections to the restored editions of the Alif Leilah, or Arabian Nights Entertainment," *Journal of the Asiatic Society* 63 (March 1837), pp. 161–68.

9. *Athenaeum* 572 (Oct. 13, 1838), p. 737.

10. Ibid., 622 (Sept. 28, 1839), p. 742.

11. Ibid., 572 (Oct. 13, 1838), pp. 738–39.

12. Ibid., p. 738. The writer for the *Asiatic Journal* n. ser. XXX, no. 117 (Sept.–Dec. 1839), p. 83, fully developed this point. The *Nights*, he noticed, "is rather a vehicle for stories, partly fixed and partly arbitrary, than a collection fairly deserving, from its constant identity with itself, the name of a distinct work, and the reputation of having wholly emanated from the same inventive mind." As for the foreign elements, he qualified von Hammer's early sweeping conclusion, postulating that a "world there may have been similar to the *Arabian Nights*, whether in Persian, Pahlavi, or Arabic, we will not dispute; but we cannot imagine that this has furnished anything but the ground-world of what we now call the *Arabian Nights*."

13. British Museum MS, no. 7, 334, fol. 136.

14. The citation was transcribed from Ibn Saʿīd who in turn cited it from al-Qurṭubī. See *Athenaeum* 622 (Sept. 28, 1839), p. 742; and Littmann, "Alf Layla wa-Layla," E. I., New ed., I, 361.

15. "The Thousand and One Nights," pt. 2, *New Quarterly Magazine* n. ser. 2 (Apr. 1879), pp. 378–80.

16. See, for instance, Littmann, "Alf Layla wa-Layla," E. I., New ed., I, 363.

17. See, for example, his "Greek Form Elements in the Arabian Nights," *Journal of the American Oriental Society* LXII (1942), pp. 277–92.

18. It is another testimony to the strong hold of the *Nights* on the European mind that around the turn of the century Biblical scholars were exceedingly rapturous to discover that the Biblical story of Ahikar crept into the body of the *Nights.* See, for instance, George A. Barton, "The Story of Ahikar and the Book of Daniel," *American Journal of Semitic Languages and Literatures* XVI (July 1900), pp. 242–47; and Eb. Nestle, "The Story of Ahikar," *Expository Times* X (1898), pp. 276–77. The latter concluded as follows: "Startling as it seemed at first, that a story from the *Thousand and One Nights* should have connexions with our Bible, not as the offspring of a Biblical book, but as an ancestor of it, it is no longer incredible, and this is reason enough for anyone who has his eyes wide open to join in Hutten's sentiment: 'Century, what a joy to live!' "

Schlegel's unsatisfactory discourse on the Sanskrit origin of the *Nights* was echoed in part by Louis H. Gray in "The Sanskrit Novel and the Arabian Nights," *Wiener Zeitschrift für die Kunde des Morgenlandes* XVIII (1904), p. 39–48. In "History as Told in the Arabian Nights," *Westm. Rev.* CXLIII (March 1895), p. 276, J. F. Hewit attempted to prove that the "Arabian Nights is not only a living picture of eastern Mahommedan life, but a storehouse of the unwritten achieves of primeval history derived from the tribal traditions and customs of northern and southern nations." More grounded in Hindu mythology, a writer for the *British and Foreign Review* XI, no. 21 (1840), pp. 224–74, studied the impact of Eastern fiction on European literature. But instead of stressing the influence of the *Nights*, he concluded that most medieval writings "were indebted to the East for many of their findings, and that the Hindus occupy an early and a prominent place in the History of Fiction" (274).

19. In this brief survey, I am mainly concerned with inquiries into the Arabic element in medieval and Renaissance writings. References to probable influences on eighteenth-century literature were too scanty to deserve special attention. Apart from Beattie's remark on Swift's indebtedness to the *Nights* and Goldsmith's allusion to the Arabian origin of Thomas Parnell's "Hermit," there appeared no other significant suggestions. In the nineteenth century and aside from the references to obvious dramatic adaptation, George Brandes devoted a chapter to "The Lake School's Oriental Romanticism," whereas W. A. Clouston and James Mew wrote on Parnell's probable indebtedness to the *Nights* and the Qurʾān. See Brandes's *Main Currents in Nineteenth Century Lit-*

erature IV (1875; rpt. London: Heinemann, 1905), pp. 90–101; William A. Clouston's *Popular Tales and Fictions* (Edinburgh: Blackwood, 1887), I, pp. 27–28; and Mew's "Some Unedited Tales from the 'Arabian Nights,'" *Tinsley's Magazine*, March 1882, pp. 235–36.

20. On Warton and his indebtedness to Huet and Warburton, see Manzalaoui, "Pseudo-Orientalism," in *William Beckfort of Fonthill, 1760–1844, Bicentenary Essays*, ed. Fatma Moussa Mahmoud (1960; 2nd ed. Port Washington, N.Y.: Kennikat Press, 1972), pp. 135–38. Clouston supplies an excellent survey of these two schools in the Introduction to his *Popular Tales.* See also T. F. Crane, "Italian Popular Tales," *North American Review* CXXIII (July 1876), esp. p. 26.

21. For an apt summary of Swan's and Douce's views, see Manzalaoui, "Pseudo-Orientalism," in *Beckfort*, pp. 138–39. For other explications, see Henry Weber, Introduction to *Tales of the East* (Edinburgh: Ballantyne, 1812); John C. Dunlop, *The History of Fiction* (1814; revised by Henry Wilson, London: G. Bell and Sons, 1888), II, pp. 29–30, 39–42, 132, 211, 476–77; Thomas Keightley, *Tale and Popular Fictions* (London: Whittaker, 1834) (esp. on the Perso-Arabian origin of "Cleomades and Claremond," "Peter of Provence and the Fair Maguelone," *Le Notti Piacevoli*, better known as the *Pleasant Nights* of Straparola), pp. 40–127; Pote, "Arabian Nights," *Foreign Quarterly Review* XXIV (Oct. 1839), pp. 144–46; and Payne, "The Thousand and One Nights," *New Quarterly Magazine* n. ser. 2 (Apr. 1879), pt. 2, pp. 379–80.

22. "Italian Popular Tales," *North American Review* CXXIII (July 1876), p. 26.

23. In *Popular Tales and Fictions*, Clouston has quite intelligently discussed the nature of this impact on European literature. While taking into account the theories advanced by other mythologists, he handled the question of influences with great tact. He began establishing the origin of some tales and examining probable ways of transmission. Throughout, he has made good use of preceding investigations into the subject.

24. See Edward Yardley, *The Supernatural in Romantic Fiction* (London: Longman & Green, 1880); E. Rehatsek, "A Few Analogies in 'The Thousand and One Nights' and in Latin Authors," *Journal of the Bombay Branch of the Royal Asiatic Society* XIV (1880), pp. 74–85; Henry Charles Coote, "Folk-Lore the Source of Some of M. Galland's Tales," *Folk-Lore Record* III, pt. 2 (1881), pp. 178–91; W. F. Kirby, "The Forbidden Doors of the Thousand and One Nights," *Folk-Lore Journal* V, pt. 2 (1887), pp. 112–24; E. Sidney Hartland, "The Forbidden Chamber," *Folk-Lore Journal* III, pt. 3 (1885) pp. 193–242; and John W. Mackail, *Lectures on Poetry* (London: Longman & Green, 1911).

25. Joseph Campbell, ed., *The Portable Arabian Nights* (1952; rpt. New York: Viking Press, 1967), pp. 35, 33, respectively.

26. For a good listing of these, see bibliography in Gerhardt, *Art of Story Telling* and *Index Islamicus* and *Supplements*, section XXXVII, "Arabic Literature," subsection "i. Legends and Stories."

27. Cecil's estimate forms part of his study of "Poe's 'Arabesque,'" *Comparative Literature* XVIII (1966), esp. pp. 63–65.

28. See Hunt's "New Translations," *Westm. Rev.* XXXIII (Oct. 1839), pp. 135–36; and for de la Mare, see "The Thousand and One," in his *Pleasures and Speculations* (1940; rpt. New York: Books for Libraries Press, 1960), pp. 71–76.

29. "Poe's 'Arabesque,'" *Comp. Lit.* XVIII (1966), p. 65.

30. On "Arabesque," see E. Kühnel in *E. I.*, new ed. I, pp. 559–61. In *Two Essays on Robert Browning* (Philadelphia: n.p., 1890), Felix E. Schelling devotes one essay to study the Arabesque in Browning's poetry. In this he explains that "Arabesque . . . was an elaborate style of ornamentation used among the earlier saracens or Arabs, in which the most indulgent play of the fancy was permitted, except that a literal interpretation of the second commandment forbade the representation of a living creature therein" (p. 1). Richard A. Moulton beautifully describes this involution in the *Nights* where it "is perfectly carried through; all the dropped threads are regularly recovered, and the whole brought into symmetry," *World Literature* (New York: Macmillan, 1927), p. 307.

31. See *The Fantastic*, trans. Richard Howard, with a Foreword by Robert Scholes (1970; rpt. Ithaca, N.Y.: Cornell University Press, 1975). Further citations will be incorporated in the text.

32. Although not a formalist, Andras Hamori deals with the story of "The Porter and the Three Ladies of Baghdad" from a similar perspective; see *On the Art of Medieval Arabic Literature* (Princeton, N.J.: Princeton University Press, 1974), pp. 164–80.

33. For the essays of Portor, Chesterton, and Newby, see "The Greatest Books of the World: The Arabian Nights," *Woman's Home Companion* XL (Feb. 1913), "The Everlasting Nights," in *The Spice of Life and Other Essays*, ed. Dorothy Collins (Beaconsfield, England: Darwen Finlayson, 1964), pp. 58–60; "The 'Thousand and One Nights,'" *The Listener* 39, Jan. 29, 1948, pp. 178–79, respectively.

34. (1927; rpt. Penguin, 1968), p. 34. Further references are to this and the following page.

35. On Flecker's grounding in Oriental studies, see Geraldine Hodgson, *The Life of James Elroy Flecker* (Oxford: Basil Blackwell, 1925).

36. It is worth mentioning that Yeats strongly disapproved of Flecker's misrepresentation of the caliph's character, condemning *Hassan* as "nothing but the perversity and petulance of the disease from which its author was already fading." In Yeats's opinion, the *Nights* provides sufficient testimony to the amiability and justice of the caliph: "We know Harun ar-Rashid through the *Arabian Nights* alone, and there he is the greatest of all traditional images of generosity and magnanimity"; from "On the Boiler," *Explorations* (London: Macmillan, 1962), pp. 447, 448.

37. See *Collected Poems* (London: Cecil Palmer, 1927), pp. 100–3. Ches-

terton's image of the East is worth contrasting with that of the Kipling. Especially in *Kim*, Kipling manifests some loving intimacy with the Orient that also contrasts quite sharply with the apathetic attitudes of Southey and Moore. In this story, the exotic is absorbed into the homely and the whole picture overflows with liveliness and breathes robust understanding of other manners. After reading the story, the reader may feel, however, that Kipling's view is fixed within the larger imperialist contention that the East is a component part of the British Empire, known and cherished as such. See *Kim* (1908; rpt. London: Macmillan, 1930).

38. Although Poe's "Thousand-and-Second Tale of Scheherazade" is often cited as a parody of Scheherazade's framing tale in the *Nights*, it was meant as "a parable which deplores the plight of the story-teller, Poe himself, in the modern world." After listening with due admiration to her early stories, the King was outraged when she reported modern discoveries and inventions. Consequently, Poe's storyteller was bowstrung. According to Levi Moffitt Cecil, "the bowstringing of the modernized Scheherazade suggests . . . Poe's own failure to gain admiration and support as an author in his day"; "Poe's 'Arabesque,'" *Comp. Lit.* XVIII (1966), pp. 62, 63.

In "A Madison Square Arabian Night," Porter is disillusioned with the public demand for mere amusement. Plumer the painter, who undertakes Scheherazade's role in the same story, explained how, after being a fashionable painter, he suddenly found himself out of business because he "had a knack of bringing out in the face of a portrait the hidden character of the original." People, he concluded, "don't want their secret meanness shown up in a picture"; *The Trimmed Lamp* (New York: Doubleday, 1919), pp. 28, 29.

39. "A Bird of Baghdad," *Strictly Business* (New York: Doubleday, 1919), p. 188.

40. See *Chimera* (New York: Random House, 1972), p. 20.

41. Richard Moulton has already advised students of literature to return to the *Nights*, for "it alone brings us in touch . . . with the process of evolution which built up romance . . . [and as such] has . . . great interest for the student of literary form," *World Literature* (New York: Macmillan, 1927), p. 306.

42. Speaking of this very aspect in an essay of 1940 and citing the framing story of the three ladies of Baghdad as an example, Walter de la Mare makes this adroit remark ("The Thousand and One," *Pleasures and Speculations*, p. 70): "Two black dogs are barbarously beaten with rods, their tears and lamentations are kissed away, the porter, egged on by his betters, addressed but one intrusive little question to the fair ladies, and presto, all but a round dozen of narratives, opening out like incense-breathing water-lilies on some moon-haunted swamp, break one after another into full bloom under our noses."

2 A Ninth-Century Fragment of the "Thousand Nights": New Light on the Early History of the *Arabian Nights*

Nabia Abbott

Introduction

The appearance of Arabic papyri on the American scene is a rare event. Scientific preoccupation with such papyri is even rarer.[1] To the author's best knowledge, only two of America's great universities, Chicago and Michigan, have a working collection of these, the earliest of Islamic documents, and, so far, Michigan has not published any of its collection.

The Oriental Institute of the University of Chicago has acquired, on several occasions since World War I, small but valuable collections of Arabic parchment and paper documents, some of which the present writer has published from time to time. The latest addition to our growing collection was purchased in 1947 through Director Thorkild Jacobsen of the Oriental Institute. The collection, like its predecessors, came out of Egypt, and like them, too, it contains but few early paper documents—6 out of a total 331 pieces. But one of these 6, incredible as it may at first seem, is an early ninth-century fragment of the *Alf Lailah* or "Thousand Nights."

Reprinted from Nabia Abbott, "A Ninth-Century Fragment of the 'Thousand Nights': New Light on the Early History of the *Arabian Nights*," *Journal of Near Eastern Studies* 8 (1949): 129–64. Reprinted by permission of the University of Chicago Press.

Arabic papyri definitely dated or readily datable as of the late seventh and early eighth centuries are generally known to be comparatively rare. But the even greater rarity of known Arabic paper documents dated or datable as of the late eighth and early ninth centuries have received little notice since Karabacek published his pioneer work on the origin and manufacture of paper in the Islamic world of that same period.[2] These rare Islamic documents, papyri or paper, represent either matters of state administration and taxation or some phase of private or commercial correspondence. Furthermore, parchment Qurʾāns excepted, known Arabic manuscripts of *book* or pamphlet length, regardless of the writing materials but dating from this same early period, are even rarer than the abovementioned documents. Unlike these latter, the book manuscripts contain literary text of *ḥadith* or Islamic tradition and related subjects.

The early Moslem world had its light and entertaining literature. But extant manuscripts representative of this class of literary productivity consist of trade or private copies, usually dating from periods considerably later than that of the original work. This is particularly the case in respect to the greatest and best-known compilation of this type of literature, namely, the *Arabian Nights.* The earliest manuscript of the *Nights* hitherto known is dated to about the mid-fifteenth century by scholars best acquainted with the complicated history of the known manuscripts of the *Nights.*[3] Controversial problems relative to the origin, content, and early literary history of the *Nights* have challenged eminent Arabists for several generations. The discovery, therefore, of a *paper* manuscript fragment, aged and tattered, but one that yields nevertheless the title page and the first page of the text of a ninth-century version of the *Nights* is an event of major importance. It presents us with the earliest known extant paper book in Islam and with a date of prime significance for the early history of the *Nights.* This being the case, it is thought best not to delay the publication of the fragment until the completion of a volume of Arabic papyri in the Oriental Institute now in its initial stages of preparation. We shall proceed, therefore, first to the task of decipherment and translation, follow up with a discussion of the contribution of the piece to Arabic paleography and to the history of paper and paper books in early Islam, and conclude with a section on the significance of the manuscript for the early history of the *Arabian Nights.*

I

Oriental Institute No. 17618

Description. Two joined folios of light-brown paper of fine texture, discolored in part and considerably damaged with much of the lower half of both folios lost. 24.2 x 13 cm. Reference to the manuscript will be by page rather than by folio.

Contents. The manuscript contains six distinctly different entries, the chronological order of which, judged by the factors of space relationships, the different types of scripts, and the overlapping of the inks, seems to be as follows:

1. The *Alf Lailah* or "Thousand Nights" fragment
2. Scattered phrases on pages 2 and 3
3. Outline drawing of the figure of a man on page 2
4. A second group of scattered phrases in different hands on page 2
5. Rough draft of a letter on page 1
6. Formulas of legal testimony dated Ṣafar A.H. 266/October, A.D. 879 written on the margins of all four pages

These will be considered below in the above order.

1. The "Thousand Nights" Fragment

The two folios on hand consist of the flyleaf, originally blank, and the first folio of the "Thousand Nights." The latter, in its turn, consists of the title page and the first page of text. Reference to the fragment will be by page rather than by folio.

Script. The script of this first entry on our pages is an excellent sample of the good book hand of the early Moslem world. It bears, in general, an overall resemblance to the so-called *kūfic-naskhī* of the book hand of the third century of Islam. It is best described as a script in which the angularity of letters generally associated with the *kūfic* script and the cursiveness usually credited to the *naskhī* script are both present to a degree. It is a light but well-schooled hand used at the time primarily for the smaller Qurʾāns[4] and occasionally for other valued works of a religious[5] and linguistic character.[6] On the other hand, the script bears a marked general resemblance to the Christian Arabic writing of the same century evolved in the Asiatic provinces of Islam under the influence of the Syriac script.[7] The main factor to note in this connection is the tendency to give the vertical strokes, particularly those of the *alif* and *l*, somewhat of the wave that is found in the Syriac script. However, when it comes to a closer analysis of the script and of the individual letters and their valued forms, the script of the "Nights" finds no close parallel in either the Islamic or Christian book hand now extant. This is not surprising, for the "Nights" manuscript is most probably the oldest Arabic book extant to come out of the Asiatic provinces if not indeed the oldest book extant of all Islam, the Qurʾāns alone excepted. We will return later to the question of the "where" and the "when" of the present manuscript after its several texts have yielded their contribution to the answers sought.

In the present entry of the manuscript, the fairly rounded letters are, for the most part, distinctly formed and, up to a point, carefully executed. Letter forms of special interest are the two *alifs*—that with and that without the bend to the right. The horizontal stroke of the second form varies considerably in extent as seen, for example, in the *basmalah* or invocation formula heading the text. Also to be noted is the use of the two forms of final *y*—that with a loop to the left and that with a horizontal stroke reversed to the right. Initial *m* has a number of minutely differentiated forms that play no mean roles in the decipherment of the text. The two letters that are most readily confused and confusing, because they are least carefully differentiated both as to form and size, are the final *n* and *r*. The *hamzah* is not indicated.

Diacritical points are used sparingly except in the first few lines of the text. Where a letter calls for two or three points these are neither consistently grouped together, nor are they accurately placed above or below the letter to which they belong. Dotted letters are, in the order of the Arabic alphabet, *b*, *t*, *j*, *z*, *ḍ*, *ẓ*, *f*, *q* (*qāf*), *n*, and *y*.

A further characteristic of the script as a whole needs to be especially emphasized, as it is not only a marked feature of all early Arabic writing, but it also plays a decisive role in the decipherment of one particularly significant word in the piece. This is the practice of writing the vertical stroke of the *alif* and of the *l* downward, regardless of these letters' position in the word.

Text
(Pls. I and II)

a) The title page:

(1) كـتـاب
(2) فيه حـذيث
(3) الف ليلة لاحول
(4) ولا قوة الا باللـه ا
(5) لعلى العـظيم

(1) A book
(2) of tales from a
(3) Thousand Nights. There is neither strength
(4) nor power except in God the
(5) Highest, the Mightiest.

Comments. It is to be noted that the title is not كتاب الف ليلة, "Book of a Thousand Nights," or كتاب حديث الف ليلة "Book of the Tales of a Thousand Nights," both of which would indicate the entire "Thousand Nights" collection of tales. The translation of the title as given above describes accurately the nature of the volume to which the present fragment originally belonged, namely, a volume containing selected tales from the "Thousand Nights." We will return later to the consideration of the significance of this fact for the early history of the *Nights*.

The paleography of these few short lines calls for but little comment over and above the observation already made under the general heading of "Script." Note should be taken of the triangular form of the final *h* of *lailah* in line 3, particularly the initial slanted stroke of the letter. This is to be contrasted with the corresponding, but in this case perpendicular, stroke in the *h* of *Allah* in line 4. Both forms appear in the text on the following page. The division of a word at the end of a line, as in line 4, is another well-known practice among the scribes of the first centuries of Islam. It is generally common when the initial letter of the word is either separate, as in the present case, or one of the letters of the alphabet that may not be joined to the letter following, for example, *dāl*, *dhāl*, etc.

b) Text of the "Thousand Nights":

(1) بسم الله الرحمن الرحيم
(2) ليلة
(3) فلما كانت تلك ال(ل)يلة القابلة
(4) قالت دينازاد يام(ل)ذتى ان كنت
(5) غير نايمة تحدثينى بالحديت
(6) الذى اوعدتينى به واضربى (المثل) عن ا
(7) لفضل والنقص والحول والجهل
(8) والسخا والبخل والشجاعة والجبن
(9) [ي]كون فى الانسان غريزة او طريفة
(10) [او] يخص معلمه او ادب شامى
(11) [او اع]رابى
(12) فحدثتها شبرازاد بحد]يث فيه حسن ظريف
(13) عن فلان ال ? [وذ]كره
(14) فت]صر احق من لم
(15) [الا امكر منهم
[traces only at the end of line] (16)

Translation

(1) In the name of Allah the Merciful, the Compassionate.
(2) NIGHT
(3) And when it was the following night
(4) said Dīnāzād, "O my Delectable One, if you are
(5) not asleep, relate to me the tale
(6) which you promised me and quote striking examples of the
(7) excellencies and shortcomings, the cunning and stupidity
(8) the generosity and avarice, and the courage and cowardice
(9) that are in man, instinctive or acquired

(10) or pertain to his distinctive characteristics or to courtly manners, Syrian
(11) or Bedouin.
(12) [And Shīrāzād related to her a ta]le of elegant beauty
(13) [of So-and-So the ? and] his [f]ame (or [c]raft)
(14) [sh]e becomes more worthy than they who are (or do) not
(15) [or] else more crafty (or malicious) than they.
(16) [(traces only at the end of the line)]

Comments, Lines 1–5. Although our scribe uses the diacritical points liberally in the first few lines of the text, he is not always particularly careful about placing them with the letters to which they belong, nor is he consistent about their group spacing: the two dots of *t* in *tilk* are far apart, and the first dot is too far out to the right; the dots of *y* in *lailah* are even farther apart, with the second dot too much to the left and so falling before the adjoining *h;* again, the two dots of *y* in *Dīnāzād*, though each is quite distinct, are crowded together and allowed to fall below the preceding *d.* Both these dots and the one above *z* are faint, but clear nevertheless. Note the use of the *y* for *hamzah* in *nāʾimah* of line 5. The omission of the second *l* in *al-lailah* of line 3 is obviously a scribal error.

Line 6. Note especially the separate reversed *y* in *al-ladhī.* The *alif* at the end of the line is similar to that of *al-raḥīm* in line 1. Attention has already been drawn, under the general characterization of the script, to the early practice of splitting a word at the end of a line. The phrase اصربى عن offers some difficulty. If one is strictly to follow the great majority of the dictionaries, the phrases should be translated as "leave aside," or "turn away," or "depart from." But quite obviously such a meaning in the present context would be strange indeed. It is extremely improbable that Dīnāzād in requesting a story should instruct the storyteller to set aside so inclusive a list of such good story materials and at the same time stop short of specifying the type of story she actually desired. Lane (*Lexicon*, "*ḍaraba,*" p. 1780, col. *c*) quotes the *Asās* of Zamakhsharī and after him the *Tāj al-ʿArūs* as explaining the phrase اصرب عنه to mean عَرَّف, "to inform about (a thing or person)," which meaning fits very well with our text. Lane, however, proceeds to point out that this is a scribal error for عرف عنه,

"to abstain from." While this error could very well be, one still cannot help wondering if it really is so, in view of the applicability of عزف عن to the present text. Be that as it may, the Arabic ضرب, as its English equivalent "to beat," is very rich in idiomatic usage. One could conceivably translate اضربي عن as "beat about"—whence beat about the bush—in the sense of "approach indirectly" as one does in a story meant to entertain in contrast with the more lucid scientific treatment of the theme of the story. Perhaps the difficulty should be resolved by assuming that المثل, "parable," "proverb," "Example," has dropped by scribal error—as the *l* of *al-lailah* in line 3—from the phrase.

Line 7. The upper stroke of the *ḍ* of the first word is very faint. The first reconstruction to suggest itself for the broken third word of the line was الحكمة. However, further examination brought to light a separate *l* as the final letter of the word and also the remaining traces of the head of the *w*.

Lines 8–9. Note the absence of *hamzah* in *sakhāʾ* of line 8. Space permits the reconstruction of only one letter at the beginning of line 9, which must obviously be a *y*. The last word of the line, like that of line 8, is crowded for space resulting in the almost miniature size of the first three letters of the word, particularly with respect to the loop of the *ṭ*. This latter should, however, be compared with the not too large loop of *ẓ* of line 12 and the almost equally small loop of *ḍ* of line 6 and ṣ in line 10.

Lines 10–11. As the passage grows, it presents a problem in punctuation and opens up the possibility of more than one rendering. I am grateful to Professor Sprengling for generous and valuable suggestions that have been incorporated in the translation of these lines and in the following comments.[8]

The stroke of the *y* in *yakhuṣṣ* appears too high but is no higher than the stroke of *n* in *insān* of line 9. Its high position above the line is the result of its being placed over the *kh* as in the case of the *b* over the *kh* in *bukhl* of line 8. At first glance the third word of line 10 appears to be بعلمه, "by his learning," in which case it would be referring to man's consciously acquired knowledge in contrast to his natural endowments or his chance environmental acquisitions. However, strong light and a microscope reveal an initial *m*, small and faded but definitely there. This suggests مَعْلَمَهُ, "his particular mark or characteristic." But it is also possible to read مُعْلَمَة and translate this as "cavalier courage" in contrast to "refined or courtly manner." It is possible to punctuate with a semicolon after *maʿlamahu* and link the second verbal clause of line 6 to the last phrase in the paragraph, and render the result as ("and quote striking examples of) courtly manners, Syrian or Bedouin."

The decipherment of the last word of line 10 as *shāmī* calls for some comment. At first sight it looks as though there are but two of the three "teeth" needed for the initial *sh*. But enlarged photographs and careful microscopic examination of the manuscript itself confirmed the writer's suspicion that the scribe, having first written the three-toothed *sh*, lifted his pen to write the *alif* from up downward in the characteristic manner of all the scribes of early Islam—a practice already referred to above under the general heading of "Script." In the crowded space at the end of the line the lower end of this downward stroke of the *alif* overlapped almost all—but not quite all—of the third tooth of the *sh*. The next letter of this word, initial *m*, broken and crowded over the final *y*, is similar to the three *m*'s of the invocation formula in line 1, but is closest to the first of these, namely, the *m* of *bism*. Both these *m*'s have a curved stroke at the right that extends at the top beyond the rest of the head of *m*, instead of either failing to meet the stroke at the left, as in the *m* of line 3, or of meeting it in a neat corner, as in the *m* of line 5.

The extent of the space lost at the beginning of line 11 would seem, at first, to call for more than the restoration given above. But, by actual measurement, the three restored letters, *a*, *w*, and *a*, occupy very little more space—5–6 mm at the most—than the three identical letters written in the very same order in line 10. This extra space can be readily accounted for either by a slight extension of the lower horizontal stroke of one or both *alif*'s or by a very little more spacing between the three separate letters themselves.

Lines 12–15. The partial restoration and translation of these lines are perforce largely a matter of scientific conjecture. They most probably held the definite answer to the Arabicized form of the storyteller's name and to her relationship to Dīnāzād. They certainly held the key to the title and nature of the tale they introduce. All these points will be fully discussed in the third section of the present article.

Line 12. Line 12 permits, at the most, a two- or three-word restoration, depending on the number and size of the letters involved, in addition to the two or three letters of the broken حديث or the more likely بحديث. The reconstructed phrase is given preference over others because it seems to meet the textual, stylistic, and paleographic requirements as indicated by the preceding lines: a new paragraph is introduced with *fa* as in line 3; the storyteller is granting the request of Dīnāzād, who asks: "relate to me the tale," حدثيني بالحديث; the remains of the broken word fit best with the noun, "tale," حديث, and this in turn calls for the most likely verb in this context, namely, "told, related," حدّثت; the feminine pronominal suffix *-ha* seems the most called for under the circumstances, though it must be pointed out that it could be replaced with the plural suffix *-hum*, if one is to keep in mind the interested king who, though not mentioned in the text on hand, is undoubtedly listening, along with Dīnāzād, to the narrator's story. Furthermore, this being the introduction to the first "Night" in this particular copy, the name of the storyteller is definitely called for. Finally, the suggested phrase can be filled in neatly with no smaller letters and no more crowding than are seen in the rest of the line. However, the *f* of the first word and the *b* of the third will have to be written in keeping with the script of the page, namely, not to the right of, but directly above the following *ḥ* as the *t* and *l* over the two *ḥ*'s in line 5, to cite the most relevant of the many comparable instances on the page.

Line 13. Here again any probable reconstruction must take careful note of the space element. The line could have started with فلان بن فلان, "So-and-so the son of So-and-so." But the alternative suggested promises to be more fruitful in the milieu of the *Nights*. For the unnamed hero or villain could be So-and-so "the porter," الحمال, or "the merchant," التاجر, or "the sage," الحكيم, or "the wag," الخليع, or "the minister," الوزير or "the king," الملك, and so forth. It is impossible to determine whether or not the *k* is joined to a preceding letter. The three-letter words *k-r-h* or *t* and *k-z-h* or *t* can be read in more than a dozen ways, as any dictionary will substantiate. But none of these three-letter words seems to fit so well as some of the many possibilities that can be formed when at least one letter, separated or joined, is placed before the *k*. Of the words thus formed ذكره, "his fame," and مكره, "his craft," are preferred for reasons that will be explained below.

Line 14. The ṣ of the first word was originally joined to one or more letters now lost. The feminine prefix *t* could be readily replaced by the masculine *y*. احق, "worthier," could also be read اخف, "lighter"; there is a bare possibility that the *alif* could be a case or adverbial ending belonging with the preceding word. A less likely alternative for لم is a very crowded لهم, "to them," with only part of the lower loop of *h* still remaining.

Line 15. Although the final *r*'s and *n*'s are not sufficiently differentiated in several instances on this one page, *r* seems to be the more probable in comparison with the several *r*'s of lines 13–15 and in contrast with the one *n* of line 14.

2. Scattered Phrases on Pages 2 and 3 (Pls. IV and I respectively)

a) Page 2, upper section, three lines in a fine and careful book hand, but different from that of the *Nights* text:

(1) بسم الله الرحمن الرحيم
(2) نحن اسرتك وانت امامنا كفى بمثلك
(3) بحلمه هادينا.

(1) In the name of Allah, the Merciful, the Compassionate.
(2) We are your kin and you are our leader. It is sufficient for us that one like you
(3) should guide us through his kindly wisdom.

b) Page 3, just below the initial entry on the title page:

(1) كلمة (2) مستحقة فى نظر [المومنين]

(1) A testimony (2) that is deemed proper by the [faithful].

This undoubtedly refers to the statement in lines 3–5 above it.

c) Below these two lines are two separate entries of the phrase بسم الله, each phrase beginning a new line, but the first *Allah* seems to have been altered to الذى with the *y* reversed. The tail end of the bend of the *alif* of the next word is still visible. The line, therefore, most probably consisted of either the usual *basmalah* or else of the slightly less familiar invocation, بسم الذى لا اله الا هو, "In the name of him than whom there is no other god." The second and last phrase seems to stand alone.

The remaining initial phrase of the *basmalah* formula seems to stand alone.

The entries (a) and (b) are neither in the same hand nor yet in the same ink. What they have in common is the pious tone of the phrases and the fact that, except for the earlier text of the *Nights*, both entries have priority to space on their respective pages. The succeeding entries are fitted into the remaining space.

3. Outline of a Figure of a Man (Pl. IV)

Page 2, lower half:

A rough outline of a man's form is crudely drawn in heavy strokes of thick blue-green ink that has grayed with time. This seems to have been filled in later with white paint, which as mixed with the ink gives the latter a greenish blue shade. It is barely possible that a name or short phrase is worked into the strokes on the left side. The misproportioned and dwarfed figure shows the outline of the head, short thick neck, folded arms, and feet that point out sideways in a straight line. Later attempts to wash out the outline of the head were not altogether successful and have left the paper damaged and slightly crinkled from the rubbing. The face is pierced through, leaving a fair-sized hole. This latter was probably intentional and in keeping with the popular belief that orthodox Islam condemned the representation of animate beings.

It seems hardly possible that this crude "work of art" has any relationship to the original, well-written manuscript of the "Nights" that is before us. Furthermore, it is difficult to tell if, when it was first introduced later, it was meant to illustrate some tale or incident in the book. It could conceivably be no more than an amateur's product in an idle moment with scrap paper ready at hand. Spacing and the overlapping of different inks "dates" the figure as "post" the scattered phrases already considered and "pre" the second group of scattered phrases appearing on this same page of the manuscript.

The lone ornament on the left top corner of the opposite page seems to be drawn in the same blue-green ink that was used in the figure.

4. A Second Group of Scattered Phrases in Different Hands (Pl. IV)

Page 2:

a) Roughly circling the head of the figure described above are some short phrases written upside down. They read, from the inner side of the page outward: عجائب, "wonders," الله كبير, "Allah is great," and الكبير الله, "the great one is Allah." The three phrases are in the same shade of ink. The strokes are uneven and the script generally poor.

b) Upper section of page, two lines of text in a later *muṭlaq* common everyday hand in contrast to the book hand of the earlier entry:

(1) قريبك ما للغلبة عنك يصبر ولا
(2) يطبق الصبر ضب محبوب

(1) Your nearest (or dearest) will not patiently endure an adverse change in your relationships;
(2) nor will patience itself endure the loved one's anger.

While there can be no question that the figure preceded the scattered phrases, the relative chronological order of either the figure alone or of the figure and the phrases to the entry below cannot be determined with equal certainty; for here neither the space element nor yet the paleography of the nondescript writing can come to our aid. The odds in favor of either order being about equal, it is preferred to treat entries 5 and 6 in succession for reasons that will be seen presently.

5. Rough Draft of a Letter on Page 1 (Pl. III)

Text

(1) [بسم الله الر حمن] الرحيم
(2) [اطـا]ل الله بقاك
(3) [وادام عز]ك وكرا متك
(4) [واتم نعم]ه عليك
(5) [وزاد فى] احسـانه
(6) [اليك] وعزك فى الدنيا و
(7) [الا]خرة برحمته كتبت اليك
(8) جعلت فداك من انطاكيه
(9) بقدوم اقجمبر مع الفرض
(10) وانا ومن قبلى فى عافية والحمد
(11) لله على ذلك وصلى الله على محمد

Translation

(1) [In the name of Allah, the Merciful,] the Compassionate,
(2) [May Allah] prolong your life
(3) [and continue you in pow]er and grace
(4) [and complete his blessin]gs toward you
(5) [and increase] his benefits
(6) [to you] and honor you in this world and
(7) [the] next by his mercy. I wrote you,
(8) may Allah make me your ransom, from Antioch
(9) of the arrival of Aqjambar together with the soldier's pay
(10) I, myself, and those who are with me are in good health and praise be
(11) to Allah for that. The blessings of Allah be upon Mohammed.

Comments. That this is but a rough copy of a letter and not the actual letter itself is evidenced by several factors. The most important of these latter are that it is still attached to the next folio and that it bears no indication of an address nor yet any signs that it had ever been folded or rolled for mailing, as was the practice of the century. The script, too, is a "rough" specimen of the *muṭlaq* or common variety of nondescript cursive current among the people. It is in a class with the script of (*a*) on page 2, but not identical with it, as a careful comparison of the *alif*'s and the *k*'s in both specimens readily reveals. In the former the head of the *alif* is either straight or shows a slight hook to the right; in the latter, the *alif* is either straight or it and the *l* show a marked hook to the left. Again, the ک in the former consists of two separate pen strokes, the initial د and the added ـ above it; in the letter it is formed in one continuous pen operation as in line 3 and in the *k* of *Antākīa* in line 8.

The greetings of lines 2–7 are among the commonest in use in the correspondence, official or private, of the third century. The present version, however, offers one difficulty, namely, the second word of line 6, which I have assumed to be a scribal error for the usually met with عزّك in similar greetings. If, however, it is to be read as a four-letter word, the following are some of the possibilities: عبّرك, "afford you passage"; عتّدك, "provide for your future"; or perhaps even an incorrect عيذك for عاذك, or اعاذك "afford you protection."

Lines 8–9. The first two words of line 8 are run together. The word read فرض and translated as "soldiers' pay" can also mean either "a share of an inheritance" or "fees"; read as قرض, it means "loan received." Any one of these three renderings can fit in with the text. The reason for giving the preference to "soldiers' pay" will be discussed later in connection with the early history of the *Nights.* For the present it is to be noted that these lines refer to a Turk who is transporting and delivering (army) funds to a second man who had but recently been in Antioch.

6. Formula of a Legal Testimony Dated Ṣafar A.H. 266/October, A.D. 879 (Pls. I–IV)

We come now to the last set of entries on these repeatedly used and much scribbled-over pages. By the time these two folios have reached the hands of a certain Aḥmad ibn Maḥfūẓ, professional witness to formal legal contracts, they had not only parted company with their fellow-folios of the "Nights" but had been deprived of their identity as folios and returned to their original state of a flat sheet of paper—only this time of waste paper. Aḥmad, therefore, proceeded to scribble the formula of his trade—legal testimony—all over the margins of the four pages, and a few more blank spaces available. He seems to have been conscious of the central division of the sheet into pages, though in one instance he disregarded this when he began his formula on the inner margin of page 4 and finished it on the adjoining inner margin of page 1. He was neither careful nor consistent in his scribbled entries, which seem to be the fruits of an idle moment.

The basic form and terminology of the legal formula with its several, but slight, variations are those most commonly met with in the third century of the Hijrah. The script, too, is true to type for the function and the period, though not so neatly executed as in some of the actual legal documents themselves. It is extremely cursive and unduly complicated with unorthodox ligatures. These latter not only join letters that should be left unconnected within the word but also frequently run several words together. Careless abbreviations and the absence of all diacritical points complicate and slow down the task of decipherment, particularly in respect to names and dates. Fortunately, the repetitions and numerous entries, of which there are at least fifteen, provide the opportunity for minute comparisons and repeated checking in respect to both the full name of the witness and the date of his testimony.

It is impossible to determine the order in which Aḥmad made his entries. But inasmuch as this order itself is of no significance for us, the simplest course is to follow the page order of the manuscript.

Page 1: (a) Inner margin, lower half of page:

(1) وشهد احمد بن محفوظ بن احمد الجرهمى على اقرارهما
(2) بجميع ما فى هذا الكتاب وكتب بـ(خـ)ط(ـه)فى اخر صفر

(1) And Aḥmad ibn Maḥfūẓ ibn Aḥmad al-Jurhamī testified to their agreement
(2) to all that is in this document. And he wrote (his testimony) with his own hand, on the last of Ṣafar.

Comments. The writing of الجرهمى is the clearest in this entry. The phrase هذا الكتاب مافى is run together as is also the phrase وكتب بخطه, with بط, serving as an abbreviation for the second word. اخرصفر is likewise run together except for the initial *alif.* These and other ligatures are quite common and will be pointed out only as they first occur. The abbreviations are used less frequently. Both practices are extremely common in third-century legal testimony.[9]

b) Part of the top margin and upper half of the inner margin:

(1) على اقرارهما
(2) بجميع ما فى هذا الكتاب
(3) هذا الكتاب هذا الكتاب

(1) to their agreement
(2) to all that is in the document.
(3) this document this document.

The fourth line in this section is upside down to the three lines above. It is the continuation of the entry of the formula begun on page 4 and will be considered in connection with that page.

It is to be further noted that the phrase هذا الكتاب, "this document," occurs twice more in between lines 8–10 of the preceding letter.

Page 2: (a) Upper margin, last three lines written upside down:

(1) شهد احمد بن محفوظ الجرهمى على اقر[ار]هما
(2) بجميع مافى هذا الكتاب وذلك فى صفر من سنة ست وستين ومئتين
(3) هذا الكتاب فى ت[اريـ]خه هذا الكتاب وكتب بـخ[ط]ه وبت[اريـ]خه

(1) Aḥmad ibn Maḥfūẓ al-Jurhamī, testified to their agreement
(2) to all that is in this document, and that in Ṣafar of the year six and sixty and two-hundred.
(3) this document as of its date. This document with his own hand and as of its date.

Comments. A line in the same ink as the formula runs through the text of line 1. The first five words of line 2 are run together, as are also فى ذلك and سنة ست; these last are at the end of the line, with the rest of the date written right below them with the following وستئين و ligatured. Note the stroke that is meant for the *hamzah* carrier—or more probably here for the tooth of the first *y*—in the last word. The stroke is long enough to be an *alif* in ligature with the following letter. In other words, we have a choice of several common practices of writing the Arabic for "two hundred"— مئتين, مايتين, or ميتين. The unorthodox ligatures met with in this line are not so extreme as in some dates yet to follow. There are very numerous illustrations in early Arabic papyri and papers of this unhappy practice of overcrowding the letters and joining several or all the words of dates meant to be written out in full.[10]

The second part of line 3 is ligatured right through except for the last word. The abbreviations, as already stated, are common.

b) About the middle of the page and toward the outer margin appears the ligatured name of the witness, محفوظ بن احمد احمد بن.

c) Below the above are traces of three lines written upside down:

(1) احم[د] (2) الجر[همى] (3) بجميع ما

(1) Aḥmad (2) al-Jurhamī (3) in all that

These three lines most probably constituted originally the complete formula.

d) Lower inner margin, touching the outline of the figure of the man:

شهد احمد بن محفوظ

Aḥmad ibn Maḥfūẓ testified.

Page 3: The title page of the "Nights."

(a) Upper margin, three lines written upside down:

(1) [شهد] احمد بن محفوظ بن احمد الجرهمى على اقرارهما
(2) [بجميع] ما فى هذا الكتاب وكتب بـخطه فى صفر من سنة ست وستين ومیتین
(3) هذا الكتاب على [illegible] ٢ ٢ [illegible]

(1) Aḥmad ibn Maḥfūẓ ibn Aḥmad al-Jurhamī testified to their agreement
(2) to all that is in this document and he wrote (his testimony) with his own hand in Ṣafar of the year six and sixty and two-hundred.
(3) (See comments below under this line.)

Comments, Lines 1–2. The name, محفوظ, written with the *w* always ligatured to the *ẓ*, is about as clear here as in any of the rest of the entries. Note in the plate the lone word شهد at the end of line 1, not introduced into the text above. The date in line 2 is extremely crowded. Having first written سنة ست و, all ligatured, Aḥmad slides his pen back to start with ستين and then completes the date in the crowded space at the end of the line.

Line 3. This line probably represents two separate "operations," the first of which is definitely linked with line 2 and consists of the clear-cut entry of the date in Coptic letter numerals. This practice of repeating the Arabic date in Greek or Coptic numerals was very common in the Egypt of the third and fourth centuries of the Hijra.[11] The σ, *sigma*, and ϛ, *stau* (digamma in the old Greek alphabet), for 200 and 6, respectively, offer no paleographic difficulty. The middle letter looks as though it might be a γ, *gamma*, or ν, *nu*. Actually however, it represents a known Coptic form of ξ, *xi*, or 60 as seen in other early documents.[12]

The second "operation" of this line relates to the rest of its contents. Here Aḥmad seems to be toying with the phrase, هذا الكتاب, and the word, على, no doubt from the familiar على اقرارهما, as he has toyed with other scattered phrases of the formula in several places in the manuscript. He seems to be doing precisely the same thing with the one Arabic and the several Greco-Coptic letters that follow. The Arabic *s* can be read either as an abbreviation for the word سنة, "year," or as the numeral 60;[13] the two letters following it are, as already seen, the Greco-Coptic numerals for 60 and 200. This still leaves two more letters that look like two *gammas* to be considered. I venture to suggest that these are no more than incomplete forms of the *xi*, or 60, needing but the extended stroke of an adjoining but here absent *sigma* to complete them, as is indeed the case with the two letters preceding them. It is my belief that Aḥmad is here scribbling the different numerals, alone or in combination, of the date 266, just as he scribbles the different words and phrases of the formula.

Page 3: (*b*) Inner margin:

(1) شهد [احمـ]ـد بن محفوظ بن احمد الجرهمى بجميع ما فى
(2) هذا الكتاب من بعد ما قراه [وشـ]ـهد على اقرارهما فى اخر صفر
(3) من سنة ست وستين [وميـ]ـتين

(1) Aḥmad ibn Maḥfūẓ ibn Aḥmad al-Jurhamī testified to all that is in
(2) this document after having read it. He testified to their agreement on the last of Ṣafar
(3) of the year six and sixty and two [hundred].

Comments. The phrase, من بعد ما قراه, introduced just this once in this set, occurs with variations in other testimony formulas.[14] اخر صفر is ligatured and extremely crowded. The date in line 3 is written in two units, the slight break coming between the ست and the ستين.

The last of Ṣafar A.H. 266 corresponds to the twentieth of October, A.D. 879.

c) Lower margin, five fragmentary lines:

(1) شا[هـ]ـد (2) على اقرارهما (3) سنة ست وستـ[ـيـ]ـن (4) شهد احمد
(5) اقرار هما بجميع ما فى هذا الكتاب

(1) testified (2) to their agreement (3) year six and sixty (4) Aḥmad testified
(5) their agreement to all that is in this document

Comments. Lines 1–3 and 4–5 represent two separate entries of the formula. What remains of the fragmentary date in line 3 is run together.

Page 4: The page of the "Nights."

(a) Upper margin, two lines upside down:

(1) شهد احمد بن محفوظ بن احمد الجرهمى
(2) على اقرارهما بجميع مافى هذا الكتاب وذلك فى صفر من سنة ست وستين وميتين

(1) Aḥmad ibn Maḥfūẓ ibn Aḥmad al-Jurhamī testified
(2) to their agreement to all that is in this document and that in Ṣafar of the year six and sixty and two hundred.

Comments. The words صفر من سنة ست are run together. The rest of the date is completed with ستين, "sixty," above this and the ميتين, "two hundred," above this again.

b) Outer margin, two lines, the first of which is broken:

(1) [بجميع] ما فى هذا الكتاب وذلك فى صفر
(2) من سنة ست وس[تين] و[مي]تين [شهد] على

(1) [to all] that is in this document and that in Ṣafar
(2) of the year six and sixty and two hundred. [Testified] to

Comments. The date here looks hopelessly broken, but in reality it offers no more serious difficulties to the experienced eye than any of the other date entries. It is written in three units, the first break in the flow of the pen coming after the first *w* and the second break after the *n* of ستين.

c) Lower margin, three broken lines:

(1) [شهد احمد بن محفوظ بن احمد الجرهمى] بجميع ما فى
(2) [هذا الكتاب شهد] احمد بن محفوظ بن احمد الجرهمى
(3) [على اقرارهما] بجميع ما فى هذا الكتاب

(1) [Aḥmad ibn Maḥfūẓ ibn Aḥmad al-Jurhamī testified] to all that is in
(2) [this document]. Aḥmad ibn Maḥfūẓ ibn Aḥmad al-Jurhamī [testified
(3) to their agreement] to all that is in this document.

Comments. The three lines quite obviously contain two separate entries of the formula. Between the three lines and the text of the "Nights" there is an extended stroke in the same light ink of the formula. It is most probably the final *b* of الكتاب. This would indicate either a very crowded third entry of the formula or a less crowded scribbling of the phrase هذا الكتاب.

d) Inner margin, one line running the length of the page:

شهد احمد بن محفوظ بن احمد الجرهمى على اقرا[ا]هما بجميع ما فى هذا الكتاب
وذلك فى صفر

The rest of the formula is entered on the inner margin of page 1 and consists of the date in Arabic words and Greco-Coptic letter numerals:

من سنة ست وستين ومئتين ϛξσ

Aḥmad ibn Maḥfūẓ ibn Aḥmad al-Jurhamī testified to their agreement to all that is in this document and that in Ṣafar of the year six and sixty and two-hundred, 266.

Comments. The writing of the date is the largest and the clearest of all the date entries. It is in three units, the first break coming after ست, and the second after ستين. The numerals overflow into the unusually large loop of the last *n*. They consist, as in the previous case discussed above, of the numbers *sigma* or 200, *xi* or 60, and *stau* or 6. However, Aḥmad has, in this instance, reversed the order of the six and the sixty. This may be a reflection of the practice, met with sometimes in early Islam, of writing the letter numerals without regard to the relative position of the units and tens.[15] Or, again, it could well be an unconscious reflection of the commoner practice, in reference to the order of the numerals in *spoken* Arabic, namely, two hundred and six and sixty. The Coptic numerals are written from left to right in this same order.

There are here fifteen separate entries of the legal formula exclusive of the several scattered phrases of the same. Seven of these entries provided a complete date, four of which are still preserved in full: manuscript page 2, section (*a*); page 3, section (*a*); and page 4, sections (*a*) and (*d*). The date of the remaining three is but partially preserved: manuscript page 3, sections (*b*) and (*c*), and page 4, section (*b*). But, as already seen, enough of the date of these three is available to make possible the complete restoration of each date as fully written out in words. Furthermore, two of the dates of the complete entries, manuscript page 3, section (*a*), and page 4, section (*d*), are reinforced with the date in Greco-Coptic numerals. Thus we have the year 266 of the Hijrah written no less than nine times in all, while the month of Ṣafar occurs seven times, and the further specification of the last day of Ṣafar is given twice: manuscript page 1, section (*a*) and page 3, section (*b*). These facts lead to a significant conclusion. The double dating along with the terminology and paleography had left no room for doubt in the mind of the writer that the third century was actually the century involved. But with the first realization that Aḥmad was merely practicing the formula of his trade, the possibility that he may have chosen at random some third-century date or dates called for consideration. That Aḥmad should be practicing the writing of dates already passed seemed less probable than that he should be considering a date or dates yet to come. Here again common sense would seem to suggest a time not too far in the future. However, as the decipherment of Aḥmad's entries progressed and the same date, the month and the day occurred repeatedly, it seemed reasonably sure that Aḥmad was actually practicing the formula as he needed it for current use, if not on the last day of Ṣafar, then during that month of the year 266 of the Hijrah, that is, October, A.D. 879. This date, therefore, is here accepted as a *terminus ante quem* for the earlier date of the *Alf Lailah* or "Thousand Nights" text.

II

With the task of decipherment and translation accomplished, the next step is to bring the results, along with other pertinent materials, to bear on the problem of the provenience and the date of the present *paper* manuscript. The questions that need to be answered are the "where" and the "when" of the first entry of the manuscript, namely, the *Alf Lailah* or "Thousand Nights" fragment.

Plate I: Oriental Institute No. 17618, page 3, title page of *Alf Lailah*

Plate II: Oriental Institute No. 17618, page 4, text page of *Alf Lailah*

Plate III: Oriental Institute No. 17618, page 1, private letter

Plate IV: Oriental Institute No. 17618, page 2, figure drawing and scattered entries

First as to the "where." The fact that the manuscript is on paper that had already become waste paper by 266/879 would seem to exclude Egypt as even a remote possibility for consideration as to provenience. For Egypt, the home of the papyrus, continued to use that writing material, almost exclusively, throughout the third century of Islam. It is true that paper as an article of trade was known in Egypt at the time, but the manufacture of paper in that country was introduced in the first half of the fourth century of Islam or the first half of the tenth century of our era.[16] Thus while one might expect a few paper *documents* to come out of third-century Egypt, no one would ever expect the Egypt of the early third century to produce a *paper book* on any subject whatsoever. This is adequately confirmed by the evidence of material remains on hand, for the third-century Arabic *paper* documents so far brought to light number about two dozen,[17] in great contrast to the hundreds, if not indeed the thousands,[18] of Arabic papyrus documents of the same century. On the other hand, the much smaller number of Islamic book manuscripts definitely known to have originated in third-century Egypt are either parchment Qurʾāns or books of traditions written on either parchment or papyrus, while third-century books coming out of the Asiatic provinces are either on parchment or paper. Not only is the present manuscript on paper, like these latter, but it also has closer paleographic affinities with them than it does with the Egyptian group, a fact that will be considered with the question of the "when" of the manuscript.

We must turn our attention, therefore, to the three Asiatic Arab provinces of the early ʿAbbāsid Empire, namely, Ḥijāz, ʿIrāq, and Syria. The first had settled down to being the "sacred province" of Islam. It lagged behind the other two in the production of strictly secular literature. But as the most distinguished province of Arabia proper, its ancient traditions and legendary heroes, both of the desert and of the sown, continued to be rich sources of material and inspiration for the Syrian and ʿIrāqī littérateurs of these fruitful centuries of early Islam. Hence, as the probable provenience of the manuscript, Ḥijāz is the least likely of the three provinces under consideration. The real choice is, therefore, reduced to one between ʿIrāq and Syria.

It is a generally well-known fact that the Persian *Hazār Afsāna* or "Thousand Fanciful Tales" is the starting point in any consideration of the early history of the *Nights*. It is equally well known that it was first translated from Old Persian or Pahlevi into Arabic sometime in the heyday of the early ᶜAbbāsids, who had promoted ᶜIrāq to the imperial province and created and maintained Baghdād as its political and cultural capital. Therefore, all things being equal, ᶜIrāq, rather than Syria, would be the logical choice as the source of our manuscript. But that all things are *not* equal in the case on hand is amply indicated by the manuscript itself.

First we learn from the draft of the letter on the flyleaf of the "Nights" that the manuscript was at that time in the possession of someone who had but recently left Antioch in northern Syria. Again, the manuscript was originally either an extract of selected tales from a then current version of the *Nights* or a new composition or compilation of tales of like character.[19]

The third significant fact is provided by the fragmentary text itself, namely, tales of Syrian and Bedouin Arab origin are singled out for special mention. The Bedouin Arab was, as he is still today, a familiar figure of fact and fiction in all the Arab provinces of the empire. His mention, significant enough for the content of the manuscript, is neither here nor there in considering its place of origin. On the other hand, the mention of Syrian tales is highly significant, for these three facts, namely, the presence in Syria of the owner of the manuscript, the selective nature of the original volume that our fragment represents, and the emphasis in its introductory paragraph on Syrian tales, must be taken together and when so taken clearly point away from ᶜIrāq and to Syria as the answer to the "where" in respect to the origin of the manuscript. Furthermore, it is difficult to consider an ᶜIrāqī origin for so "Syrian" a manuscript when one recalls the long and bitter rivalry, political and cultural, of these two great provinces of early Islam.

A legitimate question to raise at this point is, granted that this "Nights" manuscript originated in Syria, how did it find its way to Egypt? It is seldom that one is able to give more than a general answer to questions of this nature, particularly in reference to a manuscript that is at once so early and so fragmentary. Books, like other desirable articles, found their way across the provincial borders in the company of their owners, be these scholars or book collectors and traders. In the present instance we are fortunate in being able to suggest an extremely likely answer as to the how and when of the transfer of the manuscript from Syria to Egypt.

Aḥmad ibn Ṭūlūn (254–70/868–83), the founder of the Ṭūlūnid vassal dynasty of Egypt, was extremely anxious to expand his dominions at the expense of Syria. He fought, at first, a diplomatic war with the court at Baghdād, then a "cold war" with his immediate rival, Aḥmad ibn al-Mudabbir,[20] on the Egyptian scene itself, and finally broke out in open rebellion in A.H. 264–65, when he and his Turks proceeded to annex Syria. Aḥmad himself participated in the expedition and in Muḥarram of 265/September, A.D. 878 took the lead in the final and complete reduction of the key port city Antioch in northern Syria. After some fighting on the Byzantine border, he moved quickly south to complete the conquest of the entire province before he returned to Egypt that same year of A.H. 265, to nip in the bud the revolt of his own son.[21]

Once more the information in the draft of the letter on the flyleaf of the "Nights" must be put to significant use. In the light of the above historical facts, the mention of Antioch in the letter, the fact that the possessor of the manuscript had but recently left that city, the reference to money received by him as having been recently delivered by Aqjambar, obviously a Turk, and, finally, the appearance of the manuscript itself in Egypt the very next year seem, to the present writer, to total up to a reasonably certain answer to our question. To put it more directly, the manuscript was most probably both a casualty and a price of the war of 264–65 between Egypt and Syria. Broken and misused, it found its way out of Syria in the company of Aḥmad ibn Ṭūlūn's victorious Turkish army returning home to Egypt. It is thanks to this likely mishap and to the soil of Egypt, so kind to ancient documents, that we today are in possession of this fragmentary and most unexpected find with its extremely significant evidence on the early history of the *Nights*.[22]

The answer to the "when" of the origin of our manuscript must take into consideration several related yet distinct sets of facts. The first of these, as in the case of the "where," centers on the writing material, namely, paper. It is desirable, to begin with, to review briefly the history of the use and manufacture of paper in early Islam as that history is known from the literary sources and then to follow this with the testimony of the few extant paper documents and books of the third century.

It is hardly necessary to dwell here on the early Chinese origin of paper or on its spread westward to Khurāsān, where the Arabs first came into contact with it in the second half of the seventh century of our era. But it was not until A.D. 751 in the course of the final subjugation of the province and its great city of Samarqand that Chinese captives in that city were made to yield the trade secrets of paper manufacture to their Arab captors. These latter, not being themselves artisans, set their Persian freedmen to the task of its manufacture.[23] The Chinese evidently produced several types of paper differing in their basic composition from grasses and reeds to mixtures of these with hemp and other plants or to mixtures that included part rag and finally to rag paper proper.[24] The formula(s) that the Chinese passed on to the Arabs at this point is not stated. The Arab sources distinguish their own early product, generally known as Khurāsānian and Samarqandian paper, as linen-rag paper.[25] Microscopic analysis of the hitherto earliest known specimen confirms the statements in the literary sources.[26] Microscopic analysis of the paper of our "Nights" fits in with these known literary and material facts, for it, too, proved to be an all-linen paper.[27]

Although fine-quality Chinese paper continued to be sought after for generations to come, it was the paper of Samarqand that came into widespread use throughout the Asiatic provinces of the empire. It gained rapidly and steadily over the leather and parchments imported from Persia and the papyrus that came from Egypt. Its spectacular victory was accomplished in the last five years of the eighth century when Harūn al-Rashīd and his Barmakid wazirs, the brothers Faḍl and Jaʿfar, patronized the industry, adopted paper for use in the state chancellory,[28] and urged the public to use it for their needs even for Qurʾānic codices.[29] This would seem to indicate that paper had already become generally acceptable for fine books, otherwise it would not have been suggested for Qurʾānic writing.

This did not mean that other writing materials went out of use rapidly, but rather that paper soon became the preferred material[30] in the Asiatic provinces where local factories began to supplement the imported Khurāsānian variety.[31] This being the case, one should expect to find some reference to paper books originating in these parts in the first half of the ninth century.[32] One very significant reference, dating from the reign of Maʾmūn (198–218/813–33), relates to Ḥunain ibn Isḥāq and his secretary-copyist, al-Azraq, whose books, both for content and penmanship, literally commanded their weight in silver dirhams. Therefore, to increase their cash value, these books were "written in large heavy Kūfic letters with lines far apart and on paper that was three to four times the normal thickness of the paper manufactured at the time."[33] There is also the reference to a fine forty-volume work, each volume of two hundred or more pages of the Ṭalḥī variety of Khurāsānian paper—named after Ṭalḥah ibn Ṭāḥir, governor of Khurāsān (207–213/822–28)[34]—written by Mohammed ibn Ḥabīb (d. 245/860) for the wazir Fatḥ ibn Khāqān.[35]

Turning now to the testimony of the few extant third-century paper manuscripts that have so far come to light, one must keep in mind that papyrus and paper documents and books originating in these regions had small prospects, ordinarily, of long survival[36] unless chance, as with our "Nights" manuscript, carried them off to the desert of Sinai or the sands of Egypt. The wonder is not that so few have survived but that any have survived at all. The oldest dated paper manuscript hitherto known is a copy of the *Gharīb al-Ḥadīth* of Abū ʿUbaid al-Qāsim ibn al-Sallām (d. ca. 230/844) of ʿIrāq and Khurāsān. The copy now in Leiden is dated 252/866 and is illustrated in Wright's *Facsimiles*, Plate VI.[37] The only other dated paper book of the third century that has come to my attention is a copy of the *Masāʾil* of Ibn Ḥanbal (d. 241/855) as transmitted by Abū Daʾūd (d. 275/888) and dated 266/879. The manuscript is in the Ẓāhirīyah Library[38] at Damascus where I was recently privileged to see and examine it.[39]

That the Oriental Institute manuscript of the "Nights" is earlier than the last-mentioned book goes without saying. That it is earlier than 252/866 is almost equally apparent, fourteen years being far too few to age a book of its type. Book production of the time was slow and expensive, even when hastily executed by professional scribes from the author's dictation.[40] The script of the "Nights" places it among the more carefully executed and time-consuming enterprises of some author or copyist. This in turn suggests that the copy on hand was an expensive and valued possession long treasured by some owner ere time and misfortune rendered its pages scraps of paper. A conservative estimate would allow some half a century, at the least, for this aging and repeated misuse. This throws back the date of the original manuscript to about the first or, at the most second, decade of the third century of the Hijrah or, roughly, to the first quarter of the ninth century of our era. Thus on the evidence, so far, of the manuscript itself, we have here the oldest known extant *paper book* to come out of the Islamic world.

This leads to the consideration of the extant third-century Arabic books on papyrus and parchment or vellum. The second half of the century yields the *Jāmiʿ* of Ibn Wahb, a collection of Traditions written at Asnā in Egypt on papyrus and dated 276/889. The manuscript has been published in part[41] and is now in the Egyptian National Library at Cairo, where the present writer recently had the pleasure of working with it firsthand. The four other dated Arabic manuscripts from this period are all on parchment or vellum and deal with Christian literature. The first, believed to be the earliest dated Christian Arabic manuscript extant, is a treatise on Christian theology dated 264/872.[42] The second contains lives of saints and ascetic discourses copied in 272/885 by an ʿIrāqī monk in Palestine for a monastery in Mount Sinai.[43] The third is of similar nature written by the same monk in the same year of 272,[44] and the fourth is New Testament material completed in 279/892.[45]

Next to our "Nights," the only other known manuscript that dates from the first half of the third century is a manuscript now in Heidelberg. This is the story of the prophets in the tradition of Wahb ibn Munabbih and his immediate transmitters. It is of Egyptian origin, written on papyrus, and is dated 229/844.[46] Its script bears little resemblance to that of the "Nights." This difference in the scripts of two manuscripts so close together in their dates can be explained, I believe, by the fact that the one is on papyrus and represents a current Egyptian book hand while the other is on paper and represents an early variety of the book hand of the Asiatic provinces. Being also the earliest extant specimen of this latter book hand, the present manuscript affords a new landmark in the study of Arabic paleography.

To sum up our findings: the third century of Islam has yielded hitherto, parchment Qurʾāns excluded, but eight dated Arabic books of either Moslem or Christian origin. Of these, two are on papyrus, dated 229 and 276; two are on paper, dated 252 and 266; and four are on parchment, dated 264, 272, and 279. Therefore, our manuscript of the "Nights," aged and tattered by 266, is certainly older than the paper and parchment manuscripts of 252 and 264, respectively. Furthermore, this manuscript, originating most likely in the earlier decades of the century, as we have tried to show above, emerges, exclusive of parchment Qurʾāns, not only as definitely the earliest Arabic *paper* book known to come down to us out of the Moslem world but also as most probably the earliest known Arabic book extant, regardless of the writing material, to come out of the Arab world, Christian or Moslem.[47]

With continued research and new discoveries, the present manuscript may have to yield, sooner or later, some of its multiple honors. But the one distinction it is least likely to surrender at any time, if ever, is the fact of its being the earliest manuscript extant of the *Alf Lailah* or "Thousand Nights."

III

Thus far this study has been limited more or less to the evidence of the manuscript, direct or inferred, in seeking the answer to the when of this particular fragment of the *Alf Lailah* or "Thousand Nights." But the larger and more complex questions of the relationship of the ancient Persian *Hazār Afsāna* to the *Arabian Nights* and of the early history of the latter bring us to the consideration of the early Arabic sources bearing on these problems. These sources themselves now take on added significance, since they can be checked and supplemented by the very existence of our manuscript at so early a date as well as by its textual contribution. The earliest and most relevant source materials are the well-known passages from Masʿūdī's *Murūj al-Dhahab* and Nadīm's *Fihrist* written in the first and second half of the fourth century of the Hijrah, respectively, or late in the first and second half of the tenth century of our era. Hence, our manuscript is better than a century older than the earliest reference to the *Nights* hitherto known. The literary passages in question have been much quoted and discussed since von Hammer[48] first pointed them out, more than a century ago, as a sequel to Galland's spectacular introduction of *Arabian Nights* to the Western world. They have since formed the basis of searching investigations by such first-rate scholars as de Sacy, Zotenberg, Lane, Nöldeke, Oestrup, Macdonald, and Littmann. It is not intended to outline here the long history of these investigations with the numerous controversies arising out of them in regard to the origin, date, title, frame-work, and content of the early *Nights.*[49] The aim is rather to center the attention primarily on those controversial points on which the present manuscript throws sufficient light either to settle the issue involved or to point to a fresh line of approach in the search for the probable answer.

In the interest of ready reference, it is best to begin with a translation of the source passages referred to above.[50] Variant readings are in square brackets.

> Many of those well acquainted with their *akhbār* (pseudo-historical tales of ᶜAbīd [ᶜUbaid] ibn Sharyah and others of the court of Muᶜāwiyah)[51] state that these *akhbār* are apocryphal, embellished, and fabricated, strung together by those who drew nigh to the kings by relating them and who duped their contemporaries with memorizing and reciting them (as authentic. They state, furthermore), that they are of the same type as the books that have been transmitted to us and translated for us from the Persian [Pahlavi], Indian, and Greek—books composed in like manner as the above mentioned—such as the book of *Hazār Afsāna,* or translated from the Persian to the Arabic of a *Thousand Khurāfāt,* (fantastic tales), for *khurāfa* in Persian is called *afsāna.* The people call this book *A Thousand Nights [and a Night*]. It is the story of the king and the wazir and his daughter and her nurse [or maid, or sister, or the wazir and his two daughters] named Shīrāzād [Shīrazād] and Dīnāzād [Dīnārazād] and such as the *Book of Farza [Jaliᶜad] and Shīmās* and what is in it of the stories of the kings of India and their wazirs. And such as the *Book of Sindbād* and other books of this nature.[52]

The *Fihrist* passage reads as follows:

> The first who made separate compilations of *khurāfāt* into books and placed these latter into libraries and in some gave speaking parts to beasts were the early Persians. Thereafter the Ashghanian kings, who were the third dynasty of kings of Persia, became deeply absorbed in these. Thereafter that (kind of books) increased and spread in the days of the Sassanian kings. The Arabs translated these into the Arabic tongue.

Then the eloquent and the rhetoricians took them in hand and revised them and rewrote them in elegant style and composed, along the same idea, books that resembled them.

The first book that was made along this (*khurāfāt*) idea was the book of *Hazār Afsāna* which means a *Thousand Khurāfāt*. The reason for its composition was that one of their kings whenever he had married a woman and passed a night with her, killed her on the morrow. Presently he married a maiden of royal descent, possessed of understanding and knowledge, who was called Shahrāzād. And when she was first with him, she began telling him *khurāfāt* carrying the story along at the end of the night in such a way as to lead the king to preserve her alive and to ask her on the following night for the completion of the story until she had passed a thousand nights. . . . And the king had a stewardess (*qahramānah*) who was called Dīnārzād and she assisted her in that.

The truth is—Allah willing—that the first to whom stories were told at night was Alexander the Great. He had people who used to make him laugh and tell him *khurāfāt*, not that he was seeking pleasure thereby but only as a means of keeping vigilant and on his guard. After him the kings used for that purpose the book of *Hazār Afsāna*. It contains a thousand nights and less than two hundred night stories, for the narration of a story often lasted through several nights. I have seen it in its entirety several times. It is in reality a worthless book of silly tales.

Ibn ʿAbdūs al-Jahshiyārī, the author of *Kitāb al-Wuzarā*ʾ, began to compile a book in which he made choice of a thousand night-stories, *alf samar*, out of the night-stories of the Arabs, Persians, Greeks, and others, each part independent in itself and unconnected with another. He summoned the tellers of night-stories and took from them the best of what they knew and in which they excelled. Then he selected from books of the night stories and *khurāfāt* what was to his taste and what was superior. So, out of all these, he brought together 480 nights, for each night a complete story consisting of fifty pages, more or less. But death overtook him before he had accomplished his intention of completing (the collection of) a thousand night-stories. I have seen several parts of the collection in the handwriting of Abū al-Ṭaiyib the brother of al-Shāfiʿī.

Now previous to this (activity of Ibn ʿAbdūs) there were a group of men who composed night-stories and *khurāfāt* giving speaking parts to people, birds, and beasts. Among them were ʿAbd Allah ibn al-Muqaffaʿ, Sahl ibn Harūn and ʿAlī ibn Daʾūd the secretary of Zubaidah, and others.[53]

Before going any further with these and other early sources, it is possible to settle definitely, on the evidence of the earlier text of our manuscript, some of the controversies relative to the original title of the *Nights*, to the names of the two women in the frame story, and to these women's relationship each to the other.

First as to the title. Although Masʿūdī and Nadīm both equate a "thousand *afsāna*" with a "thousand *khurāfāt*," neither mentions specifically an Arabic book, translated or original, bearing the title of a *Thousand Khurāfāt*. Furthermore, Masʿūdī states that in his day the Arabic translation of the *Hazār Afsāna* circulated among the people under the Arabic title of *Alf Lailah*. Our manuscript fragment also yields the title *Alf Lailah*. This would seem to indicate that the change from a "thousand *khurāfāt*" to a "thousand nights" was made either at the time of the first translation of the *Hazār Afsāna* or more probably became currently popular soon after. This is understandable if one recalls the leading role originally given to the night in the very inception of the *Hazār Afsāna* and the long tradition of relating at night not only the *khurāfāt* or fantastic tales but also the *akhbār*—or legends and quasi-historical tales—as well as the *asmār* or night-stories proper. These three categories of tales, whatever their distinctive character and precise differences, have, nevertheless, much in common. It is therefore not surprising that they soon came to share the night between them. Perhaps in a moment of passing insight, some of the eloquent rhetoricians referred to in the passage translated above made the change to the appropriate and pleasantly alliterative title of *Alf Laila* or *A Thousand Nights*.[54] It is not clear when this title yielded in turn to the longer *Alf Lailah wa Lailah*, *A Thousand and One Nights*. But inasmuch as the number "a thousand and one" is absent in the *Fihrist* passage quoted, it is improbable that any Arabic book of night-stories bore this longer title before the end of the fourth century of the Hijrah or the tenth century of our era.[55]

It is unfortunate that our fragment does not yield the name of the storyteller herself. However, in giving the dotted form of the name of her companion, it not only settles that issue but also provides a likely clue to the original Persian name of the heroine. It makes certain that the companion's name was Dīn-āzād and not Dunyāzād nor yet Dīnārazād. Furthermore, Dīnāzād is actually met with in the greater number of the manuscripts of Masʿūdī's text, and this usually in combination with Shīrāzād—a fact which led de Sacy to accept these as the original forms.[56] Thus in eliminating Dunyāzād, "World Freer," doubt is thrown on the form neatly coupled with it, namely, Shahrāzād, "City Freer." Two such names could well belong to two sisters, though one would expect the older to be called Dunyāzād and the younger Shahrāzād. But they would hardly be bestowed, in the same household, on the daughter of the house and on her nurse or maid even in this second order, let alone the first. It is to be further noted that in the known manuscripts of Masʿūdī's text, the names Dīnāzād and Shīrāzād are met with more frequently in combination with *dāyah*, "foster-mother" or "wet-nurse" and *jāriyah*, "maid-servant," than with *ukht*, "sister."[57] These names sharing the word *āzād*, "free, pure, noble," between them are distinguished by *dīn*, "religion, faith," and by *shīr*, "lion." One may freely translate Dīnāzād as "of noble religion" or "pure in faith"—a quality much sought after in trusted personal servants for the young—and Shīrāzād as "Lionhearted." The lion itself being the symbol of Persian royalty and courage, this latter name is aptly descriptive of both the royal birth and the outstanding personal courage of the heroine of the *Nights*.

In the Oriental Institute manuscript Dīnāzād addresses the heroine as her "delectable one." Now an older sister may use this and similar romantic terms of endearment toward a younger sister; but in all oriental countries, up to very modern times, etiquette demanded that a younger sister show due respect rather than lighthearted affection in addressing an older sister or any other older person for that matter. On the other hand, wet-nurses and personal maids generally make use of a long list of fantastic and superlative endearments in speaking to or of their precious charges. Thus the use of this early ninth-century fragment of the *Nights* to control[58] and supplement the next earliest reference to the collection, namely, Masʿūdī's account of more than a century later, permits us to conclude that in the earliest Arabic version of the *Nights* the names of the two women in the frame work were Shīrāzād and Dīnāzād and that the latter was almost certainly not a younger sister but an older nurse.[59]

The contribution of the precious fragment so far, significant as it is, is minor in comparison to the light that the manuscript throws on the much wider problems of the origin and early evolution of the *Nights*. Here two major lines of approach need to be followed and explored. The first leads to the consideration of the time and the nature of the first impact of the Persian *Hazār Afsāna* on the Arabic literary world. The second seeks the steps in the subsequent development of the *Nights* up to Nadīm's time, that is, the late tenth century of our era.[60]

The passages Masʿūdī and Nadīm already translated above need to be supplemented at this point with other materials from these same early authors and from a few others. It is Masʿūdī who informs us that the first wave of literary and scientific translation among the Arabs took place in the reign and under the patronage of ʿAbbāsid caliph Manṣūr (A.H. 135–58/A.D. 754–75). Among the books then translated was that of *Kalīlah and Dimnah* which Nadīm includes, along with the *Hazār Afsāna*, in his section on *khurāfāt* and *asmār*.[61] Some of the other books mentioned in these passages as of the same category as the *Hazār Afsāna* are also known to have been translated in the eighth century. These facts led several scholars to accept the translation of the *Hazār Afsāna* itself either in Manṣūr's time or soon after as not at all improbable. Oestrup went as far as to suggest that an Arabic *Nights* bearing the title mentioned by Masʿūdī already existed at the beginning of the ninth century.[62] On the other hand, other noted scholars have insisted that Masʿūdī's passages yield nothing definite beyond the fact of the existence of an Arabic *Nights* in the early tenth century and that Ibn ʿAbdūs's (d. 331/942) unfinished collection of about the same time represents the first attempt to edit and literalize the *Arabian Nights*. Broadly stated, the two points of view have over a century as a major issue between them.[63]

The Oriental Institute manuscript, itself of the early ninth century, establishes beyond a doubt the existence of an Arabic version of the *Nights* at that time. But it does much more than that by virtue of its literary style and the nature of its text. These latter, when tested by Nadīm's three evolutionary stages of this class of Arabic literature in general and, by logical and justified inference, also of the *Nights* in particular, are seen already to have passed the initial stage of literal translation to those of literary revision and of creative imitation. For the brief passage is certainly written in an elegant style already familiar in the second century of the Hijrah or eighth century of our era. This is the literary device of *Aḍdād*, the treatment of a subject and its opposite, or the treatment of the same subject pro and con.[64] Again, the text, while not necessarily excluding tales of non-Arabic origin, does definitely specify Syrian and Bedouin stories cast within the framework of the *Hazār Afsāna*. This is evidence enough of Nadīm's third stage, namely, creative imitation. That this stage should have been already reached by the early ninth century is further evidence that the *Hazār Afsāna* must have made its first impact on the Arabic literary world in Manṣūr's time or very soon thereafter.

Again, attention must be drawn to the accumulative evidence, including the emphasis of the text on Syrian tales, that points to Syria as the provenance of our manuscript.[65] It would be strange indeed if the capital province of ʿIrāq, where Persian influence was certainly greater than in Syria, had not kept up with the latter in production of this type of literature. It becomes necessary here to consider at some length the relationship of the Oriental Institute manuscript to the still earlier Arabic manuscripts of the *Nights*, the contemporary existence of which is demanded by the very nature of our manuscript. For it is reasonable to expect that the *very first attempt* to put into written form any or all of what was to be an Arabic *Nights*, either by direct translation from or by imitation of the *Hazār Afsāna*, would certainly call for the inclusion of an adequate introduction that would give the setting and the framework for these tales. Our manuscript, intact in its title page, pious invocation, and short introductory paragraph, nevertheless lacks this necessary complete introduction. Its title is not a clear-cut *Kitāb Alf Lailah*, "Book of a Thousand Nights";[66] it plunges headlong into a "following night" without any setting for the tales; and it uses part only of a known framework that it does not itself introduce or explain. These are factors that indicate that the man behind the manuscript, be he author, compiler, or copyist, meant to produce nothing more than either an actual "selection" from the *Nights* or new tales intended to pass as a "selection" from that work. The great probability is that our manuscript is in the tradition of other likewise partial compilations, these being either descendants of or accretions to an earlier manuscript version(s) containing the necessary introduction with the complete framework. It is highly probable, therefore, that the parent Arabic

Nights originated in ʿIrāq and that ʿIrāq itself had its own "selections" in circulation by the beginning of the ninth or the end of the eighth century. It is perhaps too much to hope that any of these have survived.

Again the Oriental Institute manuscript is a starting point for the tracing of the development of the *Nights* through the ninth century and up to Ibn ʿAbdūs's collection of night-stories in the early tenth century. The accelerated speed and increasing momentum of the many faceted literary movement that had already produced an Arabic *Nights* by the late eighth, or at the most early ninth, century continued to grow throughout the period under consideration. The ninth and tenth centuries yielded a literary harvest that was not to be surpassed in the entire history of Islam. Copious literary evidence indicates that the lighter literature, the *khurāfāt* and *asmār* to which class the *Nights* belong, shared all along the way in this rapid and extensive movement, though generally on a somewhat lower level of respectability. The list of those who contributed to it is quite impressive for its continuity from the last of the reign of the Umayyad caliph Muʿāwiyah (41–60/661–80) to the reign of the ʿAbbāsid caliph Muqtadir (295–320/908–32). It is equally impressive for the rich diversity and the caliber of some of its contributors, several of whom were polyglots engaged in translations from the Greek and the Persian. There is little to be gained in giving here the long list of names and dates of all of these: suffice it to say that they included ʿAbīd ibn Sharyah of the court of Muʿāwiyah,[67] Jablah ibn Sālim[68] of the time of Hishām (105–25/724–43), Ibn al-Muqaffaʿ[69] of the reign of Manṣūr (135–58/754–75), al-ʿAtābī[70] and Hishām al-Kalbī[71] of the reign of Hārūn al-Rashīd (170–93/786–809), Mufaḍḍal ibn Salama (ca. 250–865),[72] Aḥmad ibn Abī Ṭāhir (d. 280/893),[73] Ibn ʿAbdūs (d. 321/942),[74] and Ḥamzah al-Iṣfahānī (d. 360/970).

It is the tenth century with its Masʿūdī and Nadīm, as already seen, that yields the most significant literary references to this entire class of literature. Three other references from this same century supplement, in some measure, our still too scanty knowledge. Ṣūlī, court scholar and tutor to Prince Mohammed, son of the caliph Muqtadir, writing in 320/932, reports the following incident. In the midst of a lesson on Arabic literature, tutor and pupils were rudely disturbed when servants from the palace of grandmother Shaghab walked silently in, collected all the young prince's books, and departed with them, leaving Mohammed in a rage. Sūlī calmed his young charge and future caliph, al-Rāḍī (322–29/934–40), by pointing out that the queen and her party were probably checking on his reading and that he should not object to this opportunity of letting it be known that his books were of the very best. Several hours later the servants returned with the books to be greeted by the prince with, "Tell them who sent you, 'You have seen these books and found them to be books of tradition, jurisprudence, poetry, language, history, and the works of the learned—books through the study of which God causes one to benefit and to be compete. They are not like the books which you read excessively such as *The Wonders of the Sea*, *The Tale of Sindbād*, and *The Cat and the Mouse*.'"[75]

The second reference comes from the pen of Ḥamzah al-Iṣfahānī, who informs us in his general history (finished in 350/961) that Alexander the Great, after his conquest of Persia, divided the country into petty kingdoms under the Asghanian kings who thereafter engaged not in war but in contests of difficult questions, "so that in their days were composed the books which are now in the hands of the people, such as the *Book of Marūk*, and the *Book of Sindbād*, and the *Book of Barsanās* and the *Book of Shimās* and the like, about seventy books in all."[76] Here quite obviously Ḥamzah is dealing with the same *khurāfāt* and *asmār* literature with which Masʿūdī and Nadīm are concerned. He in part confirms and in part supplements both of these author's accounts, particularly in his mentioning specific titles and in giving a general estimate of the number of foreign books of that type current in the first half of the tenth century. It would seem therefore that he was readily acquainted with the history of this literature if not indeed with its current supply. His context, he may have felt, did not call for more than this passing remark. At any rate we knew that he was interested in the Arab and Jewish counterpart of this same literature; for he is eager to add from the Persian stock of such tales one that was as yet unknown to the Arabs and places this story in the same class as the Arab tales of Luqmān ibn ʿĀd and the Jewish tales of ʿŪj and Bulūqiyā.[77] Again he selects a list of Arab *khurāfāt* that had given rise to proverbs still current in his day and appends these to his larger work of Arabic proverbs.[78] Ḥamzah, therefore, must have been acquainted with both the Persian *Hazār Afsāna* and the *Alf Lailah*, both of which, according to Masʿūdī's account, were popular among the people in Ḥamzah's own day.[79] It is therefore not unlikely that some of his unpublished works may yet reveal with certainty both the fact and the extent of his familiarity with these particular works.

The third reference is to the *Hazār Afsāna* itself, but only as typifying the entire class of *khurāfāt.* It comes from Tauḥīdī, who, writing in 374/984, characterizes these narratives as "containing unfounded statements, mixed with the impossible, conjoined to the marvelous and the entertaining, and incapable of derivation and verification." There is also the implication that such tales are particularly enjoyed by women and youths.[80]

The next problem for consideration is the absence of more frequent and specific mention of the Arabic *Alf Lailah* in works of Arabic literature. Hitherto this problem has centered largely on the scarcity of materials from the late tenth century onward, for those who interpreted Masʿūdī's reference to mean that the first Arabic *Nights* took form about his own time dismissed the question of earlier references as irrelevant. On the other hand, those who believed Masʿūdī's passage to mean an eighth-century translation of the *Hazār Afsāna* and a ninth-century Arabic *Alf Lailah* seem to have tacitly assumed the loss of earlier references to both these books including Masʿūdī's own sources. But now that we know definitely of the existence of the Arabic *Nights* between the late eighth and the early ninth centuries, attention needs to be focused as much on this lack of tangible pre-tenth-century references as on their subsequent rarity.[81] Allowing for some necessary time lag between the appearance of a literary phenomenon and its subsequent treatment by literary historians, the eighth century is obviously too early to expect much from it in this respect.[82] Not so the ninth century. One wonders, for instance, if the movement could have really escaped the attention of the encyclopedic Jāḥiẓ (d. 255/869), whose unusual talents were most certainly appreciated by Masʿūdī[83] among many others. Be that as it may, the reason for this marked rarity of reference early or late to the *Alf Lailah* is to be sought, up to a point, in influences that are common to both periods.

The main factors to consider in this respect are the very nature of this *khurāfāt* literature and its standing among the Arabs. Khurāfah, from whom this class of story takes its name, is supposed to have been a contemporary of Mohammed to whom, among others, he related his experiences in the world of the jinns. Mohammed, in turn, is said to have repeated this and similar tales to Aishah and the other members of his harem. Khurāfah's story as reported by Mufaḍḍal ibn Salama[84] (ca. 250–865) is an artless tale with no line drawn between the worlds of the jinn, man, and other creatures wherein any one of these may assume not only the characteristics but also the form of the other. Whether the Khurāfah-Mohammed link is an invention or not, the tale itself was definitely known in the last quarter of the eighth century,[85] hence affording, along with similar tales, ready basis for comparison with the Persian *Afsāna*, "wherein speaking parts were given to beasts," as Nadīm informs us. There is, of course, no question of their widespread and increasing popularity from the ninth century on, but generally on the level of folk tales that were considered good enough media for the amusement and instruction of the ignorant and frivolous and of women and children, but seldom considered sufficiently dignified for the serious attention of reputable littérateurs and scholars.[86] Thus this somewhat paradoxical situation: the *khurāfāt*, along with other imaginative and fantastic fiction, though growing more and more popular, fell increasingly to the lot of little known and/or anonymous writers. Only on rare occasions were they to be rescued for mention in the historical record by either the unusually curious or the exceptionally cosmopolitan and encyclopedic authors. Thus one can understand, at one and the same time, Rāḍī's contemptuous reference to sea adventures and animal fables, Masʿūdī's guarded yet critical account of legendary *akhbār*, and Nadīm's poor opinion of the *Hazār Afsāna*. And since all these elements were to be found in the *Alf Lailah*, this representative collection par excellence went merrily rolling along all over the Moslem world, flourishing in its anonymity, cherished by the common man, and ignored by the highbrow, down almost to our own times.

But what of the content of the earliest Arabic *Nights*? Here the evidence of the Oriental Institute fragment, direct or indirect, is more general than specific. But, as will be seen presently, it is, nevertheless, highly significant. As already stated in the section on the "when" of the fragment, this latter represents the last stage outlined in Nadīm's account, namely, imitation, and therefore presupposes an Arabic translation of the *Hazār Afsāna*. It becomes necessary now to consider its bearing on some of the points in a related group of long-standing controversial questions. Was this Arabic translation a literal one or merely a paraphrase? Was it complete or partial? And did this translated material, whatever its literary style and extent, constitute the first Arabic *Nights* or was this latter a combination of Persian and Arabic elements? Or, again, was the first Arabic collection genuinely Arabian consisting entirely of Arabic stories and borrowing only the framework and a modified version of the Introduction of the *Hazār Afsāna*. In that case there would have to be two separate but contemporary collections of the *Nights:* the earlier *Hazār Afsāna* current in Masʿūdī's time in an Arabic version titled *Alf Lailah* and an imitative but distinctly separate collection of Arabic stories bearing the same title. Were definite answers to all these general questions forthcoming, there would still be the further problem of identifying the specific tales, Persian, Arabic, or both, that would be involved at any given point.

We turn again to our fragment, this time in search of clues to the general nature of the collection it represents and to the specific story or cycle of stories that headed the manuscript itself. It will be recalled that lines 10–11 of the text emphasize Syrian and Bedouin Arab tales. However, there is nothing in the text itself that would necessarily exclude stories of other localities, Arab or otherwise, since the *insān* of line 9 is meant for MAN, *Homo sapiens.* Hence, it is quite possible that the present "selection" of the *Nights* could have contained tales of Arab and of foreign origin, the most probable source of the latter being the *Hazār Afsāna* because of its close affinity with the *Alf Lailah*. Yet there is no reason to exclude the possibility of other foreign sources of the same category as contributing to the Arabic *Nights* even at this early stage. It seems reasonably certain that the theme of the first story in the manuscript is *makr*. It is to be noted that this word *makr* and its synonym *kaid* are used in their numerous shades of meaning as artifice, cunning, trick, wile, ruse, stratagem, craft, deceit, and malice throughout the *Nights*, in connection with both men and women, though the latter are portrayed as more cunning, crafty, and malicious than the men. *Makr* is a theme alike for short anecdotes as for longer stories and for entire cycles of stories. The probability is that it is one of these latter that is involved in our manuscript. Among the tales generally considered as part of the *Hazār Afsāna* and one that also has the craft and malice of women for a theme is the story of Qamar al-Zamān and the Lady Budūr. The same theme plays a major role in two cycles of tales that existed in the eighth century as works similar to, but independent of, the *Hazār Afsāna*, but that were later incorporated into the Arabic *Nights*, though how much later is precisely the question that concerns us at this point. These two are the well-known book-sized stories of King Jalīʿād (or Farza and other variants) and his wazir Shimās (or Shīmās) and the story of Sindbād the Sage (as distinguished from Sindbād the Sailor) known also as the story of "The King and His Seven Wazirs." In this latter the long cycle of tales revolves around Sindbād's reputation as the wisest tutor and preceptor of his day and around the clever stratagems and craft of both men and women, *kaid* or *makr al-rijāl* as contrasted with *kaid* or *makr al-nisāʾ*. It is, therefore, the story of human craft par excellence. The book enjoyed an early popularity comparable to that of *Kalīlah wa Dimnah*. Along with this latter, it was cast from Arabic prose into Arabic verse by Abān al-Lāḥiqī (d. 200/815).[87] The prose version must therefore have been readily available in the period before our manuscript to which it is time to return.

The lost space in line 13 of the text could easily accommodate any one of the following phrases:

[عن قمر الزمان وذ] كره,	of Qamar al-Zamān and his fame;
[عن الملك جلبعاد وذ] كره,	of King Jalīʿād (or some variant of the name) and his fame;
[عن شيماس الوزير وذ] كره,	of Shīmās the wazir and his fame;
[عن سندباد الحكيم وذ] كره,	of Sindbād the Sage and his fame; or
[عن كيد الرجل و م]ـكره,	of the stratagem of man and his malice.

Line 15 could then be referring to the popular belief that women are craftier than men, the obvious point of all three stories. In the story of Sindbād, the palace favorite, herself guilty, seeks to prove that women are not so crafty and certainly not craftier than the men using the phrases امكر من الرجال, "more crafty than the men," or امكر منهم, "more crafty than they" (masculine plural).[88] This last phrase is actually in our text, line 15, preceded by الا, "except, or else." Now if we take lines 14 and 15 together, they would seem to be saying that either " a man becomes," if we read يصير, or "a woman becomes," if we read the feminine تصير, "more worthy," احق, "or else more crafty than other men" والا امكر منهم. This could mean that the comparison is either between men only or that it is between men and women. Considering the ever-present battle of the sexes in some form or another in the society of the *Nights*, the probability is somewhat in favor of the second alternative. In that case the text would seem to be adequately describing a situation in the story of Sindbād the Sage. For the very first tale of the first wazir dramatizes the praiseworthy conduct of a virtuous woman who by a clever stratagem restrained the king from forcing his attentions on her in her husband's absence;[89] but, ere the cycle of tales is done, woman is nevertheless proved to be more malicious than man.

If we have interpreted our meager clues correctly, then we have here the identification of the story and through the story proof that foreign sources other than the *Hazār Afsāna* formed part of the earliest collection of the *Nights* in the late eighth or early ninth century. But so weighty a conclusion demands further corroborative evidence before it can be claimed as certain.

A more positive identification of the story of the Oriental Institute manuscript and of a group of stories contemporaneous with it can perhaps be arrived at through the combination of several or all of the elements afforded by the text, only one of which remains yet to be considered. This last is the sentence, "O my delectable one, if you are not asleep, relate to me the story which you promised me," taken as a whole and also phrase by phrase. The first phrase has already been touched upon.[90] The second, "if you are not asleep," appears, though not consistently, in some of the printed editions,[91] and the last, "the story which you promised me," like the first, has not been met with so far despite a liberal sampling of the printed editions. To put to the utmost use all our manuscript's textual data, the definite, the implied, and the uncertain, requires an exhaustive study of all extant manuscripts of the *Nights* with a view to forwarding their classification chronologically and geographically. This is quite obviously a task not to be lightly undertaken; for, aside from the time element, it calls for a scholar familiar with the history of the extant manuscripts of the *Nights* and experienced in their textual criticism. It is a task for one both willing and able to put to good use the late Professor Duncan Black Macdonald's magnificent collection of manuscript and printed editions of the *Nights* now in the library of the Hartford Theological Seminary.

Fortunately, we are not entirely dependent on the results of such a project before we can exhaust the evidence of our manuscript on the question of the content of the early *Nights.* The significance of early dates mentioned in the *Nights* has been for long a center of controversy. Some hold that these early dates, specific or implied by association with historic characters and events, are either errors of figures and/or names or else are later interpolations. Others again have inclined strongly toward the view that these dates are authentic and therefore significant both as the approximate date of the entry of the particular story in which they occur in the *Nights* and of the nature of the content of the *Nights* as a whole. This latter view, fully and brilliantly presented by Oestrup,[92] points to the fisherman's statement, in the story of "The Fisherman and the Jinn," that Solomon had been dead these eighteen hundred years, to indicate that an Arabic version of the *Hazār Afsāna* existed as early as about A.D. 800, since in Moslem popular belief there is a thousand years between Solomon and Christ. Again, there is the statement of Abū Ḥasan of Khurāsān, that he fled from Baghdād to Basrah during the civil wars of Muntaṣir and Mustaᶜīn (248–52/862–66). Finally, there is exactness of the date, Friday the tenth of Ṣafar, 263/second November, 876, mentioned by the Barber of Baghdād in the Hunchback cycle. These confirmed Oestrup's belief in an early translation of the *Hazār Afsāna*, as already seen above,[93] and furthermore convinced him that a certain part of the *Nights* had already received its final form in the ninth century. Yet even he cautiously adds: "But although I am absolutely inclined to accept this, yet I dare not consider the matter as definitely certain; but it is not at all impossible that in the various manuscripts will be found materials that will provide a final solution to this complicated question."[94]

Little did anyone then dream of so dramatic a confirmation of his view and of so definite a solution to the problem as the Oriental

Institute manuscript indeed supplies. For the very existence of such an early manuscript that also lays emphasis on the Arabic tales gives just that needed extra evidence in order to give full credence to these early internal dates. These dates, it must be noted, occur alike in the thoroughly Persian tale, despite its added Islamic color, of "The Fisherman and the Jinn," the purely Arabic story of "Abū Ḥasan of Khurāsān," and in the Hunchback cycle that combines both Persian and Arabic elements. Hence, the combined evidence of our manuscript, of the literary sources, and of the text of the *Arabian Nights* as we now have them, leave no room to doubt the existence of a ninth-century version of the *Nights* that was composite in its content. The *Hazār Afsāna*, until definite proof to the contrary is forthcoming, must be considered as the one certain source of the Persian tales, with the *Book of Sindbād* and the *Book of Jaliʿād and Shimās* as further probable sources. All foreign materials seem to have been Islamized in the process of adoption. So far as the Arabic elements of such a version are concerned, the great probability is that the pre-Islamic Arab materials competed with the Persian from the start, followed closely by the tales and anecdotes of the early caliphs and of the Umayyads and their times. As for tales and anecdotes of the early ʿAbbāsids, these were probably contemporaneous, or nearly so, with the characters and events to which they belong with few exceptions, the most outstanding of which being Hārūn al-Rashīd and his times (170–93/786–809). The stories that are woven around this caliph fall into two groups: those that actually refer to him and his courtiers and those that have been transferred to him from characters and events that came either before or after his reign. The first could well have found their way into manuscripts parent to or collateral with the Oriental Institute manuscript. The stories in the second group are necessary later and the probability is that they found their way into the *Nights* singly or in groups, at different times and in different places. Those of Asiatic setting, controlled by other internal criteria, such as the absence or negligible presence of the fantastic and the supernatural, as Nöldeke pointed out[95] had probably been absorbed into the *Nights* by the time of Ibn ʿAbdūs's collection in the early tenth century. Those of Egyptian color with the supernatural in control are almost certainly of later Egyptian origin.

Ibn ʿAbdūs's cosmopolitan collection of the "night-stories of the Arabs, Persians, Greeks, and others"[96] was unquestionably meant to be more inclusive than any other single collection of its kind. This is amply indicated by the multiplicity of the editor's sources both oral and written; by the contemplated number of stories—an exact thousand in contrast to the less than two hundred of the *Hazār Afsāna;* and by the size of each story—some fifty pages more or less. It had a definite plan of organization, since the stories of each people were to be grouped together as a complete and independent unit. But unfortunately we do not know the exact title of this large collection of many volumes. Neither do we know the radical distribution of the 480 stories that were actually completed ere death overtook the editor and halted this magnificently conceived but ill-fated project. Hence, the exact relationship, in respect to specific content, of this tenth-century *Alf Samar*, "Thousand Night Stories," to the ninth-century *Alf Lailah*, "Thousand Nights," and the eighth-century *Hazār Afsāna*, "Thousand Fanciful Tales," remains uncertain to an even greater degree than does the comparable relationship of the *Alf Lailah* to the *Hazār Afsāna*. But in the overall picture there can be no doubt that the incomplete *Alf Samar* borrowed largely from its two well-known and popular predecessors and in turn contributed liberally to the international *Alf Lailah wa Lailah* that we know today.

Further rapid and certain progress relative to the what and whence of the *Nights*, particularly in the earlier stages of the collection, must await the discovery of new evidence. There still is the possibility, remote as it may seem, that the Egyptian soil or some obscure and neglected collection in either East or West may yet yield one or more of the following: the Persian *Hazār Afsāna* known to be still in existence in the eleventh century,[97] a more generous portion of the ninth-century *Alf Lailah* than our precious fragment proved to be, and a volume or more of the *Alf Samar* that were current in Nadīm's day. There is, however, the greater probability of finding an additional historical reference or two to one or all of these three works, particularly in the hitherto unpublished works of outstanding encyclopedists of the ninth and tenth centuries, such as Hishām al-Kalbī, Jāḥiẓ, Masʿūdī, and Ḥamzah al-Iṣfahānī.[98] And, finally, there is certainty of discovering an increasing number of literary parallels to the anecdotes and tales, particularly those of Arabic origin, that are in the *Nights.*

This brings us to the wider problem of the interrelationships of the *Nights* and the literary sources, using this latter phrase in the widest sense with the emphasis on literary, historical, and even scientific materials. The problem has been long recognized and in some of its many phases partly solved. But a renewed and intensified search for literary parallels is indicated, since availability of materials, published or in microfilm, is steadily increasing. The search may even bring to light some hitherto unknown or neglected manuscript that could compare to Jāḥiẓ's (pseudo) *Maḥāsin*, Masʿūdī's *Murūj* and the *Aghānī*, by far the most fruitful early sources of literary parallels yet known. Newly discovered parallels together with those already known could then be subjected to the test of textual literary criticism to determine, insofar as this is possible, which of these materials have a common source and which are most directly interdependent, being lifted, so to speak, from the literary sources into the *Nights* or even vice versa.[99] Such a project should help to set close enough limits certainly *a quo* and probably also *ad quem* for most of the largely Arabic materials of the *Nights.* Hitherto little-known anthologies containing some parallels to the *Nights*, such as the Constantinople manuscript discovered by Ritter and described by Littmann[100] may prove to have been intermediary between earlier and later versions of the *Nights* as well as between earlier and later literary sources. It was some of these later works taken at their face value, at a time when earlier materials were either unknown or unavailable, that helped in misleading Lane to assign so late a date to the *Arabian Nights.*[101] But with our present knowledge of this problem of interrelationships, it does not seem at all improbable that some of these later sources known to him had themselves borrowed from the earlier *Nights.*

Having exhausted the evidence of the Oriental Institute manuscript, direct or indirect, specific or general, it is best to give here a summary of its contribution to the early history of the *Nights.* While the fragment does not settle all the long-standing controversies in the field, it definitely confirms the title *Alf Lailah* and the name Dīnāzād and, by implication, also the name Shīrāzād and the relationship of the former to the latter as that of a nurse. It establishes with greater certainty than was hitherto possible an earlier origin and a more rapid and steady growth for the collection than was generally conceded. In these respects it confirms the general lines long discerned by von Hammer and Oestrup; for it was the former who first accepted an eighth-century Arabic translation of the *Hazār Afsāna* and the latter who was convinced that a composite section of the growing *Nights* had already attained a definite form in the ninth century.

Based on this firm foundation and the few subsequent literary references, it becomes possible to modify and supplement the general outline of the long history of the *Nights* as submitted by Macdonald.[102] The successive steps in the evolution of the collection may be stated as follows:

I. An eighth-century translation of the *Hazār Afsāna.* It is my belief this was most probably a complete and literal translation perhaps titled *Alf Khurāfāt.*

II. An eighth-century Islamized Arabic version of the *Hazār Afsāna* titled *Alf Lailah.* This could have been either partial or complete.

III. A ninth-century composite *Alf Lailah* containing both Persian and Arabic materials. While most of the former came undoubtedly from the *Hazār Afsāna*, other current storybooks, especially the *Book of Sindbād* and the *Book of Shimās*, are not improbable sources. The Arabic materials, as Littmann has already pointed out, were not so slight or insignificant as Macdonald believed them to be.

IV. The tenth-century *Alf Samar* of Ibn ʿAbdūs. Whether this was meant to include, among other materials, all the current *Alf Lailah*, and so supersede it, is not clear.

V. A twelfth-century collection augmented by materials from IV and by Asiatic and Egyptian tales of local Egyptian composition. The change of title to *Alf Lailah* belongs, in all probability, to this period.

VI. The final stages of the growing collection extending to the early sixteenth century. Heroic tales of the Islamic countercrusades are among the most prominent additions. Persia and ʿIrāq may have contributed some of the later predominantly Far Eastern tales in the wake of the thirteenth-century Mongol conquest of those lands. The final conquest of Mameluke Syria and Egypt by the Ottoman Salīm

I (1512–20) closed the last chapter of history of the *Arabian Nights* in its oriental homeland.

Although the framework and an inkling of some of the stories of the *Nights* had found their way into Europe as early as the fourteenth century,[103] it was not until the turn of the eighteenth century that the collection itself was introduced into Europe by the Frenchman Jean Antoine Galland (1646–1715). Thereafter, the history of the *Arabian Nights* in its European domicile offers in several respects a subtle yet instructive parallel to the early history of the *Nights.* The Galland manuscript, like the *Hazār Afsāna*, has been translated, literally and otherwise. It has been, up to a point, Europeanized as the *Hazār Afsāna* was likewise Islamized. The initial edition represented by the Galland manuscript has grown and multiplied from generation to generation as did indeed the original *Hazār Afsāna* from century to century. The Arabic manuscripts of Syria and Egypt, like the non-Arabic editions of the various countries of Europe, present us with a bewildering variety of versions and/or selections that abound, in part for this same reason, in difference as well as in duplications. And just as the *Hazār Afsāna* was imitated by the Arabs, so was the *Arabian Nights* at first imitated in the West. But, unlike their Arabic counterpart that united with the *Hazār Afsāna*, these Western imitations remained apart from the oriental collection. These broad historical parallels reflect a wide and steady demand and constitute an eloquent testimony to the lasting and universal appeal of the *Arabian Nights.*

If a major catastrophe—which Allah forfend!—were to overtake our world comparable in some measure to the progressive decline of the Perso-Arab world subsequent to the Mongol, Turkish, and Western conquest, the history of the *Arabian Nights* could again prove difficult indeed to piece together. And if in such a world a student of this subject, working with whatever atomic destruction may have chanced to spare, were to come on a few pages sketching a part of that history, he could hardly be more surprised or delighted than was the present writer when Oriental Institute No. 17618, a tattered paper fragment, proved to be the earliest-known manuscript of the *Alf Lailah* or "Thousand Nights" with a significance that far outweighed its size, and, for good measure, turned out to be also the earliest-known extant evidence of any *paper* book outside the ancient Far East.

Notes

1. This general unawareness, in this country, of Arabic papyri and their significance for the earliest phases of Islamic history and culture is all the more regrettable now that work on the great collections of Egypt and Central Europe has slowed down to all but a complete halt as an aftermath of World War II. Grohmann's latest volume on the Arabic papyri of the Egyptian National Library at Cairo was first published in 1939. Replies to recent inquiries about the European situation indicate that most of the well-known Arabic papyri collections have escaped the incendiary bomb. However, little work is now being done on any of the collections, and even that little is hampered by the general lack of funds and facilities for research and publication. "The fate of the Berlin collection," writes a fellow-scholar in a private letter, "is deplorable. . . . The bulk of the collection has been deported to the Soviet Union . . . and must be considered lost to the Western worlds. A small part of the collection is said to have been destroyed by bombs."

2. Josef von Karabacek, "Das arabische Papier," *Nationalbibliothek, Mittheilungen aus der Sammlung der Papyrus Erzherzog Rainer*, Parts II–III (paged continuously) (Wien, 1887), pp. 87–178.

3. Cf. M. H. Zotenberg, "Notice sur quelques manuscrits des Mille et une nuits," *Notices et extraits des manuscrits de la Bibliothèque nationale* XXVII (1887), pp. 167–218; D. B. Macdonald, "A Preliminary Classification of some MSS of the Arabian Nights," in *A Volume of Oriental Studies Presented to Edward G. Browne*, ed. Arnold and Nicholson (Cambridge, 1922), pp. 304–21, esp. p. 307 and references there cited.

4. Cf., e.g., B. Moritz, *Arabic Paleography* (Bibliothèque khédiviale, "Publications," no. 16 [Cairo, 1905]), plates 41, 45, and 46. Moritz has reproduced only these few samples. However, on a recent visit to the National (former Khedivial) Library at Cairo, whence Moritz himself drew his materials, I was privileged to see literally dozens of these small parchment Qurʾāns and permitted to examine a goodly number of them minutely. It was most gratifying to find such ample confirmation of my earlier published statement in regard to the relationships of these small Qurʾāns to the larger and more pretentious ones of the same period, particularly with reference to their widespread use and the development and character of their script. Cf. the writer's "Arabic Paleography," in *Ars islamica* VIII (1941), pp. 79–80.

I wish to take this opportunity of expressing my sincere thanks to Dr. Mohammed Sabry, director of the Egyptian National Library at Cairo and to his staff, particularly Mr. Mohammed Husain among the latter, for willing cooperation and numerous courtesies extended to me beyond the *farḍ al-kifāyah*, during the autumn months of 1946 spent in their hospitable city.

5. Cf. William Wright, ed., *Facsimilies of Inscriptions and Manuscripts* ("Oriental Series" [London: Paleographical Society, 1875–83]), plate VI; J. David-Weill, ed., *Le Djâmiʿ d'Ibn Wahb* ("Publications de l'Institute français

d'archéologie oriental: Textes Arabes," Tome III [2 vols.; Cairo, 1939–41]), plates 1 ff.

6. E.g., Oriental Institute No. 17619, a third-century fragment on grammar.

7. For a discussion of the relationship of early Christian Arabic scripts to early Moslem scripts see the writer's *The Rise of the North Arabic Script and Its Early Ḳurʾānic Development* ("Oriental Institute Publications," vol. L [Chicago, 1939]), pp. 20–21 and references there cited.

8. For a fuller list of opposite qualities that pertain to man, cf. Tauḥīdī, *Al-Imtāʿ wa al-Muʾānasah* (3 vols.; Cairo, 1939–44), I, p. 149.

9. Cf., e.g., the writer's "Arabic Marriage Contracts among the Copts," *ZDMG* XCV (1941), 67–70; Adolph Grohmann, *Arabic Papyri in the Egyptian Library (APEL)*, vol. II (1936), Index, "Abbreviations," and "Ligatures."

10. Cf. Karabacek, op. cit., pp. 93–95; Grohmann, *APEL* vol. II, nos. 88 and 90; N. Abbott, "Arabic Papyri of the Reign of Ǧaʿfar al-Mutawakkil . . ." *ZDMG* XCII (1938), pp. 110–11.

11. Cf. Grohmann, *APEL* vol. I, nos. 39, 41, 48; vol. II, nos. 89, 96, 98, 114, 126, 127; vol. III, nos. 181–88, 190, 196, and 198, dating from A.H. 209 to 293; for fourth-century specimens cf. Karabacek, op. cit., pp. 90–91.

12. Cf. Ludwig Stern, *Koptische Grammatik* (Leipzig, 1880), pp. 131 ff., and especially the table of forms at the end of the book. I am indebted to Dr. T. G. Allen for the reference to Stern and to Professor Edgerton and Wilson for the confirmation of my reading of this particular date.

13. For the early use of Arabic letter numerals cf. the writer's "Arabic Numerals," *Journal of the Royal Asiatic Society*, 1938, pp. 277–80.

14. Cf., e.g., Grohmann, *APEL* I, 74: p. 11, 88: pp. 14–15, 245: p. 20.

15. Cf. n. 13. See also Stern, op. cit., table at end of the book for the different paleographic forms of these letter numerals.

16. Karabacek, op. cit., p. 98; N. Abbott, *The Ḳurrah Papyri from Aphrodite in the Oriental Institute* ("*SAOC*," no. 15 [Chicago, 1938]), pp. 22–23, and references there cited.

17. Of these, two only are assigned to the first half of the third century. The definitely dated documents are but five, with their dates extending from A.H. 260 to 297 or A.D. 873–909 (cf. Karabacek, op. cit., pp. 90–91; *Papyrus Erzherzog Rainer, Führer durch die Ausstellung* [hereafter *PERF* (Wien, 1894)], p. 226, no. 845 and p. 246, nos. 924–26; *Corpus Papyrorum Raineri archiducis Austriae*, III, *Series Arabica*, ed. Adolf Grohmann [hereafter *CPR* III (Vindobonae, 1924 . . .)], vol. I, part 1, p. 58; Albert Dietrich, "Arabische Papyri aus der Hamburger Staats- und Universität-bibliothek," *Abhandlungen für die Kunde des Morgenlandes*, XXII, part 3 [Leipzig, 1937], pp. 49 and 63–64). A few other third-century paper documents, dated or otherwise, will no doubt come to light as research and publication on early materials progress. There is, for instance, Oriental Institute No. 13782, a paper fragment with two lines of invocation on Aḥmad ibn Ṭūlūn of Egypt (254–70/868–83).

18. To gain an idea of the wealth of Arabic papyri that came out of Egypt cf. Grohmann, *CPR* III, vol. I, part 1, p. 10.

19. Cf. p. 25, and p. 60.

20. For the bitter struggle between the two Aḥmads, cf. the writer's "Arabic Papyri of the Reign of Ǧaʿfar at-Mutawakkil . . ." *ZDMG* XCII (1938), pp. 101–4.

21. Ṭabarī, *Taʾrīkh (Annales)*, ed. de Goeje (15 vols.; Lugduni Batavorum, 1879–1901), III, 1929; Masʿūdī, *Murūj al-Dhahab (Les Prairies d'or)*, ed. C. Barbier de Meynard (9 vols.; Paris, 1861–77), VIII, pp. 67–71; Ibn Taghrībirdī, *Nujūm al-Zāhirah (Annals)*, ed. W. Poper (Berkeley, Calif., 1909), II, pp. 40–41.

22. In the light of the above, it is quite probable that the only other known third-century documents to come out of Syria and survive to our day were not unearthed in southern Syria as previously suggested but rather shared the above war mishap in Syria and later protection of the Egyptian soil. These are the three papyrus documents drawn up in Damascus in 241/855–56. They were purchased for the Oriental Institute by Professor Sprengling and have already been published by the present writer in *ZDMG* XCII (1938), pp. 88–135, under the title, "Arabic Papyri from the Reign of Ǧaʿfar at-Mutawakkil ʿalā-llāh."

23. Cf. Karabacek, *Das arabische Papier*, pp. 106–14.

24. Julius v. Wiesner, "Über die ältesten bis jetzt aufgefundenen Hadernpapiere," *Sitzungsberichte des Kais. Akademie der Wissenschaften in Wien*, vol. CLXVIII (1911), Abh. V, pp. 1–26.

25. Karabacek, *Das arabische Papier*, pp. 114–17.

26. Julius v. Wiesner, "Die Faijûmer und Uschmûneiner Papiere, *MPER* II–III (Wien, 1887), pp. 179–260, esp. pp. 191–218 and 242.

27. The fibers revealed by 250–530 magnifications are similar to linen fibers shown on pp. 195 and 198 of the preceding reference. I am indebted to Mr. P. Delougaz, curator of the Oriental Institute Museum, for technical assistance in the above analysis.

28. Cf. Karabacek, *Das arabische Papier*, pp. 117–21.

29. Qalqashandī, *Subḥ al-Aʿshā* (14 vols.; Cairo, 1913–19), II, p. 475.

30. E.g., the Ṭāhirid governor of Baghdād, finding himself short of paper during the wars of Mustaʿīn and Muʿtazz (248–51–55/862–65–69), instructed his secretaries to write a small hand and to be brief, since papyrus was not desirable (cf. Thaʿālibī, *Khāṣṣ al-Khāṣṣ* [Cairo, 1236], p. 71, and Ṭabarī, III, 1506, 1510–11).

31. Karabacek, *Das arabische Papier*, pp. 121–25, argues for the rapid spread of paper factories, while Adam Mez, *Die Renaissance des Islam* (Heidelberg, 1922), pp. 439–41, believes the progress to have been slower. More recent summaries of the history of Arabic paper draw on these two authors. New materials so far on hand suggest a modification of both positions, as I hope to be able to show at some later date. For the present, the controversy is

of no major significance here, since the widespread *use* of paper in the ninth century, regardless of its place of manufacture, is not questioned.

32. Note must be taken of the fact that the sources do not, as a rule, specify the writing material of a book mentioned in passing. Even more disconcerting is their use of *qirṭās*, *kāghid*, and *waraq* interchangeably, though the first generally means "papyrus," the second "paper," and the third is used for both papyrus and paper (cf. Qalqashandī, II, pp. 475–77).

33. Ibn Abī Uṣaibīʿah, *ʿUyūn al-Anbāʾ fī Ṭabaqāt al-Aṭibbāʾ*, ed. August Müller (2 vols.; Cairo and Königsberg, 1882–84), I, pp. 187 and 197. This was, in all probability, after Maʾmūn's return from Khurāsān to Baghdād in 204/819. It indicates the manufacture in Baghdād of paper made to order according to the buyer's specifications. It is significant to note in this connection that, in time, the paper of Baghdād came to be considered as the very best because of its *thickness* coupled with pliability, while the paper of Damascus took second place (cf. Qalqashandī, II, p. 476).

34. Cf. Karabacek, *Das arabische Papier*, p. 118; *Fihrist*, p. 21.

35. *Fihrist*, pp. 106–7. Some twenty volumes of the work survived to Nadīm's day, who is describing them firsthand.

36. Cf. the writer's "An Arabic Papyrus in the Oriental Institute," *JNES* V (1946), p. 169.

37. Cf. also M. J. de Goeje in *ZDMG* XVIII, pp. 781–807.

38. Cf. *Der Islam* XVII (1928), p. 250, and Brockelmann, *Geschichte der arabischen Litteratur* Suppl., I (1937), p. 310.

39. Thanks to the courtesy of the director of the library, Mr. ʿUmar Riḍā Kaḥḥālah, who not only put the facilities of the library at my disposal but kindly accompanied me on several trips to see some well-known private manuscript collections.

40. The famous al-Firāʿ (d. 207/822), tutor to Maʾmūn's sons, outwitted his publisher's greed, which made his book too expensive for the general public, by starting to dictate his next work directly to the people; cf. Abū Bakr al-Khaṭīb, *Taʾrikh Baghdād* (14 vols.; Cairo and Baghdād, 1931), XVI, p. 150, and Yāqūt, *Irshād* ("Dictionary of Learned Men") ("Gibb Memorial Series" [7 vols.; Leyden, 1907–27]), VII, pp. 227–28.

41. Cf. pp. 74–75, n. 5.

42. Cf. A. S. Lewis and M. D. Gibson, "Forty-One Facsimiles of Dated Christian Arabic Manuscripts," *Studia Sinaitica* vol. XII (Cambridge, 1907), plate XX.

43. Cf. Wright, op. cit., plate XX.

44. Cf. H. L. Fleischer, *Kleinere Schriften* (3 vols.; Leipzig, 1888), III, pp. 393–94.

45. Ibid., pp. 389–90.

46. Cf. the writer's "An Arabic Papyrus in the Oriental Institute," *JNES* V (1946), pp. 169–70, and references there cited.

47. There are several other undated manuscripts that are attributed to

the third century, largely on paleographic grounds alone. They are all Christian manuscripts on parchment with the exception of one that is on paper and one parchment manuscript that consists of Islamic Traditions written in Kūfic. Cf. M. D. Gibson, *Apocrypha Arabica*, *Studia Sinaitica* VIII (London, 1901), p. x and plate I; Fleischer, op. cit., III, pp. 388–94; Wright, op. cit., plates XIX and CXL; and the writer's "Arabic Paleography," op. cit., pp. 81–82, this latter for special comment on the Islamic manuscript. Oriental Institute No. 12027 is an incomplete paper copy of Baghawī's (d. 210 or 14/825 or 829) *Muʿjam al-Ṣaḥābah* and was believed by Moritz, from whom it was bought, to be an autograph copy of the author. This I very much doubt, though the manuscript itself is probably from the third century. Further work on the text itself may yet yield some clues for a more definite dating within the century. Cf. Brockelmann, *Suppl.*, I, p. 278, where the fragment there mentioned is very likely none other than that now in the Oriental Institute.

48. For his bibliography on the *Nights*, cf. Victor Chauvin, *Bibliographie des ouvrages arabes*, IV (1900), pp. 1–2.

49. See ibid., vol. IV, for the earlier bibliographical materials; for the more recent studies cf. J. Oestrup, *Studien über 1001 Nacht* (1891), trans. O. Rescher (Stuttgart, 1925), Foreword (not paginated), and pp. 5–21 (3–26 in the original Danish); Enno Littmann, *Die Erzählungen aus den Tausend und Ein Nächten* (6 vols.; Leipzig, 1928), VI, pp. 770–71.

50. There are several textual difficulties involved in these passages. This in turn has resulted in somewhat varying translations. I shall make grateful use of those offered by de Sacy and Macdonald, altering them only where the text *in its context* would seem to demand the change.

51. ʿAbīd ibn Sharyah, *Akhbār* (Hayderabad, 1347/1928–29), paginated consecutively with Wahb ibn Munabbih's *Kitāb al-Tijān*, pp. 312–13; cf. Brockelmann, *Suppl.*, I, pp. 100–101.

52. Masʿūdī, *Murūj al-Dhahab*, IV, pp. 90–91; cf. Silvestre de Sacy, "Les Mille et une nuits," *Mémoires de l'Académie royale des inscriptions et belles-lettres* X (1833), pp. 30–64, esp. pp. 38–41, 62–64; Duncan Black Macdonald, "The Earlier History of the Arabian Nights," *JRAS*, 1924, pp. 353–97, esp. pp. 362–63.

53. *Fihrist*, p. 304; Macdonald, *JRAS*, 1924, pp. 364–66. For some of the "others" mentioned by Nadīm in passing, cf. p. 61.

54. Cf. Oestrup, pp. 86–87 (119–20), where he seems at a loss to explain this change.

55. For the different early views on these numbers, their changes and their significance, cf. Oestrup, pp. 84–87 (116–21) and Littmann, VI, pp. 696–97. See also Richard Burton, *Nights*, X, p. 75. The edition available to me gives no place and date of publication. It is, nevertheless, the ten volumes of *The Book of a Thousand Nights and a Night* and the seven volumes of *The Supplemented Nights*, published by the so-called Burton Club—a nom de plume of a certain

Boston publisher—presumably in Boston, in 1903. It is, except for splitting Volume III of the *Supplemental Nights* into two volumes, a facsimile of the original Benares edition of 1885–88; cf. Norman M. Penzer, *An Annotated Bibliography of Sir Richard Francis Burton* (London, 1923), pp. 126, 130–32.

56. Op. cit., pp. 38–41, 62–64.

57. The fact that *qahramānah*, "stewardess," does not seem to appear in any copy of Masʿūdī's text would seem to indicate that the word is either a later addition or else belongs with Nadīm's version of the frame story, which makes Shīrāzād's companion not one who accompanied her from her father's home but a woman of the king's household. But in the latter case she would be a stranger and therefore not likely to be so familiar or affectionate with the heroine as our text implies.

58. It is to be noted that this control can be extended up to a point and used as a factor in determining the relative chronological age of the available manuscripts of this section of Masʿūdī's *Murūj* and of the relevant section of Nadīm's *Fihrist.*

59. De Sacy, in his reconstruction of Masʿūdī's text, arrived at these same conclusions; cf. above, p. 55.

60. The equally wide and fascinating problem of the origin and earlier history of the *Hazār Afsāna* itself, on the one hand, and of the post-tenth-century development of the *Nights,* on the other, fall outside the scope of the contribution of the Oriental Institute manuscript.

61. Masʿūdī, VIII, pp. 290–91; *Fihrist,* pp. 304–5.

62. Op. cit., p. 91 (126); cf. p. 68.

63. Oestrup summarizes the arguments, pro and con, on these points up to his time; cf. esp., pp. 9, 80–82, 91, 99, 105–6 (9, 111–14, 126, 137, 146–47) and corrects on p. 81 (112) Manṣūr's dates to read not 712–55 but 754–75. For more recent developments in both camps, cf. Littmann, VI, pp. 695–96, 705–6.

64. For late second- and early third-century works of these types produced by some of the outstanding scholars of the day, including Aṣmaʿī (d. 216/831) and Jāḥiẓ (d. 255/869), and written from linguistic and literary points of view, cf. Brockelmann, op. cit., I, pp. 103, 105, 117, 153, and *Suppl.,* I, pp. 167, 246, and 249; August Haffner, *Drei Arabische Quellenwerke über die* ʾAḍdād (Beirut, 1913).

65. Cf. p. 49.

66. Cf. p. 25.

67. Cf. p. 78, n. 51, and *Fihrist,* pp. 89–90.

68. *Fihrist,* pp. 305, 244–45.

69. Ibid., pp. 305–6, 118.

70. Ibid., pp. 308, 121.

71. Ibid., p. 97.

72. Macdonald, *JRAS,* 1924, pp. 371–72.

73. *Fihrist*, pp. 308, 146–47.

74. Ibid., p. 305; cf. Macdonald, *JRAS*, 1924, pp. 367–72, for a general analysis of *Fihrist*, pp. 305–13.

75. *Akhbār al-Rāḍī wa al-Muttaqī* (from *K. al-Awraq*, ed. J. Heyworth Dunne [Cairo, 1354/1935], pp. 5–6).

76. *Taʾrikh* ("Analium"), ed. J. M. E. Gottwaldt (2 vols.; Lipsica, 1848), I, pp. 41–42; cf. Oestrup, pp. 30–31; Macdonald, *JRAS*, 1924, pp. 361–62.

77. *Taʾrikh*, I, 64; cf. Eugen Mittwoch, "Die literarische Tätigkeit Ḥamza al-Iṣbahānīs," *Mitteilungen des Seminars für orientalische Sprachen (MSOS)* XII (1909), p. 140.

78. Mittwoch, op. cit., pp. 141–47, and in *MSOS* XVI (1913), pp. 37–50. I have been unable to discover any further work by Mittwoch on these as expected by Macdonald, *JRAS*, 1924, p. 362.

79. Cf. Macdonald, *JRAS*, 1924, pp. 361–62.

80. Tauḥīdī, *Al-Imtāʿ wa al-Muʾānasah*, I, 23. I am indebted to Professor von Grunebaum for this reference.

81. For the few later references to either the *Hazār Afsāna* or the *Alf Lailah*, cf. Macdonald, *JRAS*, 1924, pp. 367, 379–80, 390; Littmann, VI, p. 697; Oestrup, p. 98 (135–36).

82. There is a tantalizing reference to an *Alf Lailah* by al-Aṣmaʿī (122–216/739–831) that is reported by E. J. W. Gibb in Burton (*Supplemental Nights*, III, pp. 41–42) and passed over by both without comment. The reference itself is made by the Turkish author ʿAlī ʿAzīz Efendī of Crete in his *Mukhayyalāt-i Ledun-i Illāhi* ("Phantasms from the Divine Presence"), written in 1211/1796–97 and published at Constantinople in 1268/1851–52. The author cites as his source (Turkish text, p. 3), a *Khulāṣat al-Khayāl*, "Extracts of Phantasms," compiled from the Syriac, Hebrew, and other languages. He adds: "When it had been entirely perused and its strange matter considered, as one would from an esoteric strip or a philosophic volume, such as would cause heedfulness and consideration, and yield counsel and admonition, like the ʿIbret-numā of Lāmiʿī and the Elf Leyle of Aṣmaʿī (الف الليلى اصمعى in the Turkish text), certain of the strange stories and wonderful tales of the book were selected and separated, and having been arranged, dervish-fashion in simple style, were made the adornment of the pen of composition and offered to the notice of them of penetration. For all that this book is of the class of phantasms, still, as it has been written in conformity with the position of the readers of these times, it is of its virtues that its perusal will of a surety dispel sadness of heart" (cf. Burton, op. cit., III, pp. 41–47, for Gibb's extracts, in translation, and comments).

The resulting *Mukhayyalāt* contains three phantasms, each consisting of a principal story supported by several subordinate tales. These, in their style and objective, seem to have much in common with the allegorical romances in verse and prose of the famed Lāmiʿī (d. between 1530 and 1532) (cf. E. J. W. Gibb, *A History of Ottoman Poetry* [6 vols.; London, 1900–9], III, pp. 20–34,

353–74). The ʿ*Ibret-numā* (not available to me) is a prose romance characterized by Gibb as "a collection of wild and fantastic allegories" (ibid., III, p. 21). The *Mukhayyalāt* indeed justifies its title and carries out the main objective of the author who presents us with highly imaginative and fairly entertaining romances wherein pious men "yield counsel and admonition" through the exercise of supernatural powers. Not only is there a common ground between these phantasms and the didactic and supernatural elements of the *Nights*, but also the first phantasm (Turkish text, pp. 3–73) actually consists largely of tales from the following stories of the *Nights:* Qamar al-Zamān and Prince Amjad, The Enchanted Horse, and Zain al-Asnām, all woven into one cycle. Thus while the author's reference to the *Alf Lailah* is not inappropriate, his crediting Aṣmaʿī with an edition of that work remains somewhat a puzzle. That Aṣmaʿī edited a "Thousand Nights" which remained unknown and unnoticed through the centuries before and after ʿAlī ʿAzīz Efendī seems hardly possible. On the other hand, in view of the Oriental Institute manuscript confirming the existence of a "Thousand Nights" in Aṣmaʿī's own day, it does not seem improbable that this famed and prolific scholar made reference to the collection in some of his works still unknown to us. The answer may or may not be in ʿAlī ʿAzīz's source, the *Khulāṣat al-Khayāl* which title, however, is not to be found in either Ḥajjī Khalifah or Brockelmann.

Since the above note was written, Dr. von Grunebaum has kindly loaned me his "advance" complimentary copy of a more recent and critical analysis of the *Mukhayyalāt* and its sources, though this, too, throws no more light on the *Khulāṣat al-Khayāl* (cf. Andreas Tietze, "Azīz Efendis Muhayyelat," *Oriens* I [1948], pp. 248–329, esp. pp. 308 ff.).

83. *Murūj*, VIII, pp. 33–35.

84. *Fākhir*, ed. C. A. Storey (Leyden, 1915), pp. 137–40; for translation and comment, cf. Macdonald *JRAS*, 1924, pp. 372–79.

85. See preceding note.

86. Cf. Macdonald, *JRAS*, 1924, pp. 368–71, where he is right to emphasize the acceleration of these factors from the ninth century on but fails to point out that the situation was inherent in the Arab's general outlook on this as on all types of highly fantastic and imaginative fiction.

87. Cf. Nöldeke, *ZDMG* XXXIII (1879), pp. 513–27, esp. pp. 518 and 521; Oestrup, pp. 82, 99 (113, 137); Burton, X, p. 93; Josef Horovitz, *ZDMG* LXV (1911), pp. 287–88; Brockelmann, *Suppl.*, I, pp. 107, 219, 238–39.

88. Cf. *Alf Lailah wa Lailah*, ed. Maximilian Habicht (2 vols.; Breslau, 1825–43), XII, p. 299; ed. W. H. Macnaghten (4 vols.; Calcutta, 1839–42), III, p. 142; (Bulāq, 1279/1823), III, p. 92.

89. Nöldeke pointed out that this particular story had a basis in Persian history (*ZDMG* XXXIV, p. 523); cf. also Oestrup, p. 29 (38).

90. Cf. p. 58.

91. E.g., ed. Habicht, I, pp. 31–32, 36–37, 41–42, 44–45, 49–50, 55; ed. Macnaghten, I, pp. 25, 30.

92. Op. cit., pp. 88–92 (122–28).
93. Cf. p. 59.
94. Op. cit., p. 91 (126)
95. Cf. *ZDMG* XLII; pp. 68–72; Oestrup, pp. 72–79 (99–108).
96. Cf. p. 56.
97. Oestrup, pp. 7, 81–82 (6, 112–13); Burton, X, pp. 71, 93; Macdonald, *JRAS*, 1924, pp. 367, 397.
98. Cf. pp. 61–63.
99. Cf. Burton, X, pp. 132–52; *Suppl.*, VII, p. 426; C. C. Torrey, "The Story of ʿAbbās ibn el-Aḥnaf . . . ," *JAOS* XVI (1894), pp. 44–70; Oestrup, pp. 35–36 (46–47); Macdonald, *JRAS*, 1924, pp. 358–61; Littmann, VI, p. 707 ff.
100. Op. cit., VI, pp. 692, 702–4.
101. See his "Review" at the end of his Vol. III.
102. *JRAS*, 1924, pp. 390–91; cf. Littmann, VI, pp. 705–7; for earlier grouping see, Burton, X, pp. 93–94; Oestrup, pp. 106–9 (147–54).
103. Cf. Littmann, VI, pp. 687–88.

3 The Oldest Documentary Evidence for the Title *Alf Laila wa-Laila*

Solomon D. Goitein

When did the Arabian Nights, that fabulous storehouse of folktales from many countries, peoples, and social layers, get the name "One Thousand and One Nights," under which it became known in Arabic literature?

To answer this question, we still must have recourse to Duncan Black Macdonald's excellent study "The Earlier History of the Arabian Nights" (*Journal of the Royal Asiatic Society* [1924]: 353–97). In any case, I do not see that the article "*Alf Laila wa-Laila*" by the eminent authority Enno Littmann in the new edition of the *Encyclopaedia of Islam* has contributed on this particular point anything beyond Macdonald's findings.

The first element in the title of that popular book—"One Thousand Nights"—is very old, as it is an adaptation of the Persian *hezār efsāne*, which means "A Thousand Stories," according to various Muslim writers the name of a pre-Islamic collection of tales and fables. However, in some manuscripts, as well as in the printed edition, of the book *Murūj al-Dhahab* (IV, Paris, p. 90, line 3) by the eminent Arab polyhistor al-Masᶜūdī (died 956), the author states indeed that a popular rendering of that book was called "One Thousand and One Nights." Ibn al-Nadīm, who lived one generation later and compiled a bibliography of Arabic literature called *Fihrist*, speaks of a similar book, but mentions only one thousand nights (Leipzig,

Reprinted from Solomon D. Goitein, "The Oldest Documentary Evidence for the Title *Alf Laila wa-Laila*," *Journal of the American Oriental Society* 78 (1958): 301–2. Reprinted by permission of the publisher.

1871–72, I, p. 304). A marginal note in a fragmentary manuscript of the *Fihrist* states that the book was called "One Thousand and One Nights" (see D. B. Macdonald, ibid., p. 367). However, unless new evidence is forthcoming, it stands to reason that the two tenth-century authors actually spoke of a book of "One Thousand Nights," a statement that was corrected by later copyists into one thousand and one, in order to fit the title in vogue in their time.

A certain amount of vagueness impairs also the third instance of the occurrence of the title, adduced by Macdonald (ibid., 380–81) and, relying on him, by Littmann in the above mentioned article in the *Encyclopaedia of Islam*. Al-Maqrīzī (died 1442) quotes in his famous *Khiṭaṭ* (ed. Bulāq 1270, p. 485; II, p. 181; ed. Cairo 1325, I, p. 376; II, p. 290) the Spanish writer Ibn Saᶜīd (died 1274 or 1286), relating that a certain Qurṭubī (i.e., a man originating from Cordova in Spain) mentioned the title of a popular book of stories as being *Alf Laila wa-Laila*. For reasons that are not quite evident, Macdonald suggests the reading Qurṭī for Qurṭubī, the former being the name of an Egyptian historian writing under the last Fatimid Caliph al-ᶜĀḍid (1160–71). However, even if Maqrīzī actually had that name, it would not prove much, as a fifteenth-century author and the copyist of his work naturally would give the name in use in that late period.

Under these circumstances, it is fortunate that we possess now a direct documentary evidence for the title *Alf Laila wa-Laila*, coming from Cairo around the year 1150. It is included in a manuscript of the Bodleian Library, Oxford, which was brought there from the so-called Cairo Geniza; this is a repository of discarded writings in Fusṭāṭ or Old-Cairo, written mostly in Hebrew characters, but largely in Arabic language and stemming preponderantly from the Fatimid and Ayyubid periods. It contains many thousands of letters and documents and is an invaluable source for the social history of the whole Mediterranean basin, mainly during the eleventh and twelfth centuries.[1]

Ms. Heb. f. 22 (Neubauer-Cowley's *Catalogue of the Hebrew Mss. of the Bodleian*, no. 2728), fol. 25b–52b, contains the notebook of a Jewish physician, who was also a *warrāq*, i.e., a man who sold, bought, and lent out books and served at the same time also as a notary. This combination may seem strange to us, but it finds some explanation in the fact that the man dealt largely—although by no means exclusively—in medical books. On the other hand, the office of the notary often was connected with that of a bookseller, so much indeed that in a legal document, Bodleian Ms. Heb. f. 56 (*Catalogue* 2821), no. 40, which refers to the Muslim year 521 (1127), the notary who wrote another deed quoted in it, is styled simply as *warrāq*.

In addition to many entries related to the writer's trade in books, the notebook contains eight drafts or memos of legal deeds, four of which are fully dated, ranging from 1155 (fol. 42b) to 1162 (fol. 39b). The first entry on the very first page (fol. 25b) reads as follows:

ᶜInd R(abbi) Menaḥēm k(itāb) al-taʾrīkh
Majd b. al-ᶜAzīzī k(itāb) alf laila wa-lailah
Ben al-Sōfēr al-dayyān k(itāb) ᶜashr maqālāt

"R. Menaḥēm has *The Book of History;* Majd al-ᶜAzīzī, *The Thousand and One Nights.* The son of the scribe, the judge, has *The Ten Chapters.*" Which history book is referred to here cannot be made out, of course. As the man who borrowed the book is styled "rabbi," one might assume that Josippon's very popular *Jewish History* was intended. However, this item is called on p. 38 *Yosᶜ b. Gūriyōn;* therefore, another *Taʾrīkh* must have been meant here.

The Ten Chapters are no doubt Ḥunain b. Isḥāq's *Ten Treatises on the Eye*, mentioned again in full on p. 29. This famous book was translated into English by the late Dr. Max Meyerhof (Cairo, 1928). The "judge" who borrowed the book most probably practiced the medical profession for gaining his livelihood.

Last, but not least, *Alf Laila wa-Laila* was lent out to one called Majd al-ᶜAzīzī. The family name may either go back to the name of the fifth Fatimid Caliph al-ᶜAzīz (976–96), which would mean that the man concerned was the descendant of somebody belonging to the bodyguard or entourage of the Caliph, but as most probably the person was Jewish, it is more likely that the family name refers to one of the various Egyptian villages called al-ᶜAzīzīya (cf. Ibn Doukmak, *Déscription de l'Egypte*, V, p. 56 [in the Sharqīya province]; ibid., p. 84 [in the Gharbīya]). In any case, we see that a book called "One Thousand and One Nights" could be borrowed from a bookseller in Cairo around the middle of the twelfth century.

In conclusion, I should like to remark that the Taylor-Schechter Collection of Geniza papers preserved in the University Library of Cambridge (England) contains many leaves covered with popular stories of the type of *Alf Laila wa-Laila*. A scrutiny of that material possibly may contribute toward the further elucidation of the history of that marvelous book.

Note

1. Cf. the present writer's article, "The Cairo Geniza as a Source for the History of Muslim Civilisation," *Studia Islamica* 3 (Paris, 1955): pp. 75–91.

4 Neglected Conclusions of the *Arabian Nights:* Gleanings in Forgotten and Overlooked Recensions

Heinz Grotzfeld

Certainly no other work of Arabic literature has become so universally known in the West as the *Stories of Thousand and One Nights*, more commonly called *The Arabian Nights' Entertainments* or simply *The Arabian Nights*. Since their first appearance in Europe (Galland's French translation 1704 sqq.; English and German translations of Galland only a few years later), the *Nights* met with lively interest from a large public. In the latter part of the eighteenth century, this interest generated something like a run on manuscripts of the *Nights*, especially in the English world, as is documented by the relatively large number of Arabic MSS of the *Nights* that were purchased by British residents or travelers in the East and are now to be found in British libraries. Even the Calcutta I edition of the Nights of 1814 and 1818 as well as the Calcutta II edition of 1839–42 are due to British activities, since they are both based on MSS brought from Syria or Egypt to India by Englishmen.[1] On the continent, too, one library or another contains MSS of the *Nights*, most of them, however, purchased after 1800 and representing the same recension as the Bulaq edition; a considerable number of older MSS of the *Nights* are to be found only in the Bibliothèque Nationale de Paris.

Reprinted from Heinz Grotzfeld, "Neglected Conclusions of the *Arabian Nights:* Gleanings in Forgotten and Overlooked Recensions," *Journal of Arabic Literature* 16 (1985): 73–87. Reprinted by permission of Brill Academic Publishers.

The interest in MSS of the *Nights*, which is to be observed in the eighteenth century, diminished at the beginning of the nineteenth century. Arabists, anyway, did not make the most of the MSS treasured in European libraries. They were satisfied with picking out stories that had not been translated at that time and, in their own translations or expansions of Galland, simply added them to the repertoire of *Nights* stories already existing. There are two exceptions. One is Joseph von Hammer, whose French translation, made in Constantinople from 1804 to 1806 on the basis of a complete Egyptian MS and sent to Silvestre de Sacy for publication, came out only in 1823, not in its original form, but in a stylistically rather unsatisfactory German version for which his publisher Cotta was responsible. The important information given by von Hammer in his introduction about the *Nights*, the complete list of the stories, their order and segmentation into nights, as well as his view of the history of the work, had been published earlier in the *Fundgruben* and the *Journal Asiatique*. The other exception is Maximilian Habicht, "who, through close intercourse with Orientals during his long residence in Paris, had come to embrace entirely the irresponsible Oriental attitude toward MSS and editing" (Macdonald 1909, p. 687) and made out of fragments of the *Nights* and other material a compilation of his own, which he published in the years 1825–39 (vols. I–VIII of the Breslau edition; the remaining four vols. were published after Habicht's death by H. L. Fleischer, 1842–43).

The Bulaq edition of 1835, which was widely circulated both in the Arab world and in Europe, and the Calcutta II edition, which is of the same recension, superseded almost completely all other texts and formed the general notion of the *Arabian Nights*. For more than half a century it was neither questioned nor contested that the text of the Bulaq and Calcutta II editions was the true and authentic text. This opinion did not change even when in 1887 H. Zotenberg in his *Notice sur quelques manuscrits des Mille et Une Nuits et la traduction de Galland* showed that the text of the Bulaq and Calcutta II editions represented only one recension of the work[2] and that other recensions of the *Nights* were attested by manuscript evidence much older than any evidence for ZER.[3] It is not that the results of Zotenberg's research were disregarded. But a process not uncommon in the history of texts made it possible to preserve the generally accepted notion of the *Nights* more or less unaffected by them: ZER was given, by tacit convention, the status of a *canonical* text, whereas other recensions were degraded to the rank of *apocrypha*. Still another group of texts was classified as *pseudepigrapha*, e.g., the Breslau edition, which was revealed by Macdonald to be a compilation made by its editor Habicht.[4] Even texts that since Galland had been considered to be integral parts of the *Nights*, e.g., Aladdin or Ali Baba, became classified as spurious.[5] Disregarding "apocryphal" or "pseudepigraphical" material may frequently be of little or no consequence. But focusing the view on ZER rather blocked philological research concerning the text. It is one of the purposes of this paper to show that a careful study of "apocryphal" materials can throw new light on the history of the *Nights*.

The original conclusion of the *Nights* seems to be lost. Galland never had a text for the conclusion he gave to his *Mille et Une Nuits*, and he was considered—wrongly, see n. 21—to have invented this end himself. Thus it was not before the early nineteenth century, when copies of ZER came into the hands of Europeans, that an Arabic text of the end of the *Nights* became known in Europe. Hammer boasted of being the first European to have discovered the unexpected conclusion of the *Nights* (for his *unexpected* conclusion, see below). The conclusion of the *Nights* as it stands in the Bulaq and Calcutta II editions is no doubt a very simple piece of literature.[6] Nevertheless, it reflects the conclusion outlined in the latter half of the tenth century in the following famous passage of the *Fihrist:*

> . . . until she had passed a thousand nights, while he at the same time was having intercourse with her as his wife, until she was given a child by him, which she showed to him, informing him of the stratagem she had used with him. Then he admired her undertaking and inclined to her and preserved her alive. And the king had a qahramāna who was called Dīnārzād, and she assisted her in that.[7]

The central idea of the conclusion in ZER, thus, is obviously the same as that of a *Nights* recension that circulated in Baghdad 800 years earlier, though more obscured than at that time.

We do not know what the conclusion was in the Indian archetype nor in *Hazār Afsānah*, the Persian recension. Reflexes of the frame story in the popular literatures of India and its neighboring countries compel us to assume that in the original form of the frame story, Shahrazād continues to tell her stories, in the well-known manner, thus postponing her execution from one day to the other, until she has given birth to a child[8] and therefore feels safe enough to reveal her stratagem to the king, whereupon the king preserves her alive and definitely makes her his queen. The new title the work was given in the Arabic world, *alf layla*,[9] in which the number was taken literally, suggests that Shahrazād has to survive a fixed number of nights by the telling of stories, not the period until she has reached the status of mother, which then safeguards her against execution. The connection between Shahrazād's reaching this status and her ending the storytelling became obscured. That seems to be the case already in the conclusion summarized in the *Fihrist.* The wording of the *Fihrist*, however, does not exclude, even if it does not suggest, that Shahrazād needed exactly 1000 nights to become a mother. Compared with that conclusion, ZER presents a slight but not unimportant change: during the 1001 nights, Shahrazād has borne the king three children. It is difficult to decide whether Shahrazād now has three children because naive tradition could not imagine the king and Shahrazād enjoying the delight of communion 1001 nights successively without the number of children Shahrazād is plausibly to have in that time, and therefore amended the number, or whether she has them because three children were thought to touch the king's heart more effectively than only one child. The latter does not seem to be wholly incompatible with ZER, since here changed numbers occur in two other places in the frame story as well. In the well-known orgy observed by Shāhzamān, the queen enters the garden together with twenty slave girls and twenty male slaves; in G (see n. 30) and other earlier texts, the queen is escorted only by twenty slave girls, ten of whom, however, are disguised male slaves, which becomes clear to Shāhzamān only some time later, when they strip off their clothes. In ZER, the trophies of the young woman held captive in the chest are 570 seal rings; in G and most of the other texts, the number is ninety-eight. The change in both instances is no doubt due to a defective or somewhat illegible text.[10] Nevertheless, it shows the predilection of the redactor of ZER, or more likely of one of his predecessors, for strengthening essential elements of the narration by quantitative arguments.

By linking the end of Shahrazād's storytelling with the thousand and first night, the internal logic of the conclusion is lost: when Shahrazād on the 1001st night requests the king to grant her a wish, namely to exempt her from slaughter for the sake of her three children whom she presents to him, her step has not been prepared in the narrative. Nor has any reason been given—except through the title—that she should do so this very night, since the period of storytelling has nowhere previously been limited, unlike the period of seven days in the *Book of the Seven Sages*, where the span to be bridged by telling stories is set in advance by the horoscope of the hero. One or other among the copyists or compilers of *Nights* recensions also realized this lack. Von Hammer owned (and translated) a ZER-MS containing a revised ZER version. Its conclusion says that on the 1001st night, after the story of Maʿrūf the Cobbler, king Shahriyār was bored by Shahrazād's storytelling and ordered her to be executed the following morning, whereupon Shahrazād sent for her three children and asked for mercy, which was granted her, in the same way as in the other ZER versions. This surprising turn, which could have been borrowed from a parody of the frame story, fully explains why Shahrazād must proceed to act as well as why she finishes telling stories to the king.[11]

Even the author of the poor conclusion that ends the recension contained in the so-called Ṣabbāgh-MS[12] conceived such a double motivation, though one that perfectly fits the poorness of the composition: Shahrazād has related to the king all she knew (*hāḏā mā ʿindī min tawārīḫ as-sālifīn wan-nās al-awwalīn*), "and when king Shahriyār had heard all the tales of Shahrazād, and since God had blessed him by her (sc. with children) during the time he had been occupied by listening to her tales, he said to himself: 'By God, this wife is intelligent, erudite, reasonable, experienced, so I must not slay her, specially since God has blessed me by her with two children.' And he continued that night admiring her wisdom, and his love for her increased in his heart. In the following morning, he rose and went to the cabinet, bestowed a robe of honour and all kinds of favour upon her father the wazīr, and lived together with her in happiness and delight until the angel of Death came to them and made them dwell in the grave" (MS arabe 4679, fol. 401b). In these artless, simple, or poor conclusions[13] we meet the same deterioration that is often to be observed in stories transmitted by long oral tradition: the elements as such of the stories are still preserved, but the original connection between them has become distorted or totally lost. So it is reasonable to assume that the conclusions of ZER and the Ṣabbāgh-MS reproduce what was known about the end of the *Nights* from oral tradition in a more or less skillful arrangement by the respective compiler.

There exists, however, an elaborate skillful conclusion, entirely different from that of ZER. It is attested by some manuscript sources considerably older than ZER, and one printed one, namely Habicht's edition. But since this edition, following Macdonald's article in *JRAS* 1909, was discredited in its entirety, though parts of it reproduce "authentic" *Nights* material, particularly fragments of *Nights* recensions prior to ZER, its conclusion was no longer paid any attention.

So far, I know of four sources for this conclusion:

H: Habicht's edition or compilation of the *Nights;* the end of his compilation, nights 885–end, is based upon the transcript made by Ibn an-Najjār (Habicht's Tunisian friend) of a fragment of a *Nights* recension transcribed in 1123/1711 (see Macdonald 1909, p. 696).

K: MS Edebiyât 38 in Kayseri, Rašīd Efendi kütüphane; this MS is described by H. Ritter in *Oriens* 2, 1949, pp. 287–89; on the basis of its script Ritter gives the sixteenth or the seventeenth century as the date of its transcription ("frühestens 10. jh. H."). The text is divided into nights, but the nights are not numbered, the space for the numbers, which probably were to have been rubricated, not having been filled.

B: MS We. 662 in Berlin, Stiftung Preussischer Kulturbesitz-Staatsbibliothek (formerly Royal Library), Nr. 9104 in Ahlwardt's catalogue; the transcription of the part concerning us is from 1173/1759. The night-formulae and the numbering have been crossed out (see p. 100).

P: MS arabe 3619 in Paris, Bibliothèque Nationale; the MS was formerly marked "Supplément arabe 1721 II" (Zotenberg 1887, p. 214); "d'origine égyptienne écrit au XVIIe siècle ou au commencement du XVIIIe siècle."

The conclusion of these sources differs from the conclusion attested by the *Fihrist* and narrated in ZER, in that Shahrazād does not implore the king's mercy by referring to her status as mother of his child or children, but "converts" the king by telling stories that make him reflect on his own situation so that he begins to doubt whether it was right to execute his wives after the bridal night. No sooner is Shahrazād sure that her stories have taken effect than she begins to tell the prologue/frame story of the *Nights* themselves, somewhat condensed and slightly alienated in that the characters have no names, but are labeled "the king," "the wazīr," "the wazīr's daughter" and "her sister," and the scene is simply "a town":[14]

> It has reached me, o auspicious King, that someone said: People pretend that a man once declared to his mates: I will set forth to you a means of security against annoy. A friend of mine once related to me and said: We attained to security against annoy, and the origin of it was other than this; that is, it was the following: I over-travelled whilome lands and climes and towns and visited the cities of high renown. . . . Towards the last of my life, I entered a city,[15] wherein was a king of the Chosroës and the Tobbas and the Caesars. Now that city had been peopled with its inhabitants by means of justice and equity; but its then king was a tyrant dire who despoiled lives and souls at his desire; in fine, there was no warming oneself at his fire, for that indeed he oppressed the believing band and wasted the land. Now he had a younger brother, who was king in Samarcand of the Persians, and the two kings sojourned a while of time, each in his own city and stead, till they yearned unto each other and the elder king despatched his Wazir to fetch his younger brother . . . (Burton XII, pp. 192–93; I shall skip the rest of the story, which end as follows)
>
> . . . on the fifth night she told him anecdotes of Kings and Wazirs and Notables. Brief, she ceased not to entertain him many days and nights, while the king still said to himself, "Whenas I shall have heard the end of the tale, I will do her die," and the people redoubled their marvel and admiration. Also the folk of the circuits and cities heard of this thing, to wit, that the king had turned from his custom and from that which he had imposed upon himself and had renounced his heresy, wherefore they rejoiced and the lieges returned to the capital and took up their abode therein, after they had departed thence; and they were in constant prayer to Allah Almighty that He would stablish the king in his present stead. And this [said Shahrazad] is the end of that which my friend[16] related to me. Quoth Shahriyar, "O Shahrazad, finish for us the tale thy friend told thee, inasmuch as it resembleth the story of a King whom I knew;

> but fain would I hear that which betided the people of this city and what they said of the affair of the king, so I may return from the case wherein I was."[17] Shahrazad replies that, "when the folk heard how the king had put away from his malpractice and returned from his unrighteous wont, they rejoiced in this with joy exceeding and offered up prayers for him. Then they talked one with other of the cause of the slaughter of the maidens [and they told this story and it became obvious for them, that only women had caused all that][18] and the wise said, 'Women are not all alike, nor are the fingers of the hand alike.'" (Burton XII, p. 197)

The king comes to himself and awakens from his drunkenness; he acknowledges that the story was his own and that he has deserved God's wrath and punishment, and he thanks God for having sent him Shahrazād to guide him back on the right way. Shahrazād, then, lectures on the interrelation between ruler and army, between ruler and subjects, on the indispensability of a good wazīr (which is all somewhat inappropriate in this context), argues by reference to sūra 33:35 that there are also chaste women,[19] and by relating the Story of the Concubine and the Caliph (Burton XII, pp. 199–201; Chauvin's Nr. 178) and the Story of the Concubine of al-Maamun[20] (Burton XII, pp. 202–6; Chauvin's Nr. 179) she demonstrates for Shahriyār that this case is not as unique as he thought, because "that which hath befallen thee, verily, it hath befallen many kings before thee . . . all they were more majestical of puissance than thou, mightier of kingship and had troops more manifold" (Burton XII, p. 199). The king is now fully convinced that he was wrong and that Shahrazād has no equal. He arranges his marriage with her, and marries Dīnāzād to his brother Shāhzamān, who in Samarcand behaved the same way as he had done until Shahrazād entered the scene. Dīnāzād, however, stipulates that the two kings and the two sisters should live together forever. So the wazīr is sent to Samarcand as their governor. The king orders the stories told by Shahrazād to be recorded by the annalist, they fill thirty volumes. There is no mention in these texts of a child, much less three children, as an argument for granting mercy to Shahrazād.[21] The texts of the four sources mentioned above are essentially identical, the variants in number and nature being within the usual confines. But though derived from one and the same version, they constitute the end of two different recensions of the Nights. In H, this conclusion follows the "Tale of the King and his Son and his Wife and the seven Wazirs" (i.e., the Arabic version of the *Book of Sindbād* or *Book of the Seven Sages*); the transition from this tale to the conclusion is seamless and logical:

> King Shahriban (i.e., Shahriyār's name in the Breslau edition) marvelled at this history and said, "By Allah, verily, injustice slayeth its folk!"[22] And he was edified[23] by that, wherewith Shahrazad bespoke him, and sought help of Allah the Most High. Then he said to her, "Tell me another of thy tales, O Shahrazad; supply me with a pleasant story and this shall be the completion of the story-telling." Shahrazad replied, "With love and gladness! It has reached me, O auspicious King, that a man once declared . . ." (Burton XII, p. 192; see p. 93)

In the three other texts, this conclusion is interwoven with the "Tale of Baibars and the Sixteen Captains of Police"[24] as follows: the 16th Captain tells to King Baibars the prologue-story as if related to himself by a friend. The stories told in the Breslau edition by the 14th, 15th, 16th Captain (*n*, *o*, *p* in Burton's translation) in this recension of the Baibars-cycle are told by the 13th, 14th, and 15th respectively (this shift is already prepared in the first half of the cycle: the 5th Captain relates two stories, his "own" and that of the 6th Captain). The stories of the Clever Thief and of the Old Sharper (Burton's *na* and *nb*) remain in their place in the order of tales between *n* and *o*. The 5th Captain thus tells, in the first person singular, the story of the traveler who was threatened by a robber sitting on his breast with a knife drawn in his hand, but is delivered by a crocodile that came

> "forth of the river and snatching him up from off my breast plunged into the water, with him still hending knife in hand, even within the jaws of the beast which was in the river. And I praised God for having escaped from the one who wanted to slay me." The king[25] marvelled and said: "Injustice harms[26] its folk." Then he was alarmed[27] in his heart and said: "By God, I was in foolishness before these exhortations, and the coming of this maiden is nothing but (a sign of God's) mercy." Then he said: "I conjure thee, O Shahrazad, supply me with another one of these pleasant tales and exhortations, and this shall be the completion of the Story of King aẓ-Ẓāhir and the sixteen Captains." And she said: "Well, then came forward another Captain, and he was the sixteenth of the Captains, and said: 'I will set forth to you a means of security against annoy. One of

> my friends once related to me . . .' " (B, fol. 113a; I have borrowed from Burton XII, p. 44 and 192 the translations of the corresponding parts in the Breslau edition = H)

The text of the story told by the 16th Captain (see p. 95) is somewhat fuller in B than in H, which is, for its part, close to the text of K. B and K coincide, however, in minor details both internal (e.g., even the first wives of the two brother-kings are sisters) and external (e.g., the 16th Captain's story has night-divisions at the same places), so there is no doubt that B and K derive from the same version, the fuller text of B being due to a more recent polishing. In P, a considerable portion of the text is missing here: "The Tale of the two Kings," which is told by the Captain, breaks off after the words characterizing the elder kind (" . . . and wasted the land"); then follows immediately the "Tale of the Concubine of the Caliph" (fol. 163b, lines 5–6). The lacuna is superficially dissimulated by the interpolation of *fataᶜ aǧǧab al-malik aẓ-Ẓāhir min hāḏihi l-umūr, fa-lā taᶜaǧǧab ayyuhā l-malik Šahriyār* at the end of the second Concubine tale (fol. 170a). Even the division into nights continues; the numbering, however, runs thus: fol. 163a: 908; fol. 165b: 909; fol. 168a: 1000 (!). Shahrazād finishes telling her stories in that night.

Incorporating the prologue-story into the Baibars-cycle involved a threefold oblique narration, which necessitated some adjustments in the text to be transcribed. The redactor mastered this task well, but eventually, certainly because of failing attention, made a mistake, which then was copied by over-scrupulous scribes. In K, as in B (P: lacuna), the Baibars-cycle ends as follows (somewhat less abruptly than in the Breslau edition, vol. 11, p. 399):

> " . . . and this is the end of what my friend related to me, O King aẓ-Ẓāhir." Those who were attending and King aẓ-Ẓāhir marvelled, then they dispersed. And this is [said Shahrazad] what reached me from their invitation. Then King Shahriyar said: "This is indeed marvellous, but O Shahrazad, this story which the Captain related *to me* (*aḥkā lī*), resembles the story of a king whom I know . . ."

He then asks what the reaction of the subjects was, "so I may return from the case wherein I was" (K, fol. 122b). Shahrazād replies by using nearly the same words as in H (see above p. 93), though on the basis of the premises of this composition she cannot have any further information. In the text of B, the inappropriate *to me* has been eliminated. The story then continues and ends in the same way as in H.

The literary ambition and the skill of the composition—at least of parts of it—are clearly discernible in spite of the somewhat degenerated versions in which it is accessible to us. Redactional mistakes as the aforementioned one indicate that this conclusion was not originally composed for these versions, but is a "recycled" fragment.[28] Since the recensions into which this conclusion have been inserted were in all probability compiled as early as the sixteenth century,[29] the recensions to which this conclusion originally belonged must be considerably older.

Such an early date of origin is suggested by some characteristic details in which the Story of the Two Kings and the Wazīr's Daughter, i.e., the prologue-story, agrees with the prologue in Galland's MS, the earliest extant MS of the *Nights*.[30] As in G, the story immediately begins with two kings who are brothers (ZER begins with a king who divides his kingdom and assigns it to either of his two sons); the younger brother returns to his castle, as in G, to take leave of his wife (in ZER he returns because he forgot *ḥāǧa* "something" or *ḫaraza* "a pearl") and, as in G, he perceives in the garden the wife of his brother together with ten white slave girls and ten male negro slaves (in ZER the number is twenty for each group). The lover of the younger brother's wife is "a man" (*raǧul*, K and B) or "a strange man" (*raǧul aǧnabī*, H), which fits in better with the "man from the kitchen-boys" (*raǧul min ṣubyān al-maṭbaḫ*) in G than with the "negro slave" in ZER. Last not least, the epithets *ǧabbār—lā yuṣṭalā lahū bin-nār* ("a tyrant dire—there was no warming oneself at his fire," see p. 93) that characterize the elder brother occur even in G among the epithets of Shahriyār (they are not found in ZER nor in any other MS which is independent of the G group).[31] This congruence does not necessarily imply that this conclusion ever constituted the end of that recension of which G is an initial fragment, since the prologue in G, too, is most probably a literary spolium;[32] it implies, however, that a prologue like that of H and K, B, P once formed the beginning and the end of a recension of the *Nights* considerably earlier than G.

Although the conclusion incontestably bears an Islamic stamp and at first sight hardly has anything in common with the conclusion summarized by Ibn an-Nadīm, we have to ask ourselves, considering the great age of the composition, whether it is a totally new creation achieved without any knowledge of other conclusions of the *Nights*—or at least without any regard to them—or whether the author of this composition has perhaps also inserted, besides comparatively young elements such as the two concubine tales,[33] fragments of older recensions. I think we have good reasons to assume that this composition includes an element that was part not only of a very old recension of the *Nights*, but also, most probably, of the Indian archetype. Ibn an-Nadīm's words concerning the end of the *Nights*, "until she was given a child by him, which she showed to him, informing him of the stratagem she had used with him," imply, no doubt, the device by which in this composition the king is informed of the matter. For, how did Shahrazād instruct the king? It is hardly conceivable that the structural element par excellence of the (older parts of the) *Nights*, namely telling a story for the most varied purposes (to obtain ransom, to gain time, to entertain, to instruct), should not be employed here: for Shahrazād nothing is better suited to reveal her stratagem to the king than to relate to him the story in its alienated form in which Shahriyār recognizes himself and his own fate as in a mirror. I have no doubt that in the recension of the *Nights*, which the author of the *Fihrist* had before his eyes, the conclusion was introduced by this revelation story, but I consider it also very likely that this was the case already in the Indian archetype of the *Nights*.

Since the king is converted from his hatred for women to an indulgent attitude toward them, and does not simply show mercy, as he does in the *Fihrist*/ZER conclusion, there is no need for Shahrazād to produce a child, or three children respectively, as an argument to obtain pardon. Children would even mar the picture of the sumptuous wedding by which this composition is closed. Therefore I assume that the author of this conclusion dropped the children motif on purpose.

A third version of the end is found in the recension represented by the so-called MS Reinhardt.[34] After the tale of Hārūn ar-Rashīd and Abū Ḥasan, the Merchant of Oman, which is the last tale of this recension (nights 946–52 in ZER), Shahrazād immediately begins the Tale of the Two Kings and the Wazīr's Daughters, without any preparatory transition except for the usual *wa-ḥukiya*, "one relates." The first part of this tale repeats almost verbatim, without any abridgement, the prologue of this recension,[35] the two kings and their father, for instance, being given their names. Only the latter part of the tale is more condensed (the two daughters of the wazīr remain nameless here):

> (Shahrazād is still talking:) " . . . and she occupied him with tales and stories until she got pregnant and gave birth to a boy, got pregnant once again with a girl, and for a third time got pregnant with a boy. They bought white and black slave girls and populated the palace anew, as it had been before, the king not being aware of any of this." The king turned his face to her (i.e., he pricked his ears) and asked: "Where are *my* children?"—She replied: "They are here." Then he said: "So that is the way to let me know! By God, if you had not acted in this manner and caught me with your stories, you would not have remained alive until now. Well done!" Shahrazād replied: "A woman is worth only as much as her intelligence and her faith. Women are very different from one another." And she ordered (*amarat*) her sister Dunyazad to bring the children. . . . (4281, fol. 477b–78a)

The king rejoices at his children and tells Shahrazād that he loves her still more. Complying with her request, he brings back servants and domestics to the palace;[36] he writes a letter to his brother relating to him this happy ending; the brother sends his congratulations and gifts for all of them, "and King Shah Baz and the wazir's daughter abode in all solace of life and its delight until there came the Destroyer of delights and the Sunderer of societies" (the translation of this frequent end-clausula is borrowed from Burton).

I have evidence that the Reinhardt-MS is the original copy of this recension or compilation;[37] so the date of transcription, 1247/1832, is at the same time that of the compilation. In view of this recent date one is not inclined to assume that the end of this recension is a proof of another ancient conclusion of the *Nights*. Nevertheless, it cannot be contested that this conclusion comes closest to that summarized by Ibn an-Nadīm: There are children involved;[38] Shahrazād reveals her stratagem to the king; the king admires her intelligence, he inclines toward her and preserves her alive. Shahrazād's sister has, in this conclusion, the same function as Shahrazād's accomplice in the *Fihrist*-version: she is only a nurse (thus, there is no need to marry her to the king's brother); there is no trace of a "conversion" or "listening to reason." These congruences are not accidental; there must be a connection between the end of the recension known to Ibn an-Nadīm and the conclusion of the Reinhardt-MS. It is not likely that the compiler of this recension knew a version of the conclusions discussed above. It is true that he did not hesitate to recast stories radically, as is shown by the prologue, but if he had rewritten the end, there should be some traces left from the former text. As to Shahrazād's device of informing the king of her stratagem, namely relating his own story to him, there is no model for it in the finale of ZER (which was certainly known to the compiler), nor does it follow immediately from what the *Fihrist* (which the compiler can hardly have known) says about the end. On the other hand, it is obvious that the stories are gathered from very shifting traditions; even such tales as occur under the same title in ZER are not all taken from ZER fragments; the tale of Tawaddud, for instance, is from a tradition that can be traced back to the sixteenth century,[39] quite independently of ZER. Thus, we cannot but deduce that the compiler of the Reinhardt-MS knew a model stemming from a separate tradition, and we must for the present accept the curious fact that the latest recension of the *Nights* obviously presents the very conclusion that is closest to its original form.[40]

Since ZER was regarded as canonical not only in Europe but also in the Arabic world, other recensions were less appreciated even there. The *Nights* fragment B, then, less than a hundred years after its transcription was considered to be trash and was rehashed; by means of a rather superficial revision it was turned into a "new" work: *Kitāb samarīyāt wa-qiṣaṣ ʿibarīyāt*. The redactor's work, however, consisted chiefly in crossing out the Night-formulae and numbers and in adding a few excerpts from other books as well as a new title page (cf. Ahlwardt Nr. 9103 and 9104). We should not let ourselves be deluded by this procedure, any more than that unknown Arabic reader of the "new" work who wrote the following beneath its new title: *hāḏa kitāb min sīrat alf layla ilā intihāʾ as-sīra* ("this is a part of the Story of the Thousand Nights right to the end of the story").

Notes

1. Cf. D. B. Macdonald, *A preliminary classification of some MSS of the Arabian Nights*. In *A Volume of Oriental Studies, presented to E. G. Browne*, ed. T. W. Arnold and R. A. Nicholson (Cambridge, 1922), pp. 313 and 305. The "Egyptian MS brought to India by the late Major Turner Macan," from which Calcutta II was printed, is lost. I rather doubt if this MS was a *complete* ZER copy. Bulaq and Calcutta II differ chiefly in the first quarter, Calcutta presenting in its prose passages an unrevised "middle Arabic" like any other MS of ZER. In the three remaining quarters, the text of Bulaq and Calcutta II is almost identical, Calcutta presenting here the same "polished" Arabic as Bulaq, which is somewhat strange. But this can easily be explained by the—heretical—assumption that these parts of Calcutta II were printed directly or indirectly from the *printed* Bulaq text.

2. Zotenberg called this recension"la rédaction moderne d'Egypte," Macdonald introduced the abbreviation ZER = Zotenberg's Egyptian Recension.

3. All known manuscript evidences for ZER were transcribed shortly before or after 1800; in all probability, the compilation of ZER itself had been carried out only a few years earlier. Mardrus's affirmation that he owned the very MS "de la fin du XVIIe siècle" from which the Bulaq edition was printed (cf. Chauvin IV, p. 109) is a lie.

4. D. B. Macdonald, *Maximilian Habicht and his Recension of the Thousand and One Nights*, *JRAS*, 1909, pp. 685–704.

5. It was out of reverence for their first translator that Mia Gerhardt, *The Art of Story-Telling*, Leiden 1963, p. 15, did not call them so, but euphemistically spoke of "Galland's orphan stories."

6. Burton expanded it with passages taken from the Breslau edition. Lane translated the end as he had found it in his Bulaq copy.

7. Ibn an-Nadīm, *Kitāb al-Fihrist, maqāla* 8, *fann* 1; I quote the translation of D. B. Macdonald, *The Earlier History of the Arabian Nights*, *JRAS*, 1924, pp. 353–97; p. 365.

8. Or until she was pregnant, as in the frame story of the *Hundred and One Nights*, which corresponds much better to our feeling of plausibility. It is quite unreasonable of ZER to demand the audience or the reader to believe that Shahrazād managed to hide her three pregnancies from the king.

9. The oldest documentary evidence for the actual title *alf layla wa-layla* is from the twelfth century and comes from the Cairo Geniza; see S. D. Goitein in *JAOS* 78, 1958, pp. 301–2.

10. The number 570 is obviously a *taṣḥīf* of 98, the *rasm* of a carelessly written *ṯamāniya wa-tisʿīn* being very close to that of *ḫamsimi'a wa-sabʿīn*; it is to be found already in the Paris MS 3612, which is prior to the compilation of ZER. The twenty male slaves have been added in order to make plausible a text in which the passage relating the disguise had been dropped, obviously by a copyist who was unable to guess how the story could have run.

11. Burton missed the point of this modification or interpolation. Although he knew that this reading was to be found in some MSS, he accused Trébutien, the French translator of Hammer-Zinserling, that he "cannot deny himself the pleasure of a French touch" (X, p. 54, n. 2).

12. Paris, Bibliothèque Nationale, MS arabe 4678–79, formerly marked "Supplément arabe 2522–2523," transcribed at the beginning of the nineteenth century in Paris by Michel Ṣabbāgh from an unknown MS that had been transcribed in 1115/1703 in Baghdad, according to its colophon copied literally by Ṣabbāgh; cf. Zotenberg p. 202.

13. Burton says that the Wortley Montague MS in the Bodleian Library "has no especial conclusion relating the marriage of the two brother kings with the two sisters" (XV, p. 351). Does this mean that the MS has a poor conclusion, like that in ZER, or no conclusion at all?

14. This is certainly what was originally intended. The beginning of H and B is still in accord with this intention. In the sequel, names have slipped into the narration: the younger brother lives in Samarcand, the elder in Ṣīn. In K, the alleged friend who relates the story came to "a town in Ṣīn."

15. Burton has added here "of the cities of China" and explained in note 6 that this "is taken from the sequence of the prologue where the elder brother's kingdom is placed in China." He missed the point that in this tale, which he qualifies as "a rechauffé of the Introduction" (note 4), persons and places must remain nameless. *Fī āḫir al-ʿumr* (H = the text translated by Burton; B) is no doubt a corruption of *fī āḫir al-ʿumrān* (K); the best reading is to be found in P: *daḫaltu madīna fī āḫir al-ʿumrān* "I came to a town at the end of the civilized world" (fol. 163b).

16. This shortcut *isnād* is in contradiction with the longer *isnād* in the introductory passage, but it is no doubt that of the older version.

17. The words *hāḏihi l-ḥikāya tušbih li-ḥikāyat malik anā aʿrif-hu* are certainly an integral part of this revelation scene; so is the king's request to hear about the reaction of the subjects *urīd an asmaʿ mā ǧarā li-ahl hāḏihi l-madīna wa-mā qālū min amr al-malik*. But the subsequent final clause *li-arǧiʿ ʿam-mā kuntu fīhi* is not quite logical. An emendation *lammā raǧaʿ ʿam-mā kān fīhi* "when he returned from the case wherein he was," which, regarding the *rasm*, seems to suggest itself, would make the text reasonable.

18. This passage has been dropped from H, but the following statement of the wise presupposes at least *sabab hāḏā an-nisā;* the addition is from B, fol. 114b; nearly the same text is to be found in K, fol. 124b.

19. Women qualified as *muslimāt, muʾmināt, qānitāt, ṣādiqāt . . . ḥāfiẓāt* (sc. *furūǧahunna*) must exist in reality, as they are mentioned in this *āya*.

20. The name of the Caliph in this story is al-Maʾmūn al-Ḥākim bi-amrillāh. The *ism* of the historical caliph al-Ḥākim (who reigned from 996 to 1021) was al-Manṣūr. The scene of the story is Cairo.

21. The spread of this conclusion in the seventeenth century is attested

indirectly by Galland. He had tried in vain to get a complete copy of the *Nights*, nor had he ever had at his disposal an Arabic text of an end-fragment. The ending of his translation therefore has been suspected, until quite recently, to be of Galland's own invention. But from oral information he knew at least the basic concept of this conclusion: as early as August 1702, two years before he published the first volume of his translation, he outlined in a letter "le dessein de ce grand ouvrage: (. . .) De nuit en nuit la nouvelle sultane le mesne [Schahriar] jusques à mille et une et l'oblige, en la laissant vivre, de se défaire de *la prévention où il étoit généralement contre toutes les femmes.*" The words in italics are to be found in the conclusion of Galland's translation, in which Shahrazād does not present children, but is granted mercy because the king's "esprit étoit adouci," and the king is convinced of Shahrazād's chastity. (The quotation from Galland's letter in M. Abdel-Halim, *Galland, sa vie et son oevre,* Paris 1964, pp. 286–87).

22. Text: *al-baġyu yaqtulu ahlahū.* This looks like a proverb, a variant of the one recorded by al-Maydānī, *Maǧmaʿ al-amṯāl,* Cairo 1953, nr. 555 = Freytag, Proverbia Maidanii, cap. II, nr. 129: *al-baġyu āḫiru muddati l-qawmi, yaʿnī anna ẓ-ẓulma iḏā mtadda madāhu, āḏana bi-nqirāḍi muddatihim.*

23. Text: *ittaʿaẓa;* but see the parallel texts, note 27.

24. Translated by Burton from the Breslau edition, XII, pp. 2–44.

25. In K, the king is nameless; P: *al-malik aẓ-Ẓāhir;* in B, his name is Šahribāz.

26. B: *yaḍurru;* P: *yuhliku;* K: *yusriʿu* (= ?).

27. B: *irtāʿa fī nafsihī;* K: *irtadaʿa,* obviously a *taṣḥīf* instead of *irtāʿa.* This passage is not in P, nor is the following dialogue between the king and Shahrazād.

28. In most cases fragments of older recensions were inserted into the new compilation without extensive revision. So quite often it is not difficult to detect such *spolia* by inconsistent distribution of the roles (speaker, hearer, etc.), stylistic peculiarities and the like. The ZER-text however, especially the printed one, has undergone a careful revision.

29. The corruptions found in the text of K, the oldest of the four MSS and carefully calligraphed, show that already that text had been transmitted within a long written tradition.

30. Paris, Bibliothèque Nationale, arabe 3609–11 (formerly marked "ancien fonds 1508, 1507, 1506"). This MS, commonly designated as G, was transcribed after 1425, the year in which the *ašrafī*-dinar (mentioned in 3610, fol. 43b) was introduced, and before 943/1535, the earliest date of a reader's expression of thanks at the end of 3610.

31. *lā yuṣṭalā lahū bin-nār* is among the epithets of ʿUmar ibn an-Nuʿmān at the beginning of the ʿUmar-Romance.

32. It does not come up to the same stylistic and narrative level as the tales inserted into the frame, which are, by the way, far better in the version of

G than in ZER. Shahrazād's first tale however, that of the Merchant and the Jinnī, is as poor as in the printed texts, which proves that even it was part of the initial fragment left from preceding recensions.

33. The tale of the Concubine of al-Ḥākim can have taken its actual shape only after the eccentric person of the historical al-Ḥākim had been transfigured by time, so that he could become a nucleus of popular story or romance. The Zuwayla-Gate mentioned in all the texts was built in 1092; as a *terminus ante quem non*, such an early date is rather insignificant. Also six of the seven poems describing the bride's seven dresses in the Tale of Nūr al-Dīn and his Son (Burton I, pp. 217–19) are used (again?) here for the same purpose.

34. Strasbourg, Bibliothèque Nationale et Universitaire, MS 4278–81. Date of transcription 1247/1831–32. As for the date of the compilation, see note 37. Table of contents in Chauvin, *Bibliographie* IV, pp. 210–12.

35. The prologue has been considerably remodeled in its details: the seats of the two kings have been exchanged; the younger brother is deceived by his chief concubine, the elder by his wife; the number of slave girls and male slaves who accompany the queen into the garden has been raised to eighty; Shahrazād is the younger of the two daughters of the wazīr.

36. The untrue slaves had all been executed, so the palace, at least the *ḥaramlik*, had been totally depopulated.

37. The text has been divided into nights by relatively long formulae with separate spaces left for the numbers of the nights. The night-formulae always fill half a page; the nights themselves measure two and a half pages, the formulae not included. The scribe has evidently inserted the night-formula rather automatically, on every third or fourth page, into the text he was copying. But he has made a mistake, for there is one too many: after the formula used for the 1001st night, there is yet another, which was crossed out later. If the MS were a transcription from a compilation already lying before the copyist's eyes, the lines that were crossed out and the free space for the night-number would not have been copied.

38. The composition does not say how many children Shahrazād herself is supposed to have. The number of the heroine's children in Shahrazād's revelation is no doubt borrowed from ZER.

39. The version of Tawaddud is very different from that in ZER, but close to freely circulating versions of the story, e.g., that of MS We. 702 in Berlin (Ahlwardt Nr. 9179), transcribed in 1055/1645.

40. "A quite modern MS may carry a more complete tradition than one centuries older" (Macdonald 1922, p. 321).

5 The Age of the Galland Manuscript of the *Nights:* Numismatic Evidence for Dating a Manuscript?

Heinz Grotzfeld

The importance of the age of the Galland manuscript of the *Nights* derives from its being the oldest manuscript extant of this text. There is no date of transcription in the manuscript. In an earlier study, the present writer postulated 1426 as a date *post quem* because of the mention of the coin *ashrafī* (first issued by al-Ashraf Barsbāy in 1426). This date *post quem* has been rejected by Muhsin Mahdi, the editor of the manuscript, in a recent publication in which he attempted to identify the *ashrafī* mentioned in the text with the gold coin issued by al-Ashraf Khalīl (1290–93). This article shows that his identification is untenable, and that the Galland manuscript, in all likelihood, was not copied earlier than 1450.

In a few years, the West is going to celebrate the 300th anniversary of the discovery of the *Thousand and One Nights*. In recent years, some such centenaries have given cause for a new evaluation of the celebrated event; sometimes there has been a call for a devaluation of the event—as was the case with the 500th anniversary of the discovery of America.

It cannot be said that the discovery of *Alf layla wa-layla* is to be considered parallel with the discovery of America, neither in its importance for the course of world history, nor in its consequences for the "victims" of the discovery. There is a parallel insofar as the

Reprinted from Heinz Grotzfeld, "The Age of the Galland Manuscript of the *Nights:* Numismatic Evidence for Dating a Manuscript," *Journal of Arabic and Islamic Studies* 1 (1996–97): 50–64. Reprinted by permission of the author.

treasures of this New World, the world of the *Arabian Nights*, since their discovery, have become the property also of the West—where these treasures, by the way, were more highly appreciated than in the East. But the parallel is not complete: the East was never deprived of these treasures. What might be worthy of blame in this discovery is that the *Arabian Nights* have contributed, especially by their widespread reception, more than any other work to the creation of that somewhat distorted image of the East that partly still persists in the West, and hampers a deeper understanding of the East and its very nature. But I would like to emphasize that this image, though distorted, replaced another, unfavorable, image of the East, marked by the fears of an aggressive Muslim Empire.[1]

It is not the aim of this paper to make the discovery of the *Nights* nor the man who discovered them for Europe, Antoine Galland, the subject of a reevaluation—or devaluation.

From the dedication of Galland's translation of the *Nights* and from his correspondence, the circumstances of the discovery of the Nights are relatively well known. In the spring of 1701, Galland had completed his translation of the *Adventures of Sindbad the Sailor*. Before the manuscript went to the press, he was informed by Syrian friends living in Paris, that these adventures of Sindbad the Sailor were part of a far larger Arabic collection ("recueil") named "Les mille et une nuits." He tried to get a copy of this collection—"il a fallu le faire venir de Syrie"—and in the fall of 1701, he got with the aid of "un ami d'Alep, résident à Paris" three volumes of *Alf layla wa-layla*. The first volume of Galland's French translation came out in 1704, which was the beginning of a new phase in the eventful history of *Alf layla*.

Since their first appearance in Europe, the *Nights* have met with lively interest from a large public. In the latter part of the eighteenth century this interest generated something like a run on manuscripts of the *Nights*. The chief aim of this search for MSS, however, was to find a complete copy of the *Nights;* and when in the first years of the nineteenth century complete copies of the *Nights* had come into the hands of European travelers—most of them were amateurish orient-lovers, but some were qualified scholars—and when finally, in the 1830s the printed editions of the *Nights* appeared and it became clear that all these texts presented almost the same repertoire of stories, this chief aim seemed to have been achieved. The Bulaq edition of 1835, which was widely circulated both in the Arab world and in Europe, and the Calcutta II edition of 1839–42 (which is of the same recension), superseded almost completely all other texts and determined the general perception of the *Arabian Nights*. For more than half a century it was neither questioned nor contested that the text of the Bulaq and Calcutta II editions represented the true and authentic text. As a quite logical side effect, incomplete copies, such as the Galland MS, were no longer given any attention. To be precise, it cannot be said that the Arabic text of the *Nights* of whatever recension or MS, had been the object of any serious philological research until the end of the nineteenth century. It was not before 1887 that Arabists made the Arabic text—or, more precisely, the various Arabic texts (in the plural) of the *Nights*—the object of their studies. In this year, Hermann Zotenberg published an extensive study with the title "Notice sur quelques manuscrits des Mille et Une Nuits et la traduction de Galland," where he showed that the Bulaq and Calcutta II editions represented only one recension of the work and that other recensions of the *Nights* were attested by manuscript evidence much older than any evidence for what he called "la rédaction moderne d'Égypte," and what we usually call ZER, Zotenberg's Egyptian Recension.

Zotenberg's pioneering study not only introduced a pattern for understanding the differences and variations found in the MSS and printed editions of the *Nights*—variations in the repertoire of the stories, their order, and in the wording of the texts—it also gave prominence to the very MS that Galland had purchased in 1701 from Syria.

After Galland's death (1715), the three volumes of this MS were given to the Bibliothèque du Roi, later to be called the Bibliothèque Nationale (de France), where the MS, now nos. 3609, 3610, 3611, as it seems, never was paid special attention until Zotenberg not only observed that the wording and narrative of this MS were far better than in most other versions, especially better than in the parallel stories in ZER, but also realized that it was the oldest MS of the *Nights* in the Bibliothèque Nationale and the oldest one at all known to him. In his judgment, which was based on paleographic arguments, the MS was transcribed in the second half of the fourteenth century.

He published a page of the Galland MS in facsimile, and on the basis of the facsimile of this one page, Nöldeke wrote in his review of Zotenberg's book (*WZKM* 2 [1888]: p. 170) that this date was by no means too early.

The Galland MS and other old MSS of the *Nights*, the importance of which had been established by Zotenberg, were then the object of the research of Duncan Macdonald. In the beginning of this century, Macdonald announced his project for publishing a critical edition of the Galland MS as the basis for all further research about the text of the *Nights* and its history. He never achieved his project. It was Muhsin Mahdi who finally in 1984 presented his critical edition of *The Thousand and One Nights: From the Earliest Known Sources*, but we are indebted to Macdonald for some substantial preparatory studies in this field, which were published between 1909 and 1924. His preparatory studies are highly valuable contributions to the "demystification" of the matter: he could demonstrate that the "Breslau edition" was not based on a true oriental recension of the *Nights*—as its editor says on the title page—but was a compilation made by its editor Maximilian Habicht himself, a compilation that included, however, fragments of "authentic" recensions of the *Nights;* he could further demonstrate that the text of the Calcutta II print—which is said, on the title page, to be based on a MS brought from Egypt—is partly expanded by passages taken from the Calcutta I print, which is of the same recension as the Galland MS; and he was able to classify most of the MSS of the *Nights.*

A minor result of Macdonald's studies is of high relevance for this paper. He called into question the date of the Galland MS: "Local Cairene references in it indicate a date considerably younger than that assigned by Zotenberg" (1922, p. 307). In his article "The Earlier History of the *Arabian Nights*" (*JRAS*, 1924, pp. 353–97), he repeated this statement: "We shall see, I think, that both of these estimates [of Zotenberg—second half of the fourteenth century—and of Nöldeke—still older] make the MSS too old" (p. 382). But he did not assign any date to the MS; the most precise words are those found in his article "Alf Laila wa-Laila" in the supplement to *EI*[1] (1934) referring to William Popper's article "Data for Dating a Tale in the Nights" (*JRAS*, 1926, pp. 1–14): "Professor Popper considers that the reference to the Naḳīb Barakūt puts the story [of the

Christian broker in the Hunchback cycle] after 819 (1416). In addition to all this, time must be allowed for the stories to have become so popular that they were taken into a recension of the *Nights*" (21a). This statement, however, is made in a context where Macdonald is arguing against the supposition that the stories that constitute the corpus of the Galland MS formed the *Nights* recension already in Fatimid times. This is, maybe, the reason why later publications on the *Nights* completely disregarded Macdonald's doubts as to the age of this MS. Elisséeff (p. 56) and Tauer (p. 128) followed Zotenberg as to the date, without any argument in favor of this assignment or against Macdonald's choice of a later date.

Muhsin Mahdi's edition appeared in 1984. The Galland MS that is at the basis of this edition—since it is the oldest extant text—has been assigned a date of transcription in the fourteenth century.[2] The authority of Theodor Nöldeke that Muhsin Mahdi refers to, is of little weight in this connection. What he says about Macdonald[3] applies even more to Nöldeke, who is likely to have seen of the Galland MS no more than that facsimile page published by Zotenberg.

There is, however, a hidden clue in the MS itself. When working in the early 1980s on microfilms of the Galland MS and the Sabbagh MS for the study published by my wife and me in 1984, we discovered in the story told by the Jewish physician in the Hunchback cycle a key for dating the MS—at least for defining the date *post quem*. We discovered a *coin*. The hero of this story, a young man from Mosul who traveled together with his paternal uncles to Damascus, relates (3610, fol. 43r–43v = p. 319, 17–21 of Muhsin Mahdi's edition):

> Fa-nazalnā fī baʿḍi 'l-khānāti wa-waqafū aʿmāmī wa-abāʿū biḍāʿatī wa-matjarī, fa-kasaba 'l-dīnāru khamsatan, fa-fariḥtu bi-'l-ribḥi. Wa-tarakūnī ʿumūmī w-tawajjahū ilā Miṣra wa-qaʿadtu baʿdahum. Fa-lammā sāfarū, aqamtu anā wa-sakantu fī qāʿatin kabīratin bi-rukhāmin wa-fisqīyatin wa-ṭabaqatin wa-khizānatin wa-māʾin yajrī 'l-layla wa-l-nahāra, wa-tuʿrafu bi Qāʿat Sūdūn ʿAbd al-Raḥmān, fī kulli shahrin bi-ashrafīyayni.[4]

> We stayed in one of the caravansaries, and my uncles sold my goods at a profit of five dinars for each dinar, and I was delighted by this profit. Then they left me and went on to Egypt, while I stayed (in Damascus).

> After their departure, I moved to a large house, paved with marble and equipped with a fountain, a *ṭabaqa*, a *khizāna* and with water running night and day, known as Qāʿat Sūdūn ʿAbd al-Raḥmān, which I rented for two *ashrafis* a month.

The word *ashrafi* in the text put us into the situation of an archaeologist who has discovered a coin in an archaeological layer. Coins found in an untouched layer of an archaeological site or in a hoard are indisputable indicators of the date *post quem* for the origination of the layer or site or the hiding of the hoard in the ground, provided, of course, that the coins are not obliterated to such a degree that it is impossible to identify them. Coins mentioned in a text can serve the same purpose, provided that, on the basis of the name used for the coin, it is possible to identify an individual coinage. In Arabic texts, however, this is very rarely the case: coins are mentioned mostly by their generic name, e.g., *dirham* or *dīnār*. But the half *dirham* (*niṣf dirham* or simply *niṣf*) minted by the Mamluk sultan al-Muʾayyad Sayf al-Dīn Shaykh al-Maḥmūdī (815–24/1412–21) and the *dīnār* minted by al-Ashraf Sayf al-Dīn Barsbāy (825–41/1422–37) met with such a success as to make the name of these coinages *muʾayyadī* and *ashrafī* synonymous for nearly a century with their respective generic names *niṣf* and *dīnār*. As for the *muʾayyadī*, to be precise, it seems that this was the case mainly[5]—or only—among European merchants and pilgrims, who throughout the fifteenth century and still in the sixteenth century used to call the half dirham *maydin* or *meidin*. The word *ashrafi*, on the other hand, was actually used, in the later fifteenth and the beginning of the sixteenth centuries, by the Arabs themselves, Egyptians as well as Syrians, as a synonym for *dīnār*, especially when what was meant was the *dīnār* as a gold coin, not as a monetary unit. The word was also used for the *dīnārs* minted by the successors of al-Ashraf Barsbāy. European merchants and travelers, unless they called these *dīnārs* simply *ducat*, that is, by the name of its European counterpart, used to call this coin *serif*, *cerif*, or *serifi*, in the plural *serifin*, *cerifin*, or the like.

The name of this coin gave us an indisputable *terminus post quem* for the transcription of the MS, since this new type of gold coin of the same weight as the Venetian ducat had been introduced by an edict of 15 Ṣafar 829 = 27 December 1425 as a measure to replace the ducat in commercial transactions in Egypt and between Europe and Egypt. The measure itself came into effect only in 831/1427–28, when the first installment of the ransom (the total amount of which was 200,000 ducats) for the Cypriot king James was paid. This provided the Mamluk sultan with bullion for issuing a sufficient number of coins. One has to add some years before it could again become common practice to specify prices, rental rates, and the like by a number of coins—no longer by a number of theoretical or fictive currency units. We thought that we had to add at least some ten or fifteen years before this practice and the name of the new coin would be mirrored in everyday language as exemplified by the usage of Arabic authors of the latter part of the century.[6] So we concluded that the Galland MS could not have been copied before 1426 and that it was copied, in all likelihood, in the second half of the fifteenth century. This conclusion was put forward in our booklet "Die Erzählungen aus 1001 Nacht" (Darmstadt, 1984, pp. 26–27) and repeated in a very condensed form in my article "Neglected Conclusions" (*JAL*, 16 [1985], p. 85, n. 30). (This article is a slightly expanded English version of a paper I presented to the 23rd Deutscher Orientalistentag in Tübingen in the spring of 1983.)

We overlooked at that time that the same line contains a further key for defining a date *post quem:* Qāʿat Sūdūn ʿAbd al-Raḥmān, the name of the mansion that the young man hired. There can be no doubt that what the author or redactor of the story has in view is the Dār Sūdūn Ibn ʿAbd al-Raḥmān (variant: Bayt Sūdūn min ʿAbd al-Raḥmān). This building is mentioned by Ibn Ṭūlūn in a note of 900 H. = 1494 A.D. as the residence of the Ḥanbalite *qāḍī* (I, p. 161, l. 12) and in notes of 922 and 923 H. = 1516 and 1517 A.D. as the quarters of the Ottoman sultan Selim (II, p. 35, l. 1 and II, p. 70, l. 20). In the last mentioned place, the building is said to be *al-maʿrūfa qadīman bi-Dār Sūdūn* (without *Ibn* or *min*) *ʿAbd al-Raḥmān wa-yawmaʾidhin bi Tanim mamlūk Sibāy*, "which formerly was known as the mansion of Sūdūn ʿAbd al-Raḥmān and now as that of Tanim, the mamluk of Sibāy." Sūdūn min ʿAbd al-Raḥmān had been *nāʾib al-Shām* in the years 827–35/1424–32; he fell into disgrace with the sultan al-Ashraf Barsbāy, was removed, and died in 841/1438 in Damietta. He was jailed according to Maqrīzī (*Sulūk*, IV, p. 1066 f.) or simply exiled (Sakhāwī, *Ḍawʾ*, II, p. 275 f.). Sakhāwī points to his building activity during the years of his niyāba in Damascus.

I cannot see exactly what consequences dating the Galland MS in the second half of the fifteenth century would imply for the stemma of Muhsin Mahdi. As I understand his explanations, all development and ramification, all copying and loss of copies could have happened in the same way, even if the Galland MS was transcribed one hundred years later than he supposed. Muhsin Mahdi, in any case, rejected our arguments for a date of transcription in the late fifteenth century—not openly, but in a more tacit, though unmistakable way. In the third part of his edition, *Introduction and Indexes*, which appeared in 1994, he published, as a kind of frontispiece, the photo of a dinar issued in the year 690/1291 by the Mamluk sultan al-Ashraf Khalīl.

The legend

Ashrafi Dinar (see Night 133)
Damascus 690 A.H./[A.D. 1291]
Put in circulation during the reign of al-Ashraf Khalil
B. N. Lavoix 793, Phot. Bibl. Nat. de Fr., Paris

suggests that this coin is the *ashrafī* mentioned in the text, and that we were wrong in identifying the *ashrafī* of the text with the type of coin inaugurated by al-Ashraf Barsbāy and issued until the end of the Mamluk state in 922/1517, when the Ottomans conquered Syria and Egypt. This calls for a response.

My response consists of two parts. In the first part, I am going to sum up the arguments for our identification of the "two *ashrafīs*" of the text with the gold coin of al-Ashraf Barsbāy and his successors. It can be demonstrated that the text passage quoted above (pp. 109–10) fits very well into the usage of the later fifteenth and the beginning of the sixteenth centuries. In the second part, I will demonstrate why the "two *ashrafīs*" of the text cannot be identified with the "dinar" of al-Ashraf Khalīl.

First of all, we have to take a short digression into the monetary history of the Mamluk period. I quote Jere L. Bacharach:[7] "The traditional Muslim coin was the dinar with a canonical weight standard, the *mithqâl*, of 4.25 grams. With the advent of Saladin's rule in Egypt (566/1171) this traditional weight standard for individual dinars was dropped and stamped pieces of coined gold of varying weight were issued. This policy was continued under Saladin's descendants, the Ayyubids, then during the first period of Mamluk rule, the Baḥrî, and finally into the Circassian period. While the weight of individual pieces varied from under 5 to over 15 grams, almost all the issues had a very high degree of fineness." In the beginning of the fifteenth century, there were several attempts to introduce again a Muslim gold coin with a weight standard, but they failed, as is reported unanimously by the Arab historians, and the Venetian ducat remained the most common currency even in the Mamluk State. "The reassertion of a Muslim coin over its European counterpart on the Cairo, and by extension Mamluk, market took place during the sultanate of al-Ashraf Barsbāy. His coin, the ashrafī, gave its name to almost all the gold coins issued by the succeeding Mamluk sultans. Even the Ottoman sultans used the name for their Egyptian gold coins."[8]

There may have been several motives for replacing the ducat by an Islamic gold coin; in any case, making transactions possible by count was a chief aim. In this, the Mamluk sultans were successful. A second aim was the creation of a reliable reference unit for values and prices. In this, they were only partly successful. Especially in Egypt, people continued for a long time to specify values in *riṭl* or *fulūs*, as Maqrīzī remarks. Prices specified in numbers of *ashrafīs* do not occur in texts relating *ḥawādith* before the middle of the fifteenth century. In texts relating *ḥawādith* from the second half of the century and the first quarter of the sixteenth century, prices or fares in *ashrafīs* are not unusual, but they occur less frequently than prices specified in *nisf/anṣāf* or in *dirhams*. Partly, this can be explained by the nature of the merchandise or the service: if prices in general do not exceed fractions of the *ashrafī*, then it is more reasonable—for better comparison with the higher or lower prices mentioned elsewhere in the chronicle—to specify the prices in *anṣāf* or *darāhim*.

Examples of the common usage may be found in two Arabic works from the beginning of the sixteenth century: the *Badāyiʿ al-zuhūr fī waqāyiʿ al-duhūr* of the Cairene Ibn Iyās (1448–1524) and the *Mufākahat al-khillān fī ḥawādīth al-zamān* of the Damascene chronicle-writer Ibn-Ṭūlūn (1475–1546). Each author made the final redaction of his chronicle or diary after the Ottoman conquest of his own city, but in general I think that they reproduced their information about prices and the like from their sources or *muswaddāt* without any changes. The usage is also mirrored in the "Pilgrimage" of Arnold van Harff, a German nobleman from Cologne who traveled disguised as a merchant through Egypt and Syria in 1497 and visited St. Catherine Monastery and the Holy places in and around Jerusalem. He was in close connection with two Mamluk officers of German origin, and in particular the account of his stay in Cairo seems to be reliable, whereas the account of his voyage around the Red Sea and his visit to Mekka is no doubt a literary fiction.

Ibn Iyās, *Badāyiᶜ al-zuhūr*, p. 18; 858 H. = 1454 A.D.:

> In the month of Ṣafar (February 1443), the sultan issued a decree that Zayn al-Dīn al-Ustadār be exiled permanently to Jerusalem. When after his departure he had come to Sabīl Ibn Qāymāz, the sultan sent to him a person in order to control him, but only 300 *dīnārs* and a little bit of silver was found with him. He had been denounced to the sultan for carrying (a considerable sum of) money with him . . .

The word *dīnār* in this text means gold coins. The common gold coin in 858 was already the *ashrafī*, but *dīnār*, as this passage demonstrates, was still the common word in combination with higher figures.

Ibn Iyās, *Badāyiᶜ al-zuhūr*, p. 244; 859 H. = 1455 A.D.:

> In this month (Muḥarram 859 = 22.12.1454–20.01.1455), the price of gold rose so that the *ashrafī* dinar reached an exchange rate of 370 *dirhams* (= trade *dirhams*).

Ibn Iyās, *Badāyiᶜ al-zuhūr*, p. 52; 862 H. = 1458 A.D.:

> In the month of Rabīᶜ I (17.01.–15.02.1458), the exchange rates for gold and silver were made known by official announcement. The sultan had issued new silver coins. The rate for the gold dinar was set to 300 (trade dirhams) and the rate for the new silver (as follows): 25 good *nisf ᶜadadī* ("intended to circulate by number") of fine silver for each *ashrafī*.

This is nearly the same exchange rate mentioned by Harff forty years later (p. 94; trans. p. 112): "by law a man must give each housewife daily three madines, which equal twenty-six to a ducat (drij madijn, der doynt seesindtwentzich eynen ducaeten)."

Ibn Iyās, IV, p. 323; 919 H. = 1513 A.D.:

> The sultan was afflicted by a serious eye disease, and as a sign of his repentance, he distributed alms to his soldiers:
>
> "Monday the 15th of Jumādā I, the sultan distributed the pay and together with it a supplemental gift. He gave every mamluk 30 dinars, the disabled 20, the veterans 10. And he gave 5 dinars to the *mamālīk kitābīya* (i.e., those who already had a contract—*kitāba*—to be set free, but were at the service of their master until the complete amount stipulated for their liberation was paid), and to those of the orphans who were entitled to a pay of 1 *ashrafī*, he gave 2 *ashrafīs*, and to others whose pay was 1,000 (dirhams?), he gave 10 dinars . . ."

This text demonstrates the use of the word *ashrafī* side by side with the word *dīnār*. The higher amounts are specified in dinars, the bookkeeping term, the smaller ones in *ashrafīs*, the name of which evokes the image of the coin itself in the mind of the reader. The reader, so to speak, is to visualize the sultan handing over the two gold coins to the orphans.

The same contrast between these two words is to be observed in the work of Ibn Ṭūlūn (I, p. 142; ll, pp. 8–13):

> A person had bought a house, the *thāniyāt* of which required an embellishment.[9] So, he called for construction workers, made a contract with them, gave them the key and went to his work. When they were working and digging in the place, a coconut shell fell upon them from the place where they were digging. In this coconut there were 410 *dīnārs*, and they started quarreling over them. The *nāʾib* heard about this, and he took the gold and gave them ten *ashrafīs*.

The confiscated amount is specified by the more abstract bookkeeping term *dīnār*, the reward for the finders by the tangible name of the coin.

On the other hand, there are numerous cases where *ashrafī* is used simply for specifying prices, fares, or taxes.

Some evidence for prices

3 *irdabb* wheat for 1 *ashrafī* in Ramaḍān 896 = July 1491 (Ibn Iyās, III, p. 284)

1 *riṭl kumathrā* ("pears" ?) for 2 *ashrafīs* during a pestilence in Cairo in Jumādā II 897 = April 1492 (Ibn Iyās, III, p. 287)

1 *irdabb* wheat for 3 *ashrafīs* in Rabīᶜ I 903 = November 1497 (Ibn Iyās, III, p. 382)

one *ashrafī* for 30 pieces of coconut reported as a very cheap price in Mekka from Dhū 'l-Ḥijja 895 = October 1490 by Ibn Ṭūlūn (I, p. 135)

Evidence for fares

A very interesting passage is Ibn Ṭūlūn, I, p. 129; ll, pp. 14–22 (895 H. =1490 A.D.):

> Saturday the 18th of Shawwāl = 04.09.1490, the pilgrims set out for Mekka. (Silver) dirhams had become very scarce, unlike the *ashrafīs* and copper coins, which were mostly (of the type called) *qarābīṣ*,[10] but prices were low. A very strange thing happened. ᶜAyyāsha, the sister in law of Jaᶜfar al-Miṣrī, of the relationship of the *ḥājib al-kabīr*, had made a contract with a *mukārī* for travelling in a *shiqqa* (one half, or side, of a camel-litter) at a fare of fifty *ashrafīs*, with her daughter on the other side. She got in, but when she arrived a Qubbat Yilbugha, she came down with a fever and said, "I'll return." A woman said to her, "I'll get in instead of you; I am going to write an obligation to pay the fifty *ashrafīs* on my return from the Hijaz." She did so, and ᶜAyyāsha returned to her room (*ṭabaqa*, "a small room on the top floor"), looked out of her window, fell down (to the ground) and broke her neck.

I would like to call attention to the word *ṭabaqa*. It occurs in the characterization of the Qāᶜat Sūdūn that the young man in our tale had rented. It is obvious that a *ṭabaqa* is an element in the architecture of a wealthy house.

The fifty *ashrafīs* are to be seen, I think, as the fare for first-class traveling. Arnold von Harff, the young German traveler, paid in 1497 a fare of two *ashrafīs* for a journey in a camel-litter from Cairo to the Monastery of St. Catherine on Mt. Sinai. In his "Pilgrimage," he reproduces the form of a contract with a *mukārī* (I give it in the English translation of Malcolm Letts, p. 134):

> I N. Mokari will carry N., this Frank (so they call us who come from our countries) from here in Cairo to the monastery lying below Mt. Sinai on a good camel, on which he shall sit on one side in a wooden box covered with a thick pelt and carrying on the other side his provisions and the camel's food. I shall carry also for him two udders, namely goat-skins, full of water for him, myself and the camel. In addition I will assist him to get on and off the camel, and will stay by him by day and night and attend his welfare. This Frank N. is to give me two seraphin, namely two ducats, one at Cairo and the other when we reach the monastery below Mt. Sinai.

The fare for the journey from Cairo to Jerusalem was according to Harff six ducats (*vj ducaeten*).

Taxes specified in *ashrafīs* are mentioned especially in the last years of Mamluk rule and at the beginning of Ottoman rule. Ibn Iyās (V, pp. 54–55; Jumādā II 922 = July 1516) may suffice as an illustration of the attempts of Qānsūh al-Ghawrī to mobilize the last economic resources of Egypt in order to cover the pay of his soldiers and the costs of his military operations.

I would also like to call attention to a passage from the obituary note of Qānsūh al-Ghawrī, who died in Ramaḍān 922 = October 1516 (Ibn Iyās, V, p. 89).

Ibn Iyās enumerates the *masāwī*, the bad sides of the late sultan: his monetary policy was the most disastrous ever; his gold and silver coins were falsified, alloyed with copper, and debased. He imposed on the market an extra tax of 2.700 *dīnārs* per month—which led to higher prices. "And he imposed further a considerable sum per month on the mint, as a result of which they openly (*jahāran*) added copper and lead to the gold and silver. When a gold *ashrafī* was refined, then the resulting fine gold was worth only 12 *nisf* [instead of 25 silver *nisf* or 50–55 contemporary debased *nisf*?]. The sultan had handed over (*sallama*) the mint to a person named Jamāl al-Dīn, and this man acted fraudulently with the property of the people. He ruined the currency, he withdrew the gold coins of the preceding sultans and issued new coins, so that no longer a dinar or a dirham of any one of them was to be seen . . . (l, pp. 16 ff.)."

The lamentations of Ibn Iyās over the debasement of the *ashrafīs* struck under this Jamāl al-Dīn seem to be exaggerated: the exchange rates for the *ashrafī* proclaimed in Damascus Tuesday 23 Rajab 923 = 11 August 1517, after the Ottoman conquest when there was no longer any need to apply the official rates of the Mamluk sultans, were sixty (*niṣf*) for *ḍarb Qānṣūh al-Ghawrī* and fifty-six for *ḍarb Jamāl al-Dīn* (Ibn Ṭūlūn, II, p. 65). The rates proclaimed in Cairo in Dhū 'l-Qaʿda 926 = October 1520 were 50 *niṣf* for *al-ashrafī al-dhahab al-ʿuthmānī wa-l-ghawrī* and 42 *niṣf* for *al-ashrafī alladhī huwa ḍarb Jamāl al-Dīn* (Ibn Iyās, V, p. 356).

In the historical texts, the pay and the gratification of the mamluks are often specified in *ashrafīs.* From some passages in Ibn Iyās, it becomes evident that at least during the rule of Qānṣūh al-Ghawrī, the official exchange rates were applied even to the pay of the soldiers: they got instead of gold the official equivalent in silver or copper and lost in this way 20 to 25 percent. Harff, however, reports from 1497 that the mamluks who participated in the campaign against Āqbardī al-Dawādār had received "ander halff hundert ceraphin, das sijnt ducaeten, zu rustgelde ind darzoe eyme yecklichen des maentz twelff seraphen ind dat allet wael betzaelt" (p. 156; l, 26), "a hundred and fifty seraphin for equipment, and in addition each month twelve seraphin well and truly paid" (trans., p. 182).

These figures fit well with the information of Ibn Ṭūlūn (II, p. 20; Jumādā I 922 = June 1516) that the *nāʾib* of Damascus intended to pay his mamluks a *jāmakīya* of 50 *ashrafīs,* that is, 80 *ashrafīs* less than the mamluks of the sultan had received for their participation in the campaign against the Ottomans, which fact led to a revolt.

In the passage of the *Nights* quoted above (pp. 109–10), the words *bi-ashrafiyayn* presuppose that *ashrafī* is a kind of currency unit. That it is a coin cannot be demonstrated from the text.

The dinar of Barsbāy, as was shown above, had been introduced with the intention of creating an Islamic gold coin that could, like the ducat, circulate by number, and no longer, as had been necessary in the case of the earlier coin-shaped ingots, by weight. And that is just what makes the coin a currency unit. This coin was called *ashrafī.* From the historical texts, we know that the *ashrafī* was a gold coin with which a new weight standard was introduced (3.41 g). That led finally to a new definition of the unit dinar. Formerly, 1 dinar had been equal to 1 *mithqāl* (4.25 g) of gold. Now, 1 dinar was equal to 1 *ashrafī*. The words *ashrafī* and *dīnār* occur side by side in the texts, as in the passage quoted above, and they seem to have been largely interchangeable. So it could happen that people, by inadvertence, replaced the word *dīnār* with the word *ashrafī*, even when speaking of times before the introduction of the coin *ashrafī*. This happens with Ibn Iyās, who "speaking of the price of wheat in 803 A.H. anachronistically says it reached 4 Ashrafis!"[11]

Thus, I think we have all reason to accept the identification of *ashrafīyayn* in the text of the *Nights* with the coin/currency unit *ashrafī* of the later fifteenth century.

As regards the dinar of al-Ashraf Khalīl, there are no reports that this sultan who ruled for only three years and fifty-seven days (689–93/1290–93) made any attempt at a monetary reform, so that a new coin would have been nicknamed after him. On the contrary, his dinars display the same absence of a weight standard that was usual in his century and the following. The weight of the coin shown in the frontispiece of Muhsin Mahdi's third volume is 7.51 g (Balog, p. 122, no. 148). The weight of al-Ashraf Khalīl's other gold dinars listed by Balog are 4.60, 6.42, 6.80, 7.10, and 8.41. The weight of one specimen is not specified. Thus, the dinars of al-Ashraf Khalīl, as those of all Mamluk sultans until al-Ashraf Barsbāy, are not coins (I quote Balog, p. 40) "in the strict sense of the word, but only ingots (in the shape of coins), which could not have circulated by count, but had to be weighed." Thus the dual in the *Nights* passage (which implies that these *ashrafīyayn* circulated by count) would make no sense with reference to "coins" of al-Ashraf Khalīl.

There is no argument at all to identify the *ashrafī* of the *Nights* text with any other *ashrafī* than the gold coin issued by al-Ashraf Barsbāy and his successors. Consequently, there is no argument at all to date the Galland MS of the *Nights* earlier than ca. 1450 A.D.

Notes

Slightly condensed version of a public lecture held September 12, 1995, in the Orient-Institut der Deutschen Morgenländischen Gesellschaft, Beirut, Lebanon.

1. As late as 1683, Qara Mustafa had besieged Vienna; the ultimate termination of Ottoman expansion was reflected in the treaties of Karlovac/Karlowitz (1699) and Požarevac/Passarowitz (1718).

2. "Hiya ghayru muʾarrakha, . . . wa-lākinna waraqahā wa-khaṭṭahā yadullu ʿalā annahā nusikhat fī 'l-qarni 'l-thāmini mina 'l-hijrati (al-qarni 'l-rābiʿi ʿashara mina 'l-mīlādi)." I, p. 29. More detailed vol. II, pp. 239–40.

3. "Ammā Macdonald, fa-lam yaqṭaʿ fīhā raʾyan wa-lam yakun qad faḥaṣa waraqa 'l-nuskhati faḥṣa khabīrin. . . . Wa-lā yaẓharu annahu raʾāhā bi-ʿaynihi aw faḥaṣahā bi-diqqatin." II, p. 239.

4. Mahdi notes the presence of an anomalous second *alif* after the *bi-* in *bi-ashrafiyanyi*, but retains it in his text. It could be even *bi-ashrafayni*, with the extra *alif* and only one *yāʾ*.

5. Lane, *Manners and Customs*, Appendix B (p. 579 of the Everyman's Library edition) says that the smallest silver coin "faḍḍah" was called "nuṣṣ," and adds that it was also called "meyyedee." Johannes Wild, in whose few quotations of Arabic words the colloquial usage of the beginning of the seventeenth century is mirrored, speaks only about "nuss" (*Neue Reysbeschreibung eines Gefangenen Christen etc.*, Nürnberg, 1623, passim).

6. Maqrīzī has devoted in his treaty *Shudūr al-ʿuqūd fī dhikr al-nuqūd*, completed in Ramaḍān 841 = March 1438, a long passage to the dirham muʾayyadī (ed. al-Sayyid Muḥammad Baḥr al-ʿUlūm, pp. 32–36) in which he appreciates the reform aspect of this minting. On the other hand, he does not mention at all the *ashrafī*, which fact makes it evident that, as late as February 1438, the importance of Sultan al-Ashraf's monetary reform was not obvious for him.

7. "The Dinar versus the Ducat," *International Journal of Middle East Studies* 4 (1973): p. 84; cf. also the remainder of the article (pp. 77–96).

8. Ibid., pp. 87–88.

9. I do not know the meaning of the architectural term *thāniyāt*. Belot has *thāniyā* "poutrelle."

10. Ibn Ṭūlūn (I, p. 286) relates the *ibṭāl al-qarābīṣ al-nuḥās min al-fulūs*, the proclamation of discontinuing these copper coins in Shaʿbān 910 = January 1505. But I do not know exactly what kind of *fils* this is.

11. Popper, *Egypt and Syria under the Circassian Sultans*, p. 50.

References

Bacharach, Jere L. "The Dinar versus the Ducat." *International Journal of Middle East Studies* 4 (1973): pp. 77–96.

Balog, Paul. *The Coinage of the Mamluk Sultans of Egypt and Syria. Numismatic Studies*, no. 12. New York, 1964.

Elisséeff, Nikita. *Thèmes et motifs des mille et une nuits; essai de classification.* Beirut, 1949.

Harff, Arnold von. *Die Pilgerfahrt des Ritters Arnold von Harf etc.* hsg. von Dr.

E. von Groote. Cöln: J. M. Heberle (H. Lempertz), 1860. English translation by Malcolm Letts: *The Pilgrimage of Arnold von Harff, Knight, from Cologne. . . .* Works issued by the Hakluyt Society; 2nd ser., no. 94. London, 1946.

Ibn Iyās. *Badāyiʿ al-zuhūr fī waqāyiʿ al-duhūr.* Unpublished pages of the Chronicle of Ibn Iyās. Ed. Mohamed Mostafa. Cairo, 1951.

———. *Die Chronik des Ibn Iyās.* 2. Aufl., hsg. von Mohamed Mostafa. 3–5. Teil. Bibliotheca Islamica 5, c–e. Cairo, 1963, 1960, 1961.

Ibn Ṭūlūn, *Mufākahat al-khillān fī ḥawādith al-zamān.* The Chronicle of Ibn Tulun. Ed. Mohamed Mostafa. Parts 1–2. Cairo: Wizārat al-Thaqāfa wa-l-Irshād al-Qawmī, 1962–64.

Lane, Edward William. *The Manners and Customs of the Modern Egyptians.* Everyman's Library, no. 315. London; Dent; New York: Dutton, 1954.

Maqrīzī, *Shudhur al-ʿuqūd fī dhikr al-nuqūd.* Ed. al-Sayyid Muḥammad Baḥr al-ʿUlūm. Najaf: al-Maktaba al-Ḥaydarīya, 1387/1967.

Popper, William. *Egypt and Syria under the Circassian Sultans, 1382–1468 A.D.: Systematic Notes to Ibn Taghrî Birdî's Chronicles of Egypt.* Berkeley: University of California Press, 1955–57.

Tauer, Felix. "Tausendundeine Nacht im Weltschrifttum als Gegenstand der Lektüre und der Forschung." In *Irrgarten der Lust.* Insel Almanach auf das Jahr 1969 (Frankfurt/Main, 1968), pp. 122–47.

Wild, Johannes. *Neue Reysbeschreibung eines Gefangenen Christen etc.* Nürnberg, 1623.

6 The Sources of Galland's *Nuits*

Muhsin Mahdi

The history of the *Arabian Nights* took a fortunate but subsequently misunderstood turn in 1700 or shortly thereafter when Antoine Galland received a three-volume Arabic manuscript titled *Arabian Nights*,[1] which he had procured from Syria. Apparently misinformed, he assumed that there was an original containing far more material than this manuscript and he tried for many years to obtain a copy of it, in vain. He not only made questionable assumptions about the *Arabian Nights*, but he also, in writing a French adaptation of them, failed to give his readers an unambiguous account of his source. His *Mille et une Nuits* (1704–17), which qualified as a translation according to the standards of his time, misled readers in the West and even in the Middle East about the relationship between what he called the copy and the original. Yet his Oriental expertise and his narrative talent resulted, despite his modesty about the latter, in an immensely popular work.[2] The present study will investigate his sources, his use of them, and the example he set for others who would adapt the tradition for French readers.

In a letter to Huet on October 13, 1701, he describes his Syrian manuscript as "trois volumes intitulés Les Mille Nuits." Undated, but written perhaps in August of 1702, a letter to Cuper states: "Je n'ai qu'environ quatre ou cinq cents de ces nuits en cinq volumes arabes, qui me sont venus d'Alep, d'òu j'attends le reste." The dedication to the Marquise d'O in the first volume of his adaptation (1704) affirms that he has received "quatre"[3] volumes of the *Nights* from Syria, without specifying the language they were written in,

Reprinted from Muhsin Mahdi, "The Sources of Galland's Nuits," *International Journal of Islamic and Arabic Studies* 10 (1993): 13–26. Reprinted by permission of the author and the publisher.

and that the first two volumes of his adaptation will render the first volume of the manuscript. The "Avertissement" following it gives a different account: of the thirty-six parts in "l'original arabe" (N. 21), the first two volumes in the *Nuits* render only one. How many volumes, therefore, did he receive from Syria: three, four, or five? Did a fourth and a fifth arrive after the initial shipment? When he died, his manuscripts were deposited in the Bibliothèque du Roi, which would become the Bibliothèque Nationale. Of the two inventories taken, Jean Boivin did one in a hurry.[4] He cites "deux volumes" of the *Nights* in Arabic, numbers 5 and 6, and left 7 blank. A longer, more detailed and precise inventory[5] cites the *Nights* "en 3 vol." (no. 15) in Arabic and "en un vol." in Turkish (no. 37). This inventory also cites "The Story of Sindbad the Sailor" in Arabic (no. 12) and "The Story of the Forty Viziers" (no. 40) in Turkish. Galland inserted a French adaptation of "Sindbad" in his *Nuits* but he excluded the "Forty Viziers."

When he read his newly acquired manuscript, he admired the ingenuity of an author or authors who could blend so many extraordinary events into a coherent narrative.[6] The size of the complete original as he conceived of it raised his enthusiasm in the "Avertissement" to the first volume of his *Nuits:* "L'original arabe . . . a trente-six parties; et ce n'est que la traduction de la première qu'on donne aujourd'hui au public" (N. I, 21). Here he refers to the first two volumes of his adaptation, which cover the first of the four volumes in the Arabic manuscript according to his dedication to the Marquise d'O that precedes the "Avertissement." The complete original would therefore have had to consist of thirty-six volumes of the same size and the complete French adaptation, of seventy-two, each with more than three hundred duodecimo pages like the first volume published in 1704. The first volume of the Galland manuscript and the first two volumes of Galland's *Nuits* contain the same sixty-nine nights; so the entire original would have to contain thirty-six times sixty-nine or 2,484 nights, almost two and half times as many as the title indicates.

Galland gives us even less explicit or consistent information about the other manuscripts he used for his adaptation. He does not say whether they presented the stories they contained as a part of the *Nights*, whether night breaks continuously divide the text into units of similar length, or whether Shahrazad addresses the King at the beginning of each story. This negligence is surprising in view of his training in the study of manuscripts under Barthélemy d'Herbelot's guidance.[7] His long experience in procuring Arabic, Persian, and Turkish manuscripts for patrons who expected him to assess their value and verify their contents should have instilled in him a habit of inspecting and describing them carefully. Likewise his cataloguing of manuscripts for libraries. In his writings, however, he does not even state whether he had used written Arabic sources for all of the stories in his *Nuits*. What did he mean by "l'original" of which he says he is making "une copie"? The original of what? A copy of what? This mystery encouraged forgers, who always thrive on allusions to manuscripts without accurate information about their identity, contents, or location. They fabricated copies of what scholars long believed to have come from Galland's Arabic manuscripts by translating his French adaptation back into Arabic.

The responsibility for all of this fraud weights on the shoulders of Galland himself. He had taken what he presented as a complete French translation of the *Nights* from various sources, some of which had little to do with the tradition. He systematically and intentionally concealed this practice from his readers, although he had every opportunity to disclose it in the Avertissements, footnotes, and comments that he added to his *Nuits*. The precedent encouraged generations of unscrupulous scribes, editors, and adaptors to fabricate ever more complete editions and adaptations, some of them taken from his own work. His twelve volumes, which he repeatedly describes as a translation of the *Nights*, are partly an original work of fiction.[8] But he did more or less accurately paraphrase the stories in the three-volume manuscript.

In addition to the Arabic *Sindbad* he already owned, Galland apparently acquired various manuscripts of the *Nights* in Arabic and Turkish between 1701 and 1704, but definitely two of the *Nights* in Arabic: the three-volume Syrian manuscript and a volume, now lost, containing the stories of Qamar al-Zamān and perhaps Ghānim. If we credited the four to five hundred Arabic nights in five volumes claimed by his letter to Cuper in August of 1702, we would have to account for two Arabic volumes in addition to the three-volume manuscript. These two volumes could have contained about two hundred nights and he might have taken Ghānim from one of them, while the other might have contained another version of *Sindbad.* Perhaps he acquired these two volumes from Aleppo to supplement the three-volume set. He may have received them some time between October 13, 1701, the date of his letter to Huet, and August 1702, that of his letter to Cuper.

In any case, three of the four volumes mentioned in his dedication to the Marquise d'O are the same as numbers 3609–11 in the Arabic manuscript collection of the Bibliothèque Nationale. The fourth could be a volume now lost or the Turkish volume, which is Volume 11 in a set under the call number 356 in the Turkish collection of the Bibliothèque Nationale. We can account for the five volumes in Arabic mentioned in the letter to Cuper in August of 1702 by the three-volume manuscript, the volume now lost, and a volume containing *Sindbad.*[9] We can explain the discrepancy between the five volumes of 1702 and the four of 1704 by the fact that the Marquise d'O had already read Galland's adaptation of *Sindbad* and knew of the Arabic volume containing this story. In the dedication to her, he cites that volume before the other four. In the letter to Cuper, on the other hand, he simply may have added the volume containing *Sindbad* to the other four, since all five are in Arabic and came from Syria.

In his "Avertissement" he does not say that he has all thirty-six parts of the *Nights.* If he had had them, would he not have said so? In this case, why would he have interrupted his adaptation after the first two volumes containing the first part and waited for another manuscript from the Middle East? Nowhere in his correspondence, journals, or the later volumes of his adaptation does he say that he has or has ever had a complete set of the *Nights* in thirty-six parts. Thus we can dismiss the speculation about manuscripts in his possession of which we have no evidence and concentrate on those we know he acquired as well as those available to him in France. The existence of a version in thirty-six parts may have been hearsay or speculation inspired by his Turkish manuscript or an Arabic manuscript that Benoît de Maillet had acquired from Egypt early in the eighteenth century. Both belonged to the early Egyptian recension of the *Nights* and borrowing from one of them may have resulted in the differences between Galland's adaptation and the three-volume manuscript. The first part of the Maillet manuscript resembles the first volume of the Galland manuscript and corresponds to the first two volumes of Galland's *Nuits.* It contains 870 nights divided into twenty-nine parts. If we subtract 870 from 1001, we obtain 131 nights, which might have been divided into seven more parts, hence thirty-six in all.[10] There is no evidence, however, that Galland used any of these manuscripts or any others that he did not own.

Like others, he fell under the spell of the title: "A Thousand and One Nights!" Assuming that the original contained just that many, he yearned for a copy that would provide him with the ones missing in his three-volume manuscript, which ends abruptly after several nights in the Story of Qamar al-Zamān. Finally he despaired of finding this original[11] and added extraneous material to his adaptation until it reached a length that he considered equivalent to a thousand and one nights. Although he described it as complete, he did not tell his readers how he had completed it and misled them into believing that he had found a complete original. After enticing them with the promise of a thousand and one nights, therefore, he satisfied them by fabricating the necessary supplement.

His *Nuits* sold well and his readers wished for more, so writers like Denis Chavis and Michel Sabbagh sought to exploit the demand by fabricating additions to his additions. They even denied that he had the entire original, as if they had it themselves! They excused the liberties they took by vague allusions to the exotic provenance of the tradition, the orality of the transmission, the variations in content and volume. They obfuscated the relationship between their "translations" and the Arabic "original" so much that one can hardly determine what they pretend to be translating, whether any of their sources are an authentic part of the *Nights* or even Arabic sources at all. Who originated these sources? When and where did they do it? The legend of a complete original incited first the "translators" and then the "editors" of the Arabic recensions to forge expanded versions that would impede investigation of the historical, literary, and linguistic background. The Arab origination of stories like "ʿAlāʾ al-Dīn and the Magic Lamp" and "ʿAlī Baba and the Forty Thieves" remains controversial to this day.

Still, Galland had discovered what remains the most valuable Arabic manuscript of the *Nights.* It was his adaptation of this manuscript that stimulated interest and enthusiasm in the West. Yet he might have acquired as great a reputation if he had confined himself to the stories in the manuscript or, at least, acknowledged the sources of the others that he added. His style and charm as well as his popularity and his influence on Western narrative eclipsed his misuse of the Syrian recension and his ambiguity about it. He had the opportunity and the ability to write a genuine translation of the *Nights*, but impatience and laxity undermined his resolve. He admitted the liberties he was taking in his correspondence and journals, which he left to posterity. How did he expect that they would judge the disparity between his public and private testimony? Perhaps the contemporary indifference to textual integrity and especially in the case of an exotic text lulled his conscience.

Critics who apparently do not know Arabic have praised his adaptation for its originality. Aware nonetheless of the liberty he took with his principal source, they excuse him on the grounds of eighteenth-century practice. It is true that few translators attained and few readers expected the accuracy now required. Should modern standards not determine, however, the present value of such a work? Divergence from a source may result from vices rather than virtues, vices like ignorance, incompetence, and sloth rather than dishonesty, of which Galland seems innocent. Although long ignored, both the adaptation and the source now enjoy recognition by historians of literature as important contributions to the evolution of narrative prose in the West and the Middle East. Galland did introduce a new genre to French literature and expose Western readers to a valuable tradition that they would otherwise have remained unaware of. Proud of this achievement, he testified that he had tried to preserve the character of the Orientals and illustrate their culture. He deviated from his source, he claimed, only when "la bienséance" necessitated it. Readers who know Arabic and compare "l'original" avec "la copie" will agree that it "fait voir les Arabes aux Français avec toute la circonspection que demandait la délicatesse de notre langue et de notre temps" (N. I, 22). He did not intend, in other words, to translate the Arabic text as accurately as his translations of more serious works[12] required, but rather to appeal to a popular audience.

He felt free to abridge, omit, and alter as he saw fit; eliminate repetition, amplify the text, or add explanations wherever he thought readers might benefit from them; correlate different elements of the narrative and add transitions from one to another.[13] Except for occasional paraphrasing, he eliminated the many lines of poetry in his sources and proceeded as if he were adapting several Arabic sources, some real and some imaginary. In order to make his text more intelligible and coherent, he did not hesitate to take liberties with the real ones. He even managed to do these things without committing many blunders or advertising his ignorance as others did. Yet he might have produced a greater literary monument if his antiquarian, numismatic, and cultural research had left him more time and energy for his work on the *Nights.*

In his dedication for the Marquise d'O, he recommends "le dessein ingénieux de l'auteur arabe, qui n'est pas connu, de faire un corps si ample de narrations de son pays, fabuleuses à la vérité" (N. I, 20). Plausibly perhaps, he assumed that a single author had collected the stories, most of them no doubt by others, and united them in a frame story. Despite his enthusiasm for the technique, he eventually abandoned night breaks and the continuations of the frame story that accompanied them on the grounds that they were boring his readers.[14] Assuming nonetheless that the author had intended to add more stories to his collection, he introduced many stories himself, regardless of their provenance, as long as they were Arabic in origin.[15] Here again, he did not disclose what sources he had taken them from. Some of them came from the Egyptian rather than the Syrian branch of the tradition while others had nothing to do with the *Nights.* "Qamar al-Zamān" and "Ghānim" appear to have come from one or more manuscripts of the Egyptian branch, but "Sindbad" had never been a part of the *Nights* before he inserted it in his adaptation. The supplementary material he heard or read from the Maronite Hanna further complicates the situation, for nothing original remains of it except some extracts in Galland's journal.[16]

One might also ask whether he succeeded in creating a coherent whole including the material previously unrelated to the *Nights.* Critics anxious to raise it to the status of a literary masterpiece[17] must demonstrate that it has the structural integrity we expect of such an outstanding work, unless they only mean that it consists of stories deserving this recognition. Arabists can prove that he adapted sources of unequal value and from various genres. No one has ever, to my knowledge, compared each of the resulting parts in the adaptation with its source in a study of genre, structure, and style.[18] Nor has anyone determined whether Galland was able to sustain the quality of his *Nuits* when, after exhausting his three-volume manuscript, he began to exploit other sources, written and oral.[19] His work does not deserve the reputation that some would confer it unless the results of such a study confirm it.

Certainly the study would have to allow for the standards to which he conformed. Roland Mortier describes the classical conception of the relationship between imitation and originality as follows:

> L'art est conçu . . . comme une mise en forme de données préexistantes, comme un arrangement plus habile et plus heureux. Il ne doit ni surprendre, ni déranger, mais plaire. La réussite suppose une supériorité, ou tout au moins un écart par rapport au modèle, mais cet écart ne peut transgresser les limites fixées par le "bon goût." Tout se joue donc dans une marge très étroite, puisqu'il faut éviter à la fois de copier servilement et de choquer par une liberté excessive.[20]

The prestige of feminine high society in matters of literary taste inclined Galland to appeal to them in order to assure the success of his adaptation.[21] Recognition of their authority obligated him to remain within the confines of what they considered good taste, hence for example his suppression of certain licentious passages in his sources. Yet this consideration does not justify the alleged superiority of his *Nuits* over other adaptations by him such as *Les Fables indiennes de Bidpaï* (1724). Nor does it free critics from the need to ascertain the relationship between source and derivation, especially in this controversial case.

Unfortunately, some of Galland's sources have disappeared and, of those still available, all but one, his three-volume manuscript, have been altered. Critics should nonetheless compare his adaptation with them to the extent that they can, in spite of the confusion caused by what he said and did. The only original and authentic Arabic version of the *Nights* available to him and us both is the three-volume manuscript. Ironically, the very success of his *Nuits* incited other writers to add new material to the collection, thus complicating the restoration of the sources for which we have no original document. His appreciation of and dependence on the three-volume manuscript for a major portion of his text does not support the persistent speculation on the oral origin of his *Nuits*. As for the alleged oral origin of the Arabic tradition during the manuscript age, Western scholars long confused the *Nights* with oral storytelling and folklore to which they never belonged. Unable to read the three-volume manuscript, they did not realize that much of what they admired in Galland's *Nuits* is also in this source.

He adapted all of the material in the manuscript except the beginning of "Qamar al-Zamān." His reproduction of unique features in it proves his dependence on it. "Schahzenan" (e.g., N. I, 23) for instance translates Shahzanan (e.g., Mahdi I, 54), a corruption of Shahzaman. "[Le] pays de Zouman," which he locates "dans la Perse" (N. I, 72), renders Zuman (Mahdi I, 93n) which occurs only in the three-volume manuscript. All other Arabic versions contain Ruman or "Roman" by which Medieval Arabs referred to Byzantium. "The Story of the Jealous Husband and the Parrot" in Galland's *Nuits* was not available to him in France except in the version in the three-volume manuscript. In "The Story of the Hunchback," he refers to the Caliph Mustansir Billah as "Mostanser Billah" (N. II, 19),[22] which appears only in this manuscript and in a Vatican collateral not available to Galland. The latter omits "The Tale of the Third Old Man" in "The Story of the Merchant and the Jinni" and Galland does not insert a tale of his own in its place as some of the Egyptian manuscripts do. Instead he has Shahrazad say, "Je ne vous la dirai pas, car elle n'est pas venue à ma connaissance" (N. I, 63). I could add more examples.

Those I have given sufficiently demonstrate that Galland not only relied on the three-volume manuscript for this part of his *Nuits*, but also did the work expected of any editor and sometimes badly. He sought to repair defects in the text, fill in gaps, and smooth transitions. He likewise substituted names for the identification of characters by their profession. Other changes seem less useful, such as additions and notes that distract readers from the plot. Occasionally, as Hawari remarks, he interrupts Shahrazad with comments by "nous" (N. I, 210), apparently him and his fellow Frenchmen. He explains what a prayer rug is and composes a prayer for the occasion to inform his readers about Middle Eastern religion.[23] According to the same critic, he should have summarized all of the verse, for it plays an essential role in the Arabic *Nights.* He did not omit it to expedite the narrative, but rather because he found it difficult to translate (Hawari, 159–60). Jean Gaulmier finds that he omits details requiring a vocabulary "unavailable" in French, such as the colors of the seven wedding gowns in "The Story of Nūr al-Dīn ʿAlī" (N. I, 11). Although Gaulmier excuses him on the grounds that he wanted to avoid boring details, Galland reproduces other elaborate descriptions fully, such as Nūr al-Dīn's deathbed recommendations to his son (N. I, 311–12). He even elaborates on the conversations between Shahrazad and Shahriyar between the stories and partly in order to replace the night breaks he omits. Since none of this editing requires much talent or effort, critics who praise him for it are not very convincing.

A missing folio in the three-volume manuscript leaves a gap in the text from the beginning of the Night 102 until that of Night 104, or from the first sentence of "The Hunchback" to the arrival of the tailor and his wife in the Jewish doctor's house. Did the missing folio reach Galland in such bad condition that he had to recover what he could from it and imagine the rest from the context? Or, what seems more likely, was it missing when the manuscript arrived, thus necessitating a more elaborate restoration? Since, in either case, he did not have another manuscript of the *Nights,* he could have read on until the end of the story and learned the details necessary to fill in the gap by a summary in Night 169. Instead, however, he simply turned to Night 170 at the end of the story, discovered that the hunchback had apparently died from choking on a fish bone caught in his throat and rewrote the missing text in Gallandese Arabic on the margin of the manuscript. This he translated into French for insertion in his adaptation.

He assumed that the bone simply lodges in an apparently sober hunchback's throat while he is eating some of the fish served by the tailor's wife. In the Arabic *Nights,* the tailor playfully crams a piece of fish down a drunken hunchback's throat. He and his wife met him on a stroll through the city gardens and invited him to a dinner that the tailor bought already cooked. Galland had the tailor sitting in his shop when the hunchback joins him to sing and play his tambourine. The tailor takes him home where his wife has already cooked the dinner herself. All of this appears in volume 4 of the *Nuits* published in 1704. While working on volume 5, which he would publish in 1705, Galland discovered the summary in Night 169 that did not agree with his account of the accident at the beginning of the story. He therefore imagined an episode in which the tailor and some friends dine "jusqu'à la prière d'entre le midi et le coucher du soleil" (N. II, 69). He returns to his shop, although he normally would have closed it by then, and works until a drunken hunchback appears. Neither did Galland's alterations improve the story nor did he intend for them to do so, but merely to improvise an agreement between his hasty insertion of the story and the summary near the end.

When he read "The Tale of the Barber's First Brother" in the three-volume manuscript, he misunderstood the identity of several characters. Likewise a tailor, this brother falls in love with a rich man's wife, who induces him to make clothes for her and her husband without taking any pay. Every time he brings the new clothes, the husband acts as if he were going to pay, but his wife discourages the tailor from accepting the money. Galland assigned this intervention to a slave girl acting on the wife's behalf because he assumed that "al-Ṣabiyyah," young woman, referred to "al-Jāriyah" (Mahdi I, 351), slave girl, in the preceding sentence. He also confused the rich man, who has a mill in the lower part of his house, with his miller.[24] The rich man in the manuscript marries the tailor to the slave girl and tells him to spend the night in the mill before consummating the marriage. The miller in the *Nuits* invites him to dinner and, on the pretext that it is too late for him to go home, invites him to sleep on a bed in the mill. The rich man in the manuscript orders the miller, whom the tailor does not know, to go to the mill in the middle of the night and complain that his mule has stopped turning the mill. Pretending to mistake the tailor for his mule in the dark,[25] he harnesses him to the yoke and whips him around the mill. While Galland's miller wakes the tailor up in the middle of the night too, he tells him: "Ma mule est malade. . . . Vous me feriez beaucoup de plaisir si vous vouliez tourner le moulin à sa place" (N. II, 27). The tailor agrees to do it and receives the same beating as his counterpart in the manuscript. Thus Galland's errors convert a comedy into farce.

Once he discontinues night breaks and numbers, his readers have no further reason to expect a thousand and first night, despite the brief dialogue between Shahrazad and Shahriyar at the end of every story from here on. They nonetheless discover a concluding scene at the end of "The Two Sisters," the last story in his adaptation. The frame story does imply an eventual outcome for Shahrazad's vow in the prologue:

> qālat ashtahī minka an tuzawwijanī ilā al-malik Shahriyār, immā annanī atasabbab fi khalāṣ al-khalq wa-imma annanī amūt wa-ahlak wa-lī uswatan biman māt wa-halak.[26]

> Je vous conjure . . . de me procurer l'honneur de [la] couche [du sultan], . . . Si je péris, ma mort sera glorieuse; et, si je réussis . . . je rendrai à ma patrie un service important. (N. I, 35, 36)

The conclusion in the *Nuits* does provide a satisfactory resolution for the tension between the consequences of Shahriyar's oath and Shahrazad's determination to put an end to the slaughter. The further one reads without the constant reminder of night breaks and numbers, however, the less one feels the need for such a resolution. The lack of a conclusion seems appropriate under the circumstances and, in fact, no Arabic manuscript extant in Galland's day contains a thousand and one nights or a conclusion.[27] *Alf Layla wa-Layla* has in any case the idiomatic meaning of a large but imprecise number. Galland was aware of this meaning, as a dialogue he appended to "Aladdin" reveals. Here Shahriyar asks Shahrazad whether she has finished her stories. "A la fin de mes contes!" she cries, "le nombre en est si grand qu'il ne me serait pas possible à moi-même d'en dire le compte précisément" (N. III, 177–78). This passage hardly encourages the reader to expect a resolution of the antagonistic vows at the end of the twelfth and last volume. Here again, Galland did not improve the material he borrowed but rather degraded it.

Critics who justify the popularity of his *Nuits* by affirming the superiority of the adaptation over its sources without the evidence of a textual comparison or even the ability to make one mislead the public. Allegations of improvement in cases where he actually degraded the material are an abuse of criticism. Such ignorance would do harm even if it merely conferred an underserved reputation on Galland and his *Nuits*. Unfortunately, however, it condones attempts to found this reputation on the ruins of his sources sacrificed for the cause. Since these sources and the three-volume manuscript in particular have intrinsic value, they merit consideration as Arabic literature in its own right. The importance of their contribution to Middle Eastern culture surpasses that of their relationship with Western culture. This relationship itself requires as much attention as ever precisely because it has received so little from scholars competent in Arabic as well as French, English, and other Western languages.

Notes

This paper was extracted from the forthcoming *The Thousand and One Nights (Arabian Nights) from the Earliest Known Sources.* Part. 3: Introduction; Indices. Leiden: E. J. Brill.

1. Now in the Arabic manuscript collection of the Bibliothèque Nationale under the call numbers 3609–11. I will refer to it as "the three-volume manuscript."

2. "Le sixième volume commençait de paraître. . . . J'apprends qu'on n'en est pas moins content que des autres volumes. On demande déjà le septième," he wrote Cuper on July 10, 1705. *La correspondance d'Antoine Galland, édition critique et commentée,* ed. Mohamed Abdel-Halim, thèse complémentaire, Sorbonne, 1964. Bibliothèque de la Sorbonne: W 1964 (47) 4°; Bibliothèque Nationale, Imprimés: 4° Ln^{27} 88230.

3. Antoine Galland, *Les Mille et une Nuits* (Paris: Garnier-Flammarion, 1965), I, 20. Henceforth: N. Whatever the contents, the fourth volume mentioned here, if it existed, did not belong with the other three. According to Mohamed Abdel-Halim, comparison of the Galland, the Vatican, and the Patrick Russel manuscripts of the *Nights* indicates that either the original of all three ended where the three-volume one ends or, if it had a continuation, this continuation never reached Europe. See his *Antoine Galland: Sa vie et son oeuvre* (Paris, 1964), 192.

4. Henri Omont published Boivin's inventory in the *Journal parisien d'Antoine Galland* (1708–15) précédé de son autobiographie (Paris, 1920), 17–22.

5. Published by Abdel-Halim in his *Galland,* 140–43.

6. For a study of the framing device, see Tzvetan Todorov, *Grammaire du Décaméron* (Paris, 1969), 85–97.

7. Author of the *Bibliothèque orientale* (1697) completed and published by Galland after his death.

8. In 1888, Hermann Zotenberg found that his *Nuits* contain many stories of unknown provenance, some of which had become famous. They appeared neither in the editions of the *Nights* published in Calcutta and Cairo nor in the manuscripts in the Bibliothèque Nationale available to Galland.

Initially Zotenberg wondered whether all twelve volumes were the product of Galland's own imagination. See "Notice sur quelques manuscript des Mille et une Nuits et la traduction de Galland," *Notices et extraits des manuscrits de la Bibliothèque Nationale* (Paris, 1888), 167.

9. Abdel-Halim describes the lost manuscript as follows: "Ce serait celui décrit dans l'Epître dédicatoire et dans l'Avertissement, en quatre volumes divisés en trente-six parties, provenant de Syrie et contenant les Voyages de Sindbad. Il serait en outre, dans ses trois premiers volumes, assez proche [du manuscrit en trois volumes]. Le traducteur pouvait ainsi collationner les deux textes dans sa version. Et peut-être comptait-il, en parlant à Cuper de cinq volumes, le manuscrit turc" (192). There is no evidence of such a manuscript, however, and, if Galland had had so long a source, he would not have run out of material to translate.

10. "Les 870 nuits de notre manuscript sont réparties entre vingt-neuf sections. En tenant compte du nombre des nuits et des sections qui manquent, on peut admettre avec assez de vraisemblance que le tout devait former trente-six parties. C'est le chiffre indiqué par Galland" (Zotenberg, 183).

11. "Galland tentera plusieurs fois d'atteindre le mansucrit complet; s'il n'y a pas réussi, c'est peut-être qu'en pareil domaine un manuscrit à la fois intégral et incontestable relève lui-même du mythe." Raymond Schwab, *L'Auteur des "Mille et une Nuits": Vie d'Antoine Galland* (Paris, 1964), 161.

12. "Cet ouvrage de fariboles me fait plus d'honneur dans la monde que ne le ferait le plus bel ouvrage que je pourrais composer sur les médailles avec des remarques pleines d'érudition" (to Cuper, July 10, 1705).

13. Abdel-Halim gives a few examples of each in his *Galland*, 193 ff.

14. "Les lecteurs . . . ont été fatigués de l'interruption que Dinarzad apportait à leur lecture" (N. II, 257): "Avertissement," Volume VII in the original edition.

15. "On trouve de ces contes en arabe où il n'est parlé ni de Scheherazade, ni du sultan Schahriar, ni de Dinarzade, ni de distinction par nuit. Cela fait voir . . . qu'une infinité [d'Arabes] se sont ennuyés de ces répétitions, qui sont à la vérité très inutiles" (Idem).

16. See Abdel-Halim, *Galland*, 427 ff.

17. "Ayant personnellement tiré un plaisir de si haute qualité de la lecture de ce livre, autant dans notre enfance qu'au seuil de la viellesse, nous souhaitons donc l'accroître encore en attirant vers Galland tout le public qu'il mérite. En même temps qu'il accomplira la bonne action de dissiper enfin l'invisibilité de son chef-d'œuvre, ce nombreux public en sera immédiatement récompensé par l'enrichissement qu'il aura apporté à sa propre existence." Georges May, *Les Mille et une Nuits d'Antoine Galland ou le chef-d'œuvre invisible* (Paris, 1986), 231–32.

18. R. Hawari has made the only serious effort of this kind in his "Antoine Galland's Translation of the Arabian Nights," *Revue de littérature comparée* 54 (1984): 50–64.

19. He drew roughly 46 percent of his adaptation from the three-volume manuscript, 4 percent from the manuscript of *Sindbad*, 20 percent from other manuscripts known to have been transmitted in writing, and 30 percent from Hanna, either orally or in his handwriting.

20. *L'Originalité; une nouvelle catégorie littéraire au siècle des Lumières* (Genève, 1982), 29.

21. "On devine que Galland se sentit flatté par une attention aussi soutenue de la part d'un public aussi distingué, et on comprend que le jugement qu'il portait lui-même sur son ouvrage ait pu en être affecté" (May, 45).

22. "Al-Mustansir Billah" (Mahdi I, 347).

23. In the *Histoire de Zobéide;* see N. I, 210 and Hawari, 159–60.

24. "kān muqābiluh rajulin [*sic*] kathīr al-māl wa-kān fī asfal dārih ṭāḥūn" (Mahdi I, 350). This transcription and the following ones do not reproduce the true phonetic character of the Arabic text, which is not written in standard Arabic.

25. "wa-dakhal aṭ-ṭaḥḥān niṣf al-layl ilā akhī wa-jaʿal yaqūl mā qiṣṣat hādha al-baghl al-mīshūm [*sic*]" (Mahdi II, 352).

26. Mahdi I, 66. "Marry me to King Shahriyar so that I may either succeed in saving the people or perish and die like the rest." *The Arabian Nights*, trans. Husain Haddawy (New York, London, 1990), 11.

27. In his *Kitāb al-Fihrist* (377/987), Ibn an-Nadīm describes a conclusion on the thousandth night of an earlier version in which Shahrazad has an infant and shows it to Shahriyar, who then renounces his vow. See Nikita Elisséeff, *Thèmes et motifs des Mille et une Nuits* (Beirut, 1949), 21, 209.

7 Greek Form Elements in the *Arabian Nights*

Gustave E. von Grunebaum

Considerable effort has been devoted to the literary analysis of the *Arabian Nights.* The Indian contribution as well as the Persian, the Arabic element as well as the Jewish, the Babylonian and the Egyptian heritage, the influence of the Crusaders: all have been established with fair accuracy.[1] But so far no attention has been paid to the problem of possible relations between Greek literature and the *Nights*, although a priori a connection would appear likely. The failure to recognize the question is doubtlessly due to the still overly strict separation between classical and Arabic philologies. It is equally significant that two Greek scholars, familiar with the *belles-lettres* of the later periods of Hellenism, have been practically alone in realizing structural similarities of Greek and Arabic narrative literature,[2] and that the only two orientalists to make themselves conversant with postclassical Greek immediately saw the problem, even though they did not attack it. As early as 1905 Josef Horovitz stated in his book *Spuren griechischer Mimen im Orient:*[3] "Wenn auch für die arabische Literatur die engen Zusammenhänge mit Indien gesichert bleiben, so wird man nun doch den Einfluß der griechischen Unterhaltungsliteratur auf die Geschichten von '1001 Nacht' und andere Erzählungen . . . eingehend untersuchen müssen." Without expressly saying so, Horovitz makes it clear[4] that he sees Greek influence at work in the formation of the realistic urban narrative, so richly represented in the *Arabian Nights.*[5] In 1931, C. H. Becker[6]

Reprinted from Gustave E. von Grunebaum, "Greek Form Elements in the Arabian Nights," *Journal of the American Oriental Society* 62 (1942): 277–92. Reprinted by permission of the publisher.

in a somewhat sweeping statement and without pointing out any specific phenomena declared Arabic belles-lettres to be more or less Hellenistic. He then expressed the conviction that some day "Islamic literature will serve to complement our knowledge of the 'Spätantike.' "[7]

It may be said that the very nature of the Greek contribution formed the greatest obstacle to its discovery. Identical or cognate motifs can be traced with comparative ease, but motif survival seems to be only an insignificant part of the Greek heritage. The AN owe to classical literature patterns of style, patterns of presentation, and emotional conventions. And here again the influence of the Greek narrative tradition on the general outline of some AN tales, or on character and sentiments of their heroes, is much less obvious than, say, the Indian contribution of the frame-tale pattern. The classical patterns are preserved, within and adapted to, a cultural milieu to which many of their basic features have become meaningless; a certain deterioration of the cultural level of the audience takes its toll, reducing the artistic consistency; the different religious background entails numberless changes that are by no means restricted to the outward appearance and everyday lives of the characters; and, last but not least, the survivals have to be reconciled to the requirements of another literary tradition, which, for instance, is averse to the scenic-dramatic element so strongly developed in the Greek novel.[8] Yet it can be shown that classical patterns of expression, classical style elements, although no longer recognized as such, were alive when the AN were cast into their present form. The creative power of some classical patterns, or perhaps the persisting habit of using the comfortable and well-tried-out schemes, becomes particularly manifest in the none too rare event that a motif of Persian or Indian origin is presented in such a manner as to conform with some Hellenistic convention.

The rather rare reflections of classical subject matter in the AN—the geographical lore will not be considered in this study—are less important in themselves than as testimonies of actual motif transmission. The principal instances of motif survival are:

(1) Plautus, *Miles gloriosus* (the Latin redaction of one or possibly two Greek plays),[9] and the *Story of the Butcher, His Wife and*

the Soldier:[10] the mistress (or the wife in the Arabic version) deceives her lover (husband) by pretending to have an identical twin sister. The device of the secret passage dug between the houses of the two men also recurs in the story of *Qamar az-Zamān and His Beloved,*[11] where Ḥalīma meets her lover in the disguise of a slave-girl whose resemblance with his wife startles Ḥalīma's husband.[12]

(2) In the story of *Pyramus and Thisbe*[13] the tragic climax is brought about by the appearance of a lion whom Pyramus believes to have killed Thisbe. In the story of the *ʿUḏrite Lovers*[14] it is again a lion who puts an end to their romantic meetings. It is, however, characteristic of the artistic decline incident to the transmission of the motif that in the AN the lion actually devours the girl and that the lover finds her remains, "the ends of the bones of the damsel."[15]

(3) R. Goossens[16] traces the history of Abrīza,[17] the coy and bold princess whom the king drugs and then violates, to the Nikaia legend of the Sangarios district in Asia Minor that Nonnos, who calls the heroine Αὔρη, had included in his *Dionysiaká.*[18]

(4) K. Kerényi[19] rightly compares the scare, inflicted as a joke by king Apollonius[20] on his benefactor, the fisherman, before he gives him his due reward, with the similar procedure put into operation against Badr ad-Dīn Ḥasan in the story of the *Wazīrs Nūr ad-Dīn and Šams ad-Dīn.*[21] As a rule, the vitality of patterns of expression is considerably stronger than that of the ideas expressed and the life of the pattern is by no means bound up with the life of the concepts that the pattern originally communicated. This fact, while generally valid in literature, can be most easily exemplified in the sphere of religious writings—the term "religious" to be taken in its widest sense, to include magic, etc.

Much in the form of Koranic preaching could be shown to correspond to earlier conventional forms of religious speech, and thus the actual part of Muḥammad in establishing Arabic models of expression for certain subjects would be clarified. As orientalists so far have confined their interest to the origin of the contents of the Koran, it was again a Greek scholar who realized the survival of older style patterns in two Koranic passages. E. Norden[22] conclusively pointed out that the "self-predication" as employed by Muḥammad e.g., Sūra 61.5 ff.[23] has a long history in Semitic (and orientalized

Greek) religious speech. Successive religious movements, while altering the professed message, stubbornly clung to the ἐγώ εἰμι or, in other places, σὺ εἶ, οὗτος ἐστιν formula.[24]

Sūra 87 exemplifies the tenacity of another age-old Semitic pattern of religious speech:[25] the apostrophe of, or the oath by, a deity whose essence and actions are subsequently described—depending on the structure of the language—in a sequence of relative clauses or of present participles, used as substantives and always introduced by the article. The self-same stylistic mold is employed in the Psalms, the *Prophets*, the apocryphal *Odes of Solomon*, and Hellenistic incantation hymns, irreconcilable though their contents may be.[26]

Now the form pattern that in my opinion continues a somewhat precarious existence in the AN, is that of the so-called Greek novel. The position of both literary categories, the novel and the AN tales, within their respective literary and social background, shows important parallels. Both genres are essentially and originally popular.[27] Both were looked down upon by the higher literary circles.[28] Both soon took on traits of the strictly literary style without being quite able to bridge the spiritual gulf.[29] But while the ever-renewed attempt of Greek writers to raise the level of the novel sufficiently to have it accepted as serious literature at least succeeded in enriching the development of the form, the only traceable attempt by a high-class Arabic author to organize the collection of the AN was never completed and al-Jahšiyārī (ob. 942 A.D.) found no successor.[30]

The apocryphal writings of the New Testament freely used novel elements with the stress laid on the aretalogical, the miraculous, and the educational, while the novel proper emphasized the erotic (by no means neglected by the Apocrypha); both classes of literature utilized the travel or migration element as a comfortable framework.[31]

The apocryphal writings doubtlessly served as media for the transmission of Hellenistic ideas and motifs to the popular imagination of Islam,[32] but their very tendency to glorify Christian saints and Christian proselytism precluded too close and too literal contacts with Arabic literature. Nor has the Hellenistic aretalogy contributed conspicuously to the bulk of the AN.

The novel treats the fate of two lovers as an organic unit of dramatic composition, rounded off so well as not to admit substantial additions, omissions, or changes in the interlocking episodes without endangering the whole work. The aretalogy, on the other hand, like the apocryphal acts of the Apostles, follow an entirely different narrative technique: an indefinite number of independent acts (πράξεις) of the (saintly) personality whose life is recounted are grouped together like pearls on a string; the relation to the central figure is the only link between the various episodes that are simply put side by side; no attempt at dramalike composition is made; episodes may be omitted or added at will; usually the death of the hero puts an end to the story, sometimes, however, another incident in his biography is arbitrarily chosen as the end. It is evident that the AN, that is, the more substantial stories of the collection, are conceived according to the plan of the novel.

The aretalogical composition has, however, deeply affected that of the so-called *siyar*, such as the Sīra ʿAntar, the Sīra Baibars, etc.[33]

The relation of the aretalogy to historical monographs of the type of Sallust's writings is reflected in the historiographical attitude of parts of the *siyar*. The AN in their descriptions of battle continue the tradition of the novel without, however, reflecting contemporary historiography. To illustrate this point it suffices to compare AN battle scenes with parallel passages in Ṭabarī, Miskawaihi, or even much later historians. The tendency of the Greek novel to "abandon an ostensibly historical background in favor of a purely fictitious setting"[34] does not continue consistently in the AN, where sometimes even outside the group of "historical anecdotes"[35] pretense at dealing with a definite historico-geographical scene is made. But the technique by which such "historical" events are presented continues the habits of the Greek novelists that, in turn, in the final analysis stem from the conventions of classical historiography.[36] Similarity, the AN perpetuate that romantic treatment of history that was one of the "weapons" of the Greek novelist.[37]

The influence of the Near East on the formation of the Greek romance can hardly be overlooked. There is no need of repeating the arguments proffered by Rohde, Ed. Schwartz,[38] Kerényi,[39] and others. But such influence was mainly effective with regard to scenery, ethnographical lore, and, perhaps, religious attitude. The style and form patterns that from the novel have found their way into the AN are Greek; and even if they were originally not Greek, they did not pass into the AN directly from a hypothetical oriental source, but unmistakably came through the medium of later Greek literature. This paper, therefore, deliberately refrains from analyzing the genesis of the Greek forms as irrelevant to the understanding of the Greek contribution to the *Arabian Nights*.

II

The basic motif of the Greek romance has aptly been described as the "wanderings of a loving couple, persecuted by fate."[40] The love element, however, is most important in the novel inasmuch as the wanderings, the result of the vagaries of fate, never appear independently as the central idea of any story.[41] A characteristic shade in the love relations described in the romance consists in the lovers' being separated after having been united so that the novel tells of their reunion rather than of the development of their feelings, while in the description of this feature rests the prime interest of the modern novel. Fate rules supreme. There is no action springing from the peculiarities of the characters involved. Man is little more than a plaything of Chance, to which he meekly submits, not, however, without indulging in elaborate accusations of Fate for the hardships that have overcome him—rhetorical exercises, well suited to the prevailing attitude of passive despair.[42]

No one can fail to recognize the pattern and the spirit in some of the AN tales. Without referring to the Greek models, Horovitz defines the technique of *Saif al-mulūk*[43] as "insertion of adventurous sea-faring in the frame of a love story."[44] As early as 1876 Rohde[45] saw the structural identity of the Greek romance and some of the "oriental" tales.[46]

The literary situation presented two obstacles to a more precise recognition of Greek influence: (1) the novel pattern does not always occur isolated in the AN; more frequently than not only part of a story repeats the classical scheme; (2) when the Greek motifs were taken over by a literary tradition that had no understanding of their symbolism[47] they were used exclusively according to their possible value in the plot: the organic system in which, and for which, they were developed is torn asunder, some impressive details are preserved and applied where they are considered fitting but with no view to their real function. It is, therefore, not too easy to reconnect these floating details with the narrative concept to which they originally belonged.

Naturally, the separation from the source in which the literary existence of the motif had its natural place and its justification could not but result in a deterioration of the literary substance. This decline in its turn contributed its share toward hiding Greek traits and guarding them against detection. The resignation to the whims of Fate changes in the AN to resignation to the will of Allāh. The Muslim writer makes good use of the rhetorical opportunities, provided by the pattern of the narrative, to lament the instability of everything human[48] and to learn from the events the lesson of this world's transitoriness.[49] The antique motif of the rebellious accusation of Fate[50] is, however, incompatible with the conventional attitude of the pious Muslim.

It must be stressed that not every report of travel adventures in the AN represents a trace of the Greek romance:[51] from our point of view the connection of the wanderings with the main thread of the love story is the decisive criterion. As an instance of a feature, indispensable to the romance pattern but at times used by itself in "non-Greek" AN stories I refer to the motif of the ἀναγνωρισμός (recognition).[52]

The stories in which I consider the Greek romance pattern discernible are the following:

(1) *Ġānim b. Ayyūb*[53]
(2) the second part of *Qamar az-zamān*[54]
(3) the second part of the *Abū Muḥammad, the Sluggard*[55]
(4) *Uns al-wujūd and al-Ward fī 'l-akmām*[56]
(5) *the Story of the Pious Israelite Who Was Reunited With His Wife and Children*[57]
(6) *Saif al-mulūk and Badīʿat al-jamāl*[58]
(7) the second part of the story of *Ḥasan of Baṣra, the Jeweller*[59]
(8) the second part of *Nūr ad-dīn and Maryam, the Belt-Maker*[60]
(9) two episodes from the story of *Ḫudādād and His Brothers*:[61]

a. (6. 355 f.) the princess of Daryabār and her bridegroom are attacked by pirates in their wedding-night. The robbers kill each other for the possession of the princess;[62]
b. (6. 347 ff.) funeral of, and erection of a mausoleum for, the hero who, however, is still alive.[63]

The modern novel is chiefly interested in human developments, the Greek novel in events. This attitude recurs in the AN. Both in the Greek and the Arabic stories the principal consequences of this approach is a certain vagueness in the characterization of the heroes who are little more than the media in which a preconceived chain of happenings materializes. The poet's concentration on thrilling situations and breathtaking episodes dooms the acting persons to comparative insignificance and makes them somewhat interchangeable. With all this it is evident that the Greek writer paints his heroine in more vivid colors than her lover: he generally presents her as the more active part of the couple, the passivity or helplessness of the man contrasting pathetically with her initiative, resourcefulness, and even bravery. The AN usually show the lover in a slightly more creditable manner. Enough examples, however, stand out to remind one of the Greek romance pattern, especially where the knots of an intricate love-intrigue are to be tied.[64]

Greek romance is entirely, the AN practically free from aretalogical exaggeration of the hero's strength,[65] another feature sharply differentiating this line of development from that leading from the Apocryphal New Testament to the *siyar*, which both revel in descriptions of the supernatural power possessed by their protagonists.[66]

The technique of the typical love tale in the AN is strikingly reminiscent of that of the novel.[67] The novel does not encompass any gradual development of the lovers' feelings, nor is it interested in individual shades of passion. It favors love at first sight—this being not only the most convincing form of love to the popular mind, but the most easy to work with as well. The AN take the same attitude.

The kind of love from which the novel's protagonists are suffering—for suffering it is, their love being considered as a disease and a deadly one at that—is extremely sentimental, emotion for emotion's sake, always prone to tears, fainting fits, desperation, madness, and self-destruction. Chastity is glorified—the minor characters do not have to be strict on this point—but blends with latent lasciviousness. No elaborate demonstration is required to show that love as described in the AN is identical with the particular type endlessly presented by the novel. Everything recurs in these Arabic tales, but not only in the tales.[68]

This Hellenistic love conception probably contributed to the tear-indulging love-professions stereotyped in the proemia of the pre-Islamic *qaṣīda.*[69] It certainly became prominent in poetry with the rise of the Medinese school.[70] The development of this school of lyrics that introduced into Arabic poetry a new style of personal, confession-like erotic songs—at the same time playful and sentimental, lascivious and chaste—strangely coincides with the extension of Muslim dominion over Greek cultural territory, particularly over Syria. In other words, it is certainly connected with that first infiltration of Greek tradition that, in another direction, led to the early Arabic studies on alchemy.[71]

Tearful[72] love considered as disease[73] but at the same time recognized as the prime moving force,[74] leading to lack of sleep,[75] emaciation, madness, death,[76] becomes a commonplace topic of Arabic lyrics, never to disappear again. Before the ninth century, lovers turn into heroes of popular romance,[77] and a great many stories are told on the *"Liebestod"-cliché.*[78] The classical pattern is copied word by word. One example may suffice.

In the (probably spurious) twenty-third Idyll of Theocrit[79] the spurned lover when preparing to hang himself at her door asks his beloved to write on his grave (vss. 47 f.): τοῦτον ἔρως ἔκτεινεν . . . "This man love slew!"[80] Centuries later, a Greek inscription from the Ḥaurān (Syria) tells one Aurelios Wahbān, Son of Alexandros, a Hellenized Arab, whose death was caused by love: γένετο μου μόρον φιλότης.[81] And again, some centuries later, we find in a poem of the AN this verse: "By Allāh, O my people, when I am dead, write on my tombstone: this is (the grave of a) slave of love."[82]

Phraseology and imagery of this branch of Arabic poetry in many respects resemble that of classical tradition. Close scrutiny of Arabic love expressions in poetical diction would lead to the establishment of a great number of parallels that might yield a clue to the question of how deeply the Arabic erotic poem was influenced by Greek style. It must suffice here to state that the "military" love terminology so largely used in both Greek and Roman poetry recurs in Arabic song at a very early date.[83]

Another problem requiring further investigation is the relation of Arabic to classical (and to Provençal) love theory. In this paper I only wish to draw attention to the fact that theoretical discussion of love and its psychology accompanied Arabic love poetry as it did Greek. It can be assumed that the contribution of this literary genre to the opinions and attitudes, displayed in the Greek novel, was equaled by the contribution made by its Arabic counterpart to the contents of later Arabic lyrics. At the same time it can be said of both the Greek and the Arabic theorists that for their argumentation they mainly depended on the testimony of poetry.[84] All the protagonists of both the Greek romance and the AN have one quality in common: they are beautiful. Their beauty is their raison d'être, and the prime, not to say the only tangible, cause of their being loved. Consequently, the description of the hero and the heroine acquires major importance. Again, the presentation of the lovers' person in the AN reflects the elaborate descriptive techniques of the novel. Yet is seems that the AN proceed more independently when portraying human beings than when setting the scenery for their actions. This fact is probably due to the early development of a genuine model code for the ideal individual at least as far as women are concerned. The conventions of the early poetry,[85] and literature of the type of the so-called *Letter of al-Mundir* on the Perfect Woman[86] definitely support such an assumption.[87]

The more elaborate stories of the AN are careful in depicting the setting of the scenery. Like the novel the AN favor gardens as the meeting place of the lovers and the predilection for extensive descriptions, so characteristic of the Greek style, survives in full force. The descriptions of palaces and gardens are worked out for their own sake rather than for their function in the tale. It would be difficult not to recognize them as the direct descendants of the ἔκφρασις, the descriptive γένος of artistic prose.

Antithesis and parallelism of clauses, the requirements of the classical form, recur in the compositions of the AN, and as in the Greek model the manner of expression comes very close to poetry proper.[88] The ἔκφρασις was in high favor with the Byzantines: the extensive description of the hero's palace and his garden in the popular epic of Digenis Akritas (tenth century) is a typical example.[89] No less typical is the scene of Digenis with his beloved in the garden.[90] The manner in which Digenis's palace is presented is identical with that adopted by Constantin Porphyrogennetos when he describes the buildings erected by Basil I (868–86).[91] It is significant for the strength of the ἔκφρασις tradition that it was continued both on Byzantine and on Arabic soil.[92] The transplanting of the ἔκφρασις into Arabic prose roughly coincides with the rise of descriptive poetry under Greek influence, in the ninth and tenth centuries A.D.[93]

I am inclined to trace the *munāẓara* (comparison of, dispute for precedence between, two objects), of which two specimens occur in the AN, back to the Greek genre of the σύγκρισις. The style of the *munāẓara* has been definitely molded by the *declamatio.* Eristic poetry and prose were cultivated throughout antiquity.[94] Von Wilamowitz[95] lists the earliest συγκρίσεις and stresses the importance of the *Contest of Homer and Hesiod* for the development of the genre.[96]

AN 3. 602 ff. revives the old dispute about the respective rank of the sexes. The line of argument by which Budūr in male disguise tries to win over Qamar az-zamān to pederasty,[97] may represent a late echo of the classical ζήτημα whether love of men or love of women is preferable.[98] Three *munāẓarāt* are united in the AN story of the *Yamanite and His Six Slave Girls* who are paired off to praise their own attractions and to satirize the physical peculiarities of their rivals.[99]

What Norden says of the style of the *declamatio*[100] applies word for word to the Arabic "disputes for precedence": they are as passionate, as full of κακοζηλία[101] and forcible treatment, as saturated with pointed sentences and quotations as their literary ancestors. It is fairly obvious that the habit of having people improvise harangues to meet fictitious situations or to prove sententious theses stems from the ὑποθέσεις (exercises in fictitious discussion) of the schools of the rhetoricians.[102] The Arabs follow the Greek tradition even in discussing ἄδοξοι ὑποθέσεις: Lukian's *Encomium of the Fly*[103] has its counterpart in ʿAbd aṣ-Ṣamad b. al-Faḍl's speech on the *ḫalq al-baʿūḍa*, which is said to have been so long as to fill three *majlis.*[104] The Arabic *munāẓara* as represented in poetry by Ibn ar-Rūmī's (ob. 889 or 896) two contest poems: *Narcissus and Rose* and *Pen and Sword,*[105] and considerably later, in *saj*ᶜ, by the discussion of the advantages and disadvantages of Virgin and Bride in the forty-third maqāma of al-Ḥarīrī (ob. 1122),[106] gave rise to the development of the Persian *munāẓara*, which soon came to surpass by far its parent.[107]

The habit of the AN narrators of recounting the heroes' lives from the very beginning and of giving due consideration to their education goes back to Xenophon's *Cyrupaedia*, whose influence on the Greek novel—or whose position in its development—has often been noted.[108] This derivation becomes all the more conclusive as D. S. Margoliouth noted among the political work of Aḥmad b. abī Ṭāhir Ṭaifūr some treatises that, it would seem, were written "in the form of historical romances, a style initiated by Xenophon in his Cyrupaedia."[109]

The prosimetrical form of most of the AN seems to be a genuine Arabic, or at any rate an Oriental, contribution. The fact that the Menippean satire and to some extent the novels themselves present the same mixed form has tended to confuse the views. There can be little doubt, however, that prosimetry occurs in the classical sphere only many centuries after it developed in the East; its alleged initiator, Menipp, was of Oriental birth; and it is quite evident that the form must be very old in the *ᶜarabiyya*. While, then, it should be stated that the composite form of prose and verse, so characteristic of the AN, is of Near Eastern growth, it is not unlikely that the established convention of the Greek novel helped to establish the parallel convention in the AN. This view, moreover, implies that in the AN prosimetry is a popular development.[110]

It is worthy of brief notice that the bulk of the AN would meet the requirements of classical literary theory with regard to the novel: the stories are πλάσμα, not ψεῦδος. The borderline between what could but did not happen (the πλάσμα) and what could not happen is, of course, drawn at a different place in Greek and in Muslim culture: the general belief in demons, for instance, goes far to change the outlook in this respect. But we must beware of drawing the lines according to our present-day concepts. For the Muslim audience, the AN are just as much "plasmatic" material as the novels were for the Greek listener.[111]

The following details are meant to illustrate further the influence of the Greek romance on the AN. No motif or plot parallels, such as shipwrecks[112] or assault by robbers, will be indicated, nor will features common to fairy tales in general be listed, such as falling in love upon hearing the praise of the girl[113] if they do not have any particular significance.

(1) The degradation of a novel motif is well demonstrated by the substitution in the AN drugging with *banj* to the "Scheintod" of the romance.[114]

(2) As in the novel, but not as regular, the hero is accompanied by a friend who, at times, acquires considerable importance for the action of the novel. The Apocrypha follow the novel.[115]

(3) All AN tales—or parts of tales—modeled on the novel pattern follow the novel convention also in that they lead the events to an end favorable to the lovers. In this connection it must be stressed that the happy ending does not appear everywhere in the other parts of the AN.

(4) The importance of letters in the love intrigue is common to both the novel and the AN. There can hardly be any doubt that the AN continue the Alexandrine fashion of describing even mythical lovers as corresponding freely.[116]

(5) The general importance of dreams in the technique of both novels and AN.[117]

(6) In both groups of tales and in the Apocrypha, the people take an interest in the fate of the lovers.[118]

(7) The reaction of the community, or the audience, or even the individual to the events is amazement, *ʿajab*,[119] that same ἔκπληξις that in classical theory should be part of the effect of the μῦθος.[120] In the miracle tale the ἔκπληξις serves to emphasize reality and truth of the report. The τόπος originates in the aretalogical narrative.[121]

Some minor details worth noting are the following items:

a. Kerényi, loc. cit., p. 154, n. 10, rightly points to the connection of the transformation of Sidi Nuʿmān into a dog, AN 6. 268 ff., and the details of his life as a dog with the transformation into an ass of Lukios (Pseudo-Lukian) and the detailed treatment of his life as an animal. The fate of a human being transformed into an animal is nowhere else in the AN described in a manner comparable to the Sidi Nuʿmān story.

b. O. Weinreich, *Gebet und Wunder*, 1929, pp. 343 ff., discusses at length the opening of doors through the instrumentality of a magic world or formula. Without referring to the story, Weinreich thereby aptly illustrates the mental background of the "Sesame, open your door" formula that is so important in the story of *Ali Baba*, AN 2. 841 ff.

c. The ring with the killing fire-rays, AN 6. 183 ff. and 6. 640, reminds one of the fire-garment of St. Thekla.[122]

d. The significance of Qamar az-zamān's employment as gardener, AN 2. 467 ff., is explained by parallels from the novel.[123]

III

There exists no documentary evidence to prove the actual transmission of the classical elements. While the facts as presented above constitute by themselves convincing evidence of Greek survivals, it may be well to adduce indications of identical processes from related literary fields so as to demonstrate at least the likelihood of a development the individual phases of which unfortunately escape us.[124]

R. Söder[125] has conclusively shown how many romance elements have entered the apocryphal writings of the New Testament. The survivals not only include the main motifs of the novel action, but also substantial parts of its conventional scenery and—this is particularly significant—its love attitude.[126] It cannot be doubted that the apocryphal literature has been very important in preserving the older forms. There are, incidentally, at least two parallels between motifs of the Apocrypha and the AN. The draft that has the power of transforming human beings into animals that is used by Queen Lāb, AN 5. 140 ff., reminds one of the draft mentioned in the *Acts of Andrew and Matthew*, ch. 1 ff. The same *Acts*[127] introduce cannibals who before devouring their victims feed them a fattening dish which dims their consciousness, a detail familiar to us from the third travel of Sindbād.[128] The fact that tales typical of early Christian literature have found their way into Arabic narratives is amply exemplified by the stories collected by R. Basset in the third volume of his *Mille et un contes.*[129]

Syria is the geographical centre of the Apocrypha.[130] The vitality of the classical forms of life up to the very eve of the Muslim conquest is attested by the verses of Ḥassān b. Ṯābit (ca. 590–674) in which he taunts some of his adversaries by calling them "histrions of Gaza."[131] Ḥassān visited Damascus early in the seventh century and later became the "court-poet" of the Prophet.[132] The close administrative cooperation between the Arabs and the conquered Greeks is well known.[133]

To increase further the probability of Greek form infiltration into the AN, parallel transitions of Greek literary γένη and form elements into Arabic literature will be briefly discussed.

(1) C. H. Becker, *Islamstudien* 1. 501 ff. traces the development of the Ubi sunt qui ante nos in mundo fuere–motif from its origin in the diatribe of the Cynics to its application in Arabic literature.[134]

(2) The elegy for animals, a Hellenistic creation, suddenly reappears in Arabic during the first part of the ninth century.[135]

(3) E. Sachau[136] pointed out[137] that the earliest biographies of Muḥammad, which were by no means confined to a description of his campaigns, were titled *maġāzī*. This term, therefore, in the early days of Arabic historiography denoted the life story of a person of religious eminence. This use of the word *maġāzī* ("fights") stems from the Christian attitude of speaking of the great saints and martyrs as fighters, ἀθλῆται, athletes of God, and of their acts as fights, ἆθλοι, syr. *tektôšê*.[138] This usage apparently survived, especially in Medina, till about the middle of the eighth century.

(4) I. Goldziher, *Abhandlungen zur arabischen Philologie*, vol. 2, Introduction, pp. XLII f., states the connection between the Arabic *muʿammarūn* literature and the μακρόβιοι works of (Pseudo-) Lukian and Phlegon.[139]

(5) J. Horovitz, *Spuren griechischer Mimen im Orient*, has demonstrated the tenacious survival of the Greek μῖμος in the Arabic-speaking world to this present day. Although Horovitz has no Arabic evidence prior to the tenth century the continuity of the development is incontestable.[140]

(6) The influence of the *Cyrupaedia*, and (7) the Hellenistic impact on poetry in the ninth and tenth centuries, have been discussed above.[141]

(8) F. Rosenthal has traced the influence of classical tradition in the early specimens of Arabic autobiography.[142] Again, the Greek inspiration is shown to bear fruit during the ninth century A.D.[143]

(9) Obviously, the question of the Greek influence on Arabic rhetoric is beyond the scope of this paper.[144] Only four remarks on minor details may be found to the point here:

a. The Alexandrine custom of expressly alluding to somebody else's verse, or literally incorporating some phrase of another poet, in one's own poems[145] recurs in ᶜAbbāsid poetry. The technical term for this procedure is *taḍmīn.*[146]

b. The contrasting of *ingenium* and *ars* in the judgment of literature[147] is matched by the analogous contrasting of *ṭab*ᶜ and *takalluf* by Arabic experts.[148]

c. The view that the speaker or poet has it in his power "to make great things mean, to invest little things with greatness"[149] is again voiced by Niẓāmī ᶜArūḍī (twelfth century)[150] and Ibn Ḫaldūn (ob. 1406).[151]

d. It is important to realize that the Arabs possessed some vague knowledge about Greek and Byzantine rhetoric even before the great influx of Greek science.[152]

Notes

1. Cf. J. Østrup, *Studien über 1001 Nacht*, trans. O. Rescher (1925), and E. Littmann, *TausendundeineNacht in der arabischen Literatur*, 1923, pp. 13 ff.

2. R. Reitzenstein, *Die griechische Tefnutlegende*, Sitzungsberichte der Heidelberger Akademie der Wissenschaften, 1923, Heft 2, p. 31, and K. Kerényi, *Die griechisch-orientalische Romanliteratur in religionsgeschichtlicher Beleuchtung*, 1927, p. VIII.

3. Pp. 96 f.

4. P. 97.

5. Henceforth: AN.

6. *Das Erbe der Antike im Orient und Okzident*, p. 21.

7. The paper of H. H. Schaeder in *Die Antike* 4. 226 ff. to which Becker refers is not accessible to me at present.

8. Cf. e.g., Kerényi, p. 14, on Heliodor.

9. On the subject of Plautus's model cf. e.g., E. Fraenkel, *Plautinisches im Plautus*, 1922, pp. 253 ff. and A. Ernout's *Introduction* to his edition and translation of the play (1936). The conclusions of these authors are, unfortunately, irreconcilable. While disclaiming any authority in the field of Plautian studies, the writer favors the theory, upheld by Fraenkel, that the Latin comedy constitutes a *contaminatio* of two Greek plots.

10. AN, ed. M. Habicht, 1825–43, 11. pp. 140–45. Henceforth the AN will be cited from the German translation of E. Littmann, 6 vols., 1921–28,

as quotations from the original would be inconvenient for the non-Arabist. Littmann's translation, an achievement of outstanding literary merit, is based on the text edition Calcutta 1839–42, but includes also a considerable number of important tales, omitted in the Indian (and sometimes in the various Egyptian) prints. These stories are listed AN 6. 682 f. Littmann's translation is a thorough revision of that by P. F. Greve, which in turn was based on Burton. The story of the Butcher is missing in Littmann.

11. AN 6. 451 ff.

12. Cf. E. Rohde, *Der griechische Roman und seine Vorläufer*, p. 596 and n. 4 (1914), E. Rehatsek, *JRAS*, Bombay Branch 14. 77 ff. (1978–80), W. Bacher, *ZDMG* 30. 141 ff.

13. Cf. e.g., Ovid *Met.* 4. 55 ff.

14. AN 4. 677 ff.

15. Trans. E. W. Lane, 1841, 3. 251; cf. Rehatsek, loc. cit., 81 ff.

16. *Byzantion*, 9. 426 ff.

17. In the story of *ʿUmar b. an-Nuʿmān*, AN 1. 540 ff.

18. Ed. W. H. D. Rouse, 1940, 48. 238 ff. Here again one cannot fail to notice the crudeness of the Arabic story as compared with the Greek.

19. Loc. cit., 235, n. 27.

20. *Hist. Apoll. Tyrii*, ed. A. Riese, 1893, ch. 51.

21. AN 1. 299 ff.—R. Basset, *Mille et un contes*, 1924–26, 1. 525 traces an anecdote of the Juḥā circle back to Lucian's *Cynic*, ch. 18 (trans. H. W. and F. G. Fowler, 1905, 4. 180). This instance shows very well how striking details survived apart from their true context. Parallels between the Apocryphal New Testament and the AN will be discussed later. The story of the master thief, Rhampsinit, though related by Herodot (*Hist.* 2. 121, 122) is of ancient Egyptian origin. Its reflex in the picaresque stories of the AN has been demonstrated by Th. Nöldeke, *ZDMG* 42. 68 ff. and Littmann, *AN* 6. 711. C. Brockelmann, *GAL* 2. 59 n. 2, suggests more Egyptian influence without referring to any specific survivals. Reminiscences, other than literary, are beyond the scope of this paper, but cf. Littmann, *1001 Nacht* 21 f.

22. *Agnostos Theos. Untersuchungen zur Formengeschichte religiöser Rede*, 1913, 191 f.

23. Here Jesus is made to begin his sermon to the children of Israel with the words: "Of a truth I am God's apostle to you to confirm the law . . ." (trans. J. M. Rodwell); similarly, e.g., Sūra 20. 14 the Lord, 26. 162 Lot, 26. 171 Šuʿaib, are using such declarations to begin their addresses.

24. References: Norden, loc. cit., 176 ff. A. Deissmann, *Light from the Ancient East*, pp. 135 ff. (1927). R. Reitzenstein, *Poimandres* (1904), contains a great deal of helpful material. On pp. 165 ff. Reitzenstein discusses the Sabians' influence on Islamic thought and their function in the preservation of Hellenistic alchemy. T. Andrae, *Der Ursprung des Islams und das Christentum*, 1926, pp. 139 ff. suggests that the Koranic preachings on the Hereafter and the Last Judgment follow the homiletic pattern of the Syrian, St. Afrēm. Andrae,

however emphasizes thoughts and imagery rather than forms. G. P. Wetter, *Phōs* 114 (1915) traces the ἐγὼ εἰμι formula in Mandaean writings.

25. (1) "Praise the name of thy Lord the Most High, (2) Who hath created and balanced all things, (3) Who hath fixed their destinies and guideth them, etc.," (Rodwell).

26. It has been necessary to modify slightly Norden's statements, loc. cit., 201 ff., as he did not consider the peculiarities of the Arabic language. Cf. also pp. 235 ff. A. Poebel, *Das appositionell bestimmte Pronomen der 1. Person Sing. in den westsemitischen Inschriften und im Alten Testament* (1932), can be added to the literature quoted by Norden, in view of the rich non-Arabic material that the book contains.

27. The popular origin and character of the Greek novel is discussed by B. Lavagnini, *Le origini del romanzo greco,* 1921, 56 f., J. Ludvíkovský, *Řecký román dobrodružný,* 1925 (with French summary, pp. 147–58), pp. 151 ff., B. E. Perry *AJP* 51. 95, 97 (1930).

28. Cf. Perry, loc. cit., 95 n. 5; for the AN, see, e.g., Littmann, *1001 Nacht,* p. 7. *GAL Suppl.* 2. 64 n. 1, Brockelmann shows how even to this day conservative circles in Egypt consider other branches of popular literature as being beneath their notice.

29. Perry, loc. cit., 98.

30. On his work cf. Muḥammad an-Nadīm, *Fihrist,* ed. G. Flügel, 1871–72, p. 304. In an-Nadīm's private opinion (in 987) the AN were "a coarse book of pointless stories" (*wa-huwa bi'l-ḥaqīqa kitāb ġaṯṯ bārid al-ḥadīṯ*). Before him, in 934, aṣ-Ṣūlī (ob. 946) refers to the *Ḥadīṯ Sindabād* and similar books as to inferior literary products; cf. *GAL Suppl.* 2. 252 quoting *Aurāq* 2. 6[10].

31. Our list of novel elements follows that given by R. Söder, *Die apokryphen Apostelgeschichten und die romanhafte Literatur der Antike,* 1932, pp. 3 f. Miss Söder proves all of them to occur in Plato's *Utopia,* the *Cyrupaedia,* and, of course, the Alexander novel.

32. Söder, loc. cit., 216 underlines the popular character of these apocrypha.

33. On the differentiation between the composition of the novel and that of the aretalogical tale cf. R. Reitzenstein, *Hellenistische Wundererzählungen* (1906), particularly pp. 97 f., and Kerényi, loc. cit., 20. As this article will confine itself to emphasizing some basic facts of style and form relations, I only note the survival of the novel motif of the "death of a substitute" in the siyar; cf. the Sīra Baibars as told by H. Wangelin, *Das arabische Volksbuch vom König aẓẒāhir Baibars,* 1936, passim, and Kerényi, loc. cit., 32, 186 n. 39. While this motif has not been adopted in the sphere of the AN, they and the siyar share the habit of beginning their tale of the hero with the love story of his parents so as to survey his life from the earliest conceivable point.

34. R. M. Rattenbury in *New Chapters in the History of Greek Literature,* 3rd Series, ed. J. M. Powell, 1933, p. 220.

35. Littmann, AN 6. 762 ff.

36. Other than the type represented by Sallust; cf. Kerényi, loc. cit., 18, 20.

37. Rattenbury, loc. cit., 223.

38. *Fünf Vorträge über den griechischen Roman* (1896).

39. Kerényi, loc. cit., 44 f. proves by pointing to their names or pseudonyms that the later novelists either were, or wished to be considered, Orientals.

40. Kerényi, loc. cit., VIII: "Irrfahrten eines vom Geschick verfolgten Liebespaares," repeated literally by Reitzenstein, *Tefnutlegende*, p, 31.

41. Cf. Lavagnini, loc. cit., 11, where Rohde's somewhat differing views are discussed.

42. Similarly Lavagnini, loc. cit., 103 f.

43. See later.

44. *MSOS* 1903, Westasiat. Studien, p. 52.

45. Loc. cit., 49 f., 244.

46. Rohde, loc. cit., 49 n. 4, mentions *Saif al-mulūk* alone of the AN.

47. On the meaning of individual traits in the novel, cf. Kerényi, loc. cit., passim, and J. Geffcken, *Der Ausgang des griechisch-römischen Heidentums*, 88 f. (1919) on Heliodor.

48. E.g., AN 1. 136 f.

49. Cf. particularly AN 4. 215 ff.

50. Kerényi, loc. cit., 190.

51. This applies, e.g., to AN 1. 172 ff., 2. 463 ff., 601 ff. It should be recalled that we are not here concerned with the substance of the geographical and ethnological lore used by both novel and AN, but solely with the function of this lore in the narrative.

52. Cf. e.g., Kerényi, loc. cit., 16 n. 84; AN 1. 244 and again later in the same story, 2. 594 ff., etc.

53. AN 1. 496–540. Among the details reminiscent of the classical model are: the asphyxy of the heroine, pp. 512 ff.; love at first sight; stress on chastity, pp. 515 ff.; fainting fits, p. 524; in this story no travel episodes occur; the particular chastity situation recurs AN 5. 576 where the fisherman, Ḫalīfa, respects Qūt al-qulūb.

54. AN 2. 462–502. Separation after the wedding—travel adventures of both lovers—the prince earning his bread as a gardener—reunion. The first part of *Qamar az-zamān*, AN 2. 376–462, is essentially a Persian fairy tale, the third, 2. 502–601, a "Familienroman," to quote Littmann, AN 6. 717, who, however, fails to analyze the story correctly and only recognizes two parts, his first part comprising pp. 376–502.

55. AN 3. 190–200. Separation in the wedding night—travel adventures—reunion. Here the Greek pattern is used within the framework of a demon narrative of the lower type.

56. AN 3. 399–441. Separation of lovers—travel adventures of both parties—union of the lovers. The aretalogical detail, pp. 409 f., of the taming of the lion by the hero is noteworthy.

57. AN 3. 784–91. The family is scattered by shipwreck and reunited after many years. In spite of the entirely different setting it is obvious that the *Recognitions of Clement* have served as model; cf. *Clem. Rec.*, trans. Th. Smith (1867), especially VII 8–VIII 2, VIII 8, IX 32–37. The *Passio S. Eustathii* and the *Vita SS. Xenophon and Maria*, as analyzed by H. Delehaye, *Les passions des martyrs et les genres littéraires*, 317 ff. (1921), unmistakably continue the novel tradition, closely resembling the Recognitions. W. Bousset, *Nachrichten d. Ges. d. Wiss. zu Göttingen*, philos.-hist. Kl., 1916, pp. 469 ff. studies this particular form of the ἀναγνωρισμός motif. The *Pious Israelite* is discussed pp. 487 ff. Bousset makes the Eastern origin of the motif fairly probable. His results, of course, do not militate against any connection, direct or indirect, of the Arabic storyteller with Greek literary material.

58. AN 5. 237–329. This story not only preserves the general outline of the wanderings leading to the lovers' union but also the typical motif of the horoscope, p. 251, in Greek: the oracle that forecasts the difficulties and dangers as well as the ultimate success awaiting the hero, thus taking away any real tension on the part of the reader. The figure of the accompanying friend, Saʿīd, the diagnosis of the love by the physician, p. 262 (cf. Heliodor IV 1; paraphrased by Aristainetos, *Epist.* I 13), the attempt to seduce the chaste hero, p. 275, are all genuine Greek novel features for once properly employed in a story that follows the romance pattern.

59. AN 5. 400–528. Separation of the married lovers—travel adventures of the husband—reunion. Hasan's love is constantly referred to as the incentive of his travels, e.g., p. 444; typical ἀναγνωρισμός, pp. 464 ff.; the first part of the story, pp. 329–400, is a "Zaubermärchen." Littmann, AN 6. 724 f., fails to see the interlocking of two different patterns of composition.

60. AN 5. 731–98. Separation of the lovers—travel adventures—the girl is married to another man, preserves her chastity—reunion—another separation with travel motifs—final reunion. The first part, 5. 657–731, contains a love story of an entirely different type. The whole "novel," incidentally, reflects the emotions and events of the Crusades. Littmann, AN 6. 736 f., again overlooks the blending of forms in the tale.

61. AN 6. 314–53. The story is missing in the Oriental prints. Littmann took it over from Burton. Cf. AN 6. 682.

62. Cf. the beginning of Heliodor's *Aithiopiká*.

63. Cf. in Greek Achilles Tatios V 7, 8, Chariton IV 1, *Apoll. Tyr.* ch. 32.

64. Cf. beside Maryam, the Belt-Maker, in the story discussed above under (8), e.g., AN 1. 325 ff., 207 ff., 344 ff., 2. 305, 410 ff. (very outspoken on the greater strength of feminine desires), 505 ff., 3. 221 ff. On masculine passivity see e.g., AN 3. 233 ff., 574 ff., 5. 124 f.

65. The main exception is the extraordinary prowess of the fighters for the faith. Cf. the stories reflecting the Crusades, *ʿAjīb and Ġarīb* (AN 4. 448 ff.), and the like.

66. Cf. Söder, loc. cit., 51.

67. On the technique of the erotic narrative see Rohde, loc. cit., 145 ff.

68. On chastity in the novel see Rohde, loc. cit., passim, Kerényi, loc. cit., 210, 217. In the *Recognitions of Clement* chastity can be called the pivotal point; see particularly I 1 where Clement declares to have been a "lover of chastity" from his earliest age and VII 38 where the reunion with her sons is presented as reward of Matthidia's chastity. In the AN cf. e.g., 2. 407 ff. and 4. 684. Kerényi, loc. cit., 262 n. 162 considers Gānim b. Ayyūb's behavior a "parody" of the ideal attitude. For tears (sometimes combined with fainting fits) cf. e.g., AN 1. 236, 237, 2. 534, 555, 558, 578, 585, 3. 412, 418 f., 433, 5. 409 ff. In this connection Kerényi's discussion of the θρῆνοι loc. cit., 27 f., has to be mentioned. Fainting in the novel, Perry, loc. cit., 107, *Clem. Rec.* VII 21, 31, IX 35, Lukian, *Tocharis* ch. 30; in the AN e.g., 1. 183, 299, 2. 18 f., 317, 321, 5.6, 58, 69, 317 f., 810; cf. also Basset, loc. cit., 1. 139, 141. On suicide (or intended suicide) see Kerényi, loc. cit., 142. The Islamic condemnation of self-destruction reduces, but does not exclude the use of the motif; cf. AN 5. 807. For extraordinary sentimentality see e.g., AN 5. 366 ff., 585 ff. Lascivious bathing scenes in the novel Kerényi, loc. cit., 225 f., in the AN, e.g., 5. 362 ff.

69. While C. Brockelmann, *GAL Suppl.* 1. 30 f., errs in peremptorily precluding foreign influences on the formation of early Arabic poetry, C. Burdach, *Sitzungsberichte d. Berliner Akademie*, 1918, pp. 1089 ff. clearly overestimates the possible Hellenistic contribution to pre-Islamic lyrics.

70. ʿUmar b. abī Rabīʿa, al-Aḥwaṣ, al-ʿArjī, and others. On the types of love poetry in early Arabic literature cf. my book *Die Wirklichkeitweite der frühArabischen Dichtung*, 101 ff. (1937).

71. On these studies cf. the interesting paper by R. Reitzenstein, *Alchemistische Lehrschriften und Märchen bei den Arabern*, 1923.

72. It may be well to remember that tears were considered a χάρισμα; cf. e.g., A. J. Wensinck, *Sachau-Festschrift*, pp. 26–35 (1915), and especially Andrae, *Ursprung*, 117 and 124 ff. On larmoyant piety in earliest Islam see my notes, *WZKM* 44. 46 ff. where some references are listed to which Ibn ʿAbd Rabbihi, *al-ʿIqd al-farīd*, Cairo 1353/1935, 2. 137 f. should be added. T. Andrae, Zuhd und Mönchtum, *MO* 25. 302 n. 7 (1931) observes that "crying" as technical term stood for all kinds of devotional practices. Bakkāʾ as name of the Muslim ascetic imitates the Syriac "abīlā," literally, "the mourner." See further Marg. Smith, *Studies in Early Mysticism*, 155 ff. (1931).

73. Rohde, loc. cit., 27 f. and 28 n. 1 traces the origin of the love-disease concept and shows that Euripides frequently refers to passion as νόσος or νόσημα. Pp. 52 ff. Rohde points to the story of Stratonike as to the origin of the numerous tales in which a skilled physician diagnoses love as the cause of the patient's pains, a motif not infrequently met with in the AN. To Rohde's references, Niẓāmī ʿArūḍī, Čahār Maqāla, trans. E. G. Browne, 1921, 85 ff., and Basset, loc. cit., 2. 74 ff. may be added.

74. Cf. Ḥasan of Baṣra, AN 5. 432, with Pausanias, *Description of Greece*, VII 19. 5, quoted by Rohde, loc. cit., 44.

75. E.g., Ach. Tat. I 1, and often in Arabic poetry.

76. Love sickness, generally leading to death: e.g., AN 2. 303 ff., 569 f., 572 f., 656 ff., 3. 449 f., 4. 648, 5. 644 (parody). Of classical literature I only refer to Theocrit, *Idylls*, 1. 64–145 (Thyrsis sings of Daphnis's love-death) and 3. 52–54 (the spurned lover announces that he will die of his love), and Virgil, *Aeneid* 6. 440 ff. where those killed by tragic love are enumerated when Aeneas sees them in the lugentes campi of the underworld. Virgil begins:

Hic, quos durus amor crudeli tabe peredit,
Secreti celant calles at myrtea circum
Silva tegit . . .

On the passage cf. Norden, *Hermes* 28. 376–81 (1893), approved by A. Dieterich, *Nekyia*, 151 n. 2 (1913). Those listed by Virgil did not succumb to love as such, but met with a violent death (βιαιοθάνατοι) in consequence of their δυσέρως ἔρως. F. Cumont, *After Life in Roman Paganism*, 141 ff. (1922) discusses the post mortem fate of the βιαιοθάνατοι at length.

77. al-Jāḥiẓ (ob. 869), *Kitāb al-bayān wa't-tabyīn* 1. 295 (Cairo 1351/1932) refers to books on the majānīn al-ʿArab, "not on those *majānīn* like Majnūn banī ʿĀmir or Majnūn banī Jaʿda" but like Arsīmūs al-Yūnānī (who, 2. 178 f. is called: Raisamūs al-Yūnānī). In other words, al-Jāḥiẓ wishes to distinguish between books about lovers who fell victim to madness (for love stories of this and similar description, cf. *Fihrist*, pp. 306 ff.) and books about people of the Eulenspiegel type (pertinent Arabic literature: *Fihrist*, p. 313, where Arsīmūs is not listed. He recurs, however, as Rīsīmūs in Jāḥiẓ, *Kitāb al-ḥayawān*, Cairo 1323–25, 1.140, where it is stated that the learned credit him with more than eighty *nawādir*. Jāḥiẓ proceeds to quote four specimens. One of these is a replica of a saying attributed to Isokrates by Plutarch, *Moralia* 838 E. According to *Fihrist*, 295, Qusṭā b. Lūqā translated a *Kitāb nawādir al-yūnāniyyīn*. M. Steinschneider, *Centralblatt für Bibliothekswesen*, Beiheft 5. 27 (1889) identifies this book with the *Kitāb ādāb al-falāsifa*, mentioned by Ibn abī Uṣaibʿa, *ʿUyūn al-anbāʾ*, Cairo 1299/1882, 1. 245, but fails to give any reason for his assumption).

78. One of the oldest love romances is the story of ʿAlī b. Ādam al-Juʿfī and his girl, Manhala. When Manhala is sold to a Hāšimite ʿAlī dies of love. Cf. Abū 'l-Faraj al-Iṣfahānī, *Kitāb al-aġānī*, Būlāq 1285, 14. 51 f., *Fihrist*, p. 306, *GAL Suppl.* 1. 248. al-Masʿūdī, *Murūj aḏ-ḏahab*, ed. Barbier de Meynard and Pavet de Courteille, 1861–77, 7. 351 ff. tells of the "loves" of ʿUrwa b. Ḥizām and Majnūn banī ʿĀmir. Many stories are summarized by R. Paret, *Früharabische Liebesgeschichten*, 1972, pp. 9 ff. The Arabic collection of Mugulṭai, *Kitāb al-wāḍiḥ al-mubīn fī ḏikr man istašhada min al-muḥibbīn*, ed. O. Spies, 1936, begins with an alleged saying of the Prophet that gives the martyr of a chaste love equal standing with the martyr of the faith. Thus, the

new concept of love receives the "official" sanction of the highest spiritual authority.

The typological concept of the "lover" was firmly established no later than the ninth century. Jāḥiẓ, *Ḥayawān* 3. 16 introduces *baʿḍ al-ʿuššāq* as the author of a *qiṭʿa*, the reply being given by *al-maʿšūqa*. A similar dialogue loc. cit., 3. 17.

79. Ed. Chr. Wordsworth (1877).

80. Trans. A. Lang (1880).

81. *Syria. Publications of the Princeton Archaeological Expeditions to Syria in 1904–5 and 1909.* Division III, Section A, p. 390, no. 7879. For the formula the editor refers to Aesch. *Theb.* 751: ἐγείνατο μὲν μόρον αὑψῷ. Littmann translates the inscription AN 6. 739.

82. AN, ed. W. H. Macnaughten, 1839–42, 4. 100[18], Night 809, AN 5. 461; meter *ṭawīl:*

> *"fa-billāhi yā qaumī iḏā muttu fa'ktubū*
> *ʿalà lauḥi qabrī anna hāḏā mutayyamu."*

M. Smith, *Studies in Early Mysticism*, p. 192 (1931) quotes *Jāmī, Nafaḥāt al-uns*, ed. Nassau Less, p. 36, to the effect that on the grave of the famous mystic, Ḏū'n-Nūn al-Miṣrī (ob. 857) "there appeared an inscription . . . which ran: 'This is the beloved of God, who died from his love to God, slain by God,' and whenever that inscription was erased, it appeared again."

83. The following examples from classical phraseology may be useful as illustrations. The Arabic parallels are too numerous to require specific quotations.

a. The beloved person wounds the lover, his or her eyes are like arrows and similar objects; for classical references see A. Spies, *Militat omnis amans. Ein Beitrag zur Bildersprache der antiken Erotik*, 1930, especially pp. 24 ff. I. Goldziher, *Abhandlungen zur arabischen Philologie* 1. 117 (1896) lists and discusses some Arabic references. A survey of the *mujūn* and of the *airiyyāt* literature would doubtless reveal many reminiscences of classical phraseology.

b. The protagonist(s) of the Greek novel are frequently compared with statues of a deity; cf. Rohde, loc. cit., 155.

c. The likening to the moon of a beautiful face has been traced in Greek romance by Kerényi, loc. cit., 221, 221 n. 60. The comparison of the beloved surrounded by her servants to the moon with stars (AN 3. 31 in prose) goes back as far as Sappho (Ode 3. 1 ff.). ʿUmar b. abī Rabīʿa (ed. P. Schwarz) 168. 11 and al-Walīd b. Yazīd (ed. F. Gabrieli, *RSO* 15. 1 ff.) 51. 4, 5 have it, e.g., and an-Nābiġa aḏ-Ḏubyānī (ed. W. Ahlwardt) 3. 10 uses the simile in a panegyric on king an-Nuʿmān III of al-Ḥīra. al-ʿAskarī, *Dīwān al maʿānī* 1. 16 f. (Cairo 1352) lists some of an-Nābiġa's imitators.

84. Cf. Rohde, loc. cit., 56 ff. and F. Wilhelm, *Rheinisches Museum*, N. F. 57. 55 f. (1902) on the classical literature περὶ ἔρωτος, ἐρωτικὴ τέχνη,

etc. Characteristic of the Arabic way of treating the subject are Abū Dā'ūd al-Iṣfahānī (ob. 909; *GAL Suppl.* 1. 249 wrongly 898), *Kitāb az-zahra* (ed. R. A. Nykl, 1932) and Ibn Ḥazm (ob. 1064), *Ṭauq al-ḥamāma* (ed. D. K. Petrof, 1914, trans. R. A. Nykl, 1931) and the §§ 155–75 of the same author's *Kalimāt fī 'l-aṭbāq* (in the translation of M. Asín Palacios, 1916; on the book cf. Nykl, *AJSL* 40. 30ff.). The *Kitāb az-zahra* clearly shows the author's familiarity with Plato. The book was analyzed by L. Massignon, *La passion d'al-Hallaj*, 1922, 1. 169 ff.

But already long before these authors, probably toward the end of the eighth century, the Barmakid, Yaḥyà b. Ḫālid, who fell into disfavor in 803 A.D., had "philosophers" discuss in his presence the nature of love. The same topic was discussed at the courts of al-Ma'mūn (813–33) and al-Muntaṣir (861–62). For al-Ma'mūn cf. F. Rosenthal, *Islamic Culture* 14. 421 (1940) who quotes Yāqūt, *Iršād al-arīb*, ed. D. S. Margoliouth, 5. 280 f.; for al-Muntaṣir cf. Mas'ūdī, loc. cit., 6. 368 ff. and 7. 311 ff.

85. Cf. my *Wirklichkeitweite*, pp. 51 ff.

86. Ṭabarī, *Geschichte der Perser und Araber zur Zeit der Sasaniden*, trans. Th. Nöldeke, 1879, pp. 326 f.

87. More or less elaborate descriptions of the protagonists are frequent in the AN. Cf. e.g., 1. 102 f., 2. 378 ff., 393 f., 3. 271, 5. 115, 364 ff., 450 f. It must be said, however, that in spite of their relatively independent style the AN descriptions of beautiful persons bear definite resemblance in type e.g., to the Ἔκφρασις κάλλους of (Pseudo-)Libanios (ed. R. Foerster, 1903 ff., 8. 541–46; Latin translation in F. Morel's edition of Libanios, Paris 1606–27, 2. 709–12; on the spuriousness of the Ekphrasis see Foerster, loc. cit., 8. 439); §§ 12–5 in particular sound familiar to the reader of the AN. (Note also p. 541[7]: Ἔρως γὰρ ἐκ τῶν ἐκείνης ὀμμάτων ἐτόξευε). Söder, loc. cit., 96 n. 108 refers to a type of brief and precise description of persons, occasionally employed in the Apocryphal New Testament that strangely resembles the technique used in the Arabic ayyām literature. (Cf. W. Caskel, *Islamica* 3, Suppl. pp. 35 ff.) Lukian, *Alexandros of Abonuteichos*, ch. 3, provides an example from a higher literary sphere. Söder feels reminded of the style of the letter. P. Wendland, *Die hellenistisch-römische Kultur in ihren Beziehungen zu Judentum und Christentum* 23 (1907) notes the occurrence of this descriptive technique, which he characterizes as "inspired by the style of the police warrant," in both the post-Christian historians and the apocryphal Acts. It may be worth mentioning that O. Schissel von Fleschenberg undertook to reconstruct the ideal woman as conceived by the novelists: Das weibliche Schönheitsideal nach seiner Darstellung im griechischen Roman, *Zs. f. Aesthetik u. allg. Kunstwiss.* 2. 381–405 (1907).

88. Nikolaos Sophistes, in L. v. Spengel, *Rhetores Graeci*, 1853–56, 3. 491 ff. gives the theory of the ἔκφρασις. He describes its purpose—πειρᾶται θεατὰς τοὺς ἀκούοντας ἐργάζεσθαι: For a modern treatment of the subject cf. E. Norden, *Die antike Kunstprosa*, 1898, pp. 285 f., 288 ff. Examples in point

from the AN: a. gardens: 1. 467, 4. 474 f., 5. 587 f., 605, 659 ff., 6. 411, and often; b. palaces, treasures, etc.; 1. 83, 192 ff., 331 f., 2. 316, 783 ff., 842 ff., 3. 226 (curtain), 4. 256 ff., 5. 360 f. AN 6. 168 the paintings in a public bathhouse are mentioned but not described; here religious prejudice may have checked the author. There are also non-ekphrastic descriptions in the AN; e.g., 3. 6 ff., 12 f., 13 f., etc. The Apocrypha are fond of descriptions of buildings; cf. Söder, loc. cit., 202 f.

89. Ed. Sathas-Legrand, 1875, vss. 2702–859.

90. Vss. 1877–1920.

91. *Vita Basilii*, in: *Theophanes Continuatus*, ed. I. Bekker, 1838, pp. 321 ff. For the reference, to Digenis I am indebted to H. Grégoire, *Conférence sur Digénis Akritas*, 1941, p. 13 of the English typescript.

92. Rohde, loc. cit., 512 f. and 624 discusses the garden scenes in the novel; the general attitude toward nature in the Greek romance is presented loc. cit., 508 f. and 624. A. Biese, *Die Entwicklung des Naturgefühls bei den Griechen und Römern*, 1822–24, is somewhat disappointing in his treatment of the novel (1. 120 ff.) as he almost confines himself to Longos. Outside of the novel we meet with the garden as the scene of love-enjoyment e.g., in one of the letters of Aristainetos (around 450 A.D., ed. J. F. Boissonade, 1882, I 3) whose description of the garden is a typical ἔκφρασις. About one century earlier, Libanios wrote his famous Ἔκφρασις ἔαρος (loc. cit., 8. 479–82) and that of "the Garden" (ibid. 8. 485 f., spurious according to Foerster, ibid. 8. 439), both strikingly similar to the later Arabic specimens.

93. Cf. Ṭaha Ḥusain, *La rhétorique arabe de D̲jāḥiẓ à ʿAbd al-ḳāhir* (introduction to his edition of Qudāma, *Naqd an-nat̲r*, 1933) p. 9. He considers the Hellenistic influence in both the poet Abū Tammām (ob. probably 846) and the prosaist ʿAbd al-Ḥamīd (ob. 749) incontestable and borne out in Abū Tammām's work by his precision of ideas, his predilection for the description of nature, the insertion of philosophical ideas, and by his endeavors to achieve real unity in his poems. Brockelmann, *GAL Suppl.* 1. 135 n. 1 considers Ṭaha Ḥusain's view improbable. But the verses of al-Buḥturī (ed. Constantinople, 1300) 1. 133, 7–9 (trans. Ḥusain p. 10) and the passage in Ibn Qutaiba, *Adab al-kātib*, ed. M. Grünert, 1901, pp. 3 f., strongly support the theory of some Greek influence. Incidentally, both the poet al-Buḥturī and the scholar Ibn Qutaiba are hostile to this foreign trend. F. Gabrieli, *RSO* 13. 224 (1932) remarks on the Hellenistic influence noticeable in the ethical writings of Ibn al-Muqaffaʿ (ob. 757). Spring poems by al-Buḥturī (ob. 897) and Ibn al-Muʿtazz (ob. 908) are referred to by Brockelmann, *GAL Suppl.* 1. 126, 129. For the development of Arabic flower and landscape poetry in the tenth century cf. A. Mez, *The Renaissance of Islam*, trans. Khuda Bukhsh and D. S. Margoliouth, 1937, pp. 261 ff. The first signs of that new approach to nature, which is primarily represented by aṣ-Ṣanaubarī (ob. 945), can be discerned in some of Abū Nuwās's (ob. 810) verses; cf. *GAL Suppl.* 1. 145.

94. Cf. M. Haupt, *Opuscula* 3. 20 f. (1876).

95. *Antigonus von Karystos*, 1881, pp. 294 f.

96. This contest is supposed to have taken place at the funeral games held in honor of king Amphidamas of Chalkis. The work was composed during the reign of Hadrian, but is based on an account of the sophist Alkidamas of Elaea, fourth century B.C. The judge, by the way, despite the sympathy of the audience, decides in favor of Hesiod. It is of interest that Friedrich Nietzsche discussed the subject, *Rheinisches Museum*, N. F. 25. 528–40 (1870). This type of a contest between two poets survived in Arabic; cf. e.g., Imruʾulqais versus at-Tauʾam (Imruʾulqais, ed. W. Ahlwardt, poem 22) and ʿAbīd versus Imruʾulqais (ʿAbīd, ed. C. J. Lyall, App. 10). Attractive classical examples are Theocrit, *Idylls* 5, 6, 8, and 9.

97. AN 2. 495 ff.

98. Cf. Ach. Tat. II 35. 3 ff. the dialogue between Kleitophon and Menelaos, and F. Wilhelm, loc. cit., 61.

99. AN 3. 289–308.

100. *Kunstprosa*, pp. 277 ff.

101. Von Wilamowitz, *Hermes* 35. 28 (1900) explains the term, but does not share Norden's interpretation of it.

102. On the ὑπόθεσις cf. Rohde, loc. cit., 295 n. 2, 308, and 309 where the extempore character is stressed; see also Norden, *Kunstprosa*, 129 f. on the development of the "Schuldeklamation," the διατριβή, from the dialogue.

103. Trans. Fowler, 3. 261 ff. Isokrates, *Oratio* X, §12 criticizes the rhetor Polykrates for his panegyrics on bees and salt. Polykrates was also the author of an encomium on mice; cf. Aristotle, *Rhetoric* II 24. 6 Th. C. Burgess, *Chicago University. Studies in Classical Philology* 3, 1902, 157 ff. discusses the παράδοζα ἐγκώμια and lists the most noted specimens.

104. *Bayān* 1. 247.

105. *GAL Suppl.* 1. 125; the edition referred to by Brockelmann is not accessible to me.

106. Ed. F. Steingass, 1897, pp. 361–63.

107. H. Ethé, Ueber persische Tenzonen, *Verhandlg. d. 5. intern. Orientalisten-Congresses*, 1881, 1. Hälfte, p. 52 and 52 n. 1, maintains the independence of the Persian *munāẓara* on the rather futile ground that the earlier Arabic *munāẓara* is not poetic in the strict sense of the word as is the Persian, but is written in either prose or rhymed prose. The poems of Ibn ar-Rūmī referred to above, refute this contention. Incidentally, nos. 5 and 6 in Ethé's list of Arabic *munāẓarāt*, two little tracts by one Ḥāmid b. al-Ḥakkāk, are not, as Ethé believes, prose but *mawāliyā* poems. (cf. *Brit. Mus. Cat. cod. or.*, 1838, no. 640. 5 and 6). To this catalogue should be added: Aḥmad b. abī Ṭāhir Ṭaifūr (ob. 893), *Mufāḫarat al-ward wa'n-narjis;* cf. *Fihrist*, p. 146. at-Tanūḫī (ob. 994), *al-Faraj baʿd aš-šidda* 2. 196 (Cairo 1903/04), and accordingly *GAL Suppl.* 1. 210 give the title as *Faḍāʾil al-ward ʿalà 'n-narjis.* This book is said by Tanūḫī (loc. cit.,) to be more extensive than that composed by Ibn Lankak (tenth century) with the same title. Persian *munāẓarāt* are listed and discussed

by Ethé, *GIP* 2. 226–29. The direct comparison of these *munāẓarāt* with the poetical competitions of Theocrit that Ethé, *Tenzonen*, p. 54, suggests is untenable. The σύγκρισις is perpetuated in the *munāẓarā* proper, the ἀγών is reflected in the poetical contests mentioned above. It ought to be noted that the Syrian Narses (ob. after 503) composed tenzons; cf. Brockelmann, *Die syrische und die christlich–arabische Litteratur*, 1907, p. 65. C. Brockelmann, *Asia Major*, 1. 32 f. (1925), and earlier *Mélanges H. Dérenbourg*, 1909, pp. 231 ff., is inclined to assign Persian origin to the *munāẓarā*. But the earlier Arabic verses quoted, the Iranian descent of whose authors Brockelmann is careful to note, can hardly be considered even rudimentary *munāẓarāt* in the strict meaning of the term. This goes even for the verses of al-ʿAbbās b. al-Aḥnaf (ob. 803), pp. 27 f. (ed. Constantinople 1298). Thus, it is quite possible that M. Steinschneider, *SBWA* phil.-his. Kl., 155 (1908) Abh. 4, pp. 35 and 42, is right when he attributes the first Arabic *munāẓāra* to (Pseudo-?)Jāḥiẓ (ob. 869). I agree, however, with Brockelmann, *Mélanges*, pp. 231 f., that Steinschneider, loc. cit., 7, was mistaken in deriving the *munāẓāra* from the classical Arabic *faḫr* poetry. According to its latest editor, J. M. Unvala, the only extant *munāẓāra* in Pahlavī literature, the "Contest of the Palm-Tree and the Goat," ultimately goes back to another version "perhaps written in imitation of the Arabic *mufāḫara*" (*BSOS* 2. 639). The little book cannot, therefore, be quoted in support of the theory that the tenzon originated in Persia.

108. Cf. e.g., Perry, loc. cit., 104 n. 15, E. Schwartz, loc. cit. ch. 2.

109. *Lectures on Arabic Historians*, 1930, p. 115. The *Fihrist*, p. 146 records among other works of his:

(1) *Kitāb martaba Hurmuz b. Kisrà Nušīrwān* and

(2) *Kitāb al-malik al-Bābilī wa'al-malik al-Miṣrī al-bāġiyāni wa'l-malik al-ḥakīm ar-Rūmī*, which are most likely those referred to by Margoliouth.

110. Similar views concerning the AN are held by Littmann, *1001 Nacht*, pp. 28 f., and Horovitz, *Spuren*, p. 96. C. Burdach, *SBBA* 1904, p. 899, believes that the "Mischform" originated in Syria in the third century B.C. While he is mistaken in assigning this definite place and time of origin to a form so widely diffused through different civilizations, Burdach is right in insisting on its popular character, as against von Wilamowitz, loc. cit., 299. Rohde, loc. cit., pp. 407 and 622 does not contribute much to the question. Reitzenstein, *Tefnutlegende*, p. 30 also believes in the Oriental background of the "mixed form." Prof. R. H. Pfeiffer, in a letter dated April 1, 1939, kindly directed my attention to the prosimetric passages in the Book of Genesis. When O. Immisch, *Neue Jbb. f. d. klass. Altertum* 47. 420 (1921) refers to phrases like *chanter et dire*, *singen und sagen*, as proofs of the prosimetry of the works of art thus introduced, the stereotyped Arabic *anšada yaqūlu* comes to mind. For the original meaning of this phrase cf. Goldziher, *Abhandlungen zur arabischen Philologie* 1. 25 (1896).

111. On the classical theory and the concepts used there cf. Kerényi, loc. cit., ch. 1, and K. Barwick, *Hermes*, 63. 261–87 (1928). Arabic theory dislikes

the *muḥāl*, the impossible or the absurd, in poetry. Cf. e.g., al-ʿAskarī, *Kitāb aṣ-ṣināʿatain*, 1320, p. 286, al-Bāqillānī, *Iʿjāz al-Qurʾān*, Cairo 1352, p. 174[2], Ḏū 'r-Rumma (ed. C. H. H. Macartney, 1919) 57. 48, quoted *Bayān* 1. 129. Again it should be recalled that geographical lore is not considered here, although it may be said that the average Muslim would find little ψεῦδος in, say, the seafaring yarns of the AN.

112. Prominent also in the Apocrypha; cf. Söder, loc. cit., 42 and 48.

113. Cf. Ach. Tat. II 13 and Kerényi, loc. cit., 243, AN 2. 80 ff., 5. 114.

114. The Apocrypha here preserve the level of the novel, Söder, pp. 87 ff. The examples from the AN are very numerous. Religious use of banj in the Pahlavī book of *Artāk Virāž*, ed. E. West, 1872, ch. 2. Cf. West's remarks, pp. LIX ff.

115. Söder, loc. cit., 46 ff. AN e.g., 2. 434 ff. (Marzuwān; cf Kerényi's remarks, loc. cit., 254 n. 124) and 5. 252 ff. (Saʿīd).

116. For the "literary love letters" see the interesting discussion of H. Peter, "Der Brief in der römischen Literatur," *ASGW* 20 no. 3, pp. 188 ff. In the AN, cf. e.g., 3. 399 ff. The dependence of the Arabic nonliterary letter on the Greek will have to be investigated in detail. Greek letters like those reproduced by Deissmann, loc. cit., 152 ff., make the survival of Greek formulae and arrangement fairly probable. Cf. also the copious collection of Greek opening and closing formulae in F. X. J. Exler, *The Form of the Ancient Greek Letter*, 1923, pp. 23 ff. and 69 ff.

117. Cf. Kerényi, loc. cit., 165 ff.

118. Greek references: Söder, loc. cit., 101 f.; similar in the story Basset, loc. cit., 2. 100 ff. Appeal of the lover-poet to his people, e.g., ʿUmar b. abī Rabīʿa 235. 2, Jamīl (ed. F. Gabrieli, *RSO* 17. 40 ff.) 2. 1 f. Rohde, loc. cit., 495 briefly mentions the fact for the romance. In the Greek novels the people assemble in the end for an *acclamatio.* On the *acclamatio* and its different function in the novel and the "Wundererzählung" cf. E. Peterson, Εἷς θεός 140 ff. (1926). Peterson does not discuss the Byzantine acclamations as presented in Constantin Porphyrogennetos, *De caerimoniis*, ed. J. J. Reiske, 1829–30, I 2–9 (new. ed. with French translation by A. Vogt, 1935, pp. 29 ff.). It is important to realize that the *takbīr* in Muslim ritual is nothing else but a μέγας-*acclamatio* (cf. Peterson, loc. cit., 196 ff.), the best-known example of which occurs in *Acta* 19. 34: Μεγάλη ἡ Ἄρτεμις Ἐφεσίων Littmann, *ZS* 4. 320 (1926) feels "reminded" of the Muslim formula by the μέγας-*acclamatio.* In this connection the Muslim *šahāda* may be compared with *acclamationes* like that taken from the *Acta Nerei et Achillei* (quoted in Peterson, loc. cit., 186) when Petrus resuscitates a dead child: Εἷς θεός ἐν οὐρανῷ καὶ ἐπὶ γῆς ὃν Πέτρος κηρύσσει, or (Peterson, loc. cit., 187): Εἷς θεός μέγας καὶ δυνατὸς, ὃν ἡρμήνευσεν ἡμῖν ὁ καλλικέλαδος Μηνᾶς, and the like. It must, of course, be remembered that the εἷς θεός-formula is an *acclamatio*, not a creed. Yet, the combination of a εἷς θεός-formula with the statement that a specified person, say, Petrus or Muḥammad, is the herald or apostle of this God is highly suggestive of a con-

nection, the real nature of which remains to be investigated. It should be noted that even a "typically Muslim" formula like *in šāʾa ʾllāhu* is paralleled in Greek. The pious reservation "if the gods will"—τῶν θεῶν θελόντων—is frequent in pagan texts. Cf. Deissmann, loc. cit., 181 n. 16 and the literature there quoted.

In this connection it may be tentatively suggested that the so-called mystical letters at the beginning of twenty-nine Sūras, whose function has not yet been explained satisfactorily, reflect the *voces mysticae* so familiar to us from the magic papyri and from documents like the famous Mithras liturgy that A. Dieterich published. (Cf. *Eine Mithrasliturgie*, 1903, pp. 2 ff. and 32 ff.). For the Koranic letters and their proposed interpretations see Nöldeke-Schwally, *Geschichte des Qorāns*, 1919, 2. 68 ff. O. Loth. *ZDMG* 35. 603 (1881) before discussing the interpretations, listed in Ṭabarī's *Tafsīr*, appositely stresses Muḥammad's weakness for the miraculous and the obscure. His ready response to any symbolism of this type is beyond doubt.

119. On *ʿajīb* as term of literary criticism see the writer, *JAOS* 61. 55 (1941). Dionysius of Halikarnassus, *De Lysia* c. 13 remarks that Lysias's style is not θαυμαστή, that "it fails to astonish."

120. Peterson, loc. cit., 193 ff. and in particular p. 194 n. 2. Astonishment as reaction to the beauty of a person like in the AN, in the *Apocalypse of Peter*, Akhmim Fragment, ed. A. Dieterich, *Nekyia*, pp. 2[18] and 4[1]; trans. M. R. James, *The Apocryphal New Testament*, 1926, p. 508, vss. 8, 11.

121. O. Weinreich, "Fabel, Aretalogie, Novelle," *SBHA* phil.-hist. Kl. 1931, Heft 7, p. 12.

122. Cf. Kerényi, loc. cit., 147 n. 140.

123. Cf. Kerényi, loc. cit., 05 ff.

124. The methodology of establishing literary or cultural dependence whenever full documentation of the actual borrowing cannot be obtained has been brilliantly developed by J. Ribera, *Orígenes del Justicia de Aragón*, pp. 192 ff. (1897). Ribera's problem was the demonstration of Arabic influence on the judicial system of the Aragonese. Still more closely related to our difficulty is the inability of M. Asín of proving the infiltration of Dante's mind with Muslim ideas by presenting full documentation of the process, although the fact of their influence could be established beyond doubt. Consequently, Asín's sagacious reflections on the subject of transmission, *Revue de littérature comparée* 4. 388 ff. (1924) and, more briefly, in *Islam and the Divine Comedy*, 1926, pp. 237 ff. can be referred to in support of our position. Another unmistakable transfer of a literary tradition that cannot be fully documented has been discussed by T. Andrae, *MO* 25. 297 ff. On p. 327 Andrae speaks of the "intangible but indubitable" influence of the Christian ascetic legends on the stories of the Muslim *zuhhād*. In this connection Andrae notes the exact agreement of the mystical term *rāḥa* (rest) with the corresponding ἀνάπαυσις. It may be to the point to note that Goldziher, *Islam* 6. 177 (1915/16), too, feels that the proof of actual literary transmission can occasionally be dispensed with when the migration of ideas can be convincingly established by indirect methods.

125. Loc. cit., 148.

126. Söder, loc. cit., 34, 42, 95 f., 124 ff., 129, 136, 138 ff.

127. Ch. 1.

128. AN 4. 129 ff.; Söder, loc. cit., 79 n. 67.

129. I am referring especially to the following: the legend of Duraij, pp. 185 ff.; the story of the slave, pp. 288 ff., where Basset fails to recognize the Christian motif of the secret saint who, when discovered, flees from the glorification bestowed upon him, or her: cf. W. Bousset, *Archiv f. Religionswiss.* 21. 1 ff. (1922); the story reappears AN 3. 746 ff.; and the legend of the hermit falsely accused of debauchery, pp. 482 ff.

The story of the son of Hārūn ar-Rašīd who withdraws from the court to lead an ascetic life as an unknown workman, AN 3. 546 ff.—3. 347 ff. in Basset—reflects the legend of St. Alexios. (Cf. Littmann, AN 6. 751.) The story, originally Syrian, is represented several times in Arabic literature. Cf. Nöldeke, *ZDMG* 43. 327 f. (1889) where the AN version also is referred to, and *ZDMG* 53. 256 ff. (1899). Here Nöldeke suggests that the figure of the prince, who is usually called Aḥmad b. Hārūn ar-Rašīd as-Sabtī, is nothing but Alexios, the saintly son of the Christian Emperor, Theodosios, in Muslim garb. Goldziher, *JRAS* 1904, p. 133 declares the legend to be of Buddhist origin.

Another illustration of the contribution of Christian literature to Arabic tales is the disputation of St. Catherine in the third of her *Passiones* (ed. J. Viteau, 1897, pp. 44 ff., analyzed by J. Bidez, *Byzantinische Zeitschrift* 11. 388 ff. [1902]). Here the saint defends her faith against the most learned doctors of the Empire much in the same style as Tawaddud, AN 3. 651 ff., disputes with the scholars of the caliph. This story, various replicae of which were widely read during the later Middle Ages, probably was composed (or compiled) about 900 A.D.; cf. Horovitz, *ZDMG* 57. 175 (1903). Littmann, AN 6. 759, quotes Horovitz for the theory that the story was modeled on a *Book of the Philosopher who was examined by the slave-girl Qiṭār*, which was a translation from the Greek.

130. Cf. Söder, loc. cit., 38.

131. *mayāmis Ġazza*, μῖμοι of Gaza; ed. H. Hirschfeld, 193. 3.

132. Cf. Horovitz, *Spuren*, pp. 87 ff.

133. Some Greek expressions must have been familiar at least to individual Arabs. as-Suyūṭī, *Muzhir* (Būlāq, 1882) 1. 134 relates that Šuraiḥ once replied to a question of ʿAlī: "*qālūn*," i.e., καλόν, which word the commentator correctly explains by: "*aṣabta*" *bi'r-rūmiyya*. It is also important to recall the fact that the Greek School of Alexandria was alive when the Arabs conquered Egypt and that it continued under Muslim domination. Under ʿUmar II (717–20) the School moved to Antioch, later, under al-Mutawakkil (847–61), to Ḥarrān, and finally, under al-Muʿtaḍid (892–902), to Baġdād. Cf. M. Meyerhof, "Von Alexandrien nach Bagdad," *SBBA*, phil.-hist. Cl. 1930, pp. 4, 13 f., 19 ff. On p. 14 Meyerhof describes how the profane sciences, including rhetoric, were cultivated in the educational centers situated on Syrian and Persian territory.

134. Some Arabic references in O. Rescher, *Abriss der arabischen Litteraturgeschichte*, 1925–33, 1. 91 f. and 2. 7. H. S. Santesson, *The Moslem World* 32. 40 ff. (1942) quotes a poem using the motif from eighteenth-century Afghanistan.

135. G. Herrlinger, *Totenklage um Tiere in der antiken Dichtung*, 1930, has no Greek, or Byzantine, quotations later than the sixth century. Thus, a gap in chronology exists similar to that in the transmission of the form elements that later appear in the AN. The Arabic specimens in aṣ-Ṣūlī (ob. 946), *Kitāb al-awrāq* (section on contemporary poets), ed. J. Heyworth Dunne, 1934, p. 163 ff., are written by a certain Abū Muḥammad al-Qāsim b. Yūsuf, brother of the better known Abū Jaʿfar Aḥmad b. Yūsuf. Both were contemporaries of al-Maʾmūn. *Aġānī* 20. 56 f. refers to al-Qāsim and mentions that most of his poems were *fī madḥ al-bahāʾim wa-marāṯī-hā.* aṣ-Ṣūlī quotes elegies on a black goat (164 ff.), bugs and fleas (171 f.), a cat (172 f.), ants and mice (175). While these elegies have the paradoxical character that Herrlinger discusses loc. cit., 75 ff., the elegy on a dove (193 ff.) is slightly sentimental. 176 ff. the author has an elegy on the شاهمرح (?), *Aġānī* 20.57[1] reads شاهمرد (?). Jāḥiẓ, *Ḥayawān* 1. 14[21] and 3. 104[17] has شاهمرك as the name of a bird. This reading suggests the emendation شاهمرج in aṣ-Ṣūlī. The comment of aḍ-Ḍamīrī, *Ḥayāt al-ḥayawān*, trans. A. S. G. Jayakar, London and Bombay 1906–8, II 1. 117, under the heading الشامرك is hardly satisfactory. The genre continues with elegies by Ibn al-ʿAllāf (ob. 930) and Ibn al-ʿAmīd (ob. 970); cf. Mez, loc. cit., 255.

136. *SBBA* 1904, p. 498 and 498 n. 2.

137. Horovitz followed his lead, *Spuren*, p. 83 n. 4.

138. For references see Delehaye, loc. cit., 211 ff.

139. Lukian, ch. 17 (ed. C. Jacobitz, 1870–72, 3. 198) mentions a long-lived Arab chief of ʿUmān; this Arab has been identified by O. Blau, *ZDMG* 27. 315 ff. (1873).

140. Cf. particularly pp. 27 f. *Fihrist*, p. 312 not only mentions Arabic translations of Greek authorities who wrote on the various arts of jugglery, but also original Arabic treatises, such as the *Kitāb aš-šaʿbaḏa* by ʿUbaid b. Kayyis, etc. In view of the material presented by Immisch, loc. cit., 418 it seems fairly probable that the Muslim *quṣṣāṣ* have some connection with the Greek μωρολόγοι, ὑβριγελωτες, and similar folk. Horovitz, *Spuren*, pp. 22 ff. makes it clear that the typological background of the heroes of the *maqāmāt* (Hamaḏānī's Abū 'l-Fatḥ, Ḥarīrī's Abū Zaid) is to be found in the Mimus tradition. Brockelmann, *EI* 3. 161 ff., s.v. *maqāma*, does not touch upon the question of possible classical reminiscences and ignores the influence that the *qāṣṣ* has probably had on the formation of the maqāma.

141. H. Pérès, *La poésie andalouse en arabe classique au XI*[e] *siècle*, 1937, pp. 37 f. tentatively traces back the *Risāla at-tawābiʿ wa'z-zawābiʿ* by Abū ʿĀmir b. Šuhaid (about 1000 A.D.; *GAL Suppl.* 1. 479 gives the name as Ibn Šahīd and the date of the treatise as about 1030) to Greek models: Lukian, or Plato's *Kratylos* or *Phaidon*. The *risāla* is related in genre, and perhaps the model of,

Abū 'l-ʿAlāʾ al-Maʿarrī (ob. 1057) *Risāla al-ġufrān.* Both describe a journey through Paradise in a somewhat humorous vein and with a view to literary criticism.

142. *Analecta Orientalia* 14. 5 ff. (1937).

143. Andrae, *MO* 25. 322 n. 1, referring to Lohmeyer, *Diatheke*, 1913, pp. 32 ff. (not accessible to me), notes the terminological agreement of Arabic *waṣiyya* and Greek διαθήκη (originally: testamentum, will, bequest) in the sense of "Last Teaching of a Sage." It would probably be fruitful to subject this branch of Arabic didactic literature to a special investigation. Ancient Near Eastern as well as classical and Sasanian traditions are likely to have substantially contributed to the development of this very popular form. G. Richter, *Studien zur Geschichte der älteren arabischen Fürstenspiegel*, 93 ff. (1932) discusses the Greek contribution but is not interested in form problems. Another subject deserving investigation is the relationship between the Arabic *awāʾil* literature and the Greek εὑρήματα, both attempting to break up the cultural development of mankind into the invention by successive individuals of the principal elements of civilization. For the εὑρήματα cf. Wendland loc. cit., 110 and the literature there listed.

H. Bauer, *Islamische Ethik*, Heft 1, 1916, Einleitung VI, note 1, suggests that the literary type of the *maḥāsin wa-masāwī* goes back to Greek models of the last days of antiquity. In this connection, Bauer refers to the tract of Johannes Damascenus, περὶ ἀρετῶν καὶ κακῶν, *MPG* 95. 85 ff., and also recalls the treatise of Efrem Syrus with the same title, *Opera*, Rome 1732, 1. 1–18.

144. A few observations by the writer, *JAOS* 61. 51, 56 (1941).

145. Cf. Rohde, loc. cit., 92 n. 3.

146. Cf. A. F. Mehren, *Rhetorik der Araber*, 138 f. (1853). al-ʿAskarī, loc. cit., 26 pronounces in favor of this figure of speech. It should be observed that *taḍmīn* also means the distribution of one thought over two verses, a manner of style that is frequently criticized by Arabic theorists.

147. Cf. Rohde, loc. cit., 126 and 126 n. 1.

148. We learn from *Muzhir* 2. 250 and from *Bayān* 2. 11 f. that al-Aṣmaʿī (ob. about 831) favored the *maṭbūʿ*, while Abū ʿUbaida (ob. about 825) rather inclined toward the hard-working poet. *Bayān* 2. 14 and Qudāma (ob. 922), *Naqd an-naṯr*, p. 92 quote *Koran* 38. 86 against the *mutakallifīn.* For definitions of *takalluf* see e.g., H. L. Fleischer, *Kleinere Schriften*, 1885–88, 1. 74, F. Dieterici, *Mutanabbi und Seifaddaula* 53 (1847), and W. Caskel, *OLZ* 1931, p. 798.

149. Isocrates quoted by Longinus, *On the Sublime*, trans. T. G. Tucker, 1935, pp. 54 f.; further classical references, Rohde, loc. cit., 323 n. 2.

150. Loc. cit., 27.

151. *Prolegomena*, trans. de Slane, 1863, 1. 283.

152. See *Bayān* 1. 87, Ibn al-Mudabbir (ob. 879), *ar-Risāla al-ʿaḏrāʾ*, ed. Zakī Mubārak, 1931, pp. 44 and 46, and al-ʿAskarī, loc. cit., 29 f. At a much

later date, Ḍiyāʾ ad-Dīn ibn al-Aṯīr (ob. 1239), *al-Maṯal as-sāʾir*, Cairo 1312, p. 10^{25-27}, insists that any description of a battle should be patterned after the *ayyām* descriptions of the ancients thus upholding the identity of the genre so characteristic of classical literature. Cf. the lucid discussion by von Wilamowitz, *Hermes* 35. 25 ff. (1900).

8 Romance as Genre in *The Thousand and One Nights*

Peter Heath

Modern study of *The Thousand and One Nights* has followed several paths.[1] One early but continuous concern has been historical, tracing the story-collection's literary development and textual history. A second line of study, which might be termed panoramic, regards the work from a holistic perspective, combining historical, philological, folkloristic, literary, and, occasionally, sociological concerns to present an overview of the work. A third, and recently prominent, trend consists of analysis of individual tales. Early examples of this latter approach were largely historical in bent; but, reflecting the general move in literary studies from emphasis on diachronic to synchronic concerns, most recent examples concentrate on literary criticism and analysis.[2]

All these lines of inquiry are fruitful; much remains to be done in each, for mature understanding of the *Nights* is only in its initial stages. This study, however, approaches the collection from a slightly different methodological viewpoint: that of genre analysis, in particular analysis of the genre of romance. This approach is not completely new. Scholars such as Burton, Littmann, and Gerhardt all classify *Nights* stories into types, while analysis of individual tales usually at least presume that particular stories fall into some cate-

Reprinted from Peter Heath, "Romance as Genre in 'The Thousand and One Nights,'" *Journal of Arabic Literature* 18 (1987): 1–21; 19 (1988): 3–26. Reprinted by permission of Brill Academic Publishers.

gory: love story, fairy tale, rogue story, travel tale, etc. This study, however, attempts to mediate between the large-scale, and thus often superficial, classifications of panoramic presentations and the usually insufficiently formulated generic assumptions of individual tale analyses.[3] This perspective perforce entails a measure of generalization, a factor of which the critic must be aware, but it also has several advantages. Although each story and the *Nights* as a whole may be perceived as individual entities, they may also be viewed as integral parts of larger, complex literary structures. By providing a theoretical framework within which perceptions of intertextual relationships can be organized, genre study offers a useful vantage point to investigate these structures. Not the least of the advantages of this is that one does not become overwhelmed by the narrative diversity that the *Nights*, with its variegated textures and tones, represents.[4] Moreover, genre analysis also opens the work to external study. Although *The Thousand and One Nights* is an individual work, it may also be viewed as a microcosm of medieval Arabic and, to some degree, Islamic popular literature. Hence, understanding of the goals and conventions of genres found in the collection can provide a critical springboard from which to approach other examples of these genres—romance, *sīra*, pious tale, fable, ribald story, humorous anecdote, etc.—that exist outside of it. From this viewpoint, genre study of the *Nights* becomes a first step toward systematic investigation of a large body of as yet insufficiently studied medieval Arabic and Islamic popular narrative.[5] Finally, from the perspective of the study of world literature, genre analysis provides a methodological vantage point from which to offer meaningful comparisons of tales unconnected to those in the *Nights* by proven genetic links of a historical or cultural nature. In sum, the study of genre opens the *Nights* to comparison: internally, among stories and groups of stories within the work itself; externally, within the context of the study of medieval Arabic and Islamic popular literature and, on a wider scale, of world literature.[6]

Prior to embarking on an analysis of romance as it exists in *The Thousand and One Nights*, two brief theoretical excursions are necessary. Before employing the terms "genre" and "romance," it is necessary to have a clear idea of what, within the context of his study, they imply.

I

Few dispute that literary work can be classified into genres.[7] Indeed, E. D. Hirsch has persuasively argued that individual utterances and, by implication, the complex systems of utterances of which literary works consist can only be effectively understood within a context of linguistic and literary conventions, norms, and traditions shared by speaker (author) and receiver (audience).[8] Just as, to use Saussurian terminology, a child develops a conception of and competence in the *langue* of a particular language through continued exposure to individual *paroles*, the literary initiate comes to understand lyric, epic, or romance by experiencing enough examples of the phenomenon to formulate a general conception of generic conventions and rules. This conception thereafter guides and, to a certain extent, determines responses in later encounters with literary works. Shared tradition between author and audience is essential to literary communication, because it saves each from having to create and learn anew *langues* with each new literary production. Generic perception is thus an integral, if not always explicitly cognized, aspect of literary experience.[9]

Traditionally, the study of genre has wrestled with two related problems: definition and scope. Aristotle, for example, sought to define genres according to modes of imitation (i.e., the medium, objects, and manner of imitation) and their psychological effects. Because he spends most of the *Poetics* further refining his analytic framework for studying partial aspects of these modes (according to plot, character, diction, thought, spectacle, and song), however, his method—despite the obvious brilliance of his achievement—has sometimes been a source of confusion, especially when later critics came to consider his observations as "laws."[10] Analysis of parts is, of course, essential. But appropriate understanding of parts depends on a correct estimation of how they interrelate within and with the whole. From this point of view, Aristotle's exposition is marked by a surprising lack of emphasis on what he himself might term "the final clause" of a genre.[11] Genre, it seems to me, is most usefully understood and defined, on the most general level, not in terms of modes of imitation but of purpose. As Hirsch says,

> The genre purpose must be in some sense an *idea,* a notion of the type of meaning to be communicated, otherwise there would be nothing to guide the author's will . . . the author has an idea of what he wants to convey—not an abstract concept, of course, but an idea equivalent to what we call an intrinsic genre. In the course of realizing this idea, he wills the meaning which subserves it.[12]

Generic purpose may be partially conceived in terms of immediate emotional response, the "pity and fear" of tragedy, the laughter of comedy, the fear provoked by the modern chiller. But deeper understanding is necessarily based on apprehensions of more profound psychological, moral, and cosmological issues, and it is the task of genre analysis, at its broadest level, to identify and clarify these. Once a genre's purpose or, as Claudio Guillén has termed it, its "informing drive" is understood, formal and material aspects of literary works (to maintain Aristotelian terminology a moment longer)—concerns of literary composition, structure, and rhetoric—fall into proper perspective.[13] Once again, we have the hermeneutic circle. One understands the whole only through analysis of parts, one can properly evaluate the significance of the parts only by attaining an appropriate understanding of the whole.[14]

In order to analyze *Nights* romances, I rely here on a method proposed by Tzvetan Todorov. He divides internal literary analysis into three levels: the semantic, the syntactic, and the verbal. The semantic level analyses themes; the syntactic, narrative structure ("the relations which the parts of the work sustain among themselves"); and the verbal, aspects of rhetoric, voice, point of view, and so on.[15] To these must be added the concerns of external literary study: the interrelationships of works existing in a single period and culture, the historical development of genres, and the relationships of genres to the social context in which they exist and to which they relate. Obviously, these categories together form a complete program of poetics; there is no question that any measure of exhaustiveness in regard to any one of them can be achieved, or even contemplated, here.[16] But at least they provide general methodological guideposts for our discussion.

The concerns of literary history raise the second problem of genre study, that of scope. It is possible to argue that generic analysis can only be validly conducted within the context of clear and provable historical and cultural linkage; that is, it consists of tracing influences and discerning innovation. From this point of view, romance begins with the narrative of Chrétien de Troyes in twelfth-century France. Study of the genre's development would start at this point, trace this author's influence on his immediate successor, Wolfram von Eschenbach, for example, and then follow the accumulative design of influence, modification, and innovation in the genre in the centuries that followed, through the works of such writers as Boiardo, Aristo, Tasso, Malory, and Spenser, taking into account particularities of talent, intent, influence, literary heritage, and general historical environment in regard to each case. By this means one formulates the "idea" of the genre of romance in medieval and renaissance Europe.[17]

Another approach posits the existence of literary universals. It assumes that despite the different ways in which genres manifest themselves through time and place, they still possess intrinsic integrity. Romance thus exists as a potential means of literary expression at any time and place, because it is an innate option of human literary discourse, a natural way for man to organize certain perceptions of life. From this perspective, genre study consists of investigating the range of unity and diversity that the overall *langue* of a genre possesses by examining individual *paroles.* Hence Hellenistic novels, medieval chivalric romances, renaissance romantic epics and allegories, gothic novels and certain strains of historical novels, romantic poetry, and modern fantasy and science fiction, to remain for the moment only within the boundaries of Western literature, could be presumed to be different permutations, to various degrees, of the same basic generic "idea." The task of analysis, then, is to clarify the various ways historical genres and individual works represent and participate in this idea.[18]

The extent to which one becomes a proponent of either the *historical* or *theoretical* approach to the study of genre, as the two viewpoints have been termed, is influenced to some degree by one's view of human nature.[19] If one agrees with a scholar such as D. W. Robertson that human nature changes within the context of different historical environments, then the idea of literary universals is analytically absurd. But if one accepts the assumption that human nature contains universals, then the perception of literature as a unified, although still inadequately explored, system of structures containing its own universals, as critics such as Frye, Todorov, and Guillén assert, becomes a valid project.[20] The present study approaches the subject within the general framework of this second approach; but without impugning the usefulness of historical study which, from this perspective, becomes one way of studying systems of genres, of investigating specific generic *langues*, grounded in particularities of historical and cultural environment, that constitute the overall generic metalanguage.

Literary works are by nature complex. Precise generic classification can often appear difficult, for individual works frequently appear to contain elements of various genres. W. P. Ker observed long ago, for instance, that strains of romance exist in works that one would ordinarily primarily consider epics.[21] It is here that the idea of the *dominant*, as outlined by Roman Jacobson, becomes useful.[22] Romances are not pure generic entities, but ones in which romance elements dominate. Episodes in a narrative such as *Sīrat ʿAntar ibn Shaddād* or *Sīrat Saif ibn Dhī Yazan* may be primarily epic or romance; but one finally classifies the work as a whole according to the generic strain that cumulatively predominates. The idea of the dominant simplifies another problem of generic scope, the concept of the "law of genre."[23] Genre analysis is founded upon description; but it usually involves, at some point, prescription. One encounters narratives where the rules of one's definition are only partially fulfilled. As long as such observations remain analytic in nature, they constitute a natural part of the critical process. But it is a different matter if obedience or disobedience to such rules assumes evaluative connotations. The purpose of generic definition is to further critical understanding. Although it should enable one to judge stories better, such evaluation does not stem mechanically from obedience to the definition's rules. The extent to which a *Nights* tale complies or fails to comply with generic norms does not make it a better or worse story. Indeed, some of the most interesting *Nights* stories are those that only partially comply with generic standards, or even play against them.[24] In sum, laws of genre exist for clarification, not retribution. Here again the concept of the dominant proves useful, since it promotes an apprehension of genre that entails a spectrum of gradation. Romances are not stories that fulfill generic definition completely, but those in which it predominates.[25]

A final question of scope is that of analytic sample. The description of romance offered here is based, at least in the first instance, on *Thousand and One Nights* tales themselves. To widen this study's focus, as many stories are touched upon as possible. But there is no need for such references to be inclusive. As Todorov has pointed out, it is not necessary to study all of a genre's members to describe it. One works deductively:

> We actually deal with a relatively limited number of cases, from these we deduce a general hypothesis, and we verify this hypothesis by other cases, correcting (or rejecting) it as need be. Whatever the number of phenomena (or literary works in this case) studied, we are never justified in extrapolating universal laws from them; it is not the quantity of observation, but the logical coherence of the theory that finally matters.[26]

The following pages attempt to outline such a coherent theory, useful for understanding *Nights* tales in the first instance, but also relevant as a preliminary basis of comparison with other romances, initially within the context of medieval Arabic and Islamic popular literature and ultimately in the context of world literature. It is not, however, intended as a static hypothesis, but rather one that exists in a dialectical relationship with the narratives it attempts to describe.

II

The anonymous fourteenth-century author of *Sir Orfeo* begins his story thus:

> Often we read lays for the harp that were written to tell us wonderous things. Some were about joy, some of woe, some of treachery and guile, of jests and ribaldry, some of fairy things, but mostly they told of love.[27]

More recently, W. T. H. Jackson writes that romance:

> is a genre hard to define, since it includes works of widely different style and subject matter, but it may be said in general that it was written for entertainment, not instruction; that its personages were idealized; that it did not shrink from the introduction of the exotic and magical; and,

> perhaps most important, that love was one of its principle themes. All of these statements could be challenged by reference to particular poems, but in general they are true.[28]

Both these descriptions of romance ring true, but as generic definitions they are by themselves incomplete. This is because they describe romance's materials rather than its purpose, its "informing drive." Typical of the genre as they may be ("in general," as Jackson remarks), one could imagine any or all of these materials existing in other genres, put to different purposes. Most other brief definitions are similarly partial or oblique. "Romance means nothing," says W. P. Ker, one of its pioneer modern students, "if it does not convey some notion of mystery and fantasy." Patricia Parker observes that, "Romance is characterized primarily as a form which simultaneously quests for and postpones a particular end, objective, or object." Fredric Jameson argues that the most important "organizational category" in romance is "the conceptual opposition between good and evil, under which all the other types of attributes and images (light and darkness, high and low, etc.) are clearly subsumed."[29] Probably none of these statements presumes to provide a complete generic definition. But they point to the difficulties any such attempt faces. It is here that Todorov's analytic framework does double service. Not only does it organize one's own perceptions, it puts others' insights into their proper perspective. In this context, both Ker and Parker address syntactic aspects of genre, while Jameson's remark is aimed at its semantic stratum.

One modern critic who offers a theoretical account of romance that approaches completeness is Northrop Frye. His description, presented in *Anatomy of Criticism* and further developed in *The Secular Scripture*, must be viewed within the larger context of Frye's overall critical theory. To summarize the details of this theory here and romance's place in it is beyond the scope of this essay; but it is necessary briefly to review what is perhaps Frye's central insight concerning the genre: romance's place within the broad spectrum of literary discourse.[30] Reacting against what might be termed the "realistic prejudice" predominant in much modern literary thought, Frye posits literature's prime mode of discourse—historically, psychologically, and aesthetically—to be not realism but myth.[31] For

Frye "myth is the imitation of action near or at the conceivable limits of desire." It presents a "world of total metaphor, in which everything is potentially identical with everything else, as though it were all inside a single body."[32] Realism, on the other hand, presents the empirical universe, the world of the senses, with all the limitations on human activity that this entails. To use a Freudian analogy, myth offers the narrative structures of the pleasure principle while realism offers that of the reality principle. Between these two extremes lies romance. For Frye romance represents the tendency to "displace myth in the human direction and yet in contrast to 'realism,' to conventionalize content in an idealized direction."[33] Put another way, it is "the search of the libido or desiring self for a fulfillment that will deliver it from the anxieties of reality but will still contain that reality."[34] This view of romance serves both to explain and normalize essential aspects of the genre's "world": the tensions that exist within it between the particular and the conventional, the probable and the improbable, the natural and the supernatural, the moral and the amoral.

The term that Frye uses to denote the incursion of realism, with its ever-present demand for plausibility, into the domain of myth is *displacement*.[35] Displacement has two connotations for Frye, since myth and realism represent opposing literary extremes at two levels. On the fictional—the imaginative—level, realism's mimetic particularism displaces the idealized conventions that constitute literature's "formulaic units," while its preference for probable action and obedience to the laws of nature displaces the complete freedom of action that characterizes myth. On the moral level, realism's awareness of social strictures displaces myth's essential amorality; it "tries to collapse the distance between the moral and the desirable."[36]

Armed with this apprehension of how to place romance within a larger framework of literary discourse, it is now possible to attempt a definition of the genre, drawn primarily from the *Nights* itself but also from within the context of an awareness of other works usually considered its members. On the semantic level, the primary theme of romance, a fundamental aspect of the genre's "informing drive," *investigates the concerns of honor as balanced between the demands of love and social propriety, within the context of Fate:* "investigates," because matters of direction, parameter, and outcome are not necessarily prescribed; "honor," because this is a concept that represents a convergence between individual and social values (one is usually honorable if one maintains one's own standards of self-worth, but these are usually based on and congruent with those of society); "love," because this is romance's dominant, although not exclusive, realm of human interest and activity, a central arena where one's "honor" is tested; "social propriety," because society's objective rules of conduct must be dealt with, in one way or another, while one pursues one's own subjective love interest; and "Fate," because it is a prime postulate of the genre that poetic justice exists, that there is a supra-human force rewarding those who adhere to honor's dictates and punishing those who do not.[37]

Two dimensions are important on the syntactic level. The first involves the narrative setting or "world" of romance. In basic accord with Frye's description, romance here inhabits that narrative realm falling between myth and realism, fantasy and naturalism, wish fulfillment and reality. It is the tension between these polarities, as they are variously expressed, that produces much of the genre's narrative suspense. The second dimension involves patterns of action typical of romance. Put simply, these represent trials of the standards of honor posited in the definition's semantic level, and movement toward or away from such trials. Narrative tension here stems from the uncertainty involved in characters' choices about their courses of action and the degree of success or failure they encounter on their ways. Analysis of tales themselves will clarify the predominant ways in which these patterns of action are fictionally manifested in the *Nights*.[38]

On the verbal level, two primary aspects deserve consideration. The first involves the genre's dominant voice. Despite a common notion that romance's primary purpose is to entertain, *Nights* tales themselves view it as to instruct. For all of their elements of wonder, fantasy, and magic, *Nights* tales take themselves quite seriously, viewing themselves as *exempla* rather than entertainment. This aspect of the genre's voice is reinforced by a second verbal strategy, the genre's preferred "radical of presentation," to adopt another of Frye's terms. This is *epos*, direct communication between storyteller and audience.[39] One of the interesting aspects of the *Nights* is the various ways it uses its framing structures to ensure that this dimension of voice is emphasized.

All aspects of this definition find clarification and elaboration in the pages that follow. One final theoretical point, however, deserves mention. It should be by now obvious that the methodological framework of this analysis is modern and Western oriented. But the question arises as to what, if anything, the medieval Arabic theory of romance was. As far as I have been able to ascertain, medieval Arabic popular romance is a genre without a poetics; primarily, it seems, due to the genre's social provenance and context. How far this observation is in fact true, however, is a question that deserves further investigation.[40]

III

Prior to presenting general descriptions of the issues involved in each of the three strata of our definition of romance, it will be useful to examine aspects of narrative semantics and syntax (saving the verbal dimension until later) in specific, concrete contexts. To this end, let us examine these dimensions of narratives in three short tales. The first of these is "The Story of the Blacksmith Who Could Handle Fire." This story is not primarily a romance, but analysis of it is useful since it offers, through contrast, entry into certain concerns typical of the genre. A summary of this tale is as follows:

> A pious man hears of a blacksmith who can put his hands into fire without being burned. Curious about a phenomenon he is certain is a mark of Divine grace, he visits the blacksmith and eventually learns the reason for the miracle. The blacksmith relates that he was once in love with a certain slave-girl. He long tried to force himself on her, but she continually resisted. Once, famine broke out, so that she was forced to beg for food at his door. Twice he offered to give her food if she yielded herself to him; twice she refused, saying that she preferred death to dishonor.[41] The third time God touched his heart.[42] The blacksmith repented his selfishness and gave her food unconditionally. When the girl saw this she asked God to bless him and spare him from flames in this world and the next. From this moment he was able to touch fire without hurt. For herself, she prayed for the release of her spirit. This prayer was answered; she died soon afterward.

The primary intent of this tale is pious. It suggests that Divine grace befalls those who heed God's call to put priority on the spiritual dimension of life. Nonetheless, it also contains key elements of romance, since the themes it selects to test its protagonists' piety are those of love and social propriety. Narrative suspense springs from two questions. Will the blacksmith take advantage of the slave-girl's predicament to force himself upon her, even though this would be a dishonorable act, motivated purely by carnal desire? And will the slave-girl, suffering the most desperate straits of physical need, abandon her moral standards, based on love of God and compliance with the rules of His faith? For both the choice is between the concerns of this world—carnal desire, physical hunger—and those of the next, a realm where spirit transcends the body's instinctual demands. Much of the tale's emotive force stems from the way these two questions are not only posed or represented, but resolved. The girl's prayer that the blacksmith be "spared from fire in this world and the next," a phrase one initially takes as being metaphoric, at least as far as this world is concerned, becomes exactly and literally fulfilled.[43] The blacksmith does indeed become immune to the effects of fire. Moreover, the girl herself chooses the logical next step in her own spiritual development. Having been forced by physical need to beg and thus submit herself to spiritual temptation, she decides to leave the realm of matter altogether. She prays for death. But in the theme of balancing honorably the concerns of love and social propriety, the latter cast in religious terms here, are typical of romance, their structuring in the tale is not. Rather than requiring its protagonists to meet or balance the demands of both these concerns on an equal basis, the tale charts their paths along separate, although parallel, courses. The blacksmith and the slave-girl can never logically become lovers, for they begin and end the story at separate points of spiritual maturity. While his dilemma centers on the choice between carnal and spiritual love, she has transcended human love altogether; her trial focuses on falling short or meeting the demands of spiritual love and the rules of her faith. For her to accept life on the blacksmith's terms, even given the level of maturity he finally achieves, would involve spiritual regression. Providing herself no longer of his world, she wills herself out of it.

The narrative domain in which the protagonists abide is somewhat typical of romance. It is a realm where poetic justice, with its actively enforced laws of cosmic reward and punishment, reigns supreme—both characters are awarded the fate they deserve. On the other hand, important characteristics push this tale toward myth. Protagonists' contact with the Divine, for one thing, is direct. God Himself inspires the blacksmith's change of heart; He answers the girl's prayers immediately. Moreover, both characters are supernaturally transfigured by their experiences: he beyond certain of Nature's laws, she out of Nature altogether. Here, then, we encounter certain of the genre's borderlines. These can be further delineated by examining "The Story of the Envier and the Envied":

> A virtuous man is envied by his neighbor, who constantly works to do him harm. The former finally decides to move to another town, where he becomes famous for his piety. His enemy, however, pursues him and eventually manages to push him into a well. Here he overhears jinn discussing the appropriate remedy for the illness suffered by the king's daughter, who has been possessed by a jinni. Extracting himself from the well, the envied heals the princess when her father approaches him for advice on the matter. The king marries the two and eventually, by public demand, the envied becomes first wazir and then, with his father-in-law's demise, king. One day he sees the envier among a crowd, but rather than punishing him, he gives his enemy gifts.

Again, the extent to which this tale should be considered as full-fledged romance is open to question. On the semantic level, for instance, the story only treats love obliquely. Nevertheless, honorable conduct and success in love are linked here, if only indirectly. And poetic justice fully controls events. The envied is consistently rewarded for his virtuous conduct, while his enemy appears only to escape punishment through a typically magnanimous gesture on the part of the hero. From the point of view of narrative structure, however, this tale reveals features typical of romance. In contrast to the blacksmith's tale, protagonists' relation to the Divine is here indirect, displaced. The envied does attain special knowledge at one point, but he does so through a temporary, undesired, visitation to a netherworld that apparently represents the borderline between nature and supernature; communication comes through jinn rather than direct Divine inspiration. And, in spite of the hero's reputation for piety, the success he achieves is framed purely in human, social terms. He marries a princess, becomes wazir, and then king. He himself remains physically unchanged, clearly "of this world." Let us move further toward the heart of romance with "The Story of Niᶜma and Nuᶜm":

> Al-Rabīᶜ ibn Ḥātim, a wealthy notable of Kufa, one day buys a young slave-girl. His son, Niᶜma, and the slave-girl, Nuᶜm, grow up together. Loving each other dearly from babyhood, at the age of ten they become man and concubine.[44] For four years they live together in bliss. But then the local governor, al-Ḥajjāj ibn Yūsuf, learns of Nuᶜm's beauty and musical talents and decides to steal her as a gift for his master, the Caliph ᶜAbd al-Malik ibn Marwān. He sends an old woman, who disguises herself as a holy person, to befriend the young couple. She gains their confidence and one day lures Nuᶜm outside the house, where al-Ḥajjāj has her seized and sent to the Caliph. Still loving Niᶜma, the girl falls ill. The Caliph is much taken with her, but declines to sleep with her until she recovers and tries to have her cured.
>
> When Niᶜma discovers the disappearance of his beloved, he first seeks recourse with the authorities. Gaining little help from al-Ḥajjāj and his chief of police, Niᶜma also falls ill. His father discovers what has truly happened and engages a learned Persian physician to treat his son. Realizing that Niᶜma is suffering from love-sickness and hearing his tale, the physician offers his help. He and Niᶜma, now disguised as the Persian's son, set out for Damascus. Word of the physician's skill spreads there, and Nuᶜm's nurse comes to him seeking a remedy for her mistress. Niᶜma encloses a note in the prepared remedy, which indeed cures the pining girl. With the nurse's help, she tries to sneak Niᶜma, disguised as a slave-girl, into her apartments. He loses his way in the palace, however, and ends up in the rooms of the Caliph's sister. Hearing his story, she decides to help him. She calls in Nuᶜm and is in the process of enjoying her singing when the Caliph enters. His sister tells him the lovers' story in the abstract and asks his opinion of how a just ruler would handle the case. When he replies that he should be merciful and restore the lovers to each other, he traps himself. He has little choice but to follow his own counsel when his sister reveals the couple's identities. The Caliph bestows gifts upon them, makes the Persian physician an advisor, and sends the lovers home, where they enjoy life until their days' end.

This tale brings us fully within the domain of romance. Semantically, narrative suspense stems from the question of whether the couple's love will hold true in the face of apparently insurmountable obstacles, whether the justness of their case will prove indisputable, and, given affirmative answers to these points, whether the lovers will, even so, be successfully reunited. Niʿma and Nuʿm do remain faithful in love; both suffer extremes of lovesickness but ultimately prove themselves willing to risk all to be rejoined—sneaking into the Caliph's palace, after all, has its dangers! In regard to social propriety, their case seems strong as well. Having loved each other since childhood, the couple have consecrated their love in a socially acceptable fashion. Moreover, Nuʿm was deceitfully betrayed and unlawfully abducted. Not least, Niʿma has been robbed of his property. Their case would seem to be indisputable, were it not for the identity of their prospective opponent. The Caliph has a case of his own. He wields supreme authority, owns the girl himself, as far as he knows, since she was sent to him as a gift (under false pretenses perhaps, but this is not his fault), and he himself has the sanctity of his household violated. The potential complications that could arise from a conflict of two "just" cases, however, are forestalled by the Caliph himself. Offering a disinterested opinion, he suddenly finds himself an interested party; but having committed himself, he relents with good grace.

The tale's structure is that of romance as well. Realistic in outward tone and setting as it may seem (although full of coincidence, it never transgresses the laws of nature), the story presents a narrative world where the demarcation between appearance and reality is blurred. The tale is full of deceit and discovery, pretense and revelation. Al-Ḥajjāj's old hag disguises herself as her opposite, a holy woman, and on this false pretense manages to gain entrance into Niʿma and Nuʿm's home and confidence. Al-Ḥajjāj, as governor the supposed upholder of law and order, himself breaks the law to abduct the girl and then sends her to the Caliph under false auspices. Thereafter, he and his chief of police feign ignorance about the whole matter when petitioned by Niʿma. For his part, Niʿma disguises himself as well, first as the physician's son and then as a slave-girl. Nuʿm's duenna, instead of protecting her charge's chastity for her royal master as is her duty, helps her sneak her lover into the palace; while the Caliph's sister initially conceals the real import of the question she puts to her brother. The tale's action moves in a context where, as far as the characters are concerned, matters are rarely as they seem, where characters are constantly brought up short on their assumptions of reality, where veils of illusion are continuously lowered and then drawn away.

Fate also plays its usual active role. Although the lovers provide the will to resolve their crisis, Fate provides the way. The Persian physician, Nuʿm's nurse, and the Caliph's sister all "just happen" to appear at the appropriate times with the right combination of knowledge, access, and influence needed to further the lovers' cause. On the other hand, the role the lovers themselves play should not be overlooked. It is because they prove themselves deserving of help, because their love is true and their cause is just, that each of the intermediaries becomes sympathetic to their plight and offers help.[45] Niʿma and Nuʿm attain the fate they prove they deserve.

The tale's plot structure moves on a line of safety–trial–return to safety. For its characters, these stages represent movements of not just temporal but also moral progression. Their honor being tested, Niʿma and Nuʿm affirm their love but also learn from their experiences. They develop as characters. Wrapped at the story's beginning in a cocoon of childhood security and guilelessness, they wend their ways through realms of danger and deceit to emerge, at the tale's end, as adults, able to understand and cope with the ways of the world. They move from innocence, to experience, to a renewed state of innocence that encompasses experience.[46] Although they have their mentors—Niʿma's father, the Persian physician, Nuʿm's nurse, the Caliph's sister—it is ultimately the lovers themselves who risk all for their love. This progression of innocence–trial–experience has structural parallels and echoes throughout the narrative. The symbols of innocence are the state and trappings of childhood, a realm that presumes the inviolateness of the home, continuous parental protection and guidance, social status based on that of the family, and, finally, personal identity defined by the external context of one's parents' identities. But circumstances remove Nuʿm and Niʿma from this shared realm of safety out into the dangerous world-at-large. Both initially face decisions that, given their naïveté, they are incompetent to make. Niʿma foolishly allows a total stranger into his house without recognizing or guarding against the potential dangers involved; Nuʿm thoughtlessly disregards social convention and her mother-in-law's advice and goes out with the old woman unattended. Her abduction pulls the two protagonists away from parents, childhood home, and even home city; their social status and identities are temporarily called into question, obscured. And they end up in that most fearsome of all places for a child, the home of a strange adult, and in this case a particularly powerful one at that, a limbo where rules of conduct are unfamiliar, filled with the constant danger of transgression through ignorance, heedlessness, or misjudgment. But they do not despair. They cope with and eventually transcend the dangers that this world presents. Having initially been deceived by al-Ḥajjāj and his agents, they in turn resolve their dilemma by, in some sense, deceiving the Caliph. Then, having achieved their goal, they return home to be reunited with their family, their geographical context and social status reattained, their union of love recognized, even ratified, by the Caliph's goodwill and gifts. Their personas are no longer defined only by external contexts; having been tested, they have won not only each other, but also themselves. Near the tale's beginning, Nuᶜm had sung to Niᶜma:

> If you were a master on whose bounty I could live,
> A sword with which I could destroy the necks of unlucky fates,
> What need would I have of intercession with Zaid or ᶜUmar
> Instead of you, if my paths upon me became strait.[47]

By the story's end, this is the state that the couple, with their newly found maturity, have attained.

IV

Having examined aspects of romantic theme and narrative structure in regard to three brief *Nights* tales, let us now explore romance's semantic stratum in a broader way to obtain a more detailed idea of the various ways the genre "investigates the concerns of honor as balanced between the demands of love and social propriety, within the context of Fate."

Protagonists' involvement with love is evident in *Nights* romances. But the genre is less concerned with this point, which it assumes, than with the question of how they handle this involvement. If handled honorably, eventual happiness is assured; if handled dishonorably, disaster follows. Honorable conduct and its opposite, in turn, consist of two parts. The first is that one must not only love passionately, but also rightly, that one must be true and faithful in love. Almost any act stemming from true love is excused, while any deed that promotes it is accepted, indeed aided, by Fate. Qamar al-Zamān, for example, leaves evidence that he has been killed and eaten by wild beasts in order to run away from his doting father, but he is not faulted because this promotes his love quest. Al-Ḥasan al-Baṣrī deserts his widowed mother for similar reasons. ʿAlāʾ al-Dīn Abū Shāmāt breaks his legal bond when he refuses to divorce a girl he had pledged to marry for only one day, but again this is acceptable because he has fallen in love with her in the interim. ʿAzīz causes the death of his cousin ʿAzīza, who dies from lovesickness for him, but he is initially held guiltless because he himself was enthralled in the bonds of love for another. That one is considered mad because of the effects of love, as are both Qamar al-Zamān and his beloved, Princess Budūr, is of little import as long as faith in love is kept.

The second aspect of the idea of honor has to do with the boundaries imposed by social propriety. Being in love may justify many otherwise unacceptable actions, but there are limits. ʿAlāʾ al-Dīn Abū Shāmāt can break his legal agreement, but there is no question that he must pay the fine entailed. ʿAlī ibn Bakkār and Shams al-Nahār love each other truly and chastely, but they suffer the problem that Shams al-Nahār is the Caliph Hārūn al-Rashīd's concubine. The social, and in this case religious, barriers involved here are insurmountable, and they waste away in longing for one another. But they die happy since they have obeyed the rules of true love and the laws of social propriety. This story, however, presents an exceptional situation in *Nights* romances.[48] The tensions that arise from protagonists being torn between the requirements of true love and those of social propriety are often real enough, but their results are seldom so extreme. Hence in a story similar in plot to that of ʿAlī ibn Bakkār and Shams al-Nahār, the young merchant Ghānim ibn Ayyūb and Hārūn al-Rashīd's favorite concubine, Qūt al-Qulūb, fall in love. The danger inherent in their situation is symbolized by their first meeting in a graveyard, where Ghānim saves the girl from a death she will surely suffer anyway should she succumb to her love for him. They are truly involved in a risky business; but their combined strength of will saves them. For a month Qūt al-Qulūb resists Ghānim's advances, although she loves him and would dearly prefer to give in. Then, when she finally reveals her identity and her relationship with the Caliph to him, he in turn refuses to gratify her desire that they now make love, remarking, "How can the dog sit in the place of the lion; it is unlawful that I draw near to that which the Master owns."[49] This combination of intensely felt love and adherence to the dictates of social propriety ensures that their story will end happily. The point is emphasized by the inclusion in it of two embedded tales of black slaves who refuse to keep to the right side of either of these two boundaries and suffer the consequence of castration.

What the *Nights* suggests here is that while the longing of love justifies many otherwise socially unacceptable actions, there eventually comes a moment when one must return from the intense subjectivity of love to face the objective reality of the world around. And if one's love has resulted in one's falling into socially untenable circumstances, unpleasant consequences are the natural result. For example, Prince Tāj al-Mulūk, disguised as a merchant, eventually wins the heart of Princess Dunyā by means of a few harmless stratagems and some well-placed bribes. Then he sneaks into the Princess's quarters disguised as a slave-girl and enjoys his beloved's company for a month. In this way he has achieved his subjective goal of winning his beloved. Objectively, however, his position is ridiculous. Lost in the throes of love, the Prince may not want to worry about the morrow, but at some time he is going to have to rouse himself to his responsibilities to his royal father and his position as heir-apparent. Even if he could postpone this indefinitely, does he expect to spend the rest of his days in someone else's palace disguised as a slave-girl? Fate does not long leave this decision to his discretion. He is discovered and brought before Dunyā's father, who brings home to him the objective realities of his circumstances by ordering him to be put to death.

Lovers who find themselves in such predicaments (is Ghānim

ibn Ayyūb, for instance, going to live out his life sleeping in the same room as his beloved without physically fulfilling his love?) but are true to their love usually manage to survive. But they also tend to undergo an interim period of suffering and often a temporary reduction in social status. Hence Tāj al-Mulūk is on the verge of being executed as a common criminal when the timely appearance of his father with a large army saves him. It being thus concretely proven that he is not just any interloper but one of powerful royal station, and that his overall intentions are honorable (the twin story of Ardashīr and Ḥayāt al-Nufūs remarks at this point that the Princess is still a virgin), the demands of honor are met by recourse to the only socially acceptable possibility in such situations: marriage. As for Ghānim, he becomes a helpless fugitive when the Caliph finally discovers the whereabouts of Qūt al-Qulūb; starved and lovesick, he finally collapses in a mosque. Apparently this is the correct response to his situation, for a series of kind people care for him until Hārūn al-Rashīd ascertains his innocence and restores his fortunes. The tale ends with his mother and sister, who were both beggared during the Caliph's initial rage, also appearing and being financially restored. Having thus resolved his emotional predicament, restored his wealth and social position, and reunited him with his family, the storybook brings Ghānim's tale to a close.

The *Nights* often appears to suggest that when torn between the polarities of love and social propriety, passive acceptance of the latter's dictates and any consequences this entails and blind reliance on Fate to find a solution to the dilemma is the preferred course of action. In this regard, Ghānim's collapse is a credible response to his situation. Similarly, when Fate, personified by two jinn, puts Ḥasan Badr al-Dīn in the place of the hunchback bridegroom in Lady al-Ḥusn's wedding, the two young people, drawn by love, naturally make the most of their wedding night. But the fact remains that their love is based on deception, a twisting of the marriage protocol; for Ḥasan Badr al-Dīn was inserted into the situation through supernatural means. Hence when the two jinn remove the youth the next morning from his wedding bed in Cairo to the gates of Damascus, he passively suffers the crowd that gather around him because of his telling nakedness to jeer at him in the streets; then he allows himself to be taken in by a kindly restaurateur where he, son and grandson of wazirs, meekly enters his benefactor's trade and patiently spends the next few years being a cook. Only the sudden appearance of his son, an objective reminder of the physical if not legal reality of his marriage, finally manages to stir his apathy—and even then not very convincingly! But at this point Fate, having exacted its price, brings about his restoration. Having remained faithful to his love, Ḥasan Badr al-Dīn is returned to the very wedding bed from which he was removed so many years before. Thereafter, in the company of his wife, son, newly regained mother, and newly discovered uncle, he assumes his rightful place in the world, after passing one last test and obtaining an official position at the King's court.

One situation where passive response is understandably required is the familiar one in which the wife or concubine of the youth's father or benefactor falls in love with him and demands his favors. The youth naturally rebuffs this proposal and is so accused by his spurned lover of trying to rape her. Caught between the hammer of his father's anger over the accusation and the anvil of his grief if the truth be discovered, there is little the protagonist can actively do. In the story of Sindbād, the Prince is ordered by the stars to remain silent in the face of the concubine's charges while the wazirs work to ameliorate his father's anger by telling tales that reveal the innate unreliability of women. Qamar al-Zamān's sons humbly flee when they fall into the same predicament. In a slightly different twist to the situation, Saif al-Mulūk is asked to betray not his father but his beloved when a jinniyya who has taken him in after his shipwreck makes advances. But his response is similarly passive. He endures years of servitude rather than betray his fidelity. In all of these cases the protagonists' adherence to their responsibilities, whether filial or romantic, causes a period of suffering, but it also ensures their eventual happiness.

The criterion of social propriety, it should be noted, can also serve protagonists. Niʿma's case, we have seen, is strengthened by the fact that his relation to Nuʿm is lawful. Similarly, do not protagonists such as Abū Muḥammad the Lazy, ʿAlāʾ al-Dīn, and al-Ḥasan al-Baṣrī have better chances for success in their quests for retrieving lost loves because these loves are their legal spouses?

Sometimes the *Nights* uses this criterion not to create and then ease narrative tension, but as a deus ex machina to resolve otherwise troublesome predicaments. A hint of this tendency exists in the story of Abū Ḥasan of Khurasan. Similar in outline to the tales of ʿAlī ibn Bakkār and Ghānim ibn Ayyūb, the crux of this tale is the question of how Abū Ḥasan, a money changer, will manage to marry his beloved, Shajarat al-Durr, a favored slave-girl of the Caliph. That the couple love each other deeply and truly is of course a point in their favor. But nevertheless it cannot overcome the tremendous social and religious barriers that their love faces. The story attempts to weaken our sense of these barriers by emphasizing that the Caliph is currently infatuated with another. He also at one point frees Shajarat al-Durr, thus giving her a greater degree of control over her own fate. But if these points ameliorate the social barriers involved, they in no way eliminate them.[50] After all, ʿAlī ibn Bakkār and Shams al-Nahār died as a result of such a situation, while Ghānim ibn Ayyūb and Qūt al-Qulūb underwent extremes of suffering. But this story makes its protagonists suffer no such straits. When the Caliph discovers their love, he is sympathetic. He grants them clemency and gives them his blessing. In other words, the dictates of social propriety are satisfied through an extraordinary gesture of generosity.[51] The exceptional nature of this generosity is indicated in the tale's frame, which tells how when the Caliph's grandson happens to visit Abū Ḥasan's house he is enraged and suspects him of being a thief because he sees his grandfather's seal on all of its furniture. Abū Ḥasan proceeds to narrate his story, and the grandson is mollified; but his initial reaction is significant, for by the genre's normal standards something is amiss. Abū Ḥasan is indeed in some way a thief, but instead of being punished for his crime or at least suffering because of it, he is awarded the stolen goods outright. He gains his desire not through the blend of fidelity, effort, suffering, and poetic justice that is the genre's staple, but by luck. It is all too easy.

A more extreme example of this tendency occurs in the story of Masrūr and Zain al-Mawāṣif. This starts as the ribald tale of a youth seducing another man's wife. It soon metamorphoses, however, into a romance, with the couple exchanging love poems and wasting away for each other when they are separated. Yet the problem of the girl's husband remains. When he returns from his travels the tale reverts to its original purpose and portrays the two lovers plotting away to cuckold him. Obviously the tale must decide which way to go, ribald or romance. It chooses the latter but then must deal with the problem of the girl's lawful marriage. It solves it through religious finagling. Masrūr is a Christian, Zain al-Mawāṣif and her husband Jewish; the lovers convert to Islam and have Islamic judges annul Zain al-Mawāṣif's first marriage, since in Islam Muslim women may only marry Muslim men. The story also begins to verge on burlesque as it attempts to justify Masrūr's love by portraying Zain al-Mawāṣif's beauty to be such that all who see her fall in love and die pining away for her. One may find the tale offensive for its apparent amorality—not only does the girl betray her husband, she eventually has him murdered—or for the tinge of religious bigotry that emerges in its final part, for only a fanatic might contend, as the tale apparently does, that the protagonists' conversion justifies their actions. But however much these aspects weaken the story, it also suffers from the fact that it resolves its plot by introducing criteria of social propriety that are not only extraneous to the genre but also contradict one of its central tenets. It is how you feel, not who you are, that ultimately justifies your acts in *Nights* romance; but this tale attempts to justify its lovers' conduct by changing who they are. The use of religion as a deus ex machina to resolve plot tensions occurs in several stories but it is an unfortunate development in the sense that it contravenes the genre's logical and moral consistency.[52]

There are stories enough among *Nights* romances of lovers, tested in one way or another by the calamities Fate has at its disposal, finally resolving the obstacles that stand in the path of their love. But the genre does not only present the positive side of the coin. Indeed, it is just as willing to delve into situations in which the protagonist falls short of either or both of the genre's dual criteria of faithfulness in love and adherence to the standards of social propriety.[53] An example of this occurs when Qamar al-Zamān, having married his beloved, Princess Budūr, resolves to return with her to his father. On the way, as he is on the point of making love to his sleeping wife, he notices a jewel she is wearing around her waist. Just as he removes it to better examine it a bird swoops down, seizes the jewel, and flies away. Forgetting about Budūr, the Prince follows the bird, which leads him away from the camp until he becomes lost. He eventually enters a city of Magians and finds refuge with a gardener. And here we are presented with the spectacle of Prince Qamar al-Zamān, only son of King Shahrimān of the Isles of Khālidān, son-in-law of one of the mightiest monarchs of China, settling down and becoming an assistant gardener for a year or so. And yet, in the logical context of the genre, this is exactly an appropriate consequence. For by allowing himself to be distracted from his beloved in the act of lovemaking by a bauble of a jewel, Qamar al-Zamān has betrayed their love. He must therefore pay the resulting penalty of a lowering in station. And indeed once he has served his term, Fate endows him with the wherewithal to rejoin his wife. This story, by the way, offers a bevy of sexual alternatives and enticements: misogyny, androgyny, lesbian and homosexual temptations, incest, and adultery—not to mention ordinary fornication. Yet its various protagonists make the correct sexual decisions (according to the standards of the genre) and thus all ends happily for them.

Not all, however, are so prudent, nor are all lapses as minor as that of Qamar al-Zamān. In both the Lady Doorkeeper's tale and the story of Muḥammad ibn ʿAlī, the Pseudo-Caliph, the protagonists fall into favorable love matches, the first with a son of Hārūn al-Rashīd, the second with the daughter of Khālid al-Barmakī. Both swear strict oaths of fidelity and then break them under the pressure of seemingly harmless extenuating circumstances. As a result both are terribly beaten by their erstwhile lovers and then bodily thrown out of their homes. Such is the genre's punishment for those who break the strictures of love's ties of fidelity. In both stories only the Caliph's authoritative intervention into events, once they become known to him, based on his sense that the culprits have suffered enough, eases these strictures and enables the couples to be reunited.

Undeniably the most explicit warning of infidelity's consequences appears in the story of ʿAzīz and ʿAzīza. On his way home from the baths on his wedding day ʿAzīz falls in love with a mysterious lady in a window. In spite of his missing their wedding night as a result and notwithstanding her own deep love for him, ʿAzīza helps her cousin and erstwhile fiancé eventually to win the favors of his new beloved. She even promotes his cause when she dies of lovesickness for him since the mystery lady, who had planned to kill ʿAzīz once she had her way with him, refrains when she learns the extent of ʿAzīza's love for him. ʿAzīz, however, having taken his cousin's love for granted, now barely notices her death. In fact, one day he meets another woman and, upon her invitation, marries her. A year later he returns to see what has happened to his former lover. She, having been thus jilted, no longer feels bound by the constraints of pity. She seizes her chance and promptly castrates him for his faithlessness. When his present wife, in turn, sees what has happened to him, she throws him out of her house. Only now does ʿAzīz properly realize the nature of true love and perceive that only ʿAzīza really loved him. But now it is too late.

Other punishments await those who are inconstant, even in illicit love, which at times in the *Nights* occurs in unusual circumstances. The protagonists of the stories of "The Man Who Never Laughed Any More" and the Third Mendicant, whose experiences resemble each other in many respects, break their numerous beloveds' interdictions against opening a certain door. Life-long depression in one case and mutilation and sorrow in the other are the result. But in these cases punishment was only to be expected. Not only were these protagonists unfaithful to their lovers' wishes, they had also entered into circumstances that were in the long run socially untenable. Just as Tāj al-Mulūk could not realistically hope to hide in Princess Dunyā's quarters forever, these youths could not really expect to live out their lives in a limbo of communal sex. Only someone with no realistic sense of social responsibility—and in their immaturity these youths apparently had none—would imagine that one could. Similarly, the Second Mendicant could not expect to live indefinitely with his newfound beloved in an underground crypt. That he realizes this and therefore summons the jinni who is holding the girl captive there brings disaster; but it is in accordance with the genre's ethics that she, who had wanted to live this way, is killed while he, who had not, survives. Instead he suffers transformation into an ape. Only the fatal self-sacrifice of another who loves him effects his return to human form, and even then he suffers the tell-tale scar of the loss of an eye. Finally, the First Mendicant's experiences indicate that even second-hand participation in illicit love—incest in this case—can have dire consequences. On the other hand, those who dare to enter unusual realms but remain resolute and true to their loves can overcome nature and supernature alike, as the stories of Abū Muḥammad, ʿAlāʾ al-Dīn, Saif al-Mulūk, and the twin tales of al-Ḥasan al-Baṣrī and Jānshāh indicate. These last two stories also show that interdictions in themselves are not all-powerful, for the protagonists of both break them and meet, not lose, beloveds as a result. What brings disaster is not breaking interdictions per se, but breaking those imposed by lovers.

Although *Nights* romances are generally lenient about the social eccentricities of true lovers, they apparently take a more sober view of sibling rivalry. When the First Lady and ʿAbd Allāh ibn Fāḍil continually forgive their siblings their treachery, Fate, in the form of jinn, intervenes to save them by transforming the latter into dogs. On a more somber note, the good-hearted Jaudar, who repeatedly overlooks his brothers' perfidy toward not only himself but their mother as well, is finally allowed to be killed off at their hands. Perhaps he deserves it, however; the virtuous protagonist of the tale of "The Envier and the Envied" is quite prepared to forgive the evil actions of his malevolent neighbor, but he also has the good sense to get out of harm's way. Jaudar, on the contrary, goes out of his way to introduce it into his household; hence, in his own way, he transgresses accepted bounds of social propriety.

What the above discussion has attempted to suggest is that a great many of the longer *Nights* tales share thematic elements to the extent that, however much they may differ in regard to historical provenance or exterior aspects of detail, they may still be considered constituent members of a single genre. Whether they are quest stories, such as Tāj al-Mulūk, Qamar al-Zamān, or Saif al-Mulūk; tales of jinn and sorcery, such as Abū Muḥammad, ʿAlāʾ al-Dīn, or al-Ḥasan al-Baṣrī; narratives set in comparatively more realistic bourgeois surroundings, such as Nūr al-Dīn ʿAlī, Ḥasan Badr al-Dīn, or Ghānim ibn Ayyūb; or somber tales of ominous warning, such as the tales of the Three Mendicants, ʿAzīz and ʿAzīza, or Jaudar; they all share the same view of love, social responsibility, and Fate. Love and marriage—falling in love, winning one's love, and then settling down—this is the song these tales sing. Almost anything is allowed those who love deep and true. Such lovers can easily rely on Fate, often personified by various human and supernatural agents, to turn events (eventually, for we do need stories from all this, after all) to their advantage. On the other hand, faithless, inconstant, or inadequate lovers suffer various levels of punishment. Nor should lovers expect to achieve success without effort. While *Nights* lovers often enjoy a short period of bliss with their beloveds without too much effort on their part, Fate usually soon pulls the rug from under their feet. Then they must actively struggle through or patiently endure the term of their trials until they finally reattain their love. Young people, beautiful in their youth, deserve love, and it is natural that they want it. But they must choose the right kind of love, remain faithful to it, and ultimately conduct themselves with a mature awareness of the responsibilities their love and their place in society entail.

If this is the key romantic statement of these stories, it is not a complete picture of the genre's thematic modality. For this very portrayal of lovers—pure ones rewarded, tainted ones punished—presupposes, as we have indicated, a worldview founded on the assumption of the existence of a cosmic system of reward and punishment, entailing as well the existence of some active agency to enforce this system. Despite the obvious permeation of Islam in many of these tales, it is rare that one senses that Islam's monotheistic God is directly intervening in their affairs. They may move in accord with His plan, but this plan contains both the rules governing the destinies of romance protagonists and the agency that applies these rules. We have termed this agency here "Fate," the overseer of poetic justice. It is Fate that leads characters on, tests them, and, depending on their performance, rewards or punishes them. Nor are the dictates of Fate inconstant. Although they sometimes appear to bring disaster just when a character seems to have achieved success, those who are faithful to their loves and mindful of the existent norms of social propriety are eventually rewarded. We thus have the apparent irony that the primary underlying message of a genre that is full of unexpected events, fantastic occurrences, supernatural interventions, abrupt twists and turns of circumstances, and a not insignificant interest in the wonderful and bizarre, is that a Divine Plan does indeed control the cosmos. And although it may be difficult, at times even impossible, for protagonists to perceive the meaning of this Plan, those who live, and love, in accordance with its precepts have nothing to fear. In short, *Nights* romances use chance, coincidence, surprise, and reversal to affirm that order and organization, not chaos, prevail in the world. And this, the genre affirms, is why its tales are worth telling.

This helps explain why the stories' protagonists are often so passive. While they certainly are intended to take advantage of the opportunities Fate casts in their way, they are not really expected to accomplish anything completely on their own. Instead they are helped along: counseled by magicians and wise wazirs, aided by supernatural beings, favored by circumstances, or perhaps having their stories unraveled and troubles untangled by a Divine representative on earth, such as the Caliph Hārūn al-Rashīd. Indeed, one might go so far as to claim that the real hero of *Thousand and One Nights* romances is not their youthful protagonists but Fate itself. Part of these tales' attraction is first seeing what outlandish combination of circumstances Fate produces and then, the desired predicament having been created, how it resolves it. Here is a genre where narrative event truly tends to overwhelm narrative personality.[54]

V

In terms of narrative structure, the definition of romance argued here concentrates on two basic facets: the genre's typical patterns of action and the nature of its "world," or narrative setting. Conceived most simply, romance's patterns of action consist of three steps: an initial state of security, movement toward one or a series of trials, return to a state of security. It is important to note that for protagonists these steps do not represent linear movements but rather developmental progressions within moral and psychological matrices, movements from innocence to experience, ignorance to knowledge, naïveté to maturity.[55] It is for this reason that protagonists of *Nights* romances are so often adolescents, for this transition stage between childhood and adulthood is ideal for treating the themes the genre wishes to explore. It is a time of psychological and physiological flux, when new attitudes develop in regard to central concerns of life: the nature and requirements of filial duty, one's attitude toward material possessions, one's ability to care for oneself within the context of a newfound independence, one's sense of responsibility toward other individuals and society as a whole, and, not least important, one's handling of that newly emergent but startlingly powerful bundle of instincts, feelings, and ideals that constitute the emotion of love. *Nights* romances are very much concerned with portraying, sorting out, and instructing their audiences about this stage of life. To do so they adopt the somewhat pessimistic but perhaps psychologically sound attitude that it is more beneficial to hear about negative or at least trying experiences than positive or easy ones. At any rate they make better stories!

Typically, a tale's protagonist is a handsome youth of wealthy, sometimes noble background, the son of a king, wazir, or wealthy merchant.[56] Doted on by his parents, he is often an only child of their later years, sometimes born only through special exertions, spiritual or pharmacological, on their part. The *Nights* adopts this late-child motif to emphasize that from the beginning the youth is special, a child of Fate.[57] And in these tales Fate leads its children along peculiar paths, varied in detail but in reality all following similar lines. The genre begins by presenting, or at least assuming, an initial stage of security, most often symbolized by the state of childhood. In this stage a lack of knowledge or maturity is assumed, for one's geographical setting, social context, economic well-being, and even, one might argue, personal identity are defined by the external determinant of parental presence. The *Nights* sometimes goes to extremes to portray the insularity and dependence of childhood. ʿAlāʾ al-Dīn Abū Shāmāt's parents, for instance, lock him up in a cellar until he is fourteen, while Ibrāhīm ibn al-Khaṣīb's father allows him out of the house only for Friday prayers.

The attainment of puberty symbolizes protagonists' emergence from their initial stage of security and movement toward that of trial. Having relinquished childhood, they can no longer remain cut off from the adult world. They shake off parental authority. Whether someone like Tāj al-Mulūk who, having fallen in love through hearsay, runs off to seek his beloved in a far-off land; or ʿAlāʾ al-Dīn Abū Shāmāt who insists on being allowed to travel and see the world; or al-Ḥasan al-Baṣrī who defies his mother's counsel and goes off with a strange magician; or even young lazybones who refuse to work, such as ʿAlāʾ al-Dīn or Abū Muḥammad; protagonists enter a stage where parents can no longer control their actions. Often this loss of authority is made explicit by the father's death, as in the stories of Ghānim ibn Ayyūb, ʿAlī Shār and Nūr al-Dīn ʿAlī; at other times parents are left behind and forgotten until the tale's end, as in the stories of Tāj al-Mulūk and Qamar al-Zamān. This latter story, by the way, displays this abandonment of parental control in unique fashion. After the Prince refuses his father's command to marry for three consecutive years, King Shahrimān locks him up in a tower cell for being rebellious. In these unlikely surroundings he meets and falls in love with a Chinese princess, and so his adventures begin.

Concomitant with this loss of parental authority, protagonists lose their original geographical grounding; they are physically drawn out into the world. Different reasons cause them to embark on their travels: desire for union or reunion with a far-off beloved (Tāj al-Mulūk, Ibrāhīm ibn al-Khaṣīb, Qamar al-Zamān, Niʿma); desire to see the world (ʿAlāʾ al-Dīn Abū Shāmāt, the Third Mendicant); exhaustion of one's inheritance through profligacy and carousing (Nūr al-Dīn ʿAlī, ʿAlī Shār, Sindbād the Sailor); a chance meeting with an enticing lady (ʿAzīz, the Second Mendicant); an encounter with a sorcerer (al-Ḥasan al-Baṣrī, ʿAlā al-Dīn); or the sudden death of one's father resulting in a collapse of one's fortunes (the First Mendicant, Ḥasan Badr al-Dīn). However it happens, the result is the same. Protagonists are not only free of parental authority but also geographically on their own.

Finally, *Nights* protagonists tend to suffer a loss or blurring of social status. Ḥasan Badr al-Dīn, the son of a wazir, loses his home and property when the King of al-Baṣra confiscates it; the Second Mendicant, a prince, looses all in his travels; Nūr al-Dīn ʿAlī and ʿAlī Shār consume their inheritances on drunken parties.[58] Sometimes this blurring of social status is indicated by forms of disguise. Prince Tāj al-Mulūk disguises himself as a merchant, as we have seen, while Niʿma dons the role of a physician's son and apprentice, in order to win their beloveds. Occasionally one senses a touch of the symbolic in such disguises. Tāj al-Mulūk might be seen as throwing off the royal necessity of the rule of intellect to become a merchant of love; then to win final union with his beloved he further disguises himself as a slave-girl. In this guise as a lowly slave of love he is discovered by the girl's father and only saves himself by returning to his former princely state. And how else could Niʿma, a merchant's son who has lived in innocent seclusion all his life, retrieve his treacherously stolen beloved without assuming the wisdom and almost magical control over material states implied by the physician's profession.

By stripping their protagonists of prior familial, geographical, and social contexts, *Nights* romances put them in a state where they have only themselves to rely on, where they must truly assume full responsibility for the decisions they make, where they themselves must define the identity they assume. Having reached this stage, they are ready to enter what Peter Molan has called the "threshold of adventure," the "world" of romance.[59] This is a world where the line separating nature and supernature, reality and illusion, is not so much indistinguishable as irrelevant. The keynote of this world is that things are not usually as they seem. Even in tales with relatively realistic settings, such as that of Niʿma and Nuʿm, characters constantly encounter situations where their initial assumptions or estimations of people and situations prove miscalculated. Such miscalculations provide initial stepping stones into romance's world, and the larger or more frequent such miscalculations are, the further protagonists are drawn into its environs.[60] It is here that the stage of trial occurs. These trials consist of Fate, the guiding force of romance's world, using the external stimuli, which are manifold and diverse natures, that the realm has at its disposal in order to probe and test protagonists' integrities, their inner cores. Such testing tends to be continual. Frye's remark that romance is "naturally a sequential or processional form" applies to *Nights* romances where the main difference between long and short members of the genre is not differing degrees of investment in dramatic build-up toward a final climax but rather the cumulative number and variety of trials and adventures protagonists undergo. Stories such as those of al-Ḥasan al-Baṣrī and Saif al-Mulūk are good examples of the incremental series of complications that characterize this stage of the genre's narrative action. Indeed, Qamar al-Zamān's adventures, to cite another example, verge on assuming cyclical proportions when his sons, unborn when his travels first begin, grow up to be old enough to embark on romance adventures of their own.[61]

Enumerating the nature of trials protagonists undergo or cataloging their types is not necessary here. For the purposes of generic definition enumerating is less important than understanding parameters. In this regard the ratio between naturalism and supernaturalism in the genre is inconsequential. Tales that inject magic, sorcerers, and jinn into their narratives fall just as much into the genre's confines as the "realistic" stratum of tales. Fanciful coloring and magical accoutrements, such as ʿAlā al-Dīn's lamp, Prince Qamar al-Aqmār's ebony horse, or al-Ḥasan al-Baṣrī's various magical aids, are only stage props in stories that rely on the same thematic issues and narrative patterns as other members of the genre. To give but one example, all these latter tales contain the phase of their protagonists shaking off parental authority that is typical of the genre: ʿAlā al-Dīn refuses to work, al-Ḥasan al-Baṣrī disobeys his mother and goes off with a Persian magician, Jānshāh deserts his father in the midst of battle, and Qamar al-Aqmār both resists his father's decision regarding his sister's marriage and uses the ebony horse after he has been forbidden to do so. And similarly, while Fate may bring their protagonists love or riches in extraordinary or magical fashions, they must, at a certain point, grow up and begin to rely on themselves. It is because they become prepared to strive and suffer to achieve their ends that Fate provides the help, magical or otherwise, necessary for them to succeed.[62]

Having undergone their varied adventures, protagonists move to the third stage of the genre's narrative pattern: return to security. Here the familial, geographical, and social contexts of which protagonists were stripped in order to enter their term of trials are reestablished. Family reunion is a keynote of this stage of the tale, a clear sign that protagonist's adventures are drawing to a close. ʿAlāʾ al-Dīn Abū Shāmāt, for example, is for some years exiled from Baghdad, residing in Alexandria. But he never visits his aged parents in Cairo, a relatively short distance away. Only at the end of his adventures, with the restoration of his position with the Caliph, does it occur to him to send for his parents and bring them to Baghdad. Similarly, after cruelly deserting his father, Prince Qamar al-Zamān tries intermittently to rejoin him for some twenty years; but only at the story's end does this take place, amidst a chorus of family reunions that must be one of the most fabulous examples of coincidence in world literature. In like manner, characters either return to their geographical origins, as do Niʿma, Abū Muḥammad the Lazybones, or Ḥasan Badr al-Dīn, or reestablish themselves in those they have developed in the course of their trials, as is the case with ʿAlāʾ al-Dīn Abū Shāmāt or Nūr al-Dīn ʿAlī. And they reassume their social stations, whether royal, as in the case with Tāj al-Mulūk, Qamar al-Zamān, or Saif al-Mulūk; waziral, as with Ḥasan Badr al-Dīn; or bourgeois, as with ʿAlī Shār, Ghānim ibn Ayyūb, or Ibrāhīm ibn al-Khaṣīb. But by their tales' ends protagonists are no longer defined by external criteria such as family, geographical location, or social context. It is they, through the experience of their trials, who have now established these aspects of their identities through their own exertions, decisions, and qualifications.[63] Those who have made correct decisions have not only emerged unscathed but prospered; those who have chosen wrongly suffer the consequences of their miscalculations. It is here that one can see how the semantic and structural concerns of the genre converge. *Nights* romances deal with aspects of protagonists breaking free of parental authority and voyaging independently into the world—for good or ill—and with the portrayal of their various experiences and entanglements with the psychological and physiological force that dominates adolescence, sexual love. When they fall in love protagonists undergo a time of complete submersion into the realm of subjective desire. They abandon life's mundane realities for realms of magic, supernatural intervention, fantastic adventure, and extraordinary coincidence. They endure frequent losses of station and much psychological, and often physical, suffering. Simultaneously, protagonists must balance their subjective desires with the objective demands of society at large. But if they handle themselves honorably, they eventually attain their desires. Moreover, they attain or reattain positions of wealth, power, and social responsibility, recollect and set aright their relationships with hitherto forgotten relations, and of course bring their love into the accepted boundaries of social propriety by celebrating the rites of marriage. In short, they live happily ever after. On the other hand, if protagonists fail to act honorably, their adventures end negatively. They enjoy none of the above reward. Instead they lose their loves and become social pariahs, living in self-desired exile, strangers to the world, psychologically, often physically, maimed; bearing the tales of their disastrous experiences as "warnings to those who would be warned."[64]

VI

Narrative voice in *The Thousand and One Nights* as a whole has several dimensions. One of these is the desire to entertain. Prior to their first night with King Shahriyār, Shahrazād instructs her sister to say, "O my sister, tell us a wondrous tale so that we might while away with it the late hours of the night." Similarly, in the tale of ʿAlī the Persian, Hārūn al-Rashīd, unable to sleep, summons ʿAlī to entertain him with his tales.[65] A second dimension is the intent to provoke and satisfy curiosity. The work has an ambivalent attitude toward curiosity; this stems from its ambivalence toward the main object of this curiosity: the "world," as we have termed it, of romance. This world is mysterious, alluring, and attractive but also full of danger. Curiosity leads and keeps protagonists in it, but it also exposes them to manifold perils.[66] And just as curiosity, the desire to learn what comes next, leads characters into adventures, it also causes them, and us as readers, to listen to stories about them. Ḥāsib Karīm al-Dīn, for instance, enters romance's "world" through a subterranean gate. He soon wishes to leave again, but he remains, even after obtaining permission to depart, in order to hear first the tale of Bulūqiyā and then that of Jānshāh. Similarly, the Porter and the Three Mendicants are warned by their hosts not to be curious, and at one point they even face death because they have ignored this warning. Nevertheless, they remain through the night even after they have won release because they want to hear the tales of other members of the gathering.[67] King Shahriyār himself refrains from killing Shahrazād because of his desire to hear what comes next.

In spite of its twin intent to entertain and first to provoke and then satisfy curiosity, the collection's dominant voice is didactic. This statement might find ready acceptance for such *Nights* genres as fable, pious tale, or (pseudo-)historical anecdote, although it would be pointed out that each seeks to instruct in different areas of experience. But that *Nights* romances present themselves primarily as instructional might not immediately appear self-evident. The genre of romance, however, does not except itself from the general didactic voice of the collection. On the contrary, I would say that it forms its backbone. The *Nights* declares its instructional intent in its first lines:

> The life-course of those past are warnings to those who follow, so that Man sees the lessons that have occurred to others and so takes warning, and so that he who peruses the accounts of previous nations and what happened to them is restrained.[68]

This introductory statement covers the collection as a whole, but individual romances also explicitly state their didactic intent. The Second Mendicant and the Eldest Lady each describe their respective tale as one that "were it written with a needle upon the corner of the eye would be a warning to those who would be warned."[69] And at the latter tale's completion the Caliph Hārūn al-Rashīd orders that it "be written in the state records and stored in the royal treasury."[70] Moreover, romances are introduced as embedded tales produced for instructional purposes just as easily as are fables or pious tales. Just as Shahrazād's father tells her "The Story of the Bull and the Ass" to try to convince her not to marry the King, or the Second Mendicant produces "The Story of the Envier and the Envied" to convince a jinni to be merciful, in "The Story of Qamar al-Zamān," Bahrām, the (former) Magian, tells the romance of Niʿma and Nuʿm to convince Qamar al-Zamān's two sons not to weep for fear of being reunited with their beloveds.[71] Similarly, why is the tale of the unfortunate ʿAzīz inserted into that of Tāj al-Mulūk if not to serve as a warning to the young prince, in the process of seeking his beloved, of how not to act in matters of love?

But the most convincing evidence of *Nights* romances' didactic intent appears in the collection's frame story. Critics have often concentrated their attention on Shahrazād in this tale. And the image of the young girl waging a battle against death through the use of words certainly has its attractions.[72] But one should remember that her main purpose with this strategy is not procrastination. This could not be so; even she would eventually run out of stories. On the contrary, Shahrazād is narrating tales primarily to instruct the King. Fascination with the figure of Shahrazād should not blind one to the fact that by the standards of the genre it is not she but King Shahriyār who is the tale's main protagonist. It is he who is being tested by Fate concerning his conception of honorable action in the concerns of life and social propriety, and it is he who is in the process of failing this test. He had degraded love into pure lust, transformed the life-long commitment of marriage into a series of one-night stands, and interpreted his own wife's infidelity as license to be recurrently and corruptly unfaithful himself. Moreover, he has seriously misconstrued the social context and probable consequences of his actions. He may be able to continue his inhuman policy for a time, but its social consequence is that "his people clamored against him and fled with their daughters."[73] Shahrazād risks death, but the King is courting it! Moreover, she has the ultimate advantage of being favored with true knowledge about how to act in life. Even if she dies, she will do so, as she says, "as a ransom for the daughters of the Muslims and the cause of their salvation from his hand."[74] The King, however, has gone astray, lost his wits, and come to erroneous conclusions about how to act in love and life. And this being romance, where unfaithful lovers meet fitting ends, he is in terrible danger. From this viewpoint, Shahrazād steps forward not only to save the other maidens of the kingdom but also the King himself. It is he whom she is redeeming. And her method is instruction in the very area in which he is deficient, the concerns of romance. For this endeavor she is eminently qualified, since she had "perused the books, histories, and biographies of preceding kings, and the accounts of past nations. Indeed, it was said that she had collected a thousand books of histories relating to preceding nations, departed rulers, and poets."[75] Shahrazād's goal is not to make the King forget his anger through infinite procrastination, but to show him, no matter how long it takes, that his view of honor and right conduct is fundamentally wrong. Shahriyār's romance, after his initial adventures, is to a great extent displaced. He does not have adventures himself; instead he is told a thousand and one nights of the adventures of others. Final evidence in support of this interpretation of the story comes at its end. When Shahrazād finally asks that her death sentence be lifted, she first brings her children and begs the King not to make them motherless, a plea founded upon accepted standards of social propriety. Shahriyār replies that even before the arrival of the children he had decided to spare her since he found her "chaste, noble, and pious." In other words, a fitting damsel with whom to fall in true love.[76]

The preferred "radical of presentation" of *Nights* romance is *epos*, direct communication between storyteller and audience. In situations where individual tales were publicly narrated, the relevance of this choice is obvious. But what is intriguing about it is the extent to which the genre attempts to create and maintain the *illusion* of this medium. The well-known framing structure of the collection plays an important role in serving this end. But it is not unusual that even within tales a storyteller-audience situation is created. Hārūn al-Rashīd, for instance, is a frequent recipient of others' stories.[77] This rhetorical strategy is, I think, connected with the modulation of voice that *Nights* romance must maintain in preserving its balance between the realms of myth and realism. Unlike myth or naturalistic narrative, each of which in its own way can pass itself off as realistic, and unlike fable whose technique of inserting animals into basically human psychological contexts in order to exemplify a moral requires no literal belief in its narrative's realism, romance desires that its events, no matter how fantastic they may appear, be accepted as at least "possible." It is one of the genre's implicit postulates that the events it portrays at least "might" have happened. If not, then any claim on its part to having didactic value is lost.[78] Thus, in order to maintain the delicate balance between belief or disbelief that so often faces its audience, the genre finds it convenient to insert internal narrative situations into its tales, where one character tells his story to another. The adoption of first-person narration lends stories an extra aura of pseudo-autobiographical veracity, and it also places the burden of belief or disbelief upon a straw-man inside the tale. In this way the external audience can simultaneously associate and dissociate itself with the responsibility of believing the story. In a sense, readers are allowed to "overhear" the tale. That they to some degree allow themselves to believe the tale is very important, for the genre only has instructional relevance if it can claim that its stories really happened, that they belong to real life.

These two aspects of the genre's verbal level, the use of voice and the genre's preferred posture in regard to its "radical of presentation" are all that we shall touch upon here. Both these and many other aspects of this stratum of the genre—the use of point of view, modulation of tone, numerous aspects of style, for example—all deserve more detailed investigation. But the above remarks at least give a general outline of this aspect of the genre and, one hopes, will provoke further research concerning it.

VII

Up to this point this essay has attempted to chart the contours and delineate the borders of the genre of romance in *The Thousand and*

One Nights. This has necessarily been done at a fairly general level; much more detailed investigation is needed in many of the areas upon which we have touched. But in that this analysis suggests the broad outlines of the genre's concerns and practices, it at least constitutes a necessary first step. Before leaving the topic, however, it may be useful briefly to mention how the investigation undertaken here can help clarify *Nights* romance's relations to other stories and genres and, finally, to touch upon the subject of the genre's social and ideological context.

Arriving at a more precise awareness of the nature of romance not only allows one to perceive and understand the workings of its individual members more fully, it also helps clarify the status of stories whose generic nature at first sight seems ambiguous. There are stories in the *Nights* that appear to share aspects of motif or plot, but this should not lead one to believe that they necessarily belong to the same genre. The tales of Saif al-Mulūk and Sindbād the Sailor, for example, share many incidents, for their protagonists both suffer many a shipwreck. But the first, whose action is motivated by Saif al-Mulūk's love quest, is clearly a romance, while the second, sharing the genre's general conception of Fate but lacking its essential romantic dimension, falls on the genre's borders.[79] Similarly, the stories of both Ghānim ibn Ayyūb and Khalīfa the Fisherman contain the subplot of Hārūn al-Rashīd's infatuation with the slave-girl Qūt al-Qulūb causing his jealous wife to seek to dispose of her. But from the perspective of the definition of romance proposed above, it is clear that these tales fall into separate genres, for they approach this shared subplot from radically different points of view. Ghānim's tale is straight romance: he falls in love with the girl, loves her intensely and truly, suffers terribly for this love, and eventually wins his beloved's hand. The story of Khalīfa differs completely. Not only does the tale dispense with any romantic attachment between its protagonist and Qūt al-Qulūb, its whole concept of Fate is totally at odds with that adopted by romance. Khalīfa's world is truly random, ironically so—based on pure chance and luck. As such the tale falls completely outside the genre.[80]

Attaining a clear idea of *Nights* romances' generic configurations also enables one better to understand its relationship with other genres of medieval Arabic popular narrative. An epic worldview, for example, may be found in *Sīrat ʿAntar*. Confronted with overwhelming odds before a battle, ʿAntar's liege Lord, King Zuhair, remarks, "O Father of Knights! This is a dismal day, stained by the sadness and concern that will come of it." But ʿAntar replies:

> By your dear life, my Lord, appointed times of death do not fall short of or exceed their times. I have wished for something like this [being faced with overwhelming odds]. If a man's time has not come, iron blades cannot cut him off. Sire, what use is the sword my shoulder bears if I do not strike with it; or the lance that I thrust with if I do not kill men with it; or the horse that I ride if I do not charge warriors with it?[81]

This passage also presents a distinct conception of Fate, but one that implies that courage, fortitude, and self-reliance allow one to face death unafraid and thus transcend Fate's bounds. "Let Fate take care of itself," ʿAntar basically says, "for I shall do what I must." The *sīra*'s hero's desire and capability for independent action are part of the genre's credo that those strong enough to take their destinies into their own hands become its masters, free to guide their own courses, content with the consequences of their decisions. Such freedom never exists in *Nights* romances; here is the essential semantic cleft that divides the genres.[82]

A similar heroic sense of self-reliance, although one stemming from wells of craftiness and guile rather than from strength of arm, exists in the rogue tales of Aḥmad al-Danaf, Ḥasan Shūmān, ʿAlī Zaibaq, and Dalīla the Crafty. Here too protagonists are masters of their own fates. A good example of the basic difference between this genre and *Nights* romances appears in the stories the collection contains of these characters. In the first part of the tale the clever old lady Dalīla undertakes a series of frauds and stratagems that makes fools of the authorities of Baghdad, some of whom themselves, Aḥmad al-Danaf and Ḥasan Shūmān, are famed rogues. Dalīla amply displays that she is in full control of her fate. The latter part of the same story, however, reveals a shift in perspective. It portrays the young Cairene rogue ʿAlī Zaibaq striving to outwit a Jewish magician. Untrue to type, the story shows its hero failing in his task. Transformed into a variety of animals by the magician, ʿAlī's wits help him maintain the status quo, for he uses them to undo his various transformations; but they do not help him advance his claim. To extract him from this dilemma the narrative turns to romance, perhaps a not unexpected turn of events since the overall concern of this part of the tale is ʿAlī's quest to win the hand of Dalīla's daughter. ʿAlī's problem is solved through help from outside. The magician's daughter falls in love with him, is instructed through a dream to become a Muslim, murders her father when he refuses to convert, and brings ʿAlī the bridal garments that he has been seeking for his beloved's dowry. Here reliance on trickery and deceit gives way to romance's reliance on Fate's hand intervening to resolve its protagonist's affairs.[83]

The predominance of the romance strain in *The Thousand and One Nights* and the collection's history of continued growth and development over many centuries testify to the genre's enduring popularity. It is therefore perhaps worthwhile to attempt to consider briefly why this should be the case. We have seen that *Nights* romances intend to entertain, provoke, and satisfy the curiosity of, and instruct, their audiences. But they also perform a more fundamental subliminal function: they reassure and comfort. For these tales' basic message is that no matter how chaotic and disturbed events may appear to be on the surface, in reality order reigns in human affairs. Fate's hand is constantly present, guiding destinies, enforcing ordinances, ensuring eventual justice. How sirenic the call of a genre that expounds such an attractively comforting exposition of life's true basis! At the end of the story of Ḥāsib Karīm al-Dīn the protagonist drinks a vial containing a magic potion. At this

> God drew into his heart wells of wisdom and opened for him the spring of learning, so that he attained joy and happiness. . . . He lifted his head to the sky and saw the seven heavens and what was in them, until the Far Lotus Tree. He saw how the spheres resolved. God revealed all this to him. He saw the moving and fixed stars and learned how the planets coursed. He observed and became alert to the configurations of the earth and sea. He learned astrology, astronomy, the science of the spheres, calculation, and what pertained to all of these, and thus learned how to calculate lunar and solar eclipses and other things. Then he looked at the earth and knew what it contained of minerals, plants, trees, and all their properties and uses. From this he deduced the science of medicine, white magic, alchemy, and knew how to make silver and gold.[84]

The contents of the vial—interestingly enough derived from the remains of the dead Serpent Queen—obviously bestow upon Ḥāsīb man's greatest gift, the power of intellectual observations and reasoning. And as the reverent tone of the passage indicates, this represents a dimension of experience foreign—at least in an organized, systematic form—to the genre of romance. The storybook itself gives an example of the worldview more typical of the genre. Sindbād the Landsman, a porter by trade, pauses to rest outside the gates of Sindbād the Sailor's stately residence. Observing the establishment's obvious wealth and comparing its owner's happy lot with his own wretched state, the poor man bursts out:

> Praise be to You, O Lord, O Creator, O Provider! You provide whom You will, without stint. O God, I ask pardon from You for all my sins, and I repent to You my faults. O Lord, I do not oppose Your wisdom and omnipotence, for You are not to be questioned about what You do. You have power over all things. Praise to you! You enrich whom You will and impoverish whom you will; You make mighty whom You will and humble whom You will. There is no God but You. How great is Your estate, how strong Your rule, how excellent Your management! You have favored whom You will among your servants, so that the owner of this place lives in utmost comfort, enjoying pleasant smells, delicious foods, and superb drinks of all sorts. You have passed judgement among Your creatures as You desire. How great is Your power over them! Some are weary, some at ease; some happy, some, like myself, extremely tired.[85]

Sindbād the Sailor overhears this outburst, brings the weary porter into his house, and regales him with tales of how he has suffered even worse conditions than his guest, but how by trusting his destiny to Fate and God's will he has emerged from his adventures wealthy and safe. By the very process of hearing these tales and coming to understand Fate's true workings, Sindbād the Landsman's own fortunes are transformed. At the very moment when he feels his lot to be worst, Fate plucks him from his poverty and, through Sindbād the Sailor's flow of words and gifts, makes him rich. This then is the comfort that *Nights* romances offer and one that makes them appealing to audiences: that in apparent chaos there is order, in tumult, design, and in the seeming randomness of human success and failure, overall coherence. In short, that there is meaning to life. In this regard, one would posit that the genre would appeal to individuals, social groups, and classes that had a need to hear this message, for perhaps varying reasons. This might explain the lower social status of

Nights audiences in medieval times and the contempt expressed for the collection by the intelligentsia. The extent to which this hypothesis can be tested may be limited, given the lack of specific evidence available. The matter is surely complex. For one thing, it should not be forgotten that other genres offering different, even opposing worldviews, such as *sīra*, were also popular among these classes. Nor should it be ignored that individual mood might sometimes be just as important a factor in leading one to listen to or read *Nights* romances as sociological criteria. Nevertheless, the whole question deserves further consideration. Moreover, from this perspective, it is intriguing to consider why *The Thousand and One Nights* achieved the popularity it did among well-educated, generally upper-class adults in eighteenth- and nineteenth-century Europe. That the rationalism of the Enlightenment had progressed far enough for such readers not to be put off, but even fascinated, by the tales' Islamic garb, and that they felt secure enough of their political and economic superiority to adopt a position of openness to a storybook stemming from a culture previously feared and hated as a dangerous rival may help explain why the book was accepted, but not why it was popular. But perhaps members of European upper classes, witnesses to the final dissolution of the feudal system and increasingly divested of the spiritual security offered by religious faith, were themselves in need of the very message *Nights* romances insinuated. If rationalism and the rise of the Newtonian picture of the universe had pushed God that much further away from direct contact with human affairs, would it not be soothing to read tales that insinuated the existence of a Divine Plan, a grand design, the guiding hand of Fate organizing and governing life's events? *Thousand and One Nights* romances whisper this comforting message and thus continue to play their part in sustaining certain necessary illusions.[86]

Notes

1. For this article I rely principally on the Būlāq edition of *The Thousand and One Nights: Alf Layla wa Layla*, 2 vols. (Būlāq, 1252/1835), reprinted by Maktabat al-Muthannā in Baghdad (n.d.), hereafter B. I have occasionally supplemented this by consulting W. H. Macnaughten, *The Alif Lailah or Book of the Thousand Nights and One Night*, 4 vols. (Calcutta, 1839–42), hereafter

C. II: and Muhsin Mahdi, ed., *The Thousand and One Nights, From the Earliest Known Sources,* 3 pts. (Leiden, 1984–), hereafter M. For the Arabic text of ʿAlāʾ al-Dīn and His Marvellous Lamp," I have used H. Zotenberg, *Histoire de ʿAlāʾ al-Dīn ou La lampe merveilleuse; texte arabe, avec une notice sur quelques manuscrits des 1001 Nuits* (Paris, 1883). In order to avoid an unwieldy apparatus of references, I generally refer to individual stories by their protagonists' names. Below is an alphabetical list of these names and the stories in which they appear; the English titles correspond to those that M. Gerhardt uses in her *The Art of Story-Telling: A Literary Study of the Thousand and One Nights* (Leiden, 1963), 18–27.

ʿAbd Allāh ibn Fāḍil: "The Story of ʿAbd Allāh ibn Fāḍil and His Beloved," B. 2: 576–95; C. II 4: 630–76.

Abū Ḥasan: "The Story of Abū Ḥasan from Khurasan," B. 2: 543–51; C. II 4: 557–64.

Abū Muḥammad: "The Story of Abū Muḥammad Lazybones," B. 1: 473–80; C. II 2: 187–204.

ʿAlāʾ al-Dīn: "The Story of ʿAlāʾ al-Dīn and the Marvellous Lamp," Zotenberg, *Histoire,* Arabic text 1–86.

ʿAlāʾ al-Dīn Abū Shāmāt: "The Story of ʿAlāʾ al-Dīn Abū Shāmāt," B. 1: 416–44; C. II 2: 64–125.

ʿAlī ibn Bakkār: "The Story of ʿAlī ibn Bakkār and Shams al-Nahār," B. 1: 320–43; C. II 1: 761–811; M. 1: 380–433.

ʿAlī the Persian: "The Story of ʿAlī the Persian," B. 1: 468–69; C. II 2: 176–80.

ʿAlī Shār: "The Story of ʿAlī Shār and Zumurrud," B. 1: 484–503; C. II 2: 212–51.

ʿAlī Zaibaq: "The Adventures of ʿAlī Zaibaq," (in Dalīla) B. 2: 199–215; C. II 3: 444–80.

Ardashīr: "The Story of Ardashīr and Ḥayāt al-Nufūs," B. 2: 215–42; C. II 3: 480–540.

ʿAzīz: "The Story of ʿAzīz and ʿAzīza," (in Tāj al-Mulūk, which is in ʿUmar ibn al-Nuʿmān) B. 1: 235–54; C. II 1: 563–611.

Blacksmith: "The Story of the Blacksmith Who Could Handle Fire," B. 1: 645–46; C. II 2: 557–61.

Dalīla: "The Story of the Tricks of Crafty Dalīla," B. 2: 187–215; C. II 3: 416–80.

Eldest Lady: "The Story of the Eldest Lady," (in Porter and Three Ladies) B. 1: 44–47; C. II 1: 121–30; M. 1: 209–19.

Envier: "The Story of the Envier and the Envied," (in Second Mendicant, which is in Porter and Three Ladies), not in B.; C. II 1: 90–92; M. 1: 164–78.

First Mendicant: "The Story of the First Mendicant," (in Porter and Three Ladies), B. 1: 31–34; C. II 1: 74–81; M. 1: 144–55.

Ghānim ibn Ayyūb: "The Story of Ghānim ibn Ayyūb, the Distracted Slave of Love," B. 1: 125–39; C. II 1: 320–51.

Ḥasan Badr al-Dīn: "The Story of the Wazirs Nūr al-Dīn and Shams al-Dīn," B. 1: 54–73; C. II 1: 148–99; M. 1: 225–79.

Ḥasan al-Baṣrī: "The Story of Ḥasan from al-Baṣra, the Jeweller," B. 2: 294–359; C. II 4: 3–151.

Ḥāsib Karīm al-Dīn: "The Story of the Serpent Queen," B. 1: 657–711; C. II 2: 582–699.

Ibrāhīm and Jamīla: "The Story of Ibrāhīm and Jamīla," B. 2: 534–43; C. II 4: 535–57.

Jānshāh: "The Story of Jānshāh," (in Ḥāsib Karīm al-Dīn) B. 1: 672–702; C. II: 617–87.

Jaudar: "The Story of Jaudar and His Brothers," B. 2: 80–105; C. II 3: 194–236.

Khalīfa: "The Story of the Fisherman Khalīfa," B. 2: 359–77; C. II 4: 151–91.

Lady Doorkeeper: "The Story of the Lady Doorkeeper," (in Porter and Three Ladies) B. 1: 47–50; C. II 1: 130–40; M. 1: 201–9.

Man from Upper Egypt: "The Story of the Man from Upper Egypt and His Frankish Wife," B. 2: 455–57; C. II 4: 353–57.

Man Who Never Laughed: "The Story of the Man Who Never Laughed Any More in His Life," (in Sindbād) B. 2: 66–69; C. II 3: 146–54.

Masrūr and Zain al-Mawāṣif: "The Story of Masrūr and Zain al-Mawāṣif," B. 2: 377–405; C. II 4: 191–246.

Muḥammad ibn ʿAlī: "The Story of Hārūn al-Rashīd and the Pseudo-Caliph," B. 1: 459–68; C. II 2: 157–76.

Niʿma ibn al-Rabīʿ: "The Story of Niʿma ibn al-Rabīʿ and His Slave-Girl Nuʿm," (in Qamar al-Zamān) B. 1: 404–14; C. II 2: 36–59; M. 1: 652–80.

Nūr al-Dīn ʿAlī: "The Story of Nūr al-Dīn ʿAlī and Anīs al-Jalīs," B. 1: 106–25; C. II 1: 278–320; M. 1: 434–71.

Nūr al-Dīn and Maryam: "The Story of Nūr al-Dīn and Maryam the Belt-Maker," B. 2: 405–55; C. II 4: 246–353.

Porter and Ladies: "The Story of the Porter and the Three Ladies," B. 1: 25–51; C. II 1: 56–142; M. 1: 115–219.

Qamar al-Aqmār: "The Story of the Ebony Horse," B. 1: 534–46; C. II 2: 318–45.

Qamar al-Zamān: "The Story of Qamar al-Zamān," B. 1: 343–416; C. II 1: 811–12: 36; M. 1: 533–688.

Qamar al-Zamān and Beloved: "The Story of Qamar al-Zamān and His Beloved," B. 2: 551–76; C. II 4: 564–630.

Saif al-Mulūk: "The Story of Prince Saif al-Mulūk and the Princess Badīʿat al-Jamāl," B. 2: 263–94; C. II 1: 81–102.

Second Mendicant: "The Story of the Second Mendicant," (in Porter and Three Ladies) B. 1: 34–41; C. II 1: 81–102; M. 1: 155–78.

Shahriyār and Shahrazād: "The Story of King Shahriyār and His Brother King Shahzamān," B. 1: 2–6, 2: 6–19; C. II 1: 1–10, 4: 730–31; M. 1: 67–72.

Sindbād: "The Story of the Malice of Women, or of the King, His Son, His Favorite, and the Seven Wazirs," B. 2: 52–86; C. II 3: 158–94.

Sindbād the Sailor: "The Story of Sindbād the Sailor," B. 2: 3–37; C. II 3: 4–83.

Tāj al-Mulūk: "The Story of Tāj al-Mulūk and the Princess Dunyā," (in ʿUmar ibn al-Nuʿmān) B. 1: 228–90; C. II 1: 552–650.

Third Mendicant: "The Story of the Third Mendicant," (in Porter and Three Ladies) B. 1: 41–44; C. II 1: 102–21; M. 1: 178–200.

Two Black Slaves: "The Story of the Eunuch Bukhait"; "The Story of the Eunuch Kāfūr," (both in Ghānim ibn Ayyūb): Bukhait B. 1: 127–28; C. II 1: 324–25; Kāfūr B. 1: 128–30; C. II 1: 325–31.

Uns al-Wujūd: "The Story of Uns al-Wujūd and al-Ward fi'l-Akmān," B. 1: 546–62; C. II 2: 345–76.

2. Important examples of the historical approach are N. Abbott, "A Ninth-Century Fragment of the 'Thousand Nights,' New Light on the Early History of the *Arabian Nights*," *Journal of Near Eastern Studies* (1949): 129–64; D. B. Macdonald, "Lost MSS. of the Arabian Nights and a Projected Edition of that of Galland," *Journal of the Royal Asiatic Society* (1911): 219–21; id., "Maximilian Habicht and His Recension of the 1001 Nights," *Journal of the Royal Asiatic Society* (1909): 685–704; id., "A Preliminary Classification of Some Manuscripts of the Arabian Nights," in *A Volume of Oriental Studies, Presented to E. G. Browne*, ed. T. W. Arnold and R. A. Nicholson (Cambridge, 1922), 304–21; id., "The Earlier History of the Arabian Nights," *Journal of the Royal Asiatic Society* (1924): 353–97; J. Oestrup, *Studier over Tusind og en Nat* (Copenhagen, 1891); R. Paret, *Der Ritter-Roman von ʿUmar An-Nuʿmān* (Tübingen, 1927); B. Perry, "The Origin of the Book of Sindbad," *Fabula* (1960): 1–94; H. Zotenberg, *Histoire;* and most recently and deserving special

mention M. Mahdi's recent edition of the old Syrian recension of the *Nights*, which we have designated M.

Examples of "panoramic" studies include R. Burton, "Terminal Essay," in *The Book of the Thousand Nights and a Night, a Plain and Literal Translation of the Arabian Nights Entertainments* (New York: Heritage Press, 1962), 3653–871; E. Littmann, "Anhang: Zur Entstehung und Geschichte von Tausendundeiner Nacht," in *Die Erzählungen aus den Tausendundeinen Nächten*, 6 vols. (Wiesbaden, 1954), 6: 647–738; M. Gerhardt's literary critical study, *The Art of Story-Telling;* and F. Ghazoul's recent *The Arabian Nights: A Structural Analysis* (Cairo, 1980). S. Qalamāwī's *Alf lailah wa-laila* (Cairo, 1966), with its combination of historical, sociological and thematic concerns, might also be included in this category, as could N. Elisséeff's folkloristic theme study, *Thèmes et motifs des Milles et Une Nuit, essai de classification* (Beirut, 1949).

Examples of analyses of individual tales are A. Hamori's two studies in his *On the Art of Medieval Arabic Literature* (Princeton, 1974), 145–80; and his "Notes on Two Love Stories from the Thousand and One Nights," *Studia Islamica* (1966): 65–80, and "A Comic Romance from the Thousand and One Nights; The Tale of the Two Vezirs," *Arabica* (1983): 38–56; and A. Miquel, *Sept contes de Mille et Une Nuits* (Paris, 1981); and P. Molan, "Sinbād the Sailor: A Commentary on the Ethics of Violence," *Journal of the American Oriental Society* (1978): 237–47, and "Maʿrūf the Cobbler: The Mythic Structure of an Arabian Nights Tale," *Edebiyat* (1978): 121–35. For a full bibliography of early *Nights* studies, see Gerhardt, *The Art of Story-Telling.*

3. Burton divides the *Nights* into fable, fairy tale, and historical anecdote, *Thousand Nights*, 3687–718; Littmann into Märchen, Romane, Novellen (with subdivisions), Sagen und Legenden, Lehrhafte Geschichten, Humoresken, and Anekdoten, *Die Erzählungen*, 6: 682–736; Gerhardt into love stories, crime stories, travel stories, fairy tales, learning-wisdom-pious tales, *The Art of Story-Telling*, 119–374; compare also Ghazoul, "It is unnecessary and indeed cumbersome to compare every enframed story to the framing one. It suffices to compare configurations of diverse narrative genres of the enframed with the frame," *The Arabian Nights*, 20. Generic assumptions in analyses of individual tales are usually obvious, and sometimes expressly stated in their titles.

4. Panoramic critics often face this drawback unless they, like Qalamāwī, adopt a thematic approach. This is evident in such studies as Gerhardt's and Ghazoul's where analyses of individual genres or perspectives can be excellent, Ghazoul on fable, for instance, but where it is difficult to offer equally balanced or insightful portraits of all aspects of the collection.

5. Medieval Arabic romances besides those contained in the *Nights* may be found in the following collections: *Āzād Bakht* (Ten Wazirs), *al-Ṭair al-nāṭiq*, *Kitāb al-ʿanqāʾ*, *Alf yaum wa-yaum*, and *Kitāb al-ḥikāyāt al-ʿajība wa-l-akhbār al-gharība*, the latter edited by Hans Wehr (Wiesbaden, 1956). These and other stories pertinent to the study of romance still await serious study,

as do other stories and collections relevant to the study of medieval Islamic (Persian, Turkish, etc.) romance. Good overviews of the corpus of what we term medieval Arabic popular literature may be found in vols. 7 and 8 of W. Ahlwardt, *Verzeichnis der Arabischen Handschriften der Königlichen Bibliothek zu Berlin*, 10 vols. (Berlin, 1887–99) and V. Chauvin, *Bibliographie des ouvrages arabes ou relatifs aux arabes, publiés dans l'Europe chrétienne de 1810 á 1885*, 12 vols. (Liège, 1892–1922). Of pertinence to this view of the *Nights* as a microcosm of medieval Arabic popular literature is M. Mahdi's hypothesis that the late Egyptian recension of the collection, usually termed ZER, is the creation of the eighteenth century, one stemming from the desire of Arab storytellers and European tourists to have a "complete" version of the work, see M. 1: 18–19.

6. Cf. Claudio Guillén: "The search for universals will be a central task for future literary studies, as it is for linguistics today. Second, this search will surely depend on the assimilation of a great deal of knowledge concerning the non-Western literatures, or to put it in academic terms, on the work of comparative literature scholars who have been trained as Orientalists," *Literature as System: Essays toward the Theory of Literary History* (Princeton, 1971), 114. Also quoted in J. T. Monroe, *The Art of Badīʿ az-Zamān al-Hamadhānī as Picaresque Narrative* (Beirut, 1983), 15, n. 12.

7. Even Benedetto Croce did not object to the concept of genre per se, only to its use as the basis for prescriptive rules having evaluative consequences. See B. Croce, *Aesthetics: As Science of Expression and General Linguistics*, trans. D. Ainslie, (Boston, 1983; 1st ed., New York, 1909), 35–38.

8. See the section "Genre and the Idea of the Whole," in E. D. Hirsch, *Validity in Interpretation* (New Haven, 1967), 71–77.

9. Thus F. de Saussure, "In separating language [*langue*] from speaking [*parole*] we are at the same time separating: (1) what is social from what is individual; and (2) what is essential from what is accessory and more or less accidental. Language is not a function of the speaker; it is a product that is passively assimilated by the individual," *Course in General Linguistics*, trans. W. Baskin, rev. ed. (New York, 1974); compare C. Guillén, "no poet is likely to raise his voice in an environment devoid of poetic models; and today the formal model called genre exerts a normative impact, not in the old knuckle-rapping sense but insofar as it offers a challenge, a foil, a series of guidelines," *Literature as System*, 122–23. Cf. also Hirsch, *Validity*, 111 and R. Wellek and A. Warren, *Theory of Literature*, 3rd ed. (New York, 1970), 226.

The determinative nature of generic assumption within audiences may be seen from public rejection of "modern" literary works that work against them; the novels of Joyce two generations ago come to mind. Within the context of study of medieval Arabic literature, one does not have to look far to find negative reactions on the part of Western readers to work considered classics by Arabs, a response that again may be largely based on different generic assumptions within two audiences. See, for example, reactions to the *maqāmāt* genre cited in Monroe, *The Art of Badīʿ az-Zamān*, 87–89; similar attitudes toward medieval Arabic poetry also exist. For a review of Western critical attitudes toward the popular *sīra*, see P. Heath, "A Critical Review of Modern Scholarship on *Sīrat ʿAntar ibn Shaddād* and the Popular *Sīra*," *Journal of Arabic Literature* (1985): 19–44. See also Ghazoul, *The Arabian Nights*, 69–70.

10. See S. H. Butcher, *Aristotle's Theory of Poetry and Fine Art*, 4th ed. (New York, 1951), 7–17; Croce, *Aesthetics*, 35–38; Wellek and Warren, *Theory of Literature*, 229–31; and W. K. Wimsatt Jr. and C. Brooks, *Literary Criticism: A Short History* (London, 1957), 159–61, 325–26.

11. See Butcher, *Aristotle's Theory*, 23 for Aristotle's definition of tragedy itself and 119–214, esp. 207 ff., for Butcher's comments. See also Wimsatt and Brooks, *Literary Criticism*, 52–53.

12. Hirsch, *Validity*, 101. But see also n. 19 against the idea of purpose as a neo-Aristotelian entelechy. Hirsch's definition of intrinsic genre is: "It is that sense of the whole by means of which an interpreter can correctly understand any part of its determinacy," 86. Compare Guillén, "form is the presence in a created, man-made object of a 'cause,'" *Literature as System*, 111.

13. Guillén, *Literature as System*, 111–12. Cf. also F. Jameson, "Magical Narratives: Romance as Genre," *New Literary History* (1975–76): 139–40.

14. Hirsch, *Validity*, 78–79 and the definition of intrinsic genre quoted in note 12. For the concept of the hermeneutic circle, see M. Heidegger, *Being and Time*, trans. J. Macquarrie and E. Robinson (London, 1962), 188–95. See also, L. Spitzer, *Linguistics and Literary History* (Princeton, 1948), 1–29.

15. T. Todorov, *The Fantastic: A Structural Approach to a Literary Genre*, trans. R. Howard (Ithaca, 1973), 20 and 157–58.

16. For a more complete exposition of Todorov's approach, see his *Introduction to Poetics*, trans. R. Howard, *Theory and History of Literature*, vol. 1 (Minneapolis, 1981). Of course the remarks on romance in *The Thousand and One Nights* offered in the present essay could be more detailed and developed; yet incomplete as they may be, they at least offer a preliminary overview of the genre that can be used as a basis for further study.

17. See, for example, W. T. H. Jackson's chapter on French romance in his *Medieval Literature: A History and a Guide* (New York, 1966), 81–100; part one of G. Hough's *A Preface to the Faerie Queene* (New York, 1963); the various articles in R. S. Loomis, *Arthurian Literature in the Middle Ages* (Oxford, 1959); and the chapter "Romances" in R. Tuve, *Allegorical Imagery: Some Medieval Books and their Posterity* (Princeton, 1966), 335–436.

18. Cf. N. Frye, *Anatomy of Criticism* (Princeton, 1957) and also *The Secular Scripture: A Study of the Structure of Romance* (Cambridge, Mass., 1976), although the concept of genre espoused here differs from this concept of mode. See also R. Schole's revision of Frye's theory of modes in *Structuralism in Literature: An Introduction* (New Haven, 1974), 117–29; and P. Parker, *Inescapable Romance: Studies in the Poetics of a Mode* (Princeton, 1979).

19. Cf. R. Bjornson's remarks on the situation of the study of the pic-

aresque novel, "Scholarly discussions of the picaresque are generally based upon one of two assumptions: either it is regarded as a historical phenomenon, or it is viewed in terms of an ideal type. Both approaches have their disadvantages, and both must somehow resolve the difficult problems of defining a category which has no *a priori* existence and of determining which works legitimately belong in that category. If a narrow historical definition is adopted, the critic is prevented from drawing fruitful analogies among works which have much in common, despite the fact that none of them were directly influenced by the others. However, when critics derive abstract generalizations from an inductive examination of one or more novels, their definitions tend to be circular, because works drawn upon to establish the model necessarily manifest the principal characteristics of the model itself," *The Picaresque Hero in European Fiction* (Madison, 1977), 4–5. Also of interest here is C. Brookes-Rose, "Historical Genres/Theoretical Genres: Todorov on the Fantastic," in her *A Rhetoric of the Unreal: Studies in Narrative and Structure, Especially on the Fantastic* (Cambridge, 1981), 55–71, although her use of the terminology differs from what is proposed here.

20. The quarrel becomes at this point one between historicists and structuralists. For Robertson's views, see his *A Preface to Chaucer: Studies in Medieval Perspectives* (Princeton, 1962), vii–ix, 3–6. For the suggestion that genres can arise *polygenetically*, i.e., that similar historical circumstances in separate cultures can produce similar genres, see Monroe, *The Art of Badīʿ az-Zamān*, 16–18.

21. W. P. Ker, *Epic and Romance: Essays on Medieval Literature* (New York: Dover, 1957), 321–22. F. Jameson makes the important point that the concept of genre is just as useful for studying "eclectic" works, works that appear to offer a mixture of genres, as it is for studying works that appear to fall into the mainstream of one genre or another, see "Magical Narratives," 150–54.

22. R. Jacobson, "The Dominant," in *Readings in Russian Poetics: Formalist and Structuralist Views*, ed. L. Matejka and K. Pomorska (Cambridge, Mass., 1971), 82–87.

23. See notes 7 and 10. See also J. Derrida, "The Law of Genre," in *On Narrative*, ed. W. J. T. Mitchel (Chicago, 1981), 51–77. (A volume of articles that originally appeared in *Critical Inquiry*, Autumn 1980 and Summer 1981.)

24. Cf., for example, the *Nights* stories Masrūr and Zain al-Mawāṣif, Khalīfa, Sindbād the Sailor, and "The Story of ʿUmar ibn al-Nuʿmān" (is it *sīra* or romance?). Also pertinent here is the concept of *anti-genre* or counter-genre, see Guillén, *Literature as System*, 135–58; for the idea of *anti-sīra*, see Ghazoul, *The Arabian Nights*, 75–90; and, applied to the genre of *maqāmāt*, Monroe, *The Art of Badīʿ az-Zamān*, 19–38.

25. Indeed, it is difficult to entertain the notion of genre without simultaneously assuming the existence of an overall interrelated framework or system of genres. For examples of such spectrums, proposed for analytic rather than

evaluative ends, see Frye and Scholes on modes, as cited in note 18. See also Guillén, *Literature as System*, 121–22, and Jameson as cited in note 21.

26. Todorov, *The Fantastic*, 4.

27. *Sir Orfeo*, in *Medieval Romances*, ed. R. S. Loomis and L. H. Loomis (New York, 1957), 314.

28. Jackson, *Medieval Literature*, 11.

29. Ker, *Epic and Romance*, 4; Parker, *Inescapable Romance*, 4; Jameson, "Magical Narratives," 140.

30. See Frye, *Anatomy*, 33, 36–37, 56–58, 131–62, 186–206; and *The Secular Scripture*. For a useful analysis of Frye's theory, see R. D. Denham, *Northrop Frye and Critical Method* (University Park, 1978).

31. Frye, *Anatomy*, 49–52 and 62–67; and Denham, *Northrop Frye*, 47–50.

32. Frye, *Anatomy*, 136.

33. Ibid., 137.

34. Ibid., 193.

35. Ibid., 136–38 and 155–56. See also Denham, *Northrop Frye*, 64–66.

36. Frye, *Anatomy*, 134–40, for realism. For his remark on literature's "formulaic units," see idem, *The Secular Scripture*, 36 ff. The quote from Denham is in *Northrop Frye*, 64.

37. This definition is my own. Compare with W. T. H. Jackson on French romances: "Both in love-making and adventure the great motivating force was honor," *Medieval Literature*, 82. Honor, of course, is also a central element of the thematic stratum of epic, thus C. M. Bowra, "In their attempts to classify mankind into different types the early Greek philosophers gave a special place to those men who live for action and for the honor which comes of it," *Heroic Poetry* (London, 1952), 1. But the concept of honor differs in epic and romance, since the arena of activity pertaining to each differs. Hence an analogous definition of the theme epic would be: *to investigate the concerns of honor as balanced between death and social propriety, within the context of Fate.* For the epic hero masters his destiny by being willing to die for honor. One is struck by the Freudian symmetry of these two definitions, one centering on the concerns of *eros*, the other of *thanatos*.

In regard to other works usually considered romances, a partial list of works from European literature that have influenced my thinking includes: *Three Greek Romances: Longus, Xenophon, Dio Chrysostom*, trans. M. Hades (Indianapolis; New York, 1953); Chrétien de Troyes, *Arthurian Romances*, trans. W. W. Comfort (London, 1973); *Medieval Romances*, ed. R. S. Loomis and L. H. Loomis (New York, 1957); Wolfram von Eschenbach, *Parzival*, trans. M. H. Mustard and C. E. Passafe (New York, 1961); Gottfried von Strassburg, *Tristan*, trans. A. T. Hatto (Harmondsworth, Middlesex, 1967); *The Death of King Arthur*, trans. J. Cable (Harmondsworth, Middlesex, 1971); *The Quest of the Holy Grail*, trans. P. Matarasso (Harmondsworth, Middlesex, 1969); L. Ariosto, *Orlando Furioso*, 2 vols., trans. B. Reynolds (Harmondsworth, Middlesex,

1975–77); T. Tasso, *Jerusalem Delivered*, trans. Edward Fairfax (New York, 1963).

38. In terms of narrative structure, I propose that the general sequence of events in romance follows this pattern. But the combination by which this pattern can be represented varies from story to story. Some follow it in a straightforward manner, others double it, or interlace it with similar patterns, or insert imbedded episodes following it. Moreover, it is useful here to keep in mind the distinction Roland Barthes offered between narrative *functions* and *indices*. Different periods and cultures will garb their characters and set their stories in different contexts, that is, use different indices; compare, for example, the royal, bourgeoisie, or lower-class protagonists and settings found in the *Nights* itself, or compare how a *Nights* noble is portrayed with how a medieval European knight is portrayed in one of the Arthurian romances. Settings and frames of reference, I would argue, differ, but narrative structure remains basically the same. See R. Barthes, "Structural Analysis of Narratives," in *Image, Music, Text*, trans. S. Heath (New York, 1977), 79–124, esp. 91–97. For two versions of Frye's conception of romance's patterns of action, see *Anatomy*, 198–203, and *The Secular Scripture*, 97 ff.

39. For the concept of "radicals of presentation," see Frye, *Anatomy*, 246–51.

40. See Guillén, *Literature as System*, 125–26 for the idea of a "genre without a poetics." It would be interesting to investigate related Islamic traditions, such as medieval Persian and Ottoman literatures, to see the extent that the tradition of elite romance produced such a poetics.

41. Cf. the Arabic: *fa-qālat al-maut wa-lā maʿṣiyat Allāh*, B. 1: 645.

42. Cf. the Arabic: *tadāraknī Allāh taʿāla bi-luṭf-hi*, B. 1: 646.

43. Cf. the Arabic: *fa-ḥarrim ʿalai-hi al-nār fī al-dunya wa-al-ākhira*. B. 1: 646.

44. This according to C. II and M; B. is confused here (B. 1: 404) although it has their ages right later (B. 1: 408).

45. The Persian also accepts because of al-Rabīʿ's offer of a generous reward (B. 1: 408). For the nurse's and the Caliph's sister's reactions, see B. 1: 410.

46. This differs from Frye, who portrays the movement as one from innocence to experience to return-to-innocence, without positing any moral or psychological development in characters. See Frye, *Anatomy*, 161–62 and 196–206; and idem, *The Secular Scripture*, 129–56.

47. B. 1: 404. This and all following translations are my own, except note 77.

48. The ʿUdhrī-love mania for chaste self-sacrifice that appears in ʿAlī ibn Bakkār and Shams al-Nahār is relatively rare in *Nights* romance, whose general tendency is toward telling of the ways its lovers stretch, or even break, the bounds of social propriety in order to ensure their love. For an analysis of ʿAlī ibn Bakkār, see Hamori's article cited in note 2.

49. B. 1: 133.

50. Cf., again, Ghānim's remark cited previously (see note 49).

51. For a reverse situation, see the story of Nūr al-Dīn ʿAlī, who gives away his beloved to the disguised Caliph Hārūn al-Rashīd in gratitude for receiving a plate of fried fish. He does get her back eventually, however.

52. This use of religion to justify otherwise reprehensible acts appears to be a tendency that developed in the *Nights*' Egyptian phase (cf. Oestrup, *Studier*, 133–34) and may be a result of anti-Christian sentiment that arose because of the Crusades. Other examples of this tendency appear in the stories of ʿAlāʾ al-Dīn Abū Shāmāt, The Man from Upper Egypt, ʿAlī Zaibaq, and Nūr al-Dīn and Maryam. Another story that walks the line between ribald and romance is that of Qamar al-Zamān and His Beloved, but this story uses what one would today term "male chauvinism" rather than religion to justify its protagonist's actions. Lane omits this tale from his translation because he found it morally "extremely objectionable." But perhaps it suffers just as much from the problem that it tries to justify romance acts with ribald standards and vice-versa.

53. This, by the way, is a favorite area of exploration of gothic romance. Cf., for example, Horace Walpole's *The Castle of Otranto*, and many of the stories of Poe.

54. Cf. Todorov's chapter "Narrative-Men" in his *The Poetics of Prose*, trans R. Howard (Ithaca, 1977), 53–79, for the other aspects of this trait.

55. For Frye's patterns of action, see the page citations in note 38. See also note 47. It would be interesting to attempt a Proppian functional analysis of the genre. For such an analysis of a *sīra* story that is also part of the *Nights*, see André Miquel, *Un conte des Mille et Une Nuits, Ajīb et Gharīb* (Paris, 1977), 245–90. Alternatively one could compare this dimension of the genre with patterns in mythic or heroic literature formulated by such scholars as Joseph Campbell in *The Hero with a Thousand Faces* (Princeton, 1949) or Lord Raghlan in *The Hero* (New York, 1956).

56. Cf., again, Barthes's concept of *indices* as remarked in note 38. It is noteworthy that if one accepts Oestrup's historical schematization of *Nights* stories (see *Studier*, 148–52), there seems to have been a continuous, although not absolute, fall in the social status of romance heroes over the course of time, from predominantly royal or aristocratic heroes, to bourgeoisie, to lower class. The extent to which this impression is indeed valid and, if so, the reasons why this should be the case, are subjects deserving further investigation.

57. For a useful analysis of the concept of "election" in romance, see E. Auerbach's comments on Chrétien de Troyes's *Yvain*, in *Mimesis: The Representation of Reality in Western Literature*, trans. W. R. Trask (Princeton, 1968), 123–42, esp. 135–37. It should be recognized here that I use the word protagonist throughout this essay according to the meaning preferred in Fowler's *Modern English Usage*, that is, as chief or principal actor(s). For me, this usually means the romantic couple. I have given the edge to the male component of the

pair because on the whole *Nights* stories do. But female "stars" live in the same ethical and narrative world and occasionally, as in the stories of Shahrazād, Tawaddud, and even ʿAzīz and ʿAzīza, dominate their male costars. It would be fascinating to study the genre from the point of view of its heroines and see the ways it indeed uses "point of view" to portray them and their male counterparts.

58. An interesting variation of this motif appears in the story of Abū Ḥasan, whose mother, of all people, manages to save him from his wastrel habits before his love affair and adventures even begin.

59. See Molan's article on Sinbād cited in note 2, 128. He relies on J. Campbell's *The Hero with a Thousand Faces*, esp. 49–94.

60. On the notion of "erring" in romance, see Parker, *Inescapable Romance*, 16–31. Such erring in the *Nights* tends to be conscious, unlike situations as in "The Story of the Merchant and the Jinni," where the merchant unwittingly finds himself thrust into circumstances unimagined just a moment before he ate his dates.

61. Frye, *Anatomy*, 186. Qamar al-Zamān uses *entrelacement* or interlacing of stories in a way that is relatively rare in *Nights* romances, although it is a typical feature of *sīra*. On the technique in Western romances, see Hough, *A Preface to the Faerie Queene*, 25–47 and Tuve, *Allegorical Imagery*, "Chapter Five," esp. 362–63 and 368.

62. From this point of view, Gerhardt's division of tales into love stories and fairy tales needs reexamination.

63. Abū Muḥammad the Lazy, for example, rises in the service of a foreign king on his own merits in the course of his quest. Ḥasan al-Baṣrī, Jānshāh, or ʿAlāʾ al-Dīn, employ doubling. Protagonists first win their beloveds through a combination of chance and magical aid, then they lose them, and then rewin them through a combination of determination and magical aid.

64. Arabic: *ʿibra li-man yaʿtabir*, a common formula in the *Nights*. See also note 68.

65. B. 1: 6. Ghazoul's remark that, "The *raison d'être* of the *sīra* is edification, that of the *Arabian Nights* is entertainment," however, is very much an oversimplification: *The Arabian Nights*, 87.

66. The tale of the Porter and the Three Ladies is one of the most eloquent examples of the *Nights*' ambiguous attitude toward curiosity. In general, curiosity is combined with interdiction, cf. the stories of al-Ḥasan al-Baṣrī, Jānshāh, Qamar al-Aqmār, and the Man Who Never Laughed.

67. B. 1: 31, 34, 41, 43.

68. B. 1: 2. The idea that the events to be unfolded should be viewed as *ʿibar* (sing. *ʿibra*): lessons, warnings, admonishments, is a theme common in medieval Arabic romance and *sīra*. M. has a different beginning that omits the word *ʿibra* altogether, but the mixture of entertainment and edification the book intends is still apparent:

> We inform this liberal gathering and the grand and distinguished lords that the purpose of writing this delightful and pleasant book is benefit for him who peruses it, for in it are many seemly stories and excellent significances for people of rank. From it one learns the science of speech and what happened to kings in early times in a full manner. I have named it the "Book of the Thousand and One Nights." It also includes lofty stories from which the listener can learn perspicacity so that no-one can trick him. He derives entertainment and pleasure during times of sadness in ages seduced by evil. (M. 1: 56)

69. B. 1: 34, 44.

70. B. 1: 51. M. (1: 219) ends the overall story thus: "They [the assembled ladies, mendicants, etc.] marvelled at the Caliph's generosity, good-judgement, and lenience. They learned the inner meaning of their cases and recorded their stories."

71. Bahrām at this point says to them, "'Lords, prepare to travel, and I shall travel with you.' The two were pleased with this and with his conversion to Islam. Then they wept bitterly, and he said, 'Lords, do not weep; your fate is to be reunited [with your beloveds] just as Niʿma and Nuʿm were reunited.' Then they said, 'What happened to Niʿma and Nuʿm?'" B. 1: 403–4.

72. Cf. Ghazoul, *The Arabian Nights*, 37, 43–44, 52, 71–72, 131; and Miquel, *Sept contes*, 28–31.

73. B. 1: 4. M. (1: 66) has a fuller version: "Mothers wept; and women, fathers, and mothers clamored and began to pray for misfortune for the King. They complained about him to the Creator of the Heavens, and they sought help from the Hearer of Cries and Answerer of Prayers."

74. B. 1: 5.

75. B. 1: 5.

76. The Breslau edition of the *Nights* apparently has a fuller version here, one that more explicitly supports the interpretation we offer. Since Burton uses this edition at this point, I rely on his "plain and literal" translation.

> When the King heard this, he wept and straining the boys to his bosom, said, "By Allah, O Shahrazad, I pardoned thee before the coming of these children, for that I found thee chaste, pure, ingenuous, and pious! I take the Almighty to witness against me that I exempt thee from aught that can harm thee." So she kissed his hands and feet and rejoiced with exceeding joy, saying "The Lord make thy life long and increase thee in dignity and majesty!" presently adding, "Thou marvelledst at that which befel thee on the part of women; yet there betided the Kings of the Chosroës before thee greater mishaps and more grievous than that which hath befallen thee, and indeed, I have set forth unto thee that which happened to Caliphs and Kings and others with their women, but the relation is longsome and hearkening groweth tedious, *and in this is all-sufficient warning for the man of wit and admonishment for the wise.*" Then she ceased to speak, and *when King Shahrayar heard her speech and profited by that which she said, he summoned up his reasoning powers and cleansed his heart and caused his understanding to revert* . . . [emphasis mine] (Burton, *The Book of a Thousand Nights and a Night*, 3634–35)

77. The tales of Abū Muḥammad the Lazy, the Porter and Three Ladies (the Three Mendicants come to Baghdad for the explicit purpose of relating their stories to him), Nūr al-Dīn ʿAlī, Ghānim ibn Ayyūb, and Muḥammad ibn ʿAlī are some examples of this.

78. Both the frequent criticism of romance that it is fantastic and attempts to defend aspects of the genre's "realism" (cf., for example, Tuve, *Allegorical Imagery*, 338–43) miss the point. Readers do not have to think that the genre's events are "realistic," nor would they wish to, perhaps; but, on the other hand, as we have tried to show in adopting certain points of Frye's portrayal of the genre, they must be prepared to suspend disbelief, or even temporarily grant romance's "world" greater "realism" than empirical reality. Those who refuse to do this deny themselves any enjoyment or edification the genre has to offer.

79. For recent analyses of Sindbād, see P. Molan as cited in note 2; Miquel, *Sept contes*, 79–109; Ghazoul, *The Arabian Nights*, 109–29. It is interesting that both B. and C. II's version of the story introduces a minor love interest in the story of the intrepid seaman's final voyage. Could this be a subconscious attempt on the part of a storyteller to move the story further into romance? One especially wonders this because the version of the *Nights* published in Calcutta (1814–18) by Sheikh Shirwanee, generally termed "Calcutta I," omits this love interest. More work on the manuscripts of the story would be needed to clear up this point.

80. For this reason Oestrup is mistaken when he classifies Khalīfa as a twin-tale of Ghānim ibn Ayyūb. The two stories obviously share certain events and characters, but their overall intent is radically different. Cf. Oestrup, *Studier*, 153.

81. *Qiṣṣat ʿAntar ibn Shaddād* (Cairo, 1961), vol. 2, book 12, 231.

82. It should be obvious from this essay as a whole that I find Ghazoul's interpretation of the *Nights* as *anti-sīra* unconvincing. For one thing, by choosing the story of ʿUmar ibn al-Nuʿmān as the basis for her presentation of *sīra* she makes an atypical *sīra* (and how it is atypical deserves study) her standard of comparison. But more fundamentally, *Nights* romance is, as I have argued here, a genre that exists unto itself, not the ironic reworking of *sīra*. Cf. Ghazoul, *The Arabian Nights*, 75–89.

83. Miquel has also noted the resort to deus ex machina and the overall change of tone in the story at this point, without, however, giving the interpretation of this event that I offer here, cf. *Sept contes*, 55–57. It is worth noting that larger, independent versions of both the story of ʿAlī Zaibaq and that of the adventures of Aḥmad al-Danaf and his cronies exist outside of the *Nights*. The first has been published in Cairo: *al-sīra al-kubrā li al-ʿĀʾiq al-Shāṭir al-muqaddam ʿAlī al-Zaibaq al-Maṣrī* (n.d.), see also John Rylands Library, Manchester, England, Arabic Manuscript Division, No. 662. For the story of Aḥmad al-Danaf, see the manuscript in the Arabic Division of the Staatsbibliothek, Berlin, Germany, We. 664–70. A useful recent study of this

genre in Arabic literature is Muḥammad al-Najjār's *Ḥikāyāt al-Shuṭṭār wa-al-ʿAyyārīn fī al-Turāth al-ʿArabī* (Kuwait, 1981).

84. B. 1: 708–9.

85. B. 2: 3.

86. This last point is only suggested here; it of course needs further development. But it is interesting that the genre of gothic romance, initiated by authors such as Ann Radcliffe and Horace Walpole, flourished in the latter half of the eighteenth century, while the historical novel emerged in the first half of the nineteenth with authors such as Scott and Hugo. These innovations, only a minor aspect of romanticism as a whole, obviously indicate new trends and interests among Europe's readers.

9 Narrative-Men

Tzvetan Todorov

"What is character but the determination of incident? What is incident but the illustration of character? What is either a picture or a novel that is *not* of character? What else do we seek in it and find in it?"

These questions occur in a famous essay by Henry James, *The Art of Fiction* (1884). Two general ideas emerge from them; the first concerns the unbreakable link between the different elements of narrative: action and character. There is no character except in action, no action independent of character. But surreptitiously, a second idea appears in the last lines: if the two are indissolubly linked, one is more important than the other nonetheless—character, that is, characterization, that is, psychology. Every narrative is "an illustration of character."

We rarely have occasion to observe so pure a case of egocentricity presenting itself as universality. Although James's theoretical ideal may have been a narrative in which everything is subservient to the psychology of the characters, it is difficult to ignore a whole tendency in literature, in which the actions are not there to "illustrate" character but in which, on the contrary, the characters are subservient to the action; where, moreover, the word "character" signifies something altogether different from psychological coherence or the description of idiosyncrasy. This tendency, of which the *Odyssey*, the *Decameron*, the *Arabian Nights*, and *The Saragossa Manu-*

Reprinted from Tzvetan Todorov, "Narrative-Men," in *The Poetics of Prose* (Oxford: Blackwell, 1977), 66–79. English translation © 1977 by Cornell University. Originally published in French as La Poetique de la Prose © 1971 by Editions du Seuil. Reprinted by permission of Georges Borchardt, Inc., and Blackwell Publishing, Ltd., for Editions du Seuil.

script are among the most famous examples, can be considered as a limit-case of literary *a-psychologism.*

Le us try to observe this situation more closely, taking the last two works as our examples.

We are usually satisfied, in speaking of such works as the *Arabian Nights*, with saying that they lack internal analysis of the characters, that there is no description of psychological states. But this way of describing a-psychologism is tautological. To characterize this phenomenon more accurately, we should start from a certain image of narrative movement when narrative obeys a causal structure. We might then represent each moment of the narrative in the form of a simple proposition, which enters into a relation of consecution (noted by +) or a relation of consequence (noted by →) with the propositions preceding and following it.

The first opposition between the narrative James extols and that of the *Arabian Nights* can be illustrated as follows: if there is a proposition "X sees Y," the important thing for James is X; for Scheherazade, Y. Psychological narrative regards each action as a means of access to the personality in question, as an expression if not a symptom. Action is not considered in itself, it is *transitive* with regard to its subject. A-psychological narrative, on the contrary, is characterized by intransitive actions: action is important in itself and not as an indication of this or that character trait. The *Arabian Nights* derive, we might say, from a *predicative* literature: the emphasis will always fall on the predicate and not on the subject of the proposition. The best-known example of this effacement of the grammatical subject is the story of Sinbad the Sailor. Even Odysseus emerges more clearly characterized from the adventures than Sinbad. We know that Odysseus is cunning, prudent, and so forth. Nothing of the kind can be said about Sinbad, whose narrative (though told in the first person) is impersonal; we should note it not as "X sees Y" but as "Y is seen." Only the coldest travel narrative can compete with Sinbad's tales in impersonality—though we have Sterne's *Sentimental Journey* to remind us that not all travel narratives are cold.

The suppression of psychology occurs here within the narrative proposition; it continues even more successfully in the field of relations among propositions. A certain character trait provokes an action; but there are two different ways of doing this. We might speak of an *immediate* causality as opposed to a *mediated* causality. The first would be of the type "X is brave → X challenges the monster." In the second, the appearance of the first proposition would have no immediate consequence, but in the course of the narrative X would appear as someone who acted bravely. This is a diffused, discontinuous causality, which is expressed not by a single action but by secondary aspects of a series of actions, often remote from one another.

But the *Arabian Nights* does not acknowledge this second causality. No sooner are we told that the sultana's sisters are jealous than they substitute a dog, a cat, and a piece of wood for her children. Kassim is greedy; therefore he goes looking for money. All character traits are immediately causal; as soon as they appear, they provoke an action. Moreover the distance between the psychological trait and the action it provokes is minimal; rather than an opposition between quality and action, we are concerned with an opposition between two aspects of the action, durative and punctual or iterative and noniterative. Sinbad likes to travel (character trait) → Sinbad takes a trip (action): the distance between the two tends toward a total reduction.

Another way of observing the reduction of this distance is to inquire if the same attributive proposition can have, in the course of the narrative, several different consequences. In a nineteenth-century novel, the proposition "X is jealous of Y" can lead to "X withdraws from society," "X commits suicide," "X courts Y," "X hurts Y." In the *Arabian Nights*, there is only one possibility: "X is jealous of Y → X hurts Y." The stability of the relationship between the two propositions deprives the first of any autonomy, of any intransitive meaning. The implication tends to become an identity. If the consequences are more numerous, the first proposition will have a greater value of its own.

Here we touch on a curious property of psychological causality. A character trait is not simply the cause of an action, nor simply its effect: it is both at once, just as action is. X kills his wife because he is cruel; but he is cruel because he kills his wife. Causal analysis of narrative does not refer back to a first and immutable origin, which would be the meaning and law of subsequent images. In other words, in its pure state, we must be able to grasp this causality outside of linear time. The cause is not a primordial *before*, it is only one element of the "cause-and-effect" couple, in which neither is thereby superior to the other.

Hence it would be more accurate to say that psychological causality duplicates the causality of events (of actions) rather than that it takes its place. Actions provoke one another, and as a by-product a psychological cause-and-effect coupling appears, but on a different level. Here we can raise the question of psychological coherence; such psychological by-products may or may not form a system. The *Arabian Nights* again affords us an extreme example, in the tale of Ali Baba. The wife of Kassim, Ali Baba's brother, is anxious about her husband's disappearance. "She wept all night long." The next day, Ali Baba brings home the pieces of his brother's body and says, by way of consolation: "Sister-in-law, your suffering is all the greater because you had so little reason to expect it. Though the harm is past remedy, if something is yet capable of consoling you, I offer to unite what little God has granted me to whatever you possess, by marrying you." The sister-in-law's reaction: "She did not refuse the match, but rather regarded it as a reasonable cause of consolation. Drying her tears, which she had begun to shed in abundance, stifling the shrill cries customary to women who have lost their husbands, she gave Ali Baba sufficient evidence that she would accept his offer." In this fashion Kassim's wife moves from despair to joy. Similar examples are countless.

Obviously, by contesting the existence of a psychological coherence in such a case we enter the realm of common sense. There is doubtless another psychology in which these two consecutive actions form a unity. But the *Arabian Nights* belong to the realm of common sense (of folklore), and the abundance of examples suffices to convince us that we are not concerned here with another psychology, nor even with an antipsychology, but with an a-psychology.

Character is not always, as James claims, the determination of incident, nor does every narrative consist of "the illustration of character." Then what *is* character? The *Arabian Nights* gives us a very clear answer, which is repeated and confirmed by *The Saragossa Manuscript:* a character is a potential story that is the story of his life. Every new character signifies a new plot. We are in the realm of narrative-men.

This phenomenon profoundly affects the structure of narrative.

Digression and Embedding

The appearance of a new character invariably involves the interruption of the preceding story, so that a new story, the one that explains the "now I am here" of the new character, may be told to us. A second story is enclosed within the first; this device is called *embedding*.

This is obviously not the only excuse for embedding. The *Arabian Nights* already affords us a number of others: for example, in "The Fisherman and the Genie," the embedded stories serve as arguments. The fisherman justifies his pitilessness toward the genie by the story of Duban; within the latter story, the king defends his position by the story of the jealous man and the parrot; the vizier defends his by the story of the prince and the ghoul. If the characters remain the same in the embedded story and in the embedding one, this kind of motivation becomes pointless. In the "Story of the Two Jealous Sisters," the narrative of the kidnapping of the sultan's children from the palace and of their recognition by the sultan encloses the narrative of the acquisition of the magic objects; temporal succession is the only motivation. But the presence of narrative-men is certainly the most striking form of embedding.

The formal structure of embedding coincides (nor is such a coincidence an accident) with that of a syntactic form, a particular case of subordination, which in fact modern linguistics call *embedding*. To reveal this structure, let us take a German example, since German syntax permits much more spectacular examples of embedding than English or French:

> *Derjenige, der den Mann, der den Pfahl, der auf der Brücke, der auf dem Weg, der nach Worms führt, liegt, steht, umgeworfen hat, anzeigt, bekommt eine Belohnung.*

> Whoever identifies the one who upset the post which was placed on the bridge which is on the road which goes to Worms will get a reward.

In the German sentence, the appearance of a noun immediately provokes a subordinate clause that, so to speak, tells its story; but since this second clause also contains a noun, it requires in its turn a subordinate clause, and so on, until an arbitrary interruption, at which point each of the interrupted clauses is completed one after the other. The narrative of embedding has precisely the same structure, the role of the noun being played by the character: each new character involves a new story.

The *Arabian Nights* contain examples of embedding quite as dizzying. The record seems to be held by the narrative, which offers us the story of the bloody chest. Here

Scheherazade tells that
Jaafer tells that
the tailor tells that
the barber tells that
his brother (and he has six brothers) tells that . . .

The last story is a story to the fifth degree; but it is true that the two first degrees are entirely forgotten and no longer have any role to play. Which is not the case in one of the stories of *The Saragossa Manuscript*, where

Alfonso tells that
Avadoro tells that
Don Lope tells that
Busqueros tells that
Frasquetta tells that . . .

and where all the degrees, except for the first, are closely linked and incomprehensible if isolated from one another.

Even if the embedded story is not directly linked to the embedding story (by identity of characters), characters can pass from one story to the other. Thus the barber intervenes in the tailor's story (he saves the hunchback's life). As for Frasquetta, she crosses all the intermediary degrees to appear in Avadoro's story (she is the mistress of the Knight of Toledo); so does Busqueros. Such shifts from one degree to the next have a comic effect in *The Saragossa Manuscript*.

Embedding reaches its apogee with the process of self-embedding, that is, when the embedding story happens to be, at some fifth or sixth degree, embedded by itself. This "laying bare of the device" is present in the *Arabian Nights*, as Borges has pointed out: "No [interpolation] is more disturbing than that of the six hundred and second night, most magical of all. On this night, the king hears from the queen's mouth her own story. He hears the initial story, which includes all the others, which—monstrously—includes itself. . . . If the queen continues, the king will sit still and listen forever to the truncated version of the *Arabian Nights*, henceforth infinite and circular. . . ." Nothing will ever again escape the narrative world, spreading over the whole of experience.

The importance of embedding is indicated by the dimensions of the embedded stories. Can we even call them digressions when they are longer than the story from which they digress? Can we regard as an addition or as a gratuitous embedding all the tales of the *Arabian Nights* because they are embedded in Scheherazade's tale? The same is true of *The Saragossa Manusrcipt:* whereas the basic story seemed to be Alfonso's, actually it is the loquacious Avadoro's tales that spread over more than three-quarters of the book.

But what is the internal significance of embedding, why are all these means assembled to give it so much emphasis? The structure of narrative provides the answer: embedding is an articulation of the most essential property of all narrative. For the embedding narrative is the *narrative of a narrative.* By telling the story of another narrative, the first narrative achieves its fundamental theme and at the same time is reflected in this image of itself. The embedded narrative is the image of that great abstract narrative of which all the others are merely infinitesimal parts as well as the image of the embedding narrative that directly precedes it. To be the narrative of a narrative is the fate of all narrative that realizes itself through embedding.

The *Arabian Nights* reveal and symbolize this property of narrative with a particular clarity. It is often said that folklore is characterized by the repetition of the same story; and indeed it is not rare, in one of the *Nights*, for the same adventure to be related twice if not more often. But this repetition has a specific function that is unknown: it serves not only to reiterate the same adventure but also to introduce the narrative that a character makes of it. Most of the time it is this narrative that counts for the subsequent development of the plot. It is not the adventures Queen Badur survives that win her King Armanos's pardon, but the narrative of them she recounts. If Turmente cannot further his plot, it is because he is not permitted to tell his story to the caliph. Prince Firuz wins the heart of the Princess of Bengal not by having his adventure but by telling it to her. The act of narrating is never, in the *Arabian Nights*, a transparent act; on the contrary, it is the mainspring of the action.

Loquacity and Curiosity—Life and Death

The speech-act receives, in the *Arabian Nights*, an interpretation that leaves no further doubt as to its importance. If all the characters incessantly tell stories, it is because this action has received a supreme consecration: narrating equals living. The most obvious example is that of Scheherazade herself, who lives exclusively to the degree that she can continue to tell stories; but this situation is ceaselessly repeated within the tale. The dervish has incurred a genie's wrath, but by telling him the story of the envious man, he wins pardon. The slave has committed a crime; to save his life, his master, as the caliph tells him, has but one recourse: "If you tell me a story more amazing than this one, I shall pardon your slave. If not, I shall have him put to death." Four persons are accused of the murder of a hunchback; one of them, the inspector of kitchens, tells the king: "O fortunate King, will you give us the gift of life if I tell you the adventure which befell me yesterday, before I met the hunchback who was put into my room by stealth? It is surely more amazing than this man's story." "If it is as you say," replies the king, "I shall grant all four of you your lives."

Narrative equals life; absence of narrative, death. If Scheherazade finds no more tales to tell, she will be beheaded. This is what happens to the physician Duban when he is threatened by death: he asks the king permission to tell the story of the crocodile; permission is not granted, and Duban perishes. But he is revenged by the same means, and the image of this vengeance is one of the finest in all the *Arabian Nights:* he offers the pitiless king a book to read while the decapitation is taking place. The executioner does his work; Duban's severed head speaks:

> "O king, you may look through the book."
>
> The king opened the book. He found its pages stuck together. Putting his finger in his mouth, he wet it with saliva and turned the first page. Then he turned the second, and those that followed. He continued in this fashion, for the pages parted only with difficulty, until he came to the seventh leaf. He looked at the page and saw nothing written there.
>
> "Physician," he said, "I see nothing written on this leaf."
>
> "Keep turning the pages," replied the head.
>
> He opened more leaves, and still found nothing. Scarcely a moment had elapsed, when the drug entered his body; the book was impregnated with poison. Then he took a step, staggered, and fell to the ground.

The blank page is poisoned. The book that tells no story kills. The absence of narrative signifies death.

Consider, after such a tragic illustration, this pleasanter version of the power of nonnarrative. A dervish tells every passerby how to gain possession of a certain talking bird, but all have failed and been turned into black stones. Princess Parizade is the first to capture the bird, and she releases the other less fortunate candidates. "All sought to find the dervish as they passed by, to thank him for his welcome and his counsel, which they had found sincere if not salutary; but he had died and none could discover whether it had been of old age or because he was no longer necessary to teach the way to the conquest of the three things over which Princess Parizade had just triumphed." The man is merely a narrative; once the narrative is no longer necessary, he can die. It is the narrator who kills him, for he no longer has a function.

Finally, the imperfect narrative also equals, in such circumstances, death. Hence the inspector of kitchens who claimed that his story was better than the hunchback's ends it by addressing the king: "Such is the amazing tale I wanted to tell you yesterday and which I recount today in all its details. Is it not more astounding than the hunchback's adventure?" "No, it is not, and your boast bears no relation to the truth," answered the King of China, "I must have all four of you hanged."

Absence of narrative is not the only counterpart of narrative-as-life; to want to hear a narrative is also to run mortal risks. If loquacity saves from death, curiosity leads to it. This law underlies the plot of one of the richest tales, "The Porter and the Ladies." Three young ladies of Baghdad receive several unknown men in their house; they stipulate only one condition in return for the pleasures they promise to bestow: "about anything you are going to see, ask no explanation." But what the men see is so strange that they ask the three ladies to tell their story. No sooner has this desire been expressed than the ladies call in their slaves: "Each slave chose his man, rushed upon him, and cast him to the ground, striking him with the flat of his sword." The men must be killed because their request for a narrative, their curiosity, is liable to the death penalty. How do they escape? Thanks to the curiosity of their executioners. For one of the ladies says: "I shall give each of them permission to continue on his way, on condition that he tell his story, recounting the series of adventures which led to his visiting us here. If they refuse, you will cut off their heads." The listener's curiosity, when it does not mean his own death, restores life to the condemned men, who in return can escape only on condition that they tell a story. Finally, a third reversal: the caliph, who was present in disguise among the guests of the three ladies, invites them the next day to his palace; he forgives them everything, but on one condition; they must tell. . . . The characters of this book are obsessed by stories; the cry of the *Arabian Nights* is not "Your money or your life!" but "Your story or your life!"

This curiosity is the source of both countless narratives and incessant dangers. The dervish can live happily in the company of the ten young men, all blind in the right eye, on one condition: "ask no indiscreet question about our infirmity or our condition." But the question is asked, and peace is at an end. To discover the answer, the dervish ventures into a magnificent palace; there he lives like a king, surrounded be forty lovely ladies. One day they depart, telling him, if he would remain in such happiness, not to enter a certain room. They warn him: "We fear you will not be able to protect yourself against that indiscreet curiosity which will be the cause of your downfall." Naturally, faced with the choice between happiness and curiosity, the dervish chooses curiosity. Just as Sinbad, for all his misfortunes, sets out again after each voyage: he wants life to tell him stories, one narrative after the other.

The palpable result of such curiosity is the *Arabian Nights.* If its characters had preferred happiness, the book would not exist.

Narrative: Supplier and Supplied

For the characters to be able to live, they must narrate. Thus the first narrative subdivides and multiplies into a thousand and one nights of narratives. Now let us attempt to take the opposite point of view, no longer that of the embedding narrative but that of the embedded narrative, and inquire: why does the embedded narrative need to be included within another narrative? How can we account for the fact that it is not self-sufficient but requires an extension, a context in which it becomes simply a part of another narrative?

If we consider the narrative in this way, not as enclosing other narratives but as being enclosed by them, a curious property is revealed. Each narrative seems to have something excessive, a supplement that remains outside the closed form produced by the development of the plot. At the same time, and for this very reason, this something-more, proper to the narrative, is also something-less. The supplement is also a lack; in order to supply this lack created by the supplement, another narrative is necessary. Hence the narrative of the ungrateful king who puts Duban to death after the latter has saved his life has something more than this narrative itself; besides, it is for this reason, with a view to this supplement, that the fisherman tells the story, a supplement that can be summed up in a formula: never pity the ungrateful. The supplement must be integrated into another story; hence it becomes the simple argument that the fisherman employs when he becomes involved in an adventure similar to Duban's, with the genie. But the story of the fisherman and the genie also has a supplement that requires another story; and there is no reason for this process to stop anywhere. The attempt to supply is therefore vain—there will always be a supplement awaiting a narrative-to-come.

This supplement takes several forms in the *Arabian Nights.* One of the most familiar is that of the argument, as in the preceding example; the narrative becomes a means of convincing the interlocutor. Further, at higher levels of embedding, the supplement is transformed into a simple verbal formula, a sentence or proverb meant to be used by the characters as much as by the readers. Finally a wider integration of the reader is also possible (though it is not characteristic of the *Arabian Nights*). Behavior provoked by reading is also a supplement, and a law is established: The more this supplement is consumed within the narrative, the less reaction this narrative provokes on the part of its reader. We may weep when reading *Manon Lescaut*, but not when reading the *Arabian Nights*.

Here is an example of a one-sentence proverb or moral. Two friends argue about the origin of wealth: Is it enough to have some money to begin with? There follows a story illustrating one of the positions being defended, then comes a story that illustrates the other; and at the end, a conclusion is reached: "Money is not always a sure means of amassing more and becoming rich."

As in the case of psychological cause and effect, we must here conceive of this logical relation outside of linear time. The narrative precedes or follows the maxim, or both at once. Similarly, in the *Decameron*, certain novellas are created to illustrate a metaphor (for example, "scraping the bottom of the barrel") and at the same time they create that metaphor. It is pointless to ask today whether the metaphor engendered the narrative, or the narrative engendered the metaphor. Borges has even suggested an inverted explanation of the existence of the entire *Arabian Nights:* "This invention [the stories Scheherazade tells] . . . is apparently posterior to the title and was imagined in order to justify it." The question of origins need not be raised; we are beyond the origin and unable to conceive of it. The supplied narrative is no more original than the supplying narrative, nor vice versa. Each narrative refers us to another, in a series of reflections that can end only by becoming perpetual—for example, by self-embedding.

Such is the incessant proliferation of narratives in this marvelous story-machine, the *Arabian Nights*. Every narrative must make its own narration explicit; but to do so a new narrative must appear in which this narration is no more than a part of the story. Hence the narrating story always becomes a narrated story as well, in which the new story is reflected and finds its own image. Furthermore, every narrative must create new ones—within itself, in order that its characters can go on living, and outside itself, so that the supplement it inevitably produces may be consumed there. The many translators of the *Arabian Nights* all seem to have yielded to the power of this narrative machine. None has been content with a simple translation merely faithful to the original; each translator has added and suppressed stories (which is also a way of creating new narratives, narrative always being a selection); a secondary speech-act, translation represents in itself a new tale that no longer awaits its narrator. Borges has told a part of this tale in his "Translators of the *Arabian Nights*."

There are, then, so many reasons for narrative never to stop that we cannot help wondering: What happened before the first narrative? And what will happen after the last? The *Arabian Nights* have not failed to provide an answer, ironic though it may be, for those who want to know the "before" and the "after." The first story, Scheherazade's, begins with these words, meaningful on every level (but one should not open the book to look for them—it should be possible to guess what they are, so appropriate are they to their place): "It is told . . ." No need to search out the origin of narrative in time—it is time that originates in narrative. And if before the first narrative there is an "it *has been* told," after the last there will be an "it *will be* told." For the story to stop, we must be told that the marveling caliph orders it to be inscribed in letters of gold in the annals of the realm; or again that "this story . . . spread and was told everywhere down to the last detail."

10 An Analysis of the "Tale of the Three Apples" from *The Thousand and One Nights*

Roger Allen

> The great scarcity of copies . . . is, I believe, the reason why recitations of them are no longer heard; even fragments of them are with difficulty procured; and when a complete copy of "The Thousand and One Nights" is found, the price demanded for it is too great for a reciter to have it in his power to pay.

To a Western audience that is generally aware of the influence of *The 1001 Nights* on Europe at the time of its translation into French and thereafter, the above quotation from Edward Lane's *Manners and Customs of the Modern Egyptians* may come as somewhat of a surprise.[1] Until quite recently interest in this world-famous collection of narrative has tended to focus on the origins of the work, the various recensions, and other essentially external features. Indeed, if we look at scholarship written in Arabic about the narrative tradition during the earlier period, we discover that the same situation applies with regard to other genres such as the *maqāma* and even the more philosophical tales of Abū 'l-ʿAlāʾ al-Maʿarrī and Ibn Ṭufayl. Studies of these works do, of course, exist, but if they venture any comments of a literary nature, they remain very much within the framework of a literary-historical approach. As a result there is a

Reprinted from Roger Allen, "An Analysis of the 'Tale of the Three Apples' from *The Thousand and One Nights*," in *Logos Islamikos: Studia Islamica in Honorem Georgii Michaelis Wickens*, ed. Roger M. Savory and Dionisius A. Agius (Toronto: Pontificial Institute of Mediaeval Studies, 1984), 51–60. Reprinted by permission of the publisher.

shortage of material on which to make any judgments concerning what one might call a tradition of narrative or of "fictionality" in Arabic literature before the modern period.

More recently a number of scholars have begun to analyze *The 1001 Nights* collection in particular as being something more than "dialect non-literature," availing themselves among other things of the advances in the study of epic, folktale, and myth during the course of this century.[2] A variety of studies has appeared: of the larger ones, we would cite those of Gerhardt, al-Qalamāwī and Ghazoul, and in shorter form the contributions of Hamori and Molan.[3] In a recent work on a contemporary narrative genre, the novel, the present writer saw fit to question the views of those who would attribute the emergence of fictional genres in the modern Arab world entirely to Western influence.[4] It was suggested that, in view of our relatively scant knowledge about prose narrative in the earlier period, such a judgment was rash. Furthermore, the interest expressed by a number of writers and critics in the earlier tradition since the 1967 conflicts suggests that, while the influence of the West may indeed have been strong at certain points during the long process known as the *nahḍa*, or renaissance, the indigenous tradition was never completely supplanted and has indeed emerged with great vigor in recent times. All of which points to the notion that an investigation of the nature of narrative in the earlier period might not only be of interest per se but also provide a framework within which to assess new experiments in fiction being tried today and indeed to reexamine the development of modern Arabic fiction as a whole. As an illustration of a narrative that seemed suitable for such analysis, I suggested "Ḥikāyat al-ṣabiyya 'l-maqtūla" ("The Tale of the Murdered Young Woman," usually known as "The Tale of the Three Apples") from *The 1001 Nights.* In the context of this tribute to a great scholar who has devoted much of his attention to the process of analyzing and making accessible to others many of the riches of Middle Eastern literature, I would now like to make a contribution to this process by attempting an analysis of this short tale.

"The Tale of the Three Apples" is a quintessential murder mystery.[5] It begins with the Caliph Hārūn al-Rashīd deciding to go down into the city in disguise with his *wazīr*, Jaʿfar al-Barmakī, and his eunuch, Masrūr. This is, of course, a familiar theme to readers of the Hārūn tales in the *1001 Nights* collection, providing as it does an obvious means whereby "local color" can be provided to tales set in ᶜAbbāsid Baghdad, or, as Hārūn himself puts it in the tale itself, in order to ensure that his people are being justly treated by those officials whom be has appointed to office. As we will see, the events of this story make Hārūn's pronouncement not a little ironic, but for the time being we may content ourselves with the observation that the Caliph's attitude to the entire exercise is well summed up by the description of his party as "going down" (*nazala*) into the city and later of "going up" to the palace. One is reminded of the terminology of Oxford and Cambridge universities.

The first person whom the caliphal party meets is a shaykh who is bemoaning both the failure of mankind to appreciate the breadth of his learning and his own need to fish in the River Tigris in order to feed his family. Hārūn suggests to this shaykh-fisherman that he try fishing again, this time on his—Hārūn's—luck. But instead of a fish, the old man brings to shore a heavy box. Paying off the shaykh, the Caliph "goes up" to his palace carrying the heavy box and full of curiosity. The shaykh's role in the tale is at an end; this is not to be a story about the employment crises in academe.

When the box is opened, the Caliph discovers to his horror that it contains the dissected body of a beautiful woman. His horror is occasioned as much by the realization that, as ruler, he will be called to account for this crime in the next world as it is by the fact of the murder itself. He soon shifts the responsibility on to Jaᶜfar who is allowed three days to find the murderer. Unable to achieve this impossible task, Jaᶜfar (along with forty of his relatives) is taken out to be crucified; the populace of Baghdad is invited to watch the spectacle. At the crucial moment, a culprit comes forward, but this immediately poses yet another problem in that not one but two people insist that they committed the murder. One is a comely young man while the other is old. The young man then explains that the whole episode is a terrible mistake. He has obtained three apples for his sick wife at great expense of energy and money. When he sees a black slave carrying an apple and asks him where it came from, the young man is horrified to hear the slave tell him that he got it from his girlfriend while her husband was away. Suspecting his wife, the young man asks to see the three apples. She is unable to find the third one. In a rage he kills her, cuts her up and throws her body into the Tigris. Only later does he discover that his own son has taken the apple without his wife's knowledge and that the slave has snatched it from the boy.

Once again Jaʿfar is given an impossible task, namely to find this slave. Despairing of carrying out the Caliph's orders, he is again saved in the nick of time when he discovers an apple in his little daughter's pocket when bidding her a last fond farewell. Asking her where the apple came from, he discovers that the culprit slave is none other than his own slave, Rīḥān. The mystery is thus finally solved, and Hārūn orders that the remarkable string of events be recorded. For, within the framework of the telling of stories each one more remarkable than the last, this one is certainly regarded as extraordinary.

The above synopsis of the events is, of course, merely the bare bones of the tale. Even so, it clearly illustrates one of the principal features of any murder mystery, namely the sequencing of events. Any murder story that introduced the fact of the murder on its final pages or that provided a solution soon after its beginning would fail in one area that is crucial to the success of this particular subgenre: the maintenance of ironic tension for the maximum amount of time possible. Indeed some writers of this type of fiction will challenge their readers relatively late in the narrative sequence. If we put a little flesh on the bare bones of "The Tale of the Three Apples," we will see that this tension is maintained in a most skillful manner and that the process involves some novel twists. To be sure, the box with the murdered girl in it is found right at the beginning of the narrative (that is, once the background of the Hārūn and Jaʿfar segment has been provided), but in this tale we do not have to wait to the end to find out who the murderer is. Not only are Jaʿfar and Hārūn presented with a "choice" of two confessed murderers, but the actual culprit clearly identifies himself well before the conclusion of the tale. It is not so much a matter of "whodunnit?"—which is clear enough, but of who is responsible for the murder's occurrence. This leads in turn from a consideration of responsibility to that of justice. And it is here that the real irony arises through the palpable disparity between Hārūn's laudable aims expressed at the beginning of the tale and his demeanor throughout the course of events.

The reader's curiosity as to who killed the girl, who she is, how long she had been dead, and which of the two men—her husband or her father—committed the murder, is satisfied by the contents of the husband's own narrative. But throughout the tale other elements serve to maintain the tension. In the first place, the two deadlines that Hārūn gives to Jaʿfar build up a tension of their own; the first is relieved by the appearance of the husband and father of the girl just as Jaʿfar is about to be crucified; the second by the discovery that his own slave is in fact "responsible" for the entire tragedy through the theft of the apple and his own duplicity. And, if we read on beyond the end of the tale, we discover that this slave manages to escape punishment for his actions: Jaʿfar persuades the Caliph to forgive him in return for listening to the tale of Nūr al-Dīn and Shams al-Dīn. In the cause of the continuing stream of narrative, all loose ends have been conveniently tied up.

Beyond these features that seem to suggest a careful sequencing of events and their resolution so as to provide for the maximum of tension, there is another aspect of this tale that it shares with many others in *The 1001 Nights*, namely that of frames. Molan has treated some other tales from the collection in this way, and many of his points are applicable here too.[6] The outermost frame here is, of course, that of Shahrazād and Shahrayār. The situation in this frame is itself fraught with violence. In telling the vast collection of tales, Shahrazād is trying to prevent the King from killing her (as he has killed many virgin girls before her) as an act of revenge for his wife's infidelity with a black slave. In this context, the fact that a black slave in this story so close to the beginning of the collection is directly responsible for the tragic death of the girl is obviously of considerable significance.

It is Shahrazād, the potential victim of the violence of the King in the first frame of the tale, who narrates the contents of the second frame, namely the activities of Hārūn al-Rashīd and his retinue. Besides introducing a series of events, this frame provides the tale with authenticity of both place and character. The setting is Baghdad (as is the case with the tales of what Gerhardt terms "the Hārūn cycle"),[7] and this is emphasized by the use of the River Tigris as the initial focal point of the Caliph's attentions. We also have two authentic characters: Hārūn al-Rashīd and Jaʿfar. By "authentic" here I imply that two such people are familiar to students of the history of this period, but also that the means by which Ja^cfar al-Barmakī actually met his end at the hands of Hārūn—with his severed head impaled upon one of the bridges of Baghdad—seems fully reflected in this particular tale.[8] In this frame too the atmosphere is full of violence. Hārūn addresses his *wazīr* as "dog of a wazīr" and then proceeds to threaten him twice with a grotesquely public death. When Jaʿfar presents the Caliph with the dilemma of two men confessing to the murder, the latter's solution is to kill them both. He further expresses his amazement to the young man that he should have confessed without being tortured first.

Jaʿfar on the other hand emerges in a different light. He is portrayed for us by the narrator of the tale as a long-suffering servant of the Caliph—apparently a sine qua non for the office—although we must admire his one gesture of defiance when, knowing that he is to be crucified for failing to find the girl's killer, he asks his master how he is supposed to be able to "know the unseen." Jaʿfar is portrayed as a family man who "loves his little daughter more than all his other children," while to the young man who confesses to his wife's murder he is "prince of princes and haven of the poor."[9] Each time that he is charged with the impossible task of finding a particular person in Baghdad, the narrator gives us a glimpse of his thoughts through a short interior monologue, a process that arouses our sympathy, particularly when juxtaposed with the irascible and petulant comments of the Caliph.

As we noted above, this second frame begins with the discovery of the dead woman and is therefore relatively late in the time frame of the complete story. But, apart from the three-day deadlines that Jaʿfar is given, it is rather short on references to time. For that reason it stands in considerable contrast to the third and innermost frame in which the young man relates the sorry tale of how he came to kill his beloved wife. Almost every event is accompanied by a mention of when it occurred during the month or of how long it lasted. We are thus given not only the answer as to who killed the girl (although the reason for the grotesque violence with which it is done is never explained) but also a time frame for the entire tale. No sooner has the young man recounted how he and his father-in-law mourned his wife for five days and are still sorrowing "until this very day" than the nineteenth night of the 1001 is over, and the narrator takes us back through the three frames in three sentences.

This framing technique whereby one story is embedded within another is a familiar one within *The 1001 Nights*, but in this case we may observe that it illustrates clearly the interconnections between the different situations in the story and points toward certain moral conclusions that might be drawn. There is firstly the parallel between the irascibility of Shahrayār and Hārūn al-Rashīd: that of the latter is amply demonstrated in the story itself, and of the former implicit in Shahrazād's very situation. Between the outermost frame and the innermost we may point to the theme of wifely infidelity, surely a touchy topic within the context of Shahrayār's feelings on the subject. The fact that the villain in the piece is a black slave only serves to amplify the similarities, while from the point of view of structure it also links the Hārūn frame with the innermost, in that the black slave proves to be Rīḥān, a member of Jaʿfar's own household. In contrast with the scheming, deceit, and violence that punctuate this tale, the fact that two children are the agents of revealing the truth is surely not coincidental; even here violence intrudes in that the murdered girl's son is afraid that she may beat him once she discovers that the apple has been stolen. In a word, this tale might carry a subtitle "The Wages of Violence," and in that it comes so close to the beginning of the collection it may perhaps be viewed as a none-too-subtle commentary by Shahrazād herself on the very situation in which she finds herself.

Having now considered some of the structural details of the tale, let us look at the way in which some of the effects are achieved, particularly insofar as they concern language. We have already alluded to the narrator's use of interior monologue to give a more intimate picture of the character of Jaʿfar. The reader's view is also manipulated in other ways, and no more so than through the means of describing the major participants in the tale. Those with a purely peripheral role are sparsely described: the learned fisherman at the beginning is said merely to have "a net and basket on his head and a stick in his hand," while the father of the murdered girl is simply "an old man." By contrast, the young man who is the girl's husband and killer is accorded the Hollywood treatment: "a young man, handsome and in spotless clothes; radiant of visage, with gorgeous eyes, gleaming forehead, rosy cheeks, a light down of beard, and a mole on his cheek looking like a grain of ambergris." This aspect is perhaps best seen in the treatment of the girl herself. At first her description is limited to the fact that she looks "like a silver ingot." At this point the narrator is more interested in the theme of the Caliph's anger and its effect on Ja^cfar than on the personage or description of the victim herself. Later on however, when the husband relates how he came to kill her, she is described again. Once more the opportunity is used for a particular purpose; the young man characterizes his wife as an idealized life-partner, almost a stereotype: "This girl is my wife and my cousin too. This old man is her father and my uncle. She was a virgin when I married her and through God's will she gave me three sons. She used to love me and serve me, and I have never found any wrong in her." All of which makes the savagery with which he eventually kills her so seemingly inexplicable.

Our narrator then is at some pains to make his principals conform to his overall purpose. The same can be said of more detailed aspects of language. Each frame is enlivened with a generous amount of dialogue, but there are also subtle ways in which the frames are differentiated. Characteristically, the story told by Shahrazād is dotted with formulaic phrases often in *saj*ᶜ (rhyming prose), a stylistic feature beloved of Arabic prose from earliest times. On the other hand, it is surely no coincidence that the young man's story (the innermost frame) contains the use of the colloquial word "ḥaṭṭayt-hā" ("I put her"), which may well reflect the Egyptian period of the collection's compilation but may also be seen as an attempt to lend a popular touch to the inner narrative.

My aim in the preceding analysis has been to show that this tale is an interesting fusion of characteristics of traditional narrative and of features that modern critics might search for in a piece of contemporary fiction. It is, in a word, a finely crafted mystery story.

Returning to the theme with which I began, litterateurs in the Arab world showed an interest in *The 1001 Nights* from the relatively early period in the modern renaissance. For example, Mārūn al-Naqqāsh (1871–55) wrote a play titled *Abū 'l-Ḥasan al-Mughaffal*, and he was closely followed by Abū Khalīl al-Qabbānī in Syria with *Hārūn al-Rashīd ma*ᶜ*a Ghānim ibn Ayyūb wa Qūt al-Qulūb.*[10] Within the realm of drama in recent times, Alfred Faraj and Saᶜdallāh Wannūs (to name just two figures) have made successful use of tales from *The 1001 Nights* to create dramas of considerable contemporary import and popularity.[11] Some contributors to contemporary fiction are also scholars within the field of traditional narratives: we should mention Fārūq Khūrshīd, Shawqī ᶜAbd al-Ḥakīm, and Jabrā Ibrāhīm Jabrā. The first chapter of *Al-Baḥth ᶜan Walīd Masᶜūd* (*In Search of Walīd Masᶜūd*, 1978) by Jabrā contains the replay of a long message on cassette tape made by the character who is the focus of the work. In ᶜAbd al-Raḥmān Munīf's novel, *Al-Nihāyāt* (*Endings*, 1978) the action of narrative is suspended at one point while the men of a village tell each other a whole series of animal tales. Certainly Jabrā would wish to be seen through his many critical articles as drawing a firm link between the old and the new.[12]

The links between contemporary Arabic fiction and Western genres have been clearly drawn. At certain stages in the development of the fictional genres in the modern Arab world the influence of the West was certainly strong and even overwhelming. The connections between today's fiction and the narrative tradition of earlier Arabic literature, however overt or covert, conscious or unconscious they may be, are not as obvious and have been little investigated. This present study hopes to add to the relatively few works that may foster such a purpose.

Notes

1. See Edward Lane, *An Account of the Manner and Customs of the Modern Egyptians* (London: Everyman, 1954), 420. This work is discussed in some detail in Leila Ahmed, *Edward W. Lane* (London: Longman, 1978), 127–70. Among more recent studies of the reception of *The 1001 Nights*, we would mention C. Knipp, "The *Arabian Nights* in England: Galland's Translation and its Successors." *JAL* 5 (1974): 44–54.

2. Cf. Bridget Connelly, "The Structure of Four Banī Hilāl Tales," *JAL* 4 (1973): 18.

3. Mia Gerhardt, *The Art of Story-Telling* (Leiden: E. J. Brill, 1963); Suhayr al-Qalamāwī, *Alf Layla wa Layla* (Cairo: Maṭbaᶜat al-Maᶜārif, 1943); Feryal Ghazoul, *The Arabian Nights: A Structural Analysis* (Cairo: Institute for the Study and Presentation of Arab Cultural Values, 1980); Andras Hamori, *On the Art of Medieval Arabic Literature* (Princeton: Princeton University Press,

1974), 145–80. See also *Studia Islamica* 43 (1976): 65–80; Peter Molan, *JAOS* 98.3 (Jul.–Sept., 1978): 237–47 and *Edebiyat* 3.2 (1978): 121–35.

4. Roger Allen, *The Arabic Novel* (Syracuse: Syracuse University Press, 1982), 16.

5. I have used the edition of Rushdī Ṣaliḥ (Cairo: Dār al-Shaʿb, 1969), 86–90. In the older Būlāq edition (reprint 1960), the tale begins in volume I, page 66.

6. See references in note 3.

7. Gerhardt, section VI, pp. 417–70.

8. The event is described in P. Hitti, *History of the Arabs* (London: Macmillan, 1961), 295–96.

9. This reflects the historical picture of Jaʿfar. There is a good illustration of the affection in which Jaʿfar and the Barmakids were held in al-Qāḍī Abū ʿAlī al-Tanūkhī's (940–94) work, *al-Faraj baʿd al-shidda* (Baghdad: Maktabat al-Muthannà, 1955), 7: 223–26.

10. For reference to the work of Naqqāsh, see Matti Moussa in *JAL* 3 (1972): 111–14. For the work of al-Qabbānī, see Muḥammad Yūsuf Najm, *Al-Masraḥ al-ʿarabī*, vol. 7.

11. I have discussed the works of Faraj in *Edebiyat* 4.1 (1979): esp. 109–11, and of Wannūs in *JAL* 14 (1984).

12. Jabrā's articles are scattered through his collections of critical articles: *Al-Ḥurriyya wa al-Ṭūfān* (Beirut: Dār Majallat Shiʿr, 1960); *Al-Riḥla al-Thāmina* (Beirut: Al-Maktaba al-ʿaṣriyya, 1967); *Yanābīʿ al-Ruyā* (Beirut: Al-Muʾassasa al-ʿarabiyya, 1979).

11 Historical and Mythical Baghdad in the Tale of ʿAlī b. Bakkār and Shams al-Nahār, or the Resurgence of the Imaginary

Jamel Eddine Bencheikh

ʿAlī b. Bakkār is very much like a character in a novel. He is a prince, young, exceptionally handsome, and, above all, foreign. *Min awlād al-ʿajam*, the text informs us, means that he may well be Persian.[1] There were many Persians in this newly built city of Baghdad who welcomed different ethnic groups, all fighting hard for power.[2] This young man, who lives in the capital of the Muslim empire with his mother (which we only discover at the end of the tale), is the friend of a rich perfume seller in the town who freely enters the Caliph's palace and who entertains ladies in his shop who have come to select rare essences. It is here where ʿAlī meets Shams.

Later on, a jeweler takes over from the perfume seller as intermediary. This is a social choice: these are rich and delicate trades that appeal more to women than to men. But it is also for the sake of narrative style, and at the same time the first sign of a strategy of desire. The two elements of the couple have to meet. The tale uses the means of the society in which it is imagined. To exist, the tale uses a direct approach. It believes in acting quietly, without warning.

And this is precisely what happens when one of the ladies from

Reprinted from Jamel Eddine Bencheikh, "Historical and Mythical Baghdad in the Tale of ʿAlī b. Bakkār and Shams al-Nahār, or the Resurgence of the Imaginary," in *The Thousand and One Nights in Arabic Literature and Society*, ed. Richard C. Hovannisian and Georges Sabagh (Cambridge: Cambridge University Press, 1997), 14–28. Reprinted by permission of the publisher.

the palace visits the perfume shop, surrounded by her ladies-in-waiting. Her name is Shams al-Nahār, sun twice woman or woman twice fire.[3] Her name emphasizes fate, like Qamar, Badr al-Dīn, Budūr, and Shamsa. The lovers in *The Thousand and One Nights* are often named after stars or the moon.

A portrait of Shams will help us understand many things. She is surely of exceptional beauty: she has been singled out from among dozens of superb ladies-in-waiting personally by Hārūn al-Rashīd, the sovereign of sovereigns and the prince of the faithful. She is elegant and of natural distinction. Terms such as *ẓarf* and *adab* are used to describe her; they all imply sophistication, culture, and finesse.[4] Highly cultured, she writes verse and her dialogues with ʿAlī are "in a very pure form of language, agreeable and full of subtlety."[5] She is an artist, plays the lute, and sings love songs that I shall discuss below.

Shams personifies a *qayna*[6] of high rank at the court of Baghdad and is a contemporary of Badhl, ʿArīb, Mutayyam, Shāriya, to whom the *Kitāb al-Aghānī* has devoted numerous notes and who were the spouses and mothers of many a Caliph. As well as being musicians, they are also poets, says C. Pellat, "capable of writing short poems, thereby competing brilliantly with their rivals, the court poets. . . . These women had received a first-rate education; they had to show talent and extensive knowledge of the Arabic language and poetry." We are told that al-Rashīd, before reaching a decision, requested al-Asmaʿī to question one of them. She replied with such confidence "that it seemed she was reading the answers straight out of a book."[7] This, of course, reminds us of the tale of "Tawaddud" analyzed by André Miquel.[8]

As the Caliph's favorite, Shams lives in the heart of the palace, in an apartment where the inner chamber is surmounted by a dome whose capitals are sculpted with birds and wild beasts. The same colors and designs are to be found in the carpets and the dome, as if the ground reflected the vault. One is confronted with a second game of mirrors: the motifs and colors of the inner chamber can be seen again in the park in the form of flowerbeds. Thus the garden lends its horizons to the inner chamber, just as this secret enclosure prolongs the garden by the sophisticated lines of its architecture. The double perfection of two spaces that reflect each other. The illusion of space is multiplied, horizontally as well as vertically.[9]

From Baghdad to Córdoba, only the pleasure of being could imagine such residences.[10] But the text is more than a document. Description occurs at the right time, gives substance to the setting, presents a society, and begins to unravel its meanings. The text is not just a simple narrative structure. It accompanies the meaning and assumes the confrontation that is being prepared. Thus Shams, a lady of rank, lives in this sumptuous jewel case. Whenever the Caliph wants permission to see her, he sends for Masrūr, who knows his intimate secrets.[11] It is the same lady who enters a perfume shop in the bazaar and who falls in love at first sight with a young foreign prince. It does not surprise us, as it is the tempo of a tale that we have shown to have its own inherent rhythm.[12] But it so happens here that strategy and sociocultural realities enhance each other. In the social structure of an Arab town, opportunities for meeting are few and far between, especially if one ventures beyond the limits of one's background. Faces behind a gate and half-open door only appear for a few seconds. Silhouettes can scarcely be distinguished. Public premises are guarded. Encounters happen in a surprising way. What does it matter! In life, as in a tale, the waiting precedes the meeting, and the passion of loving precedes the goal. The medieval Arab lover catches fire at the first spark of desire and the fire cannot be smothered. It is not the object of the tale to narrate the circumstances of love, but to arouse the latent passion that is only waiting for the right time to be born. The lovers are united not by a stroke of luck but by the necessity within them. As soon as they identify each other, they fall in love. Their willpower is born out of their need to accomplish a necessary fate.

The lovers are totally committed to each other at once. It goes well beyond carnal pleasure, which is simply not present in this tale, it should be emphasized. No situation, no restriction, no danger—nothing will stop Shams and ʿAlī. The latter says to the jeweler who visits him: "Whatever happens, I'm destined to perish." There is no question of self-denial in the composition of this passion that completely takes over and drains the characters of everything that is not passion. Having entered a state of vertigo, they know that they are mortally affected.

Thus one of the Caliph's favorites falls in love with a foreign prince. One question guides us throughout our analysis: are we faced with a fact, a veritable reality, or fiction bearing historical semblance?

And if it turns out to be fiction, how has this been introduced into the heart of an apparently historical setting? To answer the question it is necessary to go back to the characters to see if they are identifiable, or at least if they refer to contemporaries of those days.

Shams is one of the high-ranking *qaynas* remarkably portrayed by Jāḥiẓ and al-Washshāʾ. The latter stressed a point of interest to us, namely that of love letters. He said the ladies at court "are always exchanging letters with their lovers. One sees them confined, veiled, locked up: it's in their correspondence that they find their satisfaction and in the exchange of messengers their consolation."[13] That is exactly what happens in our tale. The two lovers write to each other and, above all, express their feelings by reciting poems. Now, the role of poems in *The Thousand and One Nights* has been completely neglected—to such an extent that some translators, like Galland, have simply omitted them from their translations. For the time being, let us assume they are essential in order to understand the tale, because they either form an integral part of narrative structures or convey the essential part of significations. It would not be possible to understand enough about a tale like *ʿAzīz and ʿAzīza*, for example, if its poems were ignored. All the more so as they help to pinpoint details of the greatest interest.

We know that love poems began to flourish at the Abbasid court at the end of the second/eighth and third/ninth centuries. Without using all the sources available to us nowadays, J. C. Vadet has described this environment of princes, princesses, poets, chess players, artists, and secretaries, where the rules of the art of love are decreed.[14] Princesses and Caliph's daughters like ʿAbbāsa, ʿUlayya, and others, are sources of inspiration who gather around them poets. The first of these is alleged to have had a love affair with Jaʿfar al-Barmakī.[15] The second, Hārūn al-Rashīd's sister, who died in 210/825 during the reign of al-Maʾmūn, is the daughter of al-Mahdī and of a singer named Maknūna.[16] Furthermore, a great many sovereigns' children, girls and boys, children of *qiyān*, accede in this way to the rank of *umm walad*. To name a few in the era that concerns us: the very famous artists Ibrahim b. al-Mahdī, brother of ʿUlayya;[17] Abū ʿĪsā b. al-Rashīd, poet and fine singer, of exceptional beauty, who died at the age of nineteen of epilepsy;[18] ʿAbd Allāh b. Mūsā al-Hādi, a talented lute player, of a generous disposition but with a passion for wine that was destructive; ʿAbd Allāh b. Muḥammad al-Amīn, musician and poet.[19]

It is in this milieu that love poetry finds an ideal place to flourish. A great many ready-made scenarios are available for the tale. This milieu was open to pro-Persian influence, more favorable to certain trends in this composite society, which was still in the process of making its definitive cultural choices. The *ẓarf* is not simply an expression of sartorial or culinary elegance. It is a different way of handling language, of writing, and of contemplating existence. Social, but also moral, aspects underlie these attitudes. For too long it was only mannerism and licentiousness that were pointed out, so the deep meaning was not seen. The intention is to suggest a social and moral code of existence, different from the code that is being definitively established by the dominant Muslim ideology. That this intention is sometimes projected here and there for political aims is quite possible.

Moreover, the court is not cut off from its social and economic environment. ʿAlī b. Bakkār's two confidants—the perfume seller Abū l-Ḥasan and then the jeweler—both confirm Françoise Micheau's description of the merchants' world in the *Nights:* "These masters of the jewelry trade, of perfumes and fabrics, have access to the palace, progress socially in grand style, and have idyllic romances with princesses." In her account of Muḥammad ʿAlī, the son of the chief jeweler in Baghdad, who is in love with the sister of the wazīr Jaʿfar, the historian asks if the tale transcribes a reality or if it expresses "a dream of access to power of those who were always excluded."[20] This question does not seem to be phrased properly. Remember the portrait of the perfume seller in the text itself:

> Extremely rich, he was of high rank. His behaviour was beyond reproach and nobody doubted his word. Of great beauty, he seduced every one he met. A great honour! He could enter the Caliph's palace without being invited. There he was much appreciated by all the slave-girls and servants to whom he rendered a great many services. He was even received by the Caliph with whom he spent many an evening reciting poems and telling unheard-of anecdotes. (*Nights*, 159)

How can this portrait be attributed to a dream of access to power? The story proves that climbing the social ladder is perfectly possible in this society. I mentioned this in connection with the poets. I discussed the merchant corporation within a bourgeois class that constitutes a "lobby for the ruling class, a sort of antechamber to success, where an affluent man awaits the sudden favor that enables him to rank among the elite."[21] It is important also to specify that most members of the cultured elite belonged to this class, patrons of poets reliant on it.

Thus the tale is expressing not a dream but a reality. Abū l-Ḥasan really did exist in historical Baghdad. He is not a creature of fiction, he is true to life. Besides, is it really possible to invent the statement he made in *Nights*, p. 159: "I'm very well known for my judgement in case of problems between men and women"? He is in this way referring to a role that is perfectly authentic in the Muslim community, above all among the *ẓurafāʾ*, between rich male lovers and ladies who lead a more or less cloistered life. Moreover, the jeweler who succeeds him in this role makes a significant confession in this respect. When he learns about the full scope of the problems involved, he refuses to let the lovers meet in the palace and exclaims: "I'm a child of the people and do not have the rank of Abū l-Ḥasan. He was well known and famous. He often delivered his merchandise at the Caliph's palace. When he told me this, I trembled before him." How better to describe the social hierarchical organization and the restrictions of protocol? The jeweler is aware of his own limits. In order to pursue their love affair, the couple must leave the imperial territory and move to the other bank of the river. This is a significant shift of territory. Françoise Micheau pointed out that urban territory in Baghdad at the time was clearly split in two. "On the west bank of the Tigris, palaces and gardens, places of power and pleasure: on the east bank, districts animated by souks and disreputable suburbs."[22]

Besides, in many of the tales the intrigues take place within the imperial palace. The tale of Abū l-Ḥasan al-Khurasānī and Shajarat al-Durr[23] is told by the hero to Caliph al-Muʿtaḍid bi-llāh who ruled until 279/892. The story takes place during the reign of his grandfather al-Mutawakkil, assassinated in 232/847. A very young and very rich merchant's son is visited in his shop by a young girl who crosses the Tigris and enters the Caliph's palace. Thanks to a eunuch, he manages to track her down. She is none other than the sovereign's favorite lute player. A tailor, one of the Caliph's employees, gives an interesting account of this incident. He calls on the gods to punish the women at the palace "for casting the men into a state of inner turmoil." The tale of Hārūn al-Rashīd and Muḥammad b. ʿAlī is also of greatest interest to us.[24] The son of the jewelers' syndic in Baghdad is visited in his shop by a young girl who is the daughter of Jaʿfar, the great wazīr. She makes the young man enter the palace, marries him, and then chases him away. The great Zubayda, Hārūn's wife, knows what is going on. So it is certain that all sorts of love affairs were going on in these places dedicated, because of morality, to a terrifying virtue and, because of the exercise of power, to total immunity (or privilege). Other texts confirm this point of view—such texts as *Maṣāriʿ al-ʿUshshāq*, and also *The Hundred and One Nights*, of which two tales should be remembered in order to widen this analysis.

In the story of "The Young Man with the Pearl Necklaces" a young man from Baghdad manages to enter Caliph al-Maʾmūn's palace[25] just when "one of his dearest slave-girls" is on the point of being raped by a negro brandishing a saber. He rescues the young girl whom the sovereign offers him in marriage. How much more tragic is the admirable tale of "Waḍḍāḥ." The King of India marries his cousin, daughter of the King of Yemen, who bears him a daughter. When the daughter has grown to womanhood she receives a lover hidden in a chest. Hearing about it, her father exclaims: "What's the good of having guards and sentries? What's the good of royalty? What's the use of power if debauchery enters my home?"[26] He has the lover, Waḍḍāḥ, buried alive in the chest. The young girl dies when she discovers that her lover has suffocated. The strange thing is that, like Hārūn al-Rashīd, this king has a chamberlain called Masrūr. Even stranger, *Maṣāriʿ al-ʿUshshāq* makes Waḍḍāh al-Yaman the lover of the wife of Caliph Yazīd b. Abd al-Malik b. Marwān who reigned from 101/720.[27]

Whatever our surprise from time to time, facts must be faced. Events that occur in the tale of Shams are in no way contradictory to the customs and manners recorded by history. When Shams blindly abandons herself to an unknown person who unseals her letters and arranges to meet her in a bachelor's apartment, it is to emphasize the violence of a passion, not to mock the traditions of a society. After all, studying the tale from a purely logical point of view is like seeing the trees and not the forest. Why does Shams, who has decided to confront her fate, not go directly to ʿAlī? Why does this unknown jeweler intervene so vigorously in order to take over from the perfume seller? What did he hope for?

Admit it. Sometimes invention can be more powerful than logic. Admit, too, the other coincidence: a pack of thieves was bound to rob this very house, this very same night, only to find a couple, where the woman is none other than the Caliph's favorite. The meeting takes place in a sort of bachelor's apartment at the disposal of the jeweler, as was customary in this world of merchants who knew how to combine family and pleasure. This detail cannot be invented either. There were many thieves in Baghdad. The house had been furnished for its occupants the day before. Beggars are at all street corners ready to inform the gangs. As they suspect that the arranged feast is not particularly domestic, and that the robbery seems fruitful . . . All this is well strung together. Furthermore, the search for truth cannot do away with coincidence. What could have happened is not less true than what did happen, and vice versa. The kidnapping by the thieves is not less credible than the sudden appearance of the palace guards: the palace is not very far away, and it is normal for the police to be on patrol. If brigands can arrive unexpectedly so can the police. The apparently obscure development of the tale, in fact, contains a perfectly clear structure of space, time, and action, even if the tale does not make a point of controlling all aspects of a universe teeming with events. Why, for instance, are ʿAlī and the jeweler, fleeing Baghdad, stripped of all their belongings by Bedouins during their journey? Why have this peripety that mixes up a secondary event, which is ineffective, narratively speaking, with the unfolding of the meaning? Is it simply the recollection of a new development, of which only the beginning is described? Is it what remains of a cut in the text, the token of an excessive amount of materials without apparent futility? Or is it simply the truth of a story that events have no other justification than that of existing? Once again, is reality the most complex of all fiction?

We do not have, or no longer have, the means of knowing if this tale corresponds to a historical truth, nor is it at all possible to check up on events that took place in the Caliph's palace twelve centuries ago. We have no way of knowing if a Persian prince truly loved the favorite of the prince of the faithful. If we admit all this is true, this strange adventure catches us up on everything we know about history and contradicts any abstract idea we may have about the behavior of a Caliph. After all, the distance between ʿAlī and Shams is astronomical. It is at least as far from the imperial palace to the young man's home as it is from China to the Khālidāt Islands for Qamar and Budūr, and between Kabul and the fortress of precious stones in the case of Jānshāh and Shamsa. Hence we are to believe that the most illustrious of princes of the faithful, he who symbolized power and fame in the imaginary world of the Arabs, was publicly held up to ridicule. An absolute monarch, the vicar of God on earth, the chief of the Muslim community, accepts this major dereliction, this crime of lese majesty and lese divinity. One could have expected a logical reaction, which would lead to the execution of Shams, of her servants and slave-girls, of her palace guards, of her police, in short of any person who had the slightest knowledge of the story. The necessary punishment should have been intended as much for the culprits as for those who might remember what had happened. Nobody was to be allowed to remember what had happened. However, that is not what happens at all. Hārūn al-Rashīd has discovered everything, but still has trust in Shams. He defends her, leads her to her apartment, showers her with gifts, and feels intense sorrow at her death. He gives orders to organize a funeral worthy of her. And here it is no longer possible to pursue the historical explanation. Even if one admits the unthinkable, that is to say that Hārūn, placing himself above the laws and the world they govern and because of his deep love for the one who is going to die, shows magnanimity and compassion; even admitting that, who is going to make us believe that all of Baghdad solemnly participated in ʿAlī b. Bakkār's funeral procession? It is just as crazy to imagine Baghdad paying tribute to the person who betrayed the Caliph as it is to imagine Basra empty on a Friday at noon, in order to allow a procession of unveiled women to march through the town.[28] Here the possibility of a gossip chronicle can be ruled out.

For we are well aware that high walls scarcely protect the virtues supposedly locked up within them. This tale could have been the recollection of a sort of drama in the Caliph's palace, first murmured among the initiated and then spread to gossipmongers far from where the action took place, finally turning into a real tale. *The Thousand and One Nights* would be the only text to mention the ultimate insult to a Caliph. But precisely at this point is where the tale loses its function of secret memory to hold a very odd discourse. For even a gossip chronicle burns itself out and remains within its own limits. One retains only what one wishes to remember. However, quite the contrary, the deep memory of a dream comes up again and again and it is a dream that Baghdad never stops celebrating. I am about to prove it.

To Die for Immortality: Imaginary Resurgences

A closer look at historical references in the tale enables us to detect characteristics that are worth considering. Hārūn al-Rashīd's behavior is one of them, discussed below. First let us examine the court itself, where we find numerous signs of the situating of legends that inscribe themselves in the slow process of the creation of a myth. This concerns the characters as well as the places. In the *Encyclopedia of Islam*, it is not a coincidence that a historian begins his biographical note on Hārūn al-Rashīd with these words: "This fifth Abbasid Caliph is thanks to *One Thousand and One Nights* a so-to-speak legendary figure, hiding his authentic historical personality."[29] In fact, this phenomenon concerns several members of his entourage, in particular his sister ᶜAbbāsa, who is alleged to have had an affair with Jaᶜfar al-Barmakī, the wazīr. This liaison even became the justification for the terrible tragedy of the execution of Jaᶜfar and the imprisonment of his father Yaḥyā and of his brother Faḍl. But we know, also, that there were other, much deeper reasons for the drama of the night of January 29, 187/803. If the wazīr's corpse was exposed for an entire year, it was not only to punish him for having loved this woman. However, regarding this matter, Horovitz provided us with a first-class lead. In his study of the character of ᶜAbbāsa, he pointed out that the story of her love affair with Jaᶜfar takes on such proportions that Ibn Khaldūn questioned its authenticity. Horovitz concluded: "It therefore seems reasonable to see in this anecdote the result of popular imagination that felt it necessary to render the downfall of the favourite minister poetic. . . . Stories from the Arab pagan period contain a very similar episode: that of a minister with a king's sister."[30]

The conclusion is of particular interest to us. First of all because it expresses a desire to render poetic a death caused by the transgression of an interdict. Second, because it suggests the transference of a historical or legendary story to a character who had lived long before that time, and who is thus included in the process of mythification. Horovitz was here referring to the drama of the pre-Lakhmid sovereign of Iraq, Jadhīma al-Abrash and his sister Raqāsh.[31] Now we know that the Abbasid harem provided ample opportunity for legend to capture the story to its own advantage, or, more importantly, to bring to the surface a pattern of significations imprinted in the imaginary. J. C. Vadet, for example, remarked that the situation of *awlād al-khulafā*ʾ—the Caliph's children mentioned earlier—"can be compared to the one enjoyed by society women, singers and mawālīs in the Hijāz of the Umayyads."[32] There is a constant game of love in this milieu that profoundly influences poetry and makes a legend of a second category of people, the poets themselves. Abū Nuwās enters *The Thousand and One Nights.* Abū l-ʿAtāhiya loves ʿUtba who is a singer of al-Khayzurān, Hārūn al-Rashīd's fearsome mother. Fawz loved by al-ʿAbbās b. al Aḥnaf could be ʿUlayya, the Caliph's sister. It doesn't really matter if this is "true" or not. The fact remains that a whole *akhbār* literature develops around the court's love life. "There's every reason to believe that this poetry is directed at a certain sensitive public, mainly that of wazīrs, secretaries, singers, Caliph's friends, idle princes with a passion for literature and music, harem slaves who are just as cultured as the latter."[33] This *akhbār* literature is born in this milieu and comes back to it in completed form. Anecdotes, mostly amorous, passed on by poets, are collected by professional literary hacks who deal with them in any way they think fit. In this way they invent chains of guarantors (*isnāds*) who intervene on the story's form and who deal with its themes. "They like their anecdotes to have a pseudo-historical angle, they readily mix either eminent men, or famous poets, even if it means forcibly introducing them into a biography where they didn't exist in the first place."[34] For their part, grammarians, courtiers, "systematize old stories as they like, and whenever necessary make up new fictional heroes from start to finish."[35]

These observations are of utmost interest to us. During this operation stories will be arranged, characters sketched, themes stemming from Bedouin tradition, the Hijāzi heritage, the art of love at the court of Baghdad will be adapted. What strikes us as especially important is that some historical characters attract ancient stories. Horovitz remarks on the transfer of the story of Jadhīma to Jaʿfar, the wazīr. He adds: "What most sources attribute to the subject of ʿAbbāsa, others ascribe to two other so-called sisters of Hārūn."[36]

Work, therefore, of compilers, literary hacks, will lead to notes of *Kitāb al-Aghānī*, to *Maṣāriʿ al-ʿUshshāq*, but also, undoubtedly, to the *Nights*. Of course, I no longer, like Vadet, speak of falsifications and forgeries. For my part, I have none of the historian's preoccupations. What is important is not the individual who has had, or not had, an adventure. What is important is the process of transfer, and above all its need to give a new life to this adventure. When the hacks lie in order to unite ʿAbbāsa and Jaʿfar, they discover a possibility for the imaginary to actualize a deep-rooted scheme, namely that of two beings violating a major interdict in order to give an irrefutable example of passion. Irremediable love, doomed to failure, has selected its characters. Memory has conveyed (since when?) this story, reduced to a bare outline, which brings to mind the implacable image of an eternal drama—that of a love, which as soon as it comes into being signals death to those involved.

In this way, a Baghdad—mythical in its very reality—is going to celebrate the death of Shams and ʿAlī, no longer buried like mere culprits but as victims of an evil that even the sovereign regards as an invincible power. Baghdad buries a mortal sorrow but also a dream. The imperial city retains the memory of a fatal destiny symbolized by two tombs that an anonymous jeweler never stops visiting. The tale takes it upon itself to pay public homage and to institute a ritual celebration. From this moment on, everything must be reinterpreted, especially Hārūn al-Rashīd's attitude. He does more than express supreme indulgence. He converts a banal betrayal into a tragedy, an empty destiny into a fatal one. Here it is no longer a matter of morals being ridiculed, but of the terrifying power of a desire that violates the forbidden to demonstrate both the frailty and fatality of love and death. ʿAlī and Shams die for no other reason than that of replaying an eternal drama; in short, they die of their immortality and their everlasting desire.

Here the historical investigation ends and the literary analysis begins. Once the generative pattern is in place, it institutes its own laws of reactivation.[37] It uses an available form for a story that has become a myth. It remains markedly rigid in its narrative structure and sociocultural presentation. Or else, it reappears each time by selecting time-space-culture material that is appropriate for its regeneration. Then it can choose symbolic places and characters in order to be perpetuated. Baghdad, little by little, becomes a mythical place; a perfect symbol—Hārūn al-Rashīd—will magnify the story and raise it to its absolute imaginary form, freed of any historical contingency. In the heart of Islamic culture, and by using its own decor, a ritual that has come from elsewhere is celebrated—just as in Qamar and Ḥalīma.

For all that, had this been an author's text, it would have been an easy task to study the transfer mechanism. In her analysis of the Osiris cycle in Shakespeare's *Julius Caesar* and *Anthony and Cleopatra*, Valida Dragovitch proved how the author had given "a universal dimension to feminine myths of ancient Rome."[38] For their part, J. P. Vernant and P. Vidal-Naquet also resort to this double system of references: "That of the mythical tale that the poet has conjured up from time immemorial, and that of contemporary society that listened to and read these stories in the light of its own tensions that have turned into spectacles."[39]

What so obscurely foreshadows Hārūn al-Rashīd, and what, for that matter, the tragedy (sacrifice) of ʿAlī and Shams? And who, through the intermediary of a Baghdad crowd, celebrates such a grandiose sacrifice? The fact that no proof of historical authenticity exists does not mean that the mythical theory can be offloaded to an obscure place, from where favorable patterns can be comfortably drawn up. Hārūn al-Rashīd has become a legendary figure, in spite of his perfectly well known historical personality: in his presence, one might say. If it is possible for "Sophocles to make Oedipus return from the most distant age," why cannot a storyteller summon a Persian prince by the name of ʿAlī b. Bakkār to Baghdad, there to fall in love with the Caliph's favorite? And not just for the sake of decor. Baghdad is the center of the Muslim empire, Hārūn is the prince of the faithful and his palace represents the core of lawful intimacy. One simple and formidable transfer takes place, which in one step moves forward, projects like lightning in the center of forbidden space. The audacity has not been to tell a "true story." More than that has been done, as I have shown. The audaciousness is not to perpetuate a news item but to transform it into a story bearing the very highest significations of desire.

For in the final resort, placed between theological argument more and more decisive on the subject of passion and a bloodless poetry, where can the imaginary take refuge if not in a tale, but show the tragic nature of human love and to celebrate a cult dedicated to love? When storytellers told their tales to the audiences in the tenth, fifteenth, and eighteenth centuries, did they for one moment doubt the historical truth of the account, or did they, on the contrary, concentrate on the incandescence of the story? Did one doubt that a prince could in this way love suffering of the person who had betrayed him and sacrifice her to his people, or did one find the sacrifice even more beautiful, the sorrow deeper and more desirable, because it all took place on the biggest Arabo-Islamic stage, namely the Caliph's palace in Baghdad?

Notes

Unless otherwise indicated, all references to *Nights* refer to the edition by W. H. Macnaghten, *Book of the Thousand and One Nights Commonly Known as the 'Arabian Nights Entertainments' Now for the First Time Published Complete in the Original Arabic*, "Calcutta II" (4 vols., Calcutta, 1839–42).

1. The Arabized Persian element had been important in Abbasid Iraq, especially in court circles. It has been brought out on several occasions by historians: consult A. A. Duri, "Baghdad," in the *Encyclopedia of Islam*, I, 921–36; B. Lewis, "ʿAbbāsids," in ibid., 15–25; see also the pages devoted to "The Iranian World in the Strategy of the Fitna," in Hishem Djait, *La grande discorde* (Paris: Gallimard, 1989).

2. This refers to the *shuʿubiyya*, the struggle that put ethnic Arabs against the ethnic Iranians for the conquest of Islamic power.

3. As in Celtic, in the ancient Indo-European languages, and in German, "sun," *shams*, is feminine in Arabic, whereas *qamar*, "moon," is masculine. The feminine characters of *The Thousand and One Nights* are well inscribed in this symbolic aster: they represent the active principle, the source of vital energy, the striking beauty of which man is but the crazed reflection.

4. Regarding refinement, *ẓarf*, and the refined, *ẓurafāʾ*, see the "pioneering" article of F. Ghazi, "Un groupe social: Les raffinés," *Studia Islamica* 11 (1959); and B. al-Majdub, *Al-Ẓarf wa l-Ẓurafā bi-l-Ḥijāz fī l-ʿAṣr al-Umawi* (Tunis, 1988).

5. The women and the learned in *The Thousand and One Nights* deserve an entire study. From Tawaddud to the five young women who were presented

to King al-Nuʿmān at Baghdad, to Nuzhat al-Zamān in the same novel, the number of young women capable of reciting poems and of playing the lute is great. So also is the number of those able to speak on ethics, the art of governance, ecclesiastical science, and many other disciplines where their erudition works wonders and causes some king to fall in love with them.

6. "Slave-singer," proposes C. Pellat, in his important article in the *Encyclopedia of Islam*, IV, 853–57, with an ample bibliography; we will recognize what could have been an artist living in the caliphate circle of Baghdad between the eight and tenth centuries.

7. Ibid., 855-a. See also J. E. Bencheikh, "Les musiciens et la poésie," *Arabica* 22 (1975): 114–52; on the learned *qayna*, see H. Pérès, *La poésie andalouse en arabe classique* (Paris: Adrien-Maisonneuve, 1953), 384.

8. See *Sept contes des Mille et Une Nuits* (Paris: Sindbad, 1981).

9. Thus the perspective oversteps the limits and gives recluses the impression of being able to go beyond themselves.

10. One can compare this description with that of the music pavilion built at Córdoba for two singers from Medina and for the blond Navarrese Qalam, captured very young in the north of Spain, trained at Medina, and bought by the Umayyad Caliph ʿAbd al-Raḥmān II. See Pérès, *La poésie andalouse*, 41, and Pellat, *Encyclopedia of Islam*, IV, 855-a. A band of female musicians were playing there exactly as in our tale. Excellent books have been devoted to the various aspects of the art of Muslim life. To cite a few of the most recent: *Arabesque et jardins de paradis* (Paris: Musée du Louvre, 1989); *Tapis, présent de l'Orient à l'Occident* (Paris: Institut du Monde Arabe, 1989); *Trésors de l'Islam* (Musée d'Art et d'Historie de Genève, 1985); *Turkish Handwoven Carpets* (2 vols., Turkish Ministry of Culture, 1987).

11. The Caliph arrives in a magnificent procession that allows the reader to get to know the ceremony of a caliphal visit and to appreciate the rank of the young woman.

12. See J. E. Bencheikh, *Les Mille et Une Nuits ou la parole prisonnière*, 127.

13. *al-Muwashshā*, work analyzed at length by J. C. Vadet, in *L'Esprit courtois en Orient*, II, 317–51. The passage is translated on p. 343 n. 4.

14. Ibid., 197, 199.

15. Ibid., 198 n. 5.

16. Ibid., chap. 6, 198–208, which expatiates about whether or not ʿUlayya was the Fawz of the poet al-ʿAbbās b. al-Aḥnaf.

17. See Bencheikh, "Les musiciens et la poésie."

18. When he passed by, all of Baghdad, it is said, would sit contemplating him, which proves that the court was not isolated from the city, that the people recognized these princes.

19. Regarding these children of the Caliphs who devoted themselves to music, see *Kitāb al-Aghānī* (Beirut, 1959), x, 101 ff., which remains the richest source for the study of this family.

20. F. Micheau, "Le peuple dans *Les Mille et Une Nuits*," *Gavroche, Revue d'histoire populaire* 11 (août–sept., 1983).

21. J. E. Bencheikh, *Poétique arabe*, 2nd ed., 24.

22. Micheau, "Le peuple dans *Les Mille et Une Nuits*."

23. *Nights*, 959–63. One recalls as a matter of interest that Ardashīr, son of the King of Shiraz, enters the palace of the father of Ḥayāt al-Nufūs, King of Iraq, disguised as a merchant and, thanks to an old governess, Tāj al-Mulūk does the same to rejoin Dunya.

24. *Nights*, 286 ff.

25. See Gaudefroy-Demombynes's translation, no. VIII, 104–10. The text states curiously: "The palace was open, the guards asleep," to explain how the young man was able to enter so easily into the palace to join the young girl.

26. Ibid., 60–67.

27. It refers to Yazīd II; see the *Maṣāriʿ al-ʿUshshāq* (2 vols., Beirut: Dar Sader, n.d.), II, 192. See also the history of a parricide in the family of the Umayyads of Spain in the fourth/tenth century, under the wazīrate of Ibn Abī Manṣūr (368–92), ibid., 235–40, and the tragic story of Hind, a married woman, and her lover, Bishr, who loved each other during the Prophet's lifetime, ibid., 235–40. The *Dhamm al-Hawā* of Ibn al-Jawzī reports numerous stories of this nature.

28. See "Des rituals venus d'ailleurs," for the analysis of the tale of "Qamar et Ḥalīma."

29. Article of F. Omar, *Encyclopedia of Islam*, III, 239–41.

30. Article of Horovitz, *Encyclopedia of Islam*, I, 14.

31. Regarding this personality, see *Encyclopedia of Islam*, II, 375; Jadhīma is the husband of Zenobia of Palmyra, who inflicted on him a horrible death.

32. Vadet, *L'Esprit courtois*, 198 n. 5.

33. Ibid., 197.

34. Ibid., 195 n. 1, a remarkable analysis of the production of literary texts in this circle. See also p. 161 on the audience who "gathers the first elements of a novel or a biography."

35. Ibid., 355.

36. *Encyclopedia of Islam*, I, 14.

37. See Bencheikh, *Les Mille et Une Nuits ou la parole prisonnière*, "Texte narratif et schéma générateur," 43–95.

38. Valida Dragovitch, *Roma materna* (Paris: Les Belles-Lettres, 1989), chap. 9.

39. J. P. Vernant and P. Vidal-Naquet, *Mythe et tragédie en Grèce ancienne* (Paris: La Découverte, 1986), II, 84 and, more generally, until p. 90.

12 The Monstrous Births of "Aladdin"

Michael Cooperson

> Pétis de la Croix ("Persian and Turkish Tales"), Chavis and Cazotte ("New Arabian Nights"), Dow ("*Ináyatu llah*") and Morell ("Tales of the Genii"), with others manifold whose names are now all but forgotten, carried out the Gallandian liberties to the extreme of licence and succeeded in producing a branchlet of literature, the most vapid, frigid, and insipid that can be imagined by man,—a bastard Europeo-Oriental, pseudo-Eastern world of Western marionettes garbed in the gear which Asiatic are (or were) supposed to wear, with sentiments and opinions, manners and morals to match; the whole utterly lacking life, local colour, vraisemblance, human interest. From such abortions, such monstrous births, libera nos, Domine!
>
> Richard Burton
> from "The Translator's Foreword" to *The Supplemental Nights*

In 1712 Antoine Galland, the grandfather of Burton's "bastard" literature, published volume 11 of his French translation of *Alf laylah wa-layah* ("The Thousand and One Nights"), which contained "L'histoire d'Aladdin, ou la lampe merveilleuse." In Galland's and later versions, "Aladdin" attained an extraordinary popularity, inspiring a long line of Western-language imitations and adaptations. These include operas, stage plays, storybooks, and films, the most recent being the 1992 Walt Disney feature film *Aladdin.*[1] The Disney version, like many of its predecessors, did not so much bring "Aladdin" to the screen as present a composite of images culled from *Alf laylah wa-layah* and refracted through a number of intermediaries, among them the two classic Arabian fantasy films, Douglas Fairbanks Sr.'s *The Thief of Bagdad* (1924) and Alexander Korda's 1940 film of the same title. If, however, all three films present a

Reprinted from Michael Cooperson, "The Monstrous Births of 'Aladdin,'" *Harvard Middle Eastern and Islamic Review* 1 (1994): 67–86. Reprinted by permission of the author and the publisher.

"bastard Europeo-Oriental, pseudo-Eastern world of Western marionettes," they do not do so at the expense of a single originary "Aladdin." Galland's original—that is, the text he used as the basis for his translation—has never been located. Moreover, the Arabic "Aladdin"—in the one documented version, at least—already tells a pseudo-Oriental tale: the characters are Muslims with Arabic names, but the action takes place in China. The Western retellings eliminated the references to China and made "Aladdin" represent, first, the "real" Arab and Islamic Orient; and second, the fantasy life of the Arabs, as portrayed in the *Thousand and One Nights*. Disney's *Aladdin*, which appeared in the wake of the Persian Gulf war, marks a third transformation of these traditions of representation: it avoids the depiction of anything real, suggesting that a live-action Orient, however fantasticated, has become too realistic for comfort. Going beyond Aladdin's Jinnī, who produces monstrously improved versions of real objects, Disney has produced a monstrously improved version of a wish-fulfilling Orient.

"Aladdin" began its Western existence as an "Oriental tale," a category of story expected to be both whimsical and authentically Eastern. Galland insisted upon the Arab origin of the stories, subtitling his translation "*contes arabes*" ("Arabic tales"). For many of Galland's eighteenth-century readers, however, the "Oriental tale," including the Arabic tale, consisted simply of a fantastic narrative in a convincingly Middle Eastern setting, apart from any presumed relationship to a tale originally told in Arabic, Persian, or Turkish. Thus Galland's publisher saw no harm in filling out volume eight with two Turkish tales, an interpolation that the translator bitterly resented.[2] However, Turkish tales are at least "Oriental," and, as Ousely's 1797 *Oriental Collections* pronounces regarding variant arrangements of the tales, "If they are truly Oriental it is a matter of little importance to us Europeans whether they are strung on this night or that night."[3]

By the turn of the century, however, the inability of numerous Orientalists to locate Galland's original had prompted a series of inquiries into the authenticity—and even the existence—of his sources.[4] Galland claimed to have worked from a four-volume Syrian manuscript, but the document had not (and still has not) been found. Even so, nearly all of the individual stories Galland translated have turned up, in variant forms, in different Arabic manuscripts of *Alf laylah wa-laylah*. In a communication to the *Gentleman's Magazine* of February 1799, P. Russel, responding to the queries of several correspondents, declared that "there seems no ground to doubt that M. Galland translated from a copy similar to the MS now in my possession," although "with respect to the translation, great liberty, in accommodation to French manners, has been taken with the original."[5] Investigations by other scholars resulted in the discovery of parallel Arabic originals for most of Galland's tales, refuting earlier claims that Galland had invented the stories himself. In spite of the efforts of numerous researchers, however, certain tales, including "Aladdin," remained without Arabic originals or parallel versions.[6]

In 1887, M. H. Zotenberg, curator of Eastern manuscripts at the Bibliothèque Nationale, published two documents offering new but contradictory evidence for the authenticity of the so-called orphan tales, particularly "Aladdin." Zotenberg cited entries from Galland's diary for the period 1709–12, containing the translator's account of his meetings in Paris with an Aleppan Maronite named Ḥannā. According to Galland, Ḥannā told him a number of tales, some or all of which he (Ḥannā) also wrote out in Arabic. Galland published the Ḥannā stories as volumes eleven and twelve of the French translation of the *Mille et une nuits*, without, however, crediting Ḥannā as his informant.[7]

Having identified Ḥannā as Galland's source for the "orphan tales," Zotenberg also goes on to present a written version of "Aladdin" discovered in an Arabic manuscript copied in Paris and dated 1805–10. Galland could not have used this manuscript, given its date, but the document claims to reproduce a Baghdad manuscript of the *Nights* dated 1115 A.H. (1703 C.E.), that is, a year before the appearance of Galland's first volume. Therefore Galland may conceivably have used the Baghdad manuscript as the basis for his "Aladdin." The text of the story in Zotenberg's manuscript largely corresponds to Galland's French translation, but with significant differences in detail.[8]

British Orientalists remained suspicious of Galland's "Aladdin," but—with a few exceptions—they proved unable to resist including the tales in their English translations. Before Zotenberg's discovery, both Payne and Lane omitted "Aladdin" for the good reason that they had no Arabic originals for it. In the meantime, however, the English version of Galland's French had attained great popularity. Richard Burton, the most famous English translator of the *Nights*, noted in a preface to his *Supplemental Nights:* "Not a few readers of Mr. John Payne's admirable translation [. . .] complained that they had bought it in order to see Ali Baba, Aladdin, and others translated into classical English and that they much regretted the absence of their old favourites." Thus, says Burton, "circumstances [. . .] have now compelled me to devote the whole of this volume to the Frenchman's stories."[9] Similarly, Stanley Lane-Poole, in his supplement to Lane's translation, argued that, although they have no more than a tenuous claim to inclusion in the *Nights*, "it is generally understood that without 'Aladdin' and 'Ali Baba' the 'Arabian Nights' must be held incomplete." For his rendering of "Aladdin," Burton translated both Zotenberg's Arabic and Galland's French; Lane-Poole used Zotenberg's text alone.[10]

The pedigree of the tales remained a matter of concern for Orientalists who assumed that the *Arabian Nights* provided authentic information about the East and Easterners. Zotenberg claimed that "Aladdin" "présente un tableau assez fidèle des mœurs de l'Egypte sous le règne des derniers Sultans mamelouks, à la réserve, pourtant, de la vie intime de la cour, dont évidemment, il n'avait qu'une idée fantaisiste."[11] Yet the story's admissibility as historical evidence runs into a snag with the very first line: "It has reached me, King of the Age, that in one of the cities of China there lived a poor tailor who had a son named Aladdin."[12] In spite of the Arabic names of the characters, then, the story for its Arab audiences was already about the fantastic marvels of lands farther east. If Zotenberg is right about "Aladdin's" faithful depiction of the manners of late-medieval Egyptians, Arabic storytellers must have preceded their European counterparts in creating that "branchlet of literature, the most vapid, frigid, and insipid that can be imagined by man," or, to paraphrase Burton, "a bastard Sino-Arabic, pseudo-Chinese world of Arab marionettes garbed in the gear which the Chinese are (or were) supposed to wear, with sentiments and opinions, manners and morals to match."

Burton decried pseudo-Oriental tales of the European variety as "utterly lacking life, local colour, vraisemblance, human interest,"

Zotenberg had no similar qualms about the pseudo-Chinese "Aladdin," which he called "une œuvre littéraire d'un incontestable mérite."[13] Zotenberg applauded the French translation as well, drawing particular attention to the contribution of Galland, "qui, par les moyens les plus simples, tout comme La Fontaine dans ses fables, a su donner à la fiction orientale un tour gracieux et une portée plus généralement humaine."[14] Zotenberg's discovery of an Arabic original established the legitimacy of Galland's "Aladdin," not only as a historical document but also as a work of literature.

The "Aladdin" (ʿAlāʾ al-Dīn) story in Zotenberg's edition tells the tale of a boy who loses his father and finds a terrifying substitute in the form of a sorcerer arrived in China from North Africa.[15] The Sorcerer presents himself as ʿAlāʾ al-Dīn's long-lost uncle and sends the boy to claim a magic lamp sealed in an underground cavern. The Sorcerer attempts to kill ʿAlāʾ al-Dīn, but the latter escapes with the lamp, whose magical powers he and his mother resort to only sparingly. One day, however, ʿAlāʾ al-Dīn falls in love with Badr al-Budūr, the Sultan's daughter, and calls upon the Servant of the Lamp, a fearsome but obedient Jinnī, for help. The Jinnī kidnaps the Princess to prevent her marriage to the son of the minister, creates enormous wealth for ʿAlāʾ al-Dīn, and constructs an impressive palace for him. ʿAlāʾ al-Dīn marries Badr al-Budūr and becomes a favorite of the Sultan. Meanwhile, the Sorcerer learns of ʿAlāʾ al-Dīn's good fortune, returns to China, and manages to steal back the lamp. The Sorcerer then carries away ʿAlāʾ al-Dīn's palace with Badr al-Budūr inside it. The enraged Sultan nearly executes ʿAlāʾ al-Dīn, but eventually releases him on condition that he retrieve Badr al-Budūr. With the assistance of another Jinnī, ʿAlāʾ al-Dīn finds his wife in North Africa, where the two conspire to outwit and kill the Sorcerer. Back in China, the couple must also outwit and kill the Sorcerer's brother, who has disguised himself as a holy woman and infiltrated the palace in an attempt to avenge his brother's death.

"Aladdin" is a fantasy of escape from the terrors of apprenticeship, an institution that induces particularly strong anxiety by reason of its similarity—and in some cases, its identity—with the parent-child relationship. ʿAlāʾ al-Dīn's father wishes to teach him a trade, but the boy ignores him and waits for him to go away, which he does, dying an early death of grief. When, after the father's death, the

Sorcerer claims parental rights over ʿAlāʾ al-Dīn, the boy again expresses his unwillingness to learn a trade, consenting to his "uncle's" wishes only when the latter offers to set him up as a merchant—that is, in a profession that does not require an apprenticeship at manual labor. Although the Sorcerer's offer proves a ruse, ʿAlāʾ al-Dīn will eventually learn a trade, namely sorcery, and in particular how to create anything he wants out of thin air. This allows him to replace his mother, who has been providing meals for him in spite of his idleness: ʿAlāʾ al-Dīn learns to command the Jinnī to create food for both of them. This is consistent with ʿAlāʾ al-Dīn's attempts throughout the story to replace or occlude his parents, particularly his father, as if insistent on his own uncreatedness. However, the Sorcerer explicitly assumes the father's role, returning again and again to threaten ʿAlāʾ al-Dīn's magical constructions with the revelation of their own illegitimacy.

The lamp provides instant and complete gratification upon contact, and ʿAlāʾ al-Dīn refuses to relinquish it to his Sorcerer-Father. ʿAlāʾ al-Dīn's mother warns her son against the forbidden tokens: "I beg you, my son, by the milk which you suckled of me, throw that lamp and that ring away . . . I can't stand to look at them again . . . It's forbidden for us to live in company with [the *jinn*], because the Prophet has warned us against them." Appropriately, the productions that flow fully grown from the lamp are "like none possessed by any king": not only marvelous, but unnatural. The characters respond to them with dazed stupefaction:

> The Sultan marvelled with great admiration, and was bewildered at the splendor of the slave-women and their loveliness, which transcended praise; and his wits were turned when he looked at the golden bowls full of precious stones, which captivated the sight; and he was confounded at this marvel until he became dumb, and could not say a word from excess of wonder. And his mind was the more perplexed how all this could have come about in the space of an hour.[16]

Orientalists, formerly perplexed at the ex nihilo appearance of Galland's "Aladdin," accepted Zotenberg's discovery as evidence that the "orphan tale" had not simply arisen out of nowhere. Readers of Galland's and later translations nevertheless exercised themselves upon an analogous problem: the legitimacy of Aladdin's effortless acquisition of wealth. Douglas Fairbanks's 1924 silent film *The Thief of Bagdad,* the first film version of an "Oriental tale," domesticates its Oriental characters by demonstrating that they find unearned felicity monstrous and illegitimate. A contemporary *New York Times* feature describes the evolution of the story: the author of the feature, an unnamed "scenario writer," relates that Fairbanks "came in to us [the scenarists] one day suggesting making an *Arabian Nights* story," and that "we submerged ourselves in all the known translations of the *Arabian Nights.*"[17] The plot of the film corresponds to no single tale in the *Nights;* rather, it combines elements taken from "Aladdin," "The Tale of Prince Ahmed," "The Tale of the Magic Horse," and others. Unlike any of these tales, however, Fairbanks's story uses a thief as the protagonist. The scenarist's account explains this choice by referring to a poem from Burton's *Nights.*

The *Arabian Nights* abound in verse. One quatrain as translated by Burton reads:

> Seek not thy happiness to steal,
> 'Tis work alone will win thee weal.
> Who seeketh bliss sans toil and strife,
> The impossible seeketh and wasteth life.

This gave Mr. Fairbanks his theme. "Our hero," he said, "must be Every Young Man—of this age or any age—who believes that happiness is a quality that can be stolen; who is selfish—at odds with the world—rebellious toward conventions on which comfortable human relations are based."[18]

The Thief of Bagdad, like the contemporary Rudolph Valentino films *The Sheik* and *Son of the Sheik,* represents Arab-Islamic culture as a vaguely menacing erotic playground. Unlike Valentino's Arabian films, however, Fairbanks's *Thief* recuperates the anarchic foreigner by casting him as a convert to the rule of law and the Puritan work ethic. "By toil the sweets of human life are found," the holy man cries, reforming the thief and familiarizing the exotic characters as players in a Horatio Alger success story. The moral of the tale, spelled out by stars in the night sky at the beginning and end of the film, is "Happiness must be earned." Filmmakers and publicists had made analogous attempts to reform Valentino, whose rapacious-sheik roles combined with his suspect Italian ethnicity to make him the object of nativist and crypto-homophobic denunciation. However, Valentino's *Cobra* (1925), which cast him as a recent immigrant, failed to "Americanize" this image into one of well-earned success.[19] Fairbanks's previous film roles, as well as his unproblematic ethnicity, prevented the invidious conflation of his off-screen identity with the role of the thief. The publicity surrounding *The Thief* nevertheless still stressed Fairbanks's separateness from his Oriental subject, represented by the Asian actors who worked with him on the film. In an interview published March 2, 1924, Fairbanks discussed the difficulties he encountered "with my cosmopolitan cast," including a dispute between the "Siamese" So-Jin and the Japanese Nambu. So-Jin insisted that his salary appear larger than Nambu's. "He explained that he would lose cast [*sic*] with his own people if he deigned to work for so low a salary as Nambu. 'I am a great artist,' he went on to say, 'and he, the upstart, is only my pupil.' " In another incident, Anna May Wong, who plays the Mongol slave, refused to work until Fairbanks wrote a letter "to her honored parent" apologizing for a publicist's mistranslation of her name. The story concludes, "Mr. Fairbanks told of his great relief of having the picture finished.[20]

Fairbanks's *Thief* most profoundly influenced Disney's *Aladdin*, as indeed it influenced every Arabian fantasy film since 1924, in its visual representation of medieval Arab-Islamic culture. Fairbanks's art director, William Cameron Menzies, created the world of tiered houses, onion domes, gigantic crockery, and ornate decorations that has reappeared in every "Arabian" film since 1924.[21] The newspaper feature on the creation of *The Thief* suggests that the art direction team aspired to documentary accuracy, "Our research director brought us authorities on architecture, ornamentation, furniture, rugs, and information on many other points." But when the sets began to appear too realistic, Fairbanks objected. "They have not the light and airy quality we want," the scenarist's account quotes him as saying. "We must lift them off the earth."[22] The solution, according to the *Thief* lobby book, was to construct mirrored floors:

> First of all, there was the basic fact that when a thing is photographed, it is given substance and reality. This was overcome by building acres of glazed floor, which reflected highlights along the base line and destroyed

> the reality of solid foundations. This imparted the illusion of floating so that the magnificent structures, with their shadows growing darker as they ascend, seem to have the fantastic quality of hanging from the clouds rather than of being set firmly upon earth.[23]

Menzies's efforts to make medieval Baghdad as unreal as possible succeeded so well that the presence of real objects on the set became unbearable. For the harem scene, the property masters tried to fill a gigantic jar with real flowers: "It was a huge receptacle and they must have worked real hard to find the sort of blossoms and also the quantity to fill such a jar. But all their work went for naught. The effect of these real flowers against the highly imaginative background was grotesque."[24] Only beyond the edges of the frame did the artificiality of Menzies's constructions become apparent: as if to demonstrate his control over his creations, he constructed them so that they could only be filmed from one angle. "Menzies designed the sets and sketches for the shots; he'd tell you how high the camera should be. He'd even specify the kind of lens he wanted for a particular shot. The set was designed for one specific shot only, if you varied your angle by an inch you'd shoot over the top."[25] Like the Jinnī in Aladdin's lamp, Menzies conjured a magical world out of thin air, and like the Jinnī took care to make it like nothing anyone in the real world could ever possess. In "Aladdin," the hero asks the Jinnī to leave one of the windows of the magic palace unfinished, and the Sultan's inability to complete the work and the necessity of summoning the Jinnī to finish it only emphasize the palace's monstrous artificiality.[26] But while the magic in "Aladdin" is as monstrous to the characters in the diegesis as it is to the real-world audience, Fairbanks's Baghdad is fantastic and unreal to begin with. Menzies's fantasy world, unlike the Jinnī's, is the real world of the story, the world that medieval Muslims are supposed to have inhabited, if only in imagination.[27]

The Thief of Bagdad effected the first stage of the process by which Aladdin, who in the Arabic tale is an indolent child but not a criminal, was to become a thief in the Disney version.[28] Aladdin's great antagonist in the Disney film, the minister Jafar, as well as his magical assistant, the Genie, owe their prominence to another film, Alexander Korda's 1940 *Thief of Bagdad*. Both the Wazir or Minister and the Jinnī play significant but comparatively minor roles in the Arabic tale. The Minister resents ʿAlāʾ al-Dīn's sudden fame and fortune and repeatedly points out to the Sultan that all these wonders must be the work of a sorcerer. The two Jinnīs in "Aladdin"—the Servant of the Lamp and the Servant of the Ring—play substantial roles in moving the action forward, but occupy very little story time. The Fairbanks film omits the Minister and the Jinnīs entirely. Korda's *Thief*, on the other hand, develops both figures into prominent and complex characters.

Korda's Jaffar, played by Conrad Veidt, combines the envious Minister of the Arabic tale with the character of the Sorcerer; he is appropriately scheming, malevolent, and diabolical. The historical Jaffar, or more correctly Abū al-Faḍl Jaʿfar b. Yaḥyā b. Khālid al-Barmakī (d. 187 A.H./803 C.E.), was a member of the celebrated Barmakī family of ministers to the ʿAbbāsid caliphs. Along with his father and brother, Jaʿfar was largely responsible for the administration of the ʿAbbāsid state during the early part of the reign of the Caliph Hārūn al-Rashīd (r. 170–93 A.H./786–806 C.E.). According to the ministerial historian al-Jahshiyārī, "Jaʿfar gained an extraordinary ascendancy over al-Rashīd, to the point that al-Rashīd granted him preferential treatment over all others, and lived on terms of exceptional familiarity with him."[29] The biographer al-Dhahabī says of Jaʿfar: "He was one of the great wits of his age. He was handsome, fair-complexioned, eloquent, and cultivated. He spoke beautifully, and was generous to a fault; he was also frolicsome and much given to worldly pleasures."[30] The Barmakī family maintained its ascendancy until 187/803, when al-Rashīd unexpectedly ordered Jaʿfar executed and his father and brother imprisoned. According to al-Jahshiyārī, the Baghdādīs attributed the fall of the much-beloved Barmakīs to the Caliph's treachery and greed.[31] Poets bewailed the death of Jaʿfar, and even the Caliph is said to have regretted killing him.

In *Alf laylah wa-laylah*, Jaʿfar appears as the Caliph's companion, particularly during the Caliph's nocturnal excursions in Baghdad.[32] Korda's screenwriters would have encountered Jaʿfar in any of the translations of the *Nights*, or in some adaptation of the *Nights* stories. The Jaffar of Korda's *Thief* even mentions his nighttime rambles with Hārūn al-Rashīd. However, the transformation of "Jaʿfar the minister" into a power-hungry sorcerer is the innovation of Korda's screenwriters; Arabic literature knows Jaʿfar only as the loyal, generous, and sybaritic minister betrayed by his capricious master.

Jaffar's prominence in the Korda film arises from a directorial decision to show off the talents of Conrad Veidt.[33] Veidt had previously played "somnambulant murderers, misshapen clowns, sinister magicians, intriguing statesmen, maniacal Hindus"; later he played Nazis, notably in *Casablanca* (1942).[34] In order to showcase Veidt, scriptwriters created a major character, minister and magician combined, and gave him the name of the most celebrated minister of medieval Islam. Either Veidt's memorable performance, or the narrative economy of combining two characters into one, or both, led Disney screenwriters to import the character practically unchanged into *Aladdin*. The corresponding Disney character, called "Jaffar," plays as prominent a role in *Aladdin* as Jaffar does in Korda's *Thief*, and bears a marked resemblance to Conrad Veidt in his sorcerer costume.

Korda's second major contribution to the *Aladdin* cast is the Djinni. In the Arabic tale, the Jinnī of the Lamp is (almost always) blindly servile, despite his menacing appearance. Korda's Djinni, played by Rex Ingram, is also gigantic and menacing, but has come to resemble the wise but caustic Black slave persona familiar from period films, most notably Hattie McDaniel's Mammy character in *Gone With the Wind* (1939). The Djinni heckles his master Abu the Thief, laughing thunderously at his attempts to make proper wishes, and mockingly calling him "little master of the universe." Unlike Mammy, however, the Djinni flaunts his liberty when he receives it. When Abu accuses him of ingratitude, he replies: "Slaves are not grateful—not for their freedom." The *Aladdin* Genie, chiefly animated by Eric Goldberg and voiced by Robin Williams, also yearns for his freedom. However, his creators sidestepped the race issue, ambiguously thematized in Korda's *Thief*, by coloring their Genie a racially indeterminate blue.[35]

The creators of Disney's *Aladdin* returned, like their predecessors, to the "Aladdin" story, and, like Fairbanks, chose to thematize the illegitimacy of the character's magical acquisitions. Ron Clements, co-writer, director, and producer (along with John Musker), explained the principles that governed the Disney adaptation:

> The original story was sort of a winning the lottery kind of thing. [. . .] When we got into it, particularly coming in at the end of the 1980's, it seemed like an Eighties 'greed is good' movie. [. . .] Like having anything you could wish for would be about the greatest thing in the world and having that taken away from you is bad, but getting it back is great. We didn't really want that to be the message of the movie. We tried to put a spin on it. Like having anything you could wish for may seem like the greatest thing in the world. But things are never quite what they seem.[36]

Disney's *Aladdin* goes further than any previous version in Americanizing the characters. Whether because of a desire for authenticity or out of a felt obligation to "political correctness," the designers gave their protagonists dark skin, dark hair, and other ostensibly Middle Eastern features. But the sympathetic characters all speak perfectly American English (at least, of the characters who can speak). Among the Genie's first speeches is a campy routine that Americanizes Aladdin's name: "Aladdin! Hello, Aladdin, nice to have you on the show. Can we call you 'Al?' or maybe just 'Din?' or how 'bout 'Laddie?' " Aladdin exemplifies swagger, spunk, and optimism; his appearance was modeled on the Tom Cruise character in the patriotic film *Top Gun.* The Princess Jasmine, whose appearance was modeled on animator Mark Henn's sister Beth, becomes the mouthpiece of opposition to a vaguely defined Middle Eastern backwardness and authoritarianism. Musker described her as "rebelling against the social structure in choosing to marry someone of her own free will, and rightfully so. We're with her on that one. She should follow her heart and not to have her life dictated to her by anyone above her or in authority over her.[37]

In his preface to the *Supplemental Nights*, Burton railed against stories in which the Orientals behave just like Europeans. Such tales, he claimed, both fail to entertain and fail to depict the Orient as it really is or was. Burton nevertheless admitted that "Aladdin" had become "a household word in England," even when English readers knew the tale only through "the wretched English version of Prof. Galland's admirable French."[38] A hundred years later, the popularity of these "monstrous births" rages unabated, as in John Culhane's fustian tribute to Aladdin:

> The dream of great animated musical comedy that began with Walt Disney's *Silly Symphonies* is entering a new age with *Aladdin*. Just as the Genie shows himself capable of endless transformations, the medium itself is capable of endless permutations of words, music and designs in motion and color, making animated personalities that we suddenly discover are unforgettable. To touch our hearts, to tickle our funnybones, to remind us of where we have been before, and to transport us to whole new worlds, to remind ourselves that we can crawl in the mire or aim for the stars, for all these reasons and many more, human beings created theater. In this house of the human spirit there are many mansions. Animation lives in one of them, and currently the characters in Aladdin are holding a celebration there.[39]

But Burton also demanded that the Oriental tale speak of the real Orient. Under his scrutiny, the smallest of details yielded Oriental truths both immutable and practical. For example, upon the occurrence of the word "injustice" in a *Nights* tale, Burton noted:

> Arab[ic] Zulm, the deadliest of the monarch's sins. One of the sayings of Mohammad, popularly quoted, is "Kingdom endureth with Kufr or infidelity (i.e., without accepting Al-Islam) but endureth not with Zulm or injustice." Hence the good Moslem will not complain of the rule of Kafirs or unbelievers, like the English, so long as they rule him righteously and according to his own law.[40]

Burton's faith in the verisimilitude of the Oriental tale far outstripped that of Zotenberg, who claimed only that "Aladdin" presents a relatively faithful portrait of medieval Egyptian manners. Burton's footnote, on the other hand, effortlessly connects the appearance of a common Arabic word in a late-medieval tale with a seventh-century Prophetic dictum and, on the basis of this supposed continuity of "Moslem" thinking, offers guidance to colonial administrators, presumably including rulers of such non-Arab provinces as India.

In the 1990s, the Western spectator, far from hoping for Burton's "verisimilitude," can only dread it. Two years before *Aladdin*'s release, American armed forces had carried out the first air raids and missile attacks against Baghdad. To forestall disturbing associations, Disney changed the name of Aladdin's metropolis from "Baghdad" to the mythical but Eastern-sounding "Agrabah." Aladdin had now come almost full circle. In the Arabic tale, the hero's adventures take place in "the farthest city of China, a city called al-Qalʿās," a nonsensical name in Arabic.[41] The Western-language adaptations of the *Nights* had moved Aladdin out of China—Lang's 1916 retelling of "Aladdin," for example, settles him in Persia[42]—and Fairbanks's 1924 film had established Baghdad as the scene par excellence of Arabian film adventures. In the wake of the Gulf War, Disney moved him out of Baghdad and back into the Eastern never-never land of his birth. Had *Aladdin* depicted "Baghdad" instead of "Agrabah," American moviegoers would have had to admit that Aladdin, "a street kid who knows he was meant for bigger things in life," Abu, "a little capuchin monkey whose pickpocketing tendencies get him into trouble in the story," Jasmine, "independent, spunky, and determined to follow her heart," and many of their friends, neighbors, and fellow citizens, are the sort of figures likely to have been imprisoned, gassed, or shot by Saddam's army and secret police, or to have perished in the American bombardments or the civil war that followed them.[43]

The Arabic ʿAlā ʾal-Dīn demands from the Jinnī bigger and better versions of existing objects. The storyteller's world represents the real world (hers and ours), since the appearance of the Jinnī's monster births surprises and terrifies the characters in the story as much as it would surprise and terrify anyone who beheld such wonders in the real world. In 1924, Fairbanks demanded a bigger and better version of the Orient: not of the real Orient, but of the Orient's presumed dream of itself. *The Thief of Bagdad*'s first intertitles consist of the opening verse of the Qurʾān (albeit mistranslated), and the first line of the *Thousand and One Nights*, as if to document the film's intention to represent the best of the East. In 1924, this consists of Arabs who dream not of independence from the British and French mandates, but of magic ropes and flying carpets; or more exactly, Arabs who live in a world where magic is commonplace—that is, not the real world of the storyteller or the audience. In the late 1930s, Korda could still believe that the East's dream of itself corresponded to something in the actual East: he planned to shoot scenes for his *Thief of Bagdad* on location in Egypt and Arabia.[44] The war forced him to shoot in Arizona instead, but Korda, like the Jinnī, had the power to create worlds out of nothing. Ultimately he did produce a bigger and better version: not of the Orient, but of Fairbanks's film.

In the early 1990s, the Orient no longer exists, even as an abstraction: in its place have arisen "the Third World," "the Middle East," "the Arab World," and "the Muslim World." The "Thief of Baghdad" would now be, from an Arab nationalist point of view, Britain, which held Iraq under mandate after World War I; and from the United Nations' point of view, Saddam Hussein, who stole Kuwait. Representations of a bigger and better Third World might indeed "remind us of where we have been before, and transport us to whole new worlds," but such representations, no matter how much bigger and better than the real thing, are unlikely "to touch our hearts" or "tickle our funnybones" in the way Culhane proposes. Recognizable Third World scenes and figures have come to resemble Fairbanks's real flowers: their effect against a highly imaginative background would be grotesque. By depicting no real objects at all, the animated Aladdin completes the process Fairbanks began when he banished real flowers from the set. In the world outside the theater, the West has renounced Burton's desire for an Orient both magical and authentic, but, like Fairbanks's thief, it believes that "happiness is a quality that can be stolen," or, failing that, created out of magic lamps. Having the Orient taken away is bad, but getting it back is great.

Notes

1. I would like to thank Peter Sagal for his advice on cinematographic matters, and Dr. Rebecca Spang for her many insightful comments on an earlier draft of this paper.

2. M. H. Zotenberg, "Notice sur quelques manuscrits des *Mille et une nuits* et la traduction de Galland," *Notices et extraits des manuscrits de la Bibliothèque Nationale et autres bibliothèques* 28 (1887): 167–320, at 193.

3. Sir Gore Ousely, *Oriental Collections* (1797), 2: 25–33, cited in Burton, "Translator's Foreword" to the *Supplemental Nights to the Book of the Thousand Nights and a Night, with Notes Anthropological and Explanatory* (London, 1888), 5: 10.

4. A complete account of the manuscript traditions for "Aladdin" will be found in Zotenberg, "Notice," and of the Western reception of *Alf laylah wa-laylah* in Dwight Reynolds, "Translation and Transformation: The Fabulous History of the Western Creation of the Thousand and One Nights," to have

appeared in *Muqarnas* 12 (1995). I thank Professor Reynolds for drawing my attention to this topic.

5. P. R., "Dr. Russell on the Authenticity of the Arabian Tales," *The Gentleman's Magazine* LXIX 1:2 (February 1799): 91–92.

6. Zotenberg, "Notice sur quelque manuscrits," 167.

7. Ibid., 194–200.

8. Ibid., 201–5. The manuscript in question, B. N. Supplément arabe 2522 and 2523, is sometimes called the Sabbagh MS after its copyist Michel Sabbagh. I refer to the "Aladdin" story that it contains as "Zotenberg's Aladdin," after its editor and publisher.

9. Richard Burton, Foreword to the *Supplemental Nights*, 3: vii.

10. Edward William Lane, *The Thousand and One Nights: The Arabian Nights Entertainments*, ed. Stanley Lane-Poole, 1: xiv. "The Story of ʿAla-ed-Din and the Wonderful Lamp," trans. Stanley Lane-Poole, appears in vol. 4: 323–411.

11. "[The author of "Aladdin"] presents a fairly faithful portrait of Egyptian manners during the reign of the later Mamlūk sultans, with the exception of private life at court, of which he obviously had only the most fantasticated conception"; Zotenberg, "Notice sur quelques manuscrits," 234.

12. Ibid., 235.

13. "A literary work of indisputable merit."

14. "Who, using the simplest possible means—like La Fontaine with his fables—was able to give his Oriental fiction a gracious turn and a more universally human scope"; ibid., 234.

15. In the following accounts, names of characters are spelled as they appear in the text under discussion, and transliterated when they appear in Arabic. Thus, ʿAlāʾ al-Dīn is the protagonist of Zotenberg's story, and Aladdin of the Disney film. However, I will refer to the character abstracted from its narrative context as Aladdin, or to the core story as "Aladdin," following the most common English spelling. Jinnī, Djinni, and Genie all refer to the supernatural creature (very different in each appearance). Recurrent characters without names, such as the Sorcerer, will be capitalized.

16. Zotenberg, "Notice sur quelques manuscrits," 280, trans. Lane-Poole, "The Story of ʿAla-ed-Din," 371.

17. A Scenario Writer, "Evolution of a Picture," *New York Times*, March 16, 1924.

18. Ibid.

19. On Valentino as the ethnic Other, see Gaylyn Studlar, "Discourses of Gender and Ethnicity: The Construction and De(con)struction of Rudolph Valentino as Other," *Film Criticism* 13:2 (Winter 1989): 18–35, and Miriam Hansen, *Babel and Babylon: Spectatorship in American Silent Film* (Harvard, 1991), 245–94. On Cobra, see Studlar, 29.

20. "Troubles of a Baghdad Thief," *New York Times*, March 2, 1924.

21. John Culhane states that the backgrounds of Disney's *Aladdin* de-

rive from 1,800 photographs taken by layout director Rasoul Azadani in his hometown of Isfahan. Elsewhere, however, Culhane states that *Aladdin*'s visual style is based on "the study of Persian miniature paintings from approximately 1000 to 1500 C.E., various Victorian paintings of Eastern cultures; numerous photo-essay and coffee-table books on the Middle East; Disney animated films from the mid-Forties to the mid-Fifties, and Alexander Korda's 1940 film *The Thief of Bagdad*" (John Culhane, *Disney's Aladdin: The Making of an Animated Film* [New York: Hyperion, 1992], 89 and 100). As this account suggests, the visual texture of Fairbanks's *Thief* and its successors derives not from "Arabian" sources exclusively, but—like the "Oriental tale"—from an indiscriminate mix of Arab, Persian, and Turkish architectural and decorative elements, often refracted through nineteenth-century Orientalist representations. Both John Flanagan and Richard Foltz have drawn my attention to the important role played by images of the Ottoman world in the construction of Western representations of "Arabia."

22. "Evolution of a Picture."

23. Beverly Heisner, *Hollywood Art: Art Direction in the Days of the Great Studios* (Jefferson, N.C.: McFarland, 1990), 45.

24. "Evolution of a Picture."

25. James Wong Howe, in John Hambley and Patrick Downing, Thames Television's *The Art of Hollywood* (London: Thames Television, 1979), 96, cited in Heisner, *Hollywood Arts*, 43.

26. Zotenberg, "Notice sur quelques manuscrits," 286–87.

27. Since Menzies's world is already fantastic, the Jinnī's magical palace and the Sultan's "real" one would have to look alike. Fairbanks's script sidesteps this problem to some extent by omitting both the Jinnī and his palace from the story. *Thief* still has its magical props and ex nihilo creations, but the characters in the story perceive them as wonderful rather than monstrous.

28. Disney continues to transform Aladdin's identity: the blurb for the newly released *Aladdin* videocassette describes the protagonist as "a streetwise peasant."

29. Abū ʿAbd Allāh Muḥammad b. ʿAbdūs al-Jahshiyārī, *Kitāb al-wuzarāʾ wa l-kuttāb*, ed. M. al-Saqqāʾ, I. al-Abyārī, and ʿA. al-Shalabī, 2nd ed. (Cairo, 1401/1980), 189.

30. Shams al-Dīn Muḥammad b. Aḥmad b. ʿUthmān al-Dhahabī, *Siyar aʿlām al-nubalāʾ*, vol. 9, ed. Sh. al-Arnaʾūṭ and K. al-Kharrāṭ (Beirut, 1982), 61.

31. Al-Jahshiyārī, *Kitāb al-wuzarāʾ wa l-kuttāb*, 243.

32. In the tale of "The Porter and the Three Ladies of Baghdad," Burton translates: "The Caliph, Hārūn al-Rashīd, had gone forth from the palace, as was his wont now and then, to solace himself in the city that night, and to see and hear what new thing was stirring; he was in merchant's gear, and he was attended by Jaʿfar his Wazir, and by Masrūr his Sworder of Vengeance."

33. On Korda's script, see Karol Kulik, *Alexander Korda: The Man Who Could Work Miracles* (London: W. H. Allen, 1975), 224.

34. Theodore Strauss, "The Return of the Somnambulist," *New York Times*, May 12, 1940; Robert E. Morsberger, "The Thief of Bagdad," *Magill's Survey of Cinema.* English Language Films. First Series (Englewood Cliffs, N.J.: Salem Press, 1980), 4: 1707.

35. In addition to developing the characters of the Minister and the Djinni, Korda's film preceded Disney's *Aladdin* in attempting to cash in on merchandising spin-offs. A 1940 newspaper feature announces: "Within the next few weeks 'Thief of Baghdad' story books, coloring books, games, jewelry, masquerade costumes, 'Flying Carpet' scatter rugs, dolls, and so forth, will appear in the stores. In addition, textile fabrics, in cottons and rayons, will be available in the form of children's dresses, ladies sportswear, ladies' dresses, misses' dresses, house coats, underwear, scarfs, hats, turbans, babushkas, and other types of headgear" (Thomas E. Pryor, "Profitable Gleanings: Movies Tap New Financial and Publicity Mines through Commercial Tie-Ups," *New York Times*, January, 28, 1940).

36. Culhane, *Disney's Aladdin*, 15–16.

37. Ibid., 62 (Tom Cruise), 41 (Beth and Jasmine), 16 (Musker quote).

38. Burton, *Supplemental Nights*, 3: 51; 5: ix.

39. Culhane, *Disney's Aladdin*, 116–17.

40. Burton, *A Thousand Nights and a Night*, 1: 186.

41. Zotenberg, "Notice sur quelques manuscrits," 249.

42. Andrew Lang, ed., *Aladdin and the Wonderful Lamp, and Other Stories from the Fairy Books* (London: Longmans, 1916), 12.

43. The descriptions of the characters come from Culhane, *Disney's Aladdin*, 10.

44. Kulik, *Alexander Korda*, 240.

13 An Allegory from the *Arabian Nights:* The City of Brass

Andras Hamori

Mais les bijoux perdus de l'antique Palmyre,
Les métaux inconnus, les perles de la mer,
Par votre main montés, ne pourraient pas suffire
A ce beau diadème éblouissant et clair;

Car il ne sera fait que de pure lumière,
Puisée au foyer saint des rayons primitifs,
Et dont les yeux mortels, dans leur splendeur entière,
Ne sont que des miroirs obscurcis et plaintifs!

BAUDELAIRE, *Bénédiction*

Gloomiest of travelogues, the tale of the City of Brass engages our attention in puzzling ways. Through its maze of episodes, conventional pessimism and the old cry *ubi sunt* are staged, sensed, and at last transcended. I am attempting a few remarks here on the nature and fascination of this maze, hoping to demonstrate its coherence and to show the source of its power.[1]

The story is an account of an archaeological expedition that consists of two parts: one planned and one fortuitous. In the opening scene, the caliph ᶜAbdalmalik ibn Marwān and his courtiers are seen discussing legends of the past. The talk turns on King Solomon's dominion over the jinn, and on the still extant brass bottles in which he imprisoned the refractory ones. The caliph is overwhelmed by curiosity, and at once an expedition is organized to the country in the

Reprinted from Andras Hamori, "An Allegory from the *Arabian Nights:* The City of Brass," in *On the Art of Medieval Arabic Literature* (Princeton, N.J.: Princeton University Press, 1974), 145–63. Reprinted by permission of the publisher.

far west where such bottles may be found. The project is successful, for, in spite of losing their way in the desert, the explorers manage to reach their destination and return to Damascus with several exhibits. Of the two leaders, Ṭālib ibn Sahl falls victim to his greed in the City of Brass, and the emir Mūsā, his task done, retires to a life of piety in Jerusalem. The hub of the tale is the visit to the City of Brass. It comes about when the party strays from the direct road, and its description is simply inserted in the larger narrative. This is not, however, an instance of the usual technique of employing a frame story to bring together many stories and hold the audience's attention by tying the parts into one. In our tale, the planned and the fortuitous are linked in a number of ways, and the links are among our first clues for understanding the storyteller's overall plan.

The explorers go off on a search after flotsam that has not yet gone under in time, and that, although it is flotsam, is a reminder of Solomon's glory. But already in the initial account of the brass bottles we come upon an ironic note. It is told that when one of the Solomonic seals is broken and a demon released, he gives a loud cry of repentance—prudently, for "the notion that Solomon is alive enters his mind."[2] The ambivalence of the jinn's cry will return to haunt the listener as the story progresses.

After a whole year's journey, the expeditionary party and their guide, a wise and pious shaykh, suddenly find that they are lost in the desert. This happens in the morning, and as they have nothing better to do they push on. By the time of midday prayer they come upon an imposing black castle, which the shaykh can identify. They are on an alternate road that leads from the black castle to the City of Brass, and then to the country of the bottles. It is curious that the narrator pays no attention at all to the travelers' plight, dramatic as their straying in the desert might be. He merely makes sure of providing a displacement with a jolt; descriptions do not concern him here. After a year on the road our explorers are snatched up and set on their way to the perverted time of the City, where past and present are confused by varied dissimulations.

The black castle is a kind of ghost town. There is no one about, and only inscriptions are there to tell the story of a vanished potentate's futile—and in the end ludicrous—efforts to resist mortality.

M. Gerhardt sees the black castle as a prefiguration of the City of Brass, but she feels that "nothing happens in or because of it . . . and the whole episode serves no other purpose than to create a repository for the homilies given in the inscriptions."[3] I think that this instance of prefiguration is actually of great structural importance, all the more so because it is not the only one in the tale. With each anticipated event, we are made aware of having been drawn toward it all along, and we sense that there is a kind of law to the direction taken by our ostensibly erratic divagations.[4] The relation between the castle and the City of Brass is such that we seem lured into a dream. The first episode is in a way realistic, while in the second the implicit menace of the first is given body to create a nightmare—a nightmare thus somehow born of our own minds.

On leaving the black castle, the travelers come upon a piece of magical engineering: the figure of a horseman cast in brass, which will swivel around at the touch of a hand and indicate the direction toward the City of Brass. This machine is not in itself evil, but it is ominous, as are other robots in the *Nights*, such as the uncanny boatman in the "Third Qalandar's Tale," or the horse in "The Ebony Horse." Magic and illusionist sculpture will both have a role in the City of Brass, as parts of an ironic setting.

Continuing their passage through the desert, the explorers find a column of black stone in which a demon is wedged. He tells a curious tale, and it appears that he was punished in this fashion by Solomon whom out of pride and folly he attempted to challenge. We are now explicitly brought back to the Solomonic motif of the apparent frame story. Apparent, because in fact the entire tale is very much of one piece; for in the central episode of the City of Brass the audience must recognize a series of allusions to Solomon, and the whole journey is calculated to stand out against the Solomonic exemplum.

The exemplum has two sides. First: Solomon is an instance of mortal magnificence. The demon episode conjures up the pageantry of power from the Koran, recalling the jinn and the birds that served in the king's army, and mentioning his command of the wind. In the geographer Ibn al-Faqīh's version of the City of Brass legend, one of the inscriptions found on the city walls reads: "If any creature could attain eternal life, Solomon the son of David would have attained it."[5] It is as if the *Arabian Nights* had dropped this sentence in order to dramatize it instead.

Second: there is a darker aspect—Solomon's fall from grace and power. It is a temporary lapse according to the main line of Islamic tradition; the rabbinic opinions are more varied and more pessimistic.[6] In his *Stories of the Prophets*, Thaʿlabī tells us that Solomon possessed extraordinary powers by virtue of a ring that, in punishment for an act of idolatry committed under his roof, he once lost to a demon for a period of forty days.[7] During that time, the demon Ṣakhr impersonates the king, who, driven from his house and made unrecognizable, becomes a fugitive. The story of this demonic fraud has provided medieval Koran commentators with one of the standard interpretations of the unclear, somber verse (38:34): *wa-la-qad fatannā Sulaymāna wa-alqaynā ʿalā kursīyihi jasadan thumma anāba*, "We allowed Solomon to be seduced by temptation, and we cast a body upon his seat. Then he repented."

It is an important clue for understanding the entire tale that the demon in the rock is a close variation on Ṣakhr in the legend of the ring, and that his story is an unmistakable allusion to the demonic impersonation of Solomon. The *Arabian Nights* demon is punished because he aided and abetted a king who refused Solomon his daughter, and whose island realm Solomon then invaded. These events correspond to the exposition in the legend of the ring, where Solomon finally obtains the princess—to his grief, because it is the same princess' idolatry that later brings divine punishment upon him. Our demon is locked in a vise of stone; so is, in the legend, the impostor Ṣakhr at the end of his forty days' rule.[8] In the legend, Ṣakhr and his rock are thrown into the sea; this obviously could not be paralleled if the demon was to be a speaking character in the tale of the City of Brass.

The allusion to the outcast Solomon and to the deceptive body on the throne plays a number of essential roles. First: it strengthens the fabric of the tale because it is again a prefiguration; for in the City of Brass proper, various deceptive bodies (culminating in a body on a throne) will be the chief motifs. Second: as we shall see, the legend of Ṣakhr and Solomon is important because allegorical interpretations of it abounded in the Middle Ages. Third: the allusion is important

queen's tablet explains that a famine had set in and everyone starved when gold could no longer buy food. As Gerhardt remarks, "viewed realistically, it is absurd: a population dying of hunger would not lay itself out as tidily, even pompously, as is described here. . . ." She suggests that the explanation may be a late, rationalizing addition, provided, together with other rhetorical matter in the inscriptions, by a "prolix man of letters."[17] But it is possible to see the question in a different light, and consider Macnaghten's text an intellectually and artistically respectable whole.

The explanation on the tablet is absurd, and it is meant to be that when realistically viewed. After all, the inscriptions warn us several times to "set aside provisions," and in those phrases the word *zād* must denote other provisions than bread and meat.[18] Its Islamic source is the one Koranic occurrence of the word (2:197): *wa-mā tafᶜalū min khayrin yaᶜlamuhu l-lāhu wa-tazawwadū fa-inna khayra z-zādi t-taqwā*, "God knows of the good deeds you do. Store up provisions; for the best of provisions is the fear of God."[19] Our reading of the story must determine whether we take the *zād* mentioned in the City of Brass to mean piety, or rather food for thought: provisions for the mystic or gnostic traveler. At any rate, here the journey in the tale becomes a spiritual one; the happenings in it ripen into metaphor and the tableaux into allegory. It is, so to speak, a *qūt al-qulūb*, "food for the heart," that is meant by *min ᶜadami l-qūti mātū*, "they died for lack of food."[20] In the City of Brass life is reduced to a kind of taxidermy because it is a place of spiritual starvation. It is not unrelated that elsewhere in the *Nights* magic tends to appear as a mode of power in its utmost capriciousness, but here it is a mode of futility, a misdirected effort at transcending the limits of humanity.

That the City of Brass is meant to be allegorical becomes even clearer upon the party's subsequent arrival at Karkar, where the coveted bottles are found. Here a light shines over the face of the earth on the night before Friday, and the natives are Muslims who learned their religion from Khiḍr, the divine intermediary and prototype of the esoteric knower, ᶜārif. After the black walls—and for that matter the towers that seemed of fire—that guarded the City of Brass, Karkar offers a complete contrast. The religion of Khiḍr is the alternative to spiritual famine. There is a curious touch: the visitors are given to eat the meat of fish in human shape. This is illusion with fangs drawn; here no one mistakes the outer form for the human being.[21]

It seems to me that on the basis of the queen's tablet we can exclude a purely ethical interpretation of the allegory. It is stressed there that the queen was a good and just ruler, unlike the self-centered author of the black castle inscriptions. Khiḍr and the light of Karkar suggest that *zād* is meant to have esoteric connotations.[22]

At last the travelers return to Damascus. Of the things brought back, the jinn are released, the human-looking fish die of the heat, and the treasures are distributed among the Muslims.

We can now turn again to the question of coherence in the story. It seems to me that the attentive listener will see the sequence of ostensibly adventitious events united and made meaningful in two essential ways: (1) by the prefigurations through which the ultimate ironic experience of the City of Brass draws the voyagers toward itself, from "the notion that Solomon is alive enters his mind," through the black castle and the demon's allusion to the body on Solomon's throne, to Mūsā's perplexity before the dead queen; and (2) by the implicit presence of the Solomonic exemplum in passages that seem to stand in an accidental relation to the "frame story." It may be added here that the explicitly Solomonic sections are more or less symmetrically placed, the demon episode coming between the black castle and the City of Brass.

With its insistence on false appearances, the tale acts out the idea of the world as mirage, which one of the homilies speaks about, and it forces us to experience the concern about provisions that is reiterated in the inscriptions. It is an error to think that the tale is somehow draped around the properly homiletic passages in it and exists for their sake, but it is quite as wrong to regard them as cumbersome adjuncts devised by a pedantic litterateur. The reading of the tablets and the emir's ritualistic crying in response[23] are performative acts through which the story reaffirms, and participates in, a collective mood. At the same time, however, the allegory invites the audience to go beyond a trivial understanding of the homilies. For people who have seen (or would see) Karkar, going on a journey—the *irtiḥāl* of the homilies—will come to stand for other voyages besides that of death.[24]

But the true homiletic effect of the story springs from its structure, and particularly from the structural harmony between the line followed by Mūsā's journey on the one hand, and the affair of Solomon and the jinn on the other. If the story of the City of Brass was meant to be interpreted, one of the questions to be asked must be why the imprisoned jinn are found at Karkar, the place of light. In a none-too-clear passage, Khiḍr and the imprisoned jinn are linked in Ibn al-Faqīh's version of the legend too,[25] but the *Arabian Nights* story stresses the opposition between the City and Karkar to an extent that invites—and expects—further probing. Islamic mystical literature, not unexpectedly, abounds in references to Solomon and the demons, and a few of these will answer our question. In the "Tale of the Occident Exile," by Suhrawardī of Aleppo, the obedient jinn who served Solomon appear together with the Koranic fountain of molten brass that they fire up and fashion into a wall.[26] The Persian commentary equates the jinn with the powers of imagination and thought, the fountain with mystical wisdom, and the wall with protection against the Gog and Magog of worldliness. By a similar logic, in Ibn ʿArabī's commentary to Koran 34:12 (*wa-man yazigh minhum*, etc.), the rebellious jinn stand for the inclination toward the allurements of sensual drives (*nafs*).[27] For our story, the demon episode (with its allusion to the legend of Solomon's ring and his forty day's exile) turns out to be crucial in the light of examples like the following two from ʿAṭṭār: *dīv-rā vaqtī ke dar zindān kunī—bā Sulaymān qaṣd-i shādurvān kunī*, "If you bind the demon, you will set out for the royal pavilion with Solomon" and *az ān bar mulk-i khvīshat nīst farmān—ke dīvat hast bar jā-yi Sulaymān*, "You have no command over your self's kingdom, for in your case the demon is in the place of Solomon."[28] Finally, in Ibn ʿArabī's multilayered commentary to *wa-la-qad fatannā Sulaymāna*, etc., Solomon's changed appearance after the loss of the ring means, among other things, a distortion of original luminousness.[29] In view of these examples, we can say that the explicit statement on rebellious demons (that they are imprisoned in Karkar) and the allusion to the demon who once had the upper hand over Solomon form a neat bundle if, and only if, the story is read allegorically.

In the Islamic version of the legend of the ring, it is after the ring is recovered that Solomon asks for and receives a power unique in the world. Mūsā's journey follows a similar sequence. The deceptive bodies in the City of Brass, as mementoes of spiritual starvation, parallel the demonic impersonation of Solomon and the spiritual loss of the true self. The party's arrival at Karkar corresponds to recovering the ring and casting out the usurper and illusionist. Obviously, both storylines can be interpreted in a number of ways, whether as examples of pride and fall, or as gnostic tales of the soul's exile and return. The pattern of symbolism could accommodate the Ghazālī of the *Mishkāt al-anwār* as well as it would suit an Ismāʿīlī, Suhrawardī, or ʿAṭṭār. What matters is that the two sets of motifs are composed, not patched together.

Whatever the precise intent of the allegory, the allusive technique used in the story provides the reader with an exercise in interpretation. The journey invites a symbolic reading, *taʾwīl*, and the Solomon motif a parallel reading, *taṭbīq*.[30] The emphasis on interpretation would still fit many directions of thought, and the denotations of terms that may have been used technically—such as *maʿād*, "return," "the life to come," etc., for example—must depend on the storyteller's doctrine, if indeed he held an exact one.[31] Certain motifs, such as the glazed floor, are likely to have been inserted with a *taʾwīl* in mind, or perhaps simply as inducements to interpretation.[32]

Gerhardt lists a number of other versions of the City of Brass legend in Arabic.[33] Most interesting in regard to prototypes is the passage from Ibn al-Faqīh al-Hamadhānī, which mentions Solomon, Khiḍr, and brass creatures emerging from brass bottles. It is very striking that in this version Mūsā's men are afraid of losing their provisions to the brass men, who are demons.[34] As I have said, Ibn al-Faqīh (or the compendium of his work) leaves many aspects of the anecdote obscure. The role of Khiḍr, for instance, is quite incomprehensible. Our author obviously used a version like Ibn al-Faqīh's, but, as far as one can tell, his use of the motifs he found is quite original.

None of the versions includes the lifelike corpse of the queen, which, however, probably has a prototype in a separate quasi-historical narrative about Palmyra. In the article *Tadmur*, Yāqūt's geographical dictionary relates that the unconsumed body of a long-dead princess was found when the walls of Palmyra were broken through. In that instance the corpse was a malevolent one, with a curse that was duly fulfilled. Ṭālib (who is killed by a robot when he tries to rob the dead queen of her jewels) may have been sacrificed to propitiate this proto-queen for the abrogation of her curse in the

Arabian Nights story. It may also be to our purpose that, as the same article mentions, Tadmur was celebrated for some statues of girls that were perfectly preserved among the ruins.

Mistaking the dead for the living is not an uncommon motif. Its best-known example in Islamic literature is perhaps the anecdote of the prince who strays from his palace during his wedding feast and, drunk, spends the night in a cemetery, taking a corpse for his bride. The story is used as a gnostic parable of the soul's preexistence and return from its terrestrial sojourn, in the forty-eighth epistle of the Sincere Brethren.[35]

It complicates the problem of prototypes to compare the version of the story in the Hebrew *Maʿasēh ha-n^{e}mālāh*,[36] where Solomon himself comes to a desolate castle whose inhabitants died of famine. Even the inscribed counsels tally: *qaḥ l^{e}kā ṣēdāh la-derek*, "provide for the road," it reads over a lintel. In this castle, however, our cadavers are reduced to illusionist statuary inhabited by demons. There is no land of light; the midrash is essentially about the folly of pride and worldliness. It is possible that a common prototype of the "City of Brass" and the *Maʿasēh ha-n^{e}mālāh* existed once, in which the motifs of famine (with properly disintegrated bodies) and of statues with moralistic inscriptions already appeared. Such statues may even have brought on the association of Tadmura.

In their epistle about themselves, the Sincere Brethren define certain stations through which the would-be initiate must pass. At the station that follows formal affirmation and precedes verification by the heart, *at-taṣdīq biḍ-ḍamīr*, matters of doctrine must be pictured in the mind by means of *amthāl*, "parables."[37] Such was the job our author chose when he took his legends and images and made them into provisions for the imagination.[38] The job, to be sure, did not diminish his delight in telling a tale to set our hair on end.

Notes

1. I am using the Macnaghten text, *The Alif Laila* (Calcutta, 1839–42), III, 83–115. In some places the Habicht-Fleischer edition, *Tausend und Eine Nacht* (Breslau, 1825–43), VI, 343–401, is more complete, notably in the episode of the hill, where the Calcutta text promises seven tablets but fails to deliver all of them. Macnaghten's version shows not only more polish but also

a sharper sense for dramatic detail. Habicht, for instance, lacks the striking observations about the ladder or the palace halls in the City of Brass. The queen's name is, I think, correct in Habicht's text and garbled in Macnaghten's, cf. p. 288. In any case, the differences between the two versions are not essential to the interpretation I am suggesting. Translators (Burton, Littmann, etc.) have generally followed Macnaghten and used Habicht to fill in lacunae.

The *City of Brass* is discussed at some length in M. I. Gerhardt, *The Art of Story-Telling* (Leiden, 1963), 195–235, where valuable historical data may be found. Gerhardt and I are at complete variance in our evaluations of structure, cohesion, and meaning in the story.

2. Macnaghten, 85.

3. Gerhardt, *Art*, 207.

4. The *Faerie Queene* offers a good parallel. Guyon's progress through Phaedria's Island to Acrasia's Bower works this way, and so does Britomart's from Malecasta's pictures to Busirane's. Prefigurations give direction to our explorers' travels, and the same kind of thing happens to Spenser's protagonists on their rarely differentiated plain. The resulting feeling is described in Spenser's own line: "For who can shun the chance that destiny doth ordaine" (*FQ* III: i: 37).

5. Ibn al-Faqīh al-Hamadhānī, *Compendium libri Kitab al-boldan*, ed. de Goeje (Leiden, 1885), 90. Quoted in Gerhardt, *Art*, 219–21.

6. Cf. *Gittin*, 68b. It is debated whether Solomon was king and then commoner, or king, commoner, and king again. Rashi, ad loc., explains that only rule over the spirit world is meant. For the flawed figure of Solomon, cf. *Pesiqta Rabbati* 6: 4, to the effect that Solomon would be one of the kings without a share in the world to come had he not built the Temple. An early example of the motif of Solomon's decline can be found near the end of the *Testament of Solomon*, trans. F. C. Conybeare, *Jewish Quarterly Review* XI (1899): 45: "my spirit was darkened, and I became the sport of idols and demons." For a more far-flung instance, cf. Lidzbarski, *Ginzā, der Schatz, oder das grosse Buch der Mandäer* (Göttingen, 1925), 28 and 46. In the Islamic version, Solomon does very well after recovering his ring, but a shadow remains. Cf. ʿAṭṭār's reminder that Solomon entered Paradise five hundred years later than the other prophets because of his ring of power, *Manṭiq aṭ-ṭayr*, ed. Gowharin (Tehran, 1964), 51.

7. Thaʿlabī, *Qiṣaṣ al-anbiyāʾ* (Būlāq, 1869), 253–56. The story is at times questioned, e.g., Zamakhsharī, *Kashshāf*, to *wa-la-qad fatannā Sulaymāna* (IV, 94 in the Beirut, 1947 ed.). Zamakhsharī actually implies that it was in some way Solomon's idea to have an image of the girl's father made (vs. Thaʿlabī, where the girl asks for the image that she then secretly worships), but he still finds it difficult to accept the whole affair as moral justification for Solomon's punishment. There are of course other available explanations for the verse. Some commentators have no interest at all in the moral reasons for Solomon's fall, cf. Qummī, ad loc. (II, 236–37 in the Najaf ed.).

8. In the quoted passage by Qummī, several rebellious demons are locked into rocks, and several into bottles after this incident.

9. Macnaghten, 101: *wa-qad ṣuwwira d-dunyā bayna ʿaynayh*. The phrase is missing in Habicht.

10. Macnaghten, 103.

11. It is interesting to contrast this motif with the belief that it is the bodies of the just that remain uncorrupted. For examples from midrash and *ḥadīth*, cf. R. Mach, *Der Zaddik in Talmud und Midrasch* (Leiden, 1957), 169.

12. Macnaghten, 109; Habicht, 392–93.

13. Macnaghten, 108.

14. Cf. Gerhardt, *Art*, 216–21.

15. This motif is missing in Habicht's text.

16. Gerhardt, *Art*, 205, is mistaken in considering the name arbitrary. For Solomon as the builder of Tadmur, cf. Yāqūt, *Muʿjam al-buldān*, ad loc., Yāqūt's quote from Nābigha Dhubyānī is I: 21–23 in Derenbourg's Paris 1869 edition of the dīwān. Islamic lands may have been acquainted with versions of the Solomon legend in which rule over Tadmur is one of the stages in the shrinking of the king's power. Cf. *Aggadat shir ha-shirim* 3: 33–34, ed. Schechter, *IQR*, VII (1895), 150. Referred to in L. Ginzberg, *The Legends of the Jews* (Philadelphia, 1936), VI, 301.

The name Tadmura is also important for the provenience of the lifelike queen motif, cf. p. 292.

17. Gerhardt, *Art*, 205.

18. Macnaghten, 111 for instance.

19. The idea of spiritual provisions is not, of course, limited to Islam. Cf. Mach, *Zaddik*, 190–94.

20. Macnaghten, 105.

21. For mystical initiation by Khiḍr, cf. L. Massignon, *Essai sur les origines du lexique technique de la mystique musulmane* (Paris, 1954), 131–32.

22. By itself, the death-in-life motif occurs in ethical contexts; cf. the saying attributed to Shaqīq ibn Ibrāhīm in Sulamī, *Kitāb ṭabaqāt aṣ-ṣūfiya*, ed. J. Pedersen (Leiden, 1960), 59: "God has made those who obey Him live in their death, and He has made those who rebel against Him dead during their lives." Esoteric uses of the motif are not particularly rare. For the story of the prince who mistakes a corpse for his bride, see p. 293. The Ismāʿīlī *Haft Bāb* describes the state of those who have missed the right path as "nonexistence dissembling existence," *nīstī-yi hastmānī*, cf. Abū Isḥāq Quhistānī, *Haft Bāb*, ed. and trans. W. Ivanow (Bombay, 1959), 49.

In an allegorical exegesis that is of some interest for unraveling our story, the same book equates pure food with an interpretation (*taʾwīl*) of the Koran that is free of confusions caused by literal understanding, *ẓāhir* (p. 56, to verse 4:160). Ibn ʿArabī's *Tafsīr* interprets the *ṭayyibāt* of 4:160 as divine manifestations.

In Habicht's Karkar, a column of light rises from the sea on the night before Friday, and a man walks on the water, reciting a creed formula. These two motifs are definitely mystical (or theosophic). They are linked in one passage, for example, in the *Kitāb al-mashāriʿ wal-muṭāraḥāt*, cf. Shihāb ad-Dīn Yaḥyā s-Suhrawardī, *Opera Metaphysica et Mystica*, ed. H. Corbin (Istanbul, 1945), I, 505, and the commentary to *ʿamūd aṣ-ṣubḥ* in the *Kitāb at-talwīḥāt*, p. 108 in the same volume.

23. Cf. the article *bakkāʾ*, by F. Meier, in the second edition of the *Encyclopaedia of Islam.*

24. I do not mean that the world-renouncing aspect is invalidated, but that it is kept as a first level, while the story implies that one must pass beyond it. To see the world of experience as a sort of shell or model, and to realize that it is to the intelligible world as darkness is to light is a "first ascent," *al-miʿrāj al-awwal*, for the man starting out toward the divine presence, cf. Ghazālī, *Mishkāt al-anwār* (Cairo, 1964), 50.

25. *K. al-buldān*, 91.

26. Cf. *Qiṣṣat al-ghurba al-gharbīya*, in *Oeuvres philosophiques et mystiques de Shihabaddin Yahya Sohrawardi* [*Opera Metaphysica et Mystica*, II], ed. H. Corbin (Tehran, 1952), 285.

27. II, 303–5 in the Beirut, 1968 edition.

28. *Manṭiq aṭ-ṭayr* 35 (line 612), and *Ilāhī-nāme*, ed. H. Ritter (Istanbul, 1940), 289 (line 12). Reference to the second passage in H. Ritter, *Das Meer der Seele* (Leiden, 1955), 625.

29. II, 356 in the Beirut, 1968 edition.

30. Cf. I. Goldziher, *Die Richtungen der islamischen Koranauslegung* (repr. Leiden, 1952), 244.

31. Cf. *maʿād* in *Rasāʾil Ikhwān aṣ-ṣafāʾ* (Beirut, 1957), IV, 50; *Haft Bāb*, 47; and Daylamī, *Bayān madhhab al-bāṭinīya wa-buṭlānih*, ed. Strothmann (Istanbul, 1939), 37 and 78.

32. For the glazed floor, cf. Ibn ʿArabī's *Tafsīr*, II, 205, or Ḍiyāʾ ad-Dīn Ismāʿīl ibn Hibatallāh al-Ismāʿīlī s-Sulaymānī, *Mizāj at-tasnīm*, ed. Strothmann as *Ismailitischer Koran-Kommentar* (Göttingen, 1944; Abh. Ak. Wiss. Gött., Phil.-Hist. Kl., Dritte Folge, Nr. 31), 334.

The death of Ṭālib could be interpreted in various ways. Politically, for Ṭālib wants to earn the Umayyad caliph's favor by making him a gift of the queen's jewels. Esoterically, if we take the *amāna*, "trust," which Ṭālib breaks as an allusion to Koran 33:72. For *amāna* = *maʿrifa*, "gnosis," cf. Fakhr ad-Dīn ar-Rāzī, *At-tafsīr al-kabīr*, ad loc. Admittedly, it is an old device of plots that only one of two bold heroes escapes unscathed; in this sense Ṭālib is of the line of Enkidu and Pirithous.

It is perhaps more than an accident that the queen is found in the seventh room of the palace, although the author does not mention the number.

Finally, although the City of Brass is traditionally placed in North Africa—which makes arguments about geographical symbolism unsafe—it is tempting to think that the author is telling us something by giving the name

Tadmura (or keeping it if there is a separate prototype for her figure) to a Maghribine princess from beyond the desert of Qayrawān, even though the name is clearly linked to Palmyra. Qayrawān, according to the *Burhān-i Qāṭiʿ*, is among other things a term for the edges of the world; one is tempted to think of Alexander's search for the spring of life in the land of darkness. Quite specifically, in Suhrawardī's *Qiṣṣat al-ghurba al-gharbīya*, 277, Qayrawān is *al-qarya aẓ-ẓālim ahluhā*, "the town of iniquitous inhabitants" (Koran 4: 75), where the protagonist is held in captivity. The place is explained by the commentator: *Qayrawān yaʿnī ʿālam va bi-ẓālim ʿālamīyān khvāste and*, "Qayrawān means the world, and the people of the world are meant by 'the iniquitous.'" One wonders whether there is any implication that one *must* pass through the dark walls of the City of Brass before one may come to the Karkar of the mind. Was the route originally planned at all possible? Corbin interprets the *barzakh* in Avicenna's *Risālat Ḥayy ibn Yaqẓān* as such a necessary passage through the dark, cf. *Avicenna and the Visionary Recital*, trans. W. Trask (New York, 1960), 142 and 159, but against that view cf. A. M. Goichon, *Le récit de Ḥayy ibn Yaqẓān* (Paris, 1959), 86–90. The text of the passage in question is in *Traités mystiques d'Abou Alī al-Hosain b. Abdallah b. Sīnā*, ed. M. A. F. Mehren (Leiden, 1889), fasc. I, p. 8 of the Arabic text.

33. Gerhardt, *Art*, 210–30.

34. Ibn al-Faqīh, *K. al-buldān*, 88–91.

35. IV, 162–64. The *Epistles of the Sincere Brethren* are a tenth-century compendium of science, philosophy, and religion, Ismāʿīlī in politics and Neoplatonic-emanationist in metaphysics. The story also occurs in ʿAṭṭār's *Ilāhī-nāme*, as pointed out by Ritter, *Meer*, 47. The basic motif is widespread. For a curious example from Europe, cf. C. Nodier, *Infernaliana* (Paris, 1966), 96–97.

36. A. Jellinek, *Bet ha-Midrasch* (repr. Jerusalem, 1967), pt. v, 22–26. Referred to in Ginzbergs, *Legends*, VI, 298.

37. IV, 58. I think that, considering the Sincere Brethren's predilection for allegorical tales, *amthāl* must mean "parables" or "allegories" here, and not "maxims," *gnōmai*. (The latter are a means of the rhetorical method of *taṣdīq* according to Averroes. Cf. H. A. Wolfson, "The Terms *Taṣawwur* and *Taṣdīq* in Arabic Philosophy and Their Greek, Latin and Hebrew Equivalents," *The Moslem World* XXXIII [1943]: 118.)

38. The Iranian tradition of the Brazen Hold seems to have no direct bearing on our tale. The travelers' route is unlike the seven stages Isfandiyār must traverse. Sinbādh (*Siyāsat-nāme*, 45) proclaimed that Abū Muslim, the Mahdī, and Mazdak were waiting to return together from a brazen fort, but our City is anything but Messianic. On the Iranian motif, cf. K. Czeglédy, "Bahrām Čōbīn and the Persian Apocalyptic Literature," *Acta Orientalia Acad. Sci. Hung.* VIII (1958): 21–43. For the references to Isfandiyār and Bahrām Chūbīn, I am indebted to Prof. M. Dickson of Princeton.

14 From History to Fiction: The Tale Told by the King's Steward

Muhsin Mahdi

Questions regarding the *Nights*' origin and sources have occupied the attention of literary critics and Orientalists ever since the work was translated into French at the beginning of the eighteenth century. Yet despite the efforts of Schlegel, Hammer-Purgstall, de Sacy, Nöldeke, Macdonald, and other investigators, there are few if any definite answers. Was the work composed in ancient India, in ancient Iran, in Baghdad in Abbasid times, in Cairo in Fatimid times, in Damascus or Cairo in Mamluk times, or in Cairo in the eighteenth century? Each one of these places and periods seems to have its defenders; and "origin" and "source" have been used in so many senses that they evoke only the vaguest of meanings. It is thus understandable that students of the *Nights* have turned away from questions of literary and textual history toward the more profitable study of the work in the light of contemporary literary criticism. Like those who enjoy contemplating antiquities sold by grave robbers, some critics even find rarified delight in purely formal features of stories of unknown authorship, times, and places. Those still eager to know the cultural and literary context so as to form a clearer idea of the social and political intentions of the *Nights* are left to deal with the frequently contradictory guesses and conjectures of the past two centuries.

There is a pressing need to make a fresh start in the study of the *Nights*, combining the approaches of literary history and literary

Reprinted from Muhsin Mahdi "From History to Fiction: The Tale Told by the King's Steward," in *The Thousand and One Nights (Alf Layla wa-Layla) from the Earliest Known Sources*, ed. Muhsin Mahdi, vol. 3 (Leiden: E. J. Brill, 1984), 164–80, 254–62. Reprinted by permission of the author.

criticism. To do so, it is perhaps best to turn away from questions of origins and sources for which no answers seem to be forthcoming and raise instead questions about issues for which tangible evidence can be found. Such, I believe, is the question of the formation of the narrative tradition that has come down to us in the earliest known version of the *Nights*, the fourteenth-century Mamluk version, which for brevity's sake will be called the *Nights* simply. Here, where we have a recension created within a relatively defined historical, geographical, cultural, and linguistic environment, we can begin to raise questions that may contribute to grasping the character of the literary activity that transforms earlier material into a new creation. What can one learn about the formation of the narrative tradition that culminated in this recension of the *Nights*? Can we learn something about the manner in which the storyteller went about transforming earlier models and his reasons for doing what he did? Was it because he functioned within a different linguistic medium, addressed a different audience, or had a different point of view or a larger purpose?

A famous and widely read work of fiction, the *Nights* must attract interest in clarifying the question of possible transformation of the stories contained in it. It is usually taken for granted that such transformation was constantly taking place as the stories were retold one generation after another and as they crossed cultural and linguistic boundaries, and that the formation of the narrative tradition consisted largely of the transformation of earlier models. Yet in spite of the enormous literature on the origins and sources of the *Nights*, very little is known about how this activity actually took place, how narrators or storytellers handled inherited models and reshaped them into new narratives, and how the narrative tradition reached the advanced stage exemplified in the surviving manuscripts. Were the stories merely translated from one language to another with only an Arabic-Islamic patina added in the process of translation and transmission, and then merely copied from one period to another with only minor additions of local names and contemporary customs? Or was the older narrative material—foreign, translated, or of Arabic origin—so thoroughly transformed that the author of the new narrative at each stage used his sources as models, as any imaginative artist does when creating a new work of art?

Since none of the complete stories and cycles of stories in Arabic known to have been translations or close adaptations of foreign models forms part of the earliest surviving recension of the *Nights*, and not a single story—as distinct from stray themes or motifs and short, embedded tales—belonging to this recension can be compared to an existing ancient Indian, Middle Persian, or Byzantine original, it is not possible to venture anything but guesses and suspicions about the transformation of foreign stories in this recension. We are more fortunate with respect to some of the stories composed during the Mamluk period in Damascus or Cairo that used material, or were modeled after stories, originating in Baghdad. The tale that will be analyzed here—the tale told by the king of China's steward in "The Hunchback and the King of China"[1]—is adapted directly from a report about events said to have occurred early in the tenth century in Baghdad and written down during the second half of the tenth century not as fiction but as history. A comparison of the two accounts of the events—the historical and the fictional—will show the manner in which the storyteller went about transforming history into fiction.[2] This is perhaps a unique example; yet I hope to show that it tells us something about the extent and, above all, the nature of the transformation of some earlier stories and the manner in which the narrative tradition of the *Nights* was formed. It cannot, of course, be claimed that this is all that happened in every case, nor can it be claimed that everything that happened in this case happened in every other case; yet something of this sort no doubt happened in the majority of cases.

There is, to be sure, another tale in "The Hunchback and the King of China," that of the barber and the highwaymen,[3] which can be traced to a report transmitted as history by the tenth-century historian al-Masʿūdī about an incident that occurred at the court of the Caliph al-Maʾmūn (ruled 189–218 A.H./813–33 A.D.);[4] but this report deals with a relatively short episode that could have been easily transformed from history into fiction and from one fictional form into another many times between the ninth and the fourteenth centuries. Also, while the general theme of this historical incident is present in the *Nights* version, the transformation of the characters and linguistic surface is so complete that one cannot speak of the historical account except as a distant, indirect model. All the other sources identified so far as having served as models for stories in the *Nights* are themselves fictional. Of these only the well-known *maqāmah*, seance, of the tenth-eleventh century author Badīᶜ al-Zamān al-Hamadhānī named after the dish called *al-maḍīrah*[5] belongs to high literature; and in this case it is certain that the storyteller adapted his version, not from al-Hamadhānī's *maqāmah*, but from a thirteenth-century anonymous collection of stories known as *al-Ḥikāyāt al-ᶜajībah* ("Wonderful Stories"),[6] where he found the structure, characters, and language of al-Hamadhānī's *maqāmah* already transformed. The rest of the fictional sources, whether whole tales or individual incidents, are to be found in this thirteenth-century collection, or else in independently transmitted stories whose language and fictional form could be adapted by the storyteller with only slight modification.

In the case of the tale of the King of China's steward, however, the storyteller was faced with a report that had been transmitted as history, formed part of high literature, contained accurate and detailed references to historical personages and places, and presented linguistic and dialectal peculiarities unfamiliar to him and to his audience.[7] He was no doubt adept at adapting and transforming fictional material when composing his stories, altering, transposing, and inventing incidents to suit his purpose and design. But this historical report must have presented him with additional challenges, not all of which he was trained to meet. A comparison of the *Nights* version of the tale told by the King's steward with its immediate model is likely to provide as full an account as can be expected of the way the storyteller went about refashioning the models he found before him, subjecting them to the rules of his art, and making them fit for incorporation into his longer and more complex stories. We shall be considering a case in which the storyteller had his model literally before his eyes—I suspect he was actually looking at a written copy and writing or dictating his new creation—but a memorized perfect or near-perfect copy would do just as well for my purpose. I suspect, further, that he did not have the opportunity to revise his work in order to cover his tracks and remove the signs pointing to his model.[8] What is certain is that he was no singer of tales, which does not mean that his creation does not contain strong oral features, but oral features in writing and oral composition are not the same thing.

The historical report he used was the version reported by al-Muḥassin al-Tanūkhī (329–84 A.H./940–94 A.D.), a well-known figure of the second half of the tenth century, first as judge in various cities in Mesopotamia, and later in Baghdad as prominent aide to the Buyid king ʿAḍud al-Dawlah (ruled in Iraq 367–72 A.H./978–83 A.D.)[9] in his book *al-Faraj baʿd al-shiddah* or *Deliverance after Stress.* Another version was transmitted on the authority of his son ʿAlī,[10] but the son's version is sufficiently different from his father's to make it easy to identify (for example, the main dish in the report is called *dīgparīgah*[11] instead of *zīrbājah*) and to ascertain that it was not the version used by the storyteller. The following outline shows how closely the storyteller follows the historical version in al-Tanūkhī's *al-Faraj:*

1. Frame: transmission and setting in Baghdad and in China, respectively.[12]
2. Setting: family and business background in Baghdad.[13]
3. The maiden's first visit to the shop.[14]
4. The maiden's second visit.[15]
5. The maiden's third visit: mutual love revealed.[16]
6. The servant's visit to the shop: the maiden's identity and arrangements for entering the Caliph's palace revealed.[17]
7. Adventures on the way to the maiden's apartment in the palace.[18]
8. Meeting with Lady Zubaydah and Lady Shaghab, respectively.[19]
9. Stay in the palace.[20]
10. Eating the *zīrbājah.*[21]
11. First meeting and punishment.[22]
12. Second meeting and punishment.[23]
13. Epilogue: marriage consummated; the happy couple leave the palace and reside in the city.[24]

1. The framing of the historical account in al-Tanūkhī[25] follows the pattern of historical reports. The frame consists of a chain of authorities, beginning with the last link in the chain—the person who transmitted the report to the living narrator who in turn is transmitting it orally or writing it down in a book—and ending with the first link, the person who made the statements or experienced

the events being narrated. A certain amount of information about each link in the chain—the occasion for or the setting of the report's transmission and a reference to the transmitter's reliability—can be added where available or useful in confirming the report's authenticity. In this case, the living narrator was al-Tanūkhī the author. He heard the report from the jurisconsult and judge Ibn al-Narsī.[26] Ibn al-Narsī, in turn, heard the report narrated by a certain merchant—whom he designated by name, but al-Tanūkhī admits to have forgotten the merchant's name—to his father. At the time, Ibn al-Narsī was a young man (*ḥadath*) attending his father, who was receiving a group of people in a social gathering.[27] It is assumed that this took place in Baghdad and that the men attending the gathering were Baghdadi notables listening to a report about events that took place in their city not more than a generation before. The merchant reported that he once attended a banquet given by a colleague, a famous cloth merchant.[28] A number of dishes were served, including the dish known as *zīrbājah*. The host did not eat of this particular dish, and his guests followed his example. He asked them to eat of it and allow him to abstain, but they kept after him until he ate of it. Instead of washing his hands afterward along with everyone else, however, he stood apart to wash his hands by himself, and he continued to wash until the attendant told him he had washed his hands forty times. The guests asked him why he washed his hands so many times; he wouldn't say; they insisted; and he began to tell his story.

In the *Nights* version, the chain of authorities is reduced from four to two: the King's steward (substituting for al-Tanūkhī, Ibn al-Narsī, and the unnamed merchant who narrated the historical report) and the cloth merchant from Baghdad (substituting for the cloth merchant who gave the banquet in Baghdad and told his own story). This type of framing—a character in a story tries to save his life not by telling his own tale, but merely reporting a tale told by someone else attending a banquet where he, the narrator, happens to be present but is not otherwise involved in the tale at all—had not occurred before in the *Nights*. It will occur again in "The Hunchback and the King of China" as the frame of the tale told by the tailor, but nowhere else in the *Nights*, as far as I recall. It is not farfetched to think that it was patterned after the historical report—where the reporter hears the story at a banquet but is not otherwise involved in what happened—and substituted a chain of framing stories for the chain of transmission.[29] Thus the most complex story in the *Nights* seems to be formally patterned after the chain of transmitters of historical reports in the wider sense.[30]

The banquet is moved from Baghdad to a city called China, where "The Hunchback and the King of China" is in progress. It takes place at a particular time in the story, the night before the day the King's steward was narrating the tale to the King of China, and concurrently with other events in "The Hunchback and the King of China": the hunchback's presumed death and the transportation of his body to the house of the Jewish doctor and from there to that of the King's steward. And the setting is transformed from a pleasant occasion, in which a prosperous merchant, the main character in the historical report, invites his colleagues for a meal after which they pass the time listening to his marvelous story, to a solemn occasion. Koran recitations are performed in the presence of the doctors of the religious law and of a large crowd. Then a meal is served. The King's steward happens to be there and so does the cloth merchant from Baghdad, with no explanation how or why he got there. Then, when he refuses to eat of the *zīrbājah* and host and guests insist that he do so, the storyteller changes the sequence of the actions in the historical report, giving rise to an inconsistency in his tale that does not seem to have been noticed by scribes, editors, or translators.[31]

In the historical report, we recall, the cloth merchant first eats the *zīrbājah*, then stands aside and washes his hands forty times. The guests inquire why, and he tells his story. The guests follow the story to satisfy their curiosity about this strange affair—their host's refusal to eat of a dish he offers his guests and his having to stand aside and wash his hands forty times after eating of it. The storyteller is not inattentive to the importance of this incident, and as is his wont whenever he notices something interesting—a good meal, an attractive place, a beautiful maiden—he ornaments, elaborates, or exaggerates. In this case he multiplies the number by three: the cloth merchant is made to wash his hands forty times with potash, forty times with cyperus,[32] and forty times with soap. But the point is that he does the washing *before*, instead of after he eats the *zīrbājah* as in the historical report and as the storyteller's own version requires,[33] since the extraordinary number of washings was a punishment meted out in the story for having eaten the *zīrbājah* and forgotten to wash his hands after, not before, eating it.[34]

The storyteller understood the importance of the number of washings as a kind of punishment. He seized on it as an appropriate place to revise the historical report and add the mutilation theme required by "The Hunchback and the King of China" as a whole. The cloth merchant will pay more dearly for having eaten the *zīrbājah.* Not only will he have to wash his hands three times forty times—that is, one hundred and twenty times—but his thumbs and great toes will have to be cut off as well. All this will be interpolated by the storyteller at the appropriate place in the tale.[35] The entire company will see the mutilation, have its curiosity aroused, center its attention on it, inquire about it, and follow the story to find out how and why it happened, *before* the cloth merchant tells his tale. None of this could happen until the cloth merchant begins to eat of the *zīrbājah*, a stew hard to eat with four fingers. They notice how he stretches out his hand to eat, trembling, full of fear and anger; and they notice the sinister way the food falls from between his fingers. They ask him about his maimed thumb, and he tells them about the other maimed thumb and the maimed great toes. Now they are doubly amazed. They ask him how it came about that he was so maimed and had to wash his hands one hundred and twenty times. The washing incident is preserved but pushed to the background. Attention is focused on the mutilation.[36] The company in the *Nights* version, like the company in the historical report, wishes to know the reason for the excessive number of washings; what causes their "amazement," however, is the mutilation,[37] of which there is no trace in the historical report.

2. The storyteller shifts the historical setting backward, from the time of the Caliph al-Muqtadir (ruled 295–320 A.H./908–32 A.D.) and the lifetime of the cloth merchant who narrated his own story in the historical report, to the time of Harun al-Rashid (ruled 170–93 A.H./785–809 A.D.), the timeless, mythical caliph of the *Nights.* He replaces the two historical characters, the Caliph al-Muqtadir and his mother, Lady Shaghab, with the Caliph Harun al-Rashid and his wife, Lady Zubaydah. The storyteller will fall prey to another inconsistency before "The Hunchback and the King of China" is done. The fourth narrator, the tailor, will say that he was present at a banquet earlier the same day in the same city, China.

At that banquet a young man met an old barber. The young man and the old barber had come from Baghdad also, but after the death of the Caliph al-Mustanṣir (ruled 623–40 A.H./1226–42 A.D.) and after having first met in Baghdad in the year 653 A.H./1255 A.D.[38] This inconsistency—that is, characters living four centuries and a half apart are made to be contemporaries of one another—would only attract the attention of mundane historians, unlike the inconsistency mentioned earlier, which should have drawn the attention of the audience of the *Nights*. The fourteenth-century audience of the *Nights* in Syria and Egypt seemed to have been not only ignorant of the historical topography of Baghdad, but so disinterested in the history of the Abbasid dynasty in Baghdad that Caliphs who had lived centuries apart could be presented to them as contemporaries.

The cloth merchant's father, a modest merchant who gives his son sensible advice and leaves him a modest legacy in the historical report,[39] is transformed by the storyteller into a great merchant who dissipates his wealth through addiction to drinking and music, leaving his son little by way of capital and much by way of debts. The son's character, on the other hand, is modified to emphasize his piety and devotion to the memory of his father and his cleverness as a merchant. He succeeds in repaying the father's many debts and building his own fortune. The respective qualities and attributes of merchants and palace dwellers is a theme that will run throughout the tale. Both in contrast to his father and in his own right, the youth is presented by the storyteller as a pillar of filial piety and a mercantile virtue.

3. The four successive visits to the youth's humble shop in the marketplace are adapted by the storyteller from the historical report with only minor improvements in dramatic presentation. On her first visit, the maiden,[40] a stunning beauty magnificently dressed and adorned, arrives on a she-mule—rather than the favorite riding beast of the Abbasid Caliphs' households, the donkey, as in the historical report[41]—early in the morning, when neighboring shops are still closed. She greets the youth and sits down at his shop. Since the youth does not carry the expensive garments she asks for, he makes her wait until he can get them for her from the other cloth merchants. This provides him with the occasion to converse with her and be "drowned in the sea of her love." When the neighboring shops are opened, he procures all she wants; she takes clothing worth 5,000

pieces of silver and leaves without a word about where she resides or about the price. Love stricken and bewildered, he is too distracted to demand payment. Here, the two versions diverge in describing the youth's reaction. As soon as she departs in the historical report, he recovers his senses, blames himself for allowing a trickstress to dupe him and take advantage of his youth and inexperience, and begins to worry about his impending bankruptcy. In the *Nights* version, the impression she makes on him does not fade as fast from his memory. He remains intoxicated with her love, unable to eat or drink or sleep for a whole week and, after returning to the shop, asks his creditors for more time. His worry about impending bankruptcy is postponed until after the second visit.

4. The second visit takes place two weeks after the first—that is, the youth is made to wait two weeks in the *Nights* version instead of the one week he had to wait in the historical report. She apologizes for the delay and makes the payment, and they converse until the other merchants open their shops. She makes him purchase for her from the merchants goods worth twice as much as on the first visit and leaves, again without a word about the price. This time she is absent for more than a month; creditors begin to press him for payment; he worries about the impending bankruptcy that now seems unavoidable, and offers his possessions for sale. Thus while the historical report repeats the young cloth merchant's concern with bankruptcy a second time, the *Nights* version does not make him turn to his business concerns until he is forced to do so by his creditors.

5. But the trickstress, who had carefully planned the whole affair, returns in time to make the payment and save him from ruin. On this third visit, she does not waste time on merchandise, but engages in such free and pleasant conversation that the youth nearly dies with joy, and then she asks him, "Are you married?"—at which point the poor virgin youth weeps. Still unaware of the trap she has been carefully laying for him, too young and inexperienced to divine her feeling in her actions, face, or speech, and being the merchant he is, he goes to offer her servant some money and ask him to act as go-between. The servant has to explain that she is more in love with him than he with her, that buying garments was merely an excuse on her part, and that he should go back and speak to her himself. She

is, of course, ready to be pleased. Having accomplished her aim, she leaves the shop after telling the youth that the servant will bring him the necessary instructions.

The incident in which the cloth merchant tries to bribe the servant to act as go-between is truncated in the *Nights* version in a manner that shows an effort on the part of the storyteller to modify the maiden's character in a significant way. In the historical report, the youth gets up, tells the maiden he is going to repay the other merchants what he owes them, but goes instead to offer money to the servant. "I went back [to the maiden]—I had told her 'I am going to pay [the other merchants] the gold pieces [I owe them]'—so when I went back [to her] she asked 'Have you paid them the gold pieces!?' and laughed. She had seen that I was with the servant [all the time]." The *Nights* version begins with the phrase "She saw me offer the gold pieces to the servant" and omits the rest of the incident, the only one in the historical report in which the maiden expresses herself jocularly and laughs. This is in keeping with the youth's point of view of the maiden in the *Nights* version: he is impressed with her riches, high rank, and beauty; but he does not experience her refined, relaxed, smiling, and forgiving character as does the youth in the historical report.[42] The *Nights* version is more serious, just as it is more grim, than the historical report.

6. A few days later, the servant arrives at the shop to reveal that the maiden is sick with love of him, that she had been raised by and is the favorite maiden of Lady Zubaydah, the queen-consort of the Caliph Harun al-Rashid, and that she is the stewardess of the harem, the one who has the privilege of going in and out of the palace at pleasure to fetch things for her mistress.[43] He reveals also that she has spoken to Lady Zubaydah about him and asked to be allowed to marry him, but that Lady Zubaydah's permission is contingent on seeing him and deciding whether he is worthy of her. Finally, the servant reveals how the maiden (who seems to have made all the necessary arrangements already) will smuggle him into the Caliph's palace so that he can meet Lady Zubaydah. Should the plan succeed, he can hope to marry the maiden; but should he be discovered, the guards will of course strike off his head. He has to decide on the spot, and he decides to submit to the test.

In the *Nights* version, the servant then instructs him to "walk to the mosque built by Lady Zubaydah on the bank of the Tigris." He arrives there in the evening, performs his prayers, and passes the night in the mosque. In this episode the storyteller systematically removes from the historical report all details about the historical topography of Baghdad.

In the historical report, the youth, who presumably lived somewhere in the Karkh area on the west side of the Tigris where the cloth market was located, is instructed to "cross [the Tigris] to al-Mukharrim [a well-known quarter in tenth-century Baghdad situated slightly to the north of the area where the Caliphs' Residence, Dār al-Khulafāʾ, was located][44] and enter the mosque built by the Lady [the mother of the Caliph al-Muqtadir][45] on the bank of the Tigris, on the outer wall of which, facing the Tigris, the Lady's name is incised in cut brick, and wait there. Abū al-Faraj Ibn al-Narsī [al-Tanūkhī adds at this point] said: This was the mosque whose gate has now [that is, at the time Ibn al-Narsī narrated the report] been blocked by Subuktakīn[46] the Chief Chamberlain, freedman of [the Buyid king] Muʿizz al-Dawlah [ruled in Baghdad 334–56 A.H./945–67 A.D.], known as Jāshangīr, who connected the mosque to the [walled!] space [or courtyard] of his house, making it the place of prayer for his soldier-slaves." The addition of this information to the historical report was necessary. Ibn al-Narsī's learned audience in Baghdad knew that the mosque he named was not open to the public. He had to explain that, while this was true at the time he was narrating the report, it was not the case during the lifetime of the woman who built the mosque as a pious foundation; it was then open to the public and could have easily remained open all night. Neither the storyteller nor his audience, on the other hand, knew anything or cared about the historical layout of Baghdad; and none of this information made sense to them. "Walk to the mosque built by Lady Zubaydah on the bank of the Tigris" was good enough for an audience that knew nothing of the topography of a city long in ruins.

7. The youth spends the night in the mosque, waiting for the adventures that will terminate in the satisfaction of his desires or his death. He is to cross over from the familiar everyday world of the marketplace to the unfamiliar closed world of the Caliph's palace and harem, isolated from the outside world and protected by doorkeep-

ers and guards. When at the break of dawn the maiden's servants arrive with empty boxes followed by the maiden herself, they converse and she weeps, but they do not embrace and she does not shower him with kisses as in the historical report. Then she places him inside the box in which he is to be transported to the palace along with the other boxes in which she pretends to be bringing clothes and other effects for Lady Zubaydah. As the boat floats downstream on its way to the palace, the youth regrets his decision when it is too late, wonders whether he will achieve his desire, weeps, prays to God to save him. Yet he does not abjure his desire or calculate whether its fulfillment would have been worth losing his life, as he does in the historical report: "I said to myself, 'I let myself run the danger of being killed for the sake of a desire that may not be fulfilled after all, and were it to be fulfilled, it would not have been worth dying for.' " When the boxes arrive at the door guarded by the chief servant,[47] he insists on inspecting their contents and begins with the box in which the youth is hidden. The youth is so frightened he cannot control himself. His water runs out of the box. The maiden, whose presence of mind and wits never leave her, accuses the chief servant of having been responsible for spilling the flask of holy water from the well of Zamzam in Mecca and spoiling the colors of her Lady's garments. Then the Caliph himself arrives and wants to inspect the contents of the boxes; the youth nearly dies of fear many times over. After the Caliph has inspected all the other boxes, the maiden again saves the day by insisting that this particular box contains her Lady's special secret effects, which he will soon see when she opens it for him. The box is carried in. The youth is taken out of the box and placed in a secluded room, and the box is filled with other goods for the Caliph to see when opened.

Throughout these breathtaking adventures, and in part because they involve a number of characters in the palace and numerous bits of dialogue, the historical report is full of dialectal expressions. These are removed by the storyteller or else replaced by dialectal expressions current in Mamluk times in Syria and Egypt.[48] The same is true of names of material objects and names of the ranks of the palace guards. In trying to embellish the scene in which the box is carried through the palace corridors, the storyteller presents the chief servant as having "started up from his slumber" when it was broad daylight and even the Caliph was up and about. The scene with the Caliph, which in the historical report is short and the dialogue crisp and rapid, is elaborated far beyond what the audience of the historical report would have found believable, making the Caliph open the boxes one after another and looking at everything in them. Finally, the storyteller deprives the youth of the food, drink, and other amenities[49] with which the maiden provides him in his secluded room: this sign of the maiden's kindness did not conform to the severe aspect of her character soon to be exhibited in the *Nights* version.

8. The storyteller had yet another reason for depriving the youth of food and drink. In the historical report, the meeting with the queen mother takes place the day following his arrival. The storyteller, however, decided to move rapidly and have him meet Lady Zubaydah, the queen consort, soon after his arrival at the harem.

The meeting in the historical report is a private affair; the queen mother dismisses all but one of her handmaidens. In a brief scene, he kisses the ground before her and invokes God's blessings on her. Without speaking to him, she turns to the maiden her stewardess, praises her for the choice she had made, and gets up and leaves. The storyteller's Lady Zubaydah, who can hardly walk from the weight of her raiments and ornaments, receives him surrounded by thirty handmaidens, converses with him, questions him about his condition, is pleased with his answers, praises him, and commits her stewardess, the maiden she esteems as though she were her own child, to his care. None of this would have been believable to knowledgeable men or to the audience of the historical report in Baghdad. But it is nowhere as unbelievable as what follows next.

9. As an additional favor, the storyteller's Lady Zubaydah orders that the youth spend ten days "with them," that is, in the harem apartments in the palace, and he has the youth repeat that he remained there ten days and nights, without catching sight of the maiden, however. Lady Zubaydah then asks for and receives the Caliph's permission to marry her stewardess, and apparently arranges for the marriage ceremony to be performed in the harem, again without the Caliph being involved in any way in the affair. Another ten days and nights elapse while the handmaidens prepare the necessary sweets and foods and equip the maiden for the wed-

ding night. For twenty days the youth, an unmarried commoner, total stranger to the Caliph's household, smuggled into the palace without the Caliph's knowledge, is made to hide in the harem. The Caliph gives permission that a stewardess be married without being told to whom, a marriage ceremony is arranged in the palace, men are brought in to write and witness the marriage contract, and for ten days the whole palace is in uproar preparing for the wedding night. The Caliph must have been blind indeed. If the storyteller meant to accentuate the youth's impatience after spending ten days hidden in a room and another ten days smelling the sweets and exquisite dishes being prepared for the wedding night, and to make believable his forgetting to wash his hands after eating the *zīrbājah*, he could not have invented a less likely story to achieve his purpose. No tenth-century resident of Baghdad with the most rudimentary knowledge of the customs of the palace would have believed such a story.

The historical report contained information about the topography of the palace and about court ceremonies that were no longer comprehensible to the storyteller and his audience. The day after meeting the queen mother, the youth had to be smuggled out of the palace, hidden in the same box. The exit was somewhat easier than the entrance, the inspection requirements being more perfunctory. He is taken back to the mosque and left there to regain his house on his own. A few days later, one of the maiden's servants arrives with a letter from her and 3,000 gold pieces, a gift from the queen mother who had ordered that he buy appropriate clothes, a suitable mount, a slave to march before him, and in general dress and equip himself as befits someone who is to be presented before the Caliph. He is to proceed to the Commoners' Gate[50] of the Caliph's Residence on the day of the Mawkib when the Caliph receives officials of high rank and the public's business is conducted in his presence,[51] and to wait there until he is summoned to be presented and married before the Caliph (the Caliph having already consented that the ceremony be performed in his presence). He does as instructed, rides his she-mule to the Commoners' Gate on the assigned day, an attendant calls his name and presents him before the Caliph al-Muqtadir sitting on his throne surrounded by courtiers, judges, and military chiefs. Hardly is the awe-stricken youth inside the audience hall when a judge pronounces the marriage formula and he is conducted out. Upon leaving the audience hall, he is taken to a sumptuous and richly furnished apartment, made to sit down, and left there by himself.

10. This is the apartment in which the maiden was to be conducted to him that night. All day long no one pays any attention to him and he does not notice anyone he knows, only servants moving about and exquisite food being carried in and out. Toward nightfall the doors of the apartment are closed, there is no sign of his bride, and he feels very hungry. He wanders about the empty apartment and hits on the kitchen; the cooks do not recognize him and think he is an insignificant agent. He asks for food and is given a bowl of *zīrbājah*. In his embarrassment, and afraid the cooks may recognize him, he eats, hurriedly washes his hands with some potash he finds in the kitchen, and, thinking that was enough to remove the *zīrbājah*'s odor, returns to the spot where he was asked to wait.

This episode conforms to the young merchant's character in the historical report and is quite adequate as preparation for what was to follow there. But it is too plain and "realistic" to conform to his character in the *Nights* version. His filial piety, his success as a merchant, his trials in entering the palace—all these prepare him for greater reward and greater punishment. Since entering the palace twenty days earlier, he has been resting in his apartment in the harem, where he has been well fed and cared for all along as befits the future bridegroom of Lady Zubaydah's stewardess. In preparation for being introduced to him as wife, the maiden is conducted to the bath. That night he is offered an elaborate meal,[52] including a bowl of *zīrbājah* so sumptuously prepared and highly sweetened[53] that he neglects all the other dishes and immediately attacks the *zīrbājah* and eats his fill of it, wipes his hands, forgets to wash them or, as he likes to explain his lack of refinement, "God the Most High made me forget to wash them," and sits and waits.

11. The next episode is again more elaborate in the *Nights* version, which emphasizes the maiden's high position in the Caliph's palace: the music, the singing, the display of the bride as she moves about the entire palace where she is showered with gold pieces and given presents of silk garments—all meant to prepare for the major episode that follows and explain the maiden's reaction. After all, she was brought up by Lady Zubaydah herself and had been her chief confidante, accustomed to a most refined company and way of life

imaginable. This is the high point of her life, a time in which she is reminded of her worth and position in the palace. Proud and full of herself, she was looking forward to the greatest moment a maiden in her position is said to look forward to, the moment of embracing her beloved—a youth she had gone through so much trouble to seduce and ran great dangers to smuggle into the palace. She is disrobed and left alone with him in bed. Impatient, scarcely believing that the union is finally taking place, he throws his arms around her neck. She smells the strong odor of the *zīrbājah* in the hands embracing her!

What happened next in the historical report was too mild to fit with the storyteller's plans. For there she merely repulses him, accuses him of being unable to rise above his station as a lowly commoner, and gets up to leave the bridal room. He begs her to inform him of his sin. He is told he had eaten the *zīrbājah* but had not properly washed his hands; how then does he expect to embrace a maiden in her station of life! He begs her to listen to his story; she allows him to tell it; and he swears that henceforth he will never eat the *zīrbājah* without washing his hands forty times afterward. Once she has reminded him that from now on he must conform to the social proprieties of his new station in life, she is neither resentful nor cruel, but smiles, forgives him, orders a sumptuous meal "fit for the caliphs' tables," and they eat, drink, and move to the bed where the marriage is consummated.

In the *Nights* version, on the other hand, the storyteller has now arrived at the episode where the youth had to be maimed for eating the *zīrbājah*, not due to any fault of his, but so that his tale can be made to fit inside the "The Hunchback and the King of China." He has prepared for the maiming by having the youth forget to wash his hands, not merely wash in a hurry and therefore inadequately, as he did in the historical report. He moves now in measured steps to elaborate the episode as fully as he can. The maiden is beside herself. She lets out a loud cry, her handmaidens come running in, and the youth is left utterly frightened and bewildered about her strange behavior. At first she orders the handmaidens to throw "this madman" out. Upon inquiring what evidence of his madness she has, he finds out that he is a madman because he ate the *zīrbājah* and did not wash his hands, knowing full well that he was about to be in bed with someone of her august rank. Then she asks her handmaidens to hold him down, whips him on his back and buttocks, and asks her handmaidens to send him off to the magistrate of the city police to cut off the hand with which he ate the *zīrbājah* but forgot to wash. The youth, who still does not appreciate the enormity of his deed, his sin against the aristocratic social conventions of palace dwellers, can only curse the *zīrbājah*. The handmaidens entreat their mistress to spare the ignorant youth, but she insists on teaching him a lesson by maiming something of his extremities so that he will never again eat the *zīrbājah* and not wash his hands. The handmaidens again entreat her to forgive his lapse of memory. She turns to rebuke and curse him, and then leaves the room. For ten days a slave-girl brings him something to eat and drink and tells him the maiden is sick because he ate the *zīrbājah* and did not wash his hands. Still unable to comprehend his fault, he is angry and keeps wondering "what kind of damned manners are these?"

12. Then the maiden returns, furious as ever, and insists on having her revenge. The handmaidens tie him up, and she takes a sharp razor and cuts off his thumbs and great toes. When he is able to open his eyes and speak again, he declares he will never again eat the *zīrbājah* without washing his hands one hundred and twenty times. She approves and makes him promise and swear to fulfill his pledge.[54]

13. After the first blissful night, the youth in the historical report is able to enjoy the company of the maiden day and night for a whole week without interruption. Then the festivities celebrating the end of the first week of marriage take place.[55] The next day she explains to him that they cannot go on living in the Caliph's palace; it was only because of the queen mother's interest in her that it was possible for him to consummate the marriage in the palace, something that had not happened to anyone else before. She gives him 10,000 gold pieces—the queen mother had just given her 50,000 gold pieces on the occasion of her marriage and the maiden's own wealth in the city is many times that sum—and asks him to buy a spacious house with many rooms and a large garden, and not be tightfisted as merchants are apt to be;[56] she is used to living in palaces and will not agree to live in a small house. He buys a suitable house. She moves to it with her possessions and handmaidens and bears him many sons. He continues to trade with success ("for I just could not

abandon the business and stop gaining a living"). After many happy years in which he continues to prosper, she dies. But the obligation to wash his hands forty times every time after he eats the *zīrbājah* remains. His sons, whom he points out, are sitting around him; they are the evidence and proof of his story. The audience—all fellow merchants—knew about his wealth and probably were listening to his story in the very spacious house he bought for his departed wife. The only doubt they could have entertained would have been this: how could all this take place to a fellow cloth merchant without his friends and associates, indeed everyone in the marketplace, learning about it earlier? His absence from his shop, his newly gained wealth, his buying a spacious house, a wife and handmaidens used to the life of palace dwellers—could all of this have remained a secret until the day he decided to tell his story? Perhaps they did know the outward features of his new life. They could not, of course, have known about his adventures in the palace, which had to be kept a secret until after 320 A.H./932 A.D. at least, the year of the Caliph al-Muqtadir's and of his mother's death.[57]

In the *Nights* version the merchant concludes his story once he has satisfied the audience's curiosity about how he came to have his thumbs and great toes cut off and why he had to wash his hands one hundred and twenty times. The audience is now curious about what happened next, and he continues his story. First he had to wait for his wounds to heal. Once healed, the maiden came to him and, finally, the marriage was consummated. He stayed with her "the rest of the month" and it was he who was impatient to leave the palace. The storyteller then follows the historical report until they settle in their new home but omits the fact that he went back to trading and gaining his own living or the fact that she gave him many sons. Finally, there is no explanation of how or why he left Baghdad, or why he happens to be in China.

Ever since Aristotle spoke of the respective merits of history and poetry, history as something that actually took place has been distinguished from fiction as something that could possibly take place but may not have in fact happened. It was always known that certain kinds of poetry or fiction dealt with strange and impossible things, strange and impossible at least to an audience not credulous enough to believe everything it hears. The *Nights* is of course full of strange and impossible stories. But the tale told by the King's steward (and "The Hunchback and the King of China" as a whole) is not such a story. It claims to be an account of historical events involving historical persons in a well-known time and place, and it does not even hint at anything that is impossible in itself.

Nevertheless, we have seen in how many places the audience of the historical report would have found that report credible but would have laughed the fictional version out of court. For them, the fictional version was impossible. Although derived from historical reality, it was an outrageous distortion and corruption of history. Nor would they have found it particularly interesting or amusing. On the contrary, they would have found it silly and cold, not because they lacked imagination or were ignorant, but because they knew too much.[58] It was a tale about their city and history and institutions and customs, and it was ridiculously inaccurate.[59] Had it been a tale told about China or some inaccessible region at some remote time, they might have been amused by it, for it told of nothing that was inherently impossible. Possible and impossible do not seem to have to do only with things but with the audience as well. What would have seemed impossible to the audience of the historical report in tenth-century Baghdad could very well seem possible to the audience of the *Nights* version in fourteenth-century Damascus or Cairo, semiliterate men and women who remembered nothing to gainsay what they had heard about what might have happened in eighth- or ninth-century Baghdad. For all they knew, this was history, or else they were only too willing to transform the fictional version back into history. The same would prove to be true of audiences in later times and other countries or cultures. But it seems to have been especially true of learned Orientalists who have used the *Nights* as a source for the study of the manners and customs of Oriental societies.

Notes

1. M 1:304–15; N 121:22–130:11.

2. Amedroz made a number of judicious remarks on the differences between the version of the historical report he found in a manuscript of Ibn

al-Jawzī's *al-Muntaẓam* and the versions of the *Nights* he read in the second Calcutta edition (*C* II) and in a Cairo printing of 1297 A.H./1880 A.D. (reproducing *Q*), and in Lane's English translation. "It is interesting to contrast the two narratives, and to note how the story in the 'Nights' differs from the original as told by Ibn al-Jauzī. The inevitable loss to truth caused by the exercise of the imagination should find its compensation in the heightened interest of a picturesque narrative, but in this instance the original seems to be in every way the better story. Indeed, in the reversion from fiction to fact, the tale will be found to have lost all its evil, whilst retaining all its grossness—the latter, however, being quite inconsiderable. It depicts the course of true love, not a wholly smooth one, but marred by no such traits of excessive temper and wanton cruelty as disfigure the Steward's Story. Nor do any of the minor deviations from the original amount to improvements" (Amedroz 1904, 276). Amedroz had little sympathy for, or understanding of, the *Nights* version and made no effort to appreciate the respective merits of the two accounts when contrasting them. He seems not to have noticed that in the *Nights* the tale told by the King's steward is part of the larger "The Hunchback and the King of China" or that this fact explains certain aspects of the "evil" he detected in the fictional version. The similarity between the historical report found in another manuscript of Ibn al-Jawzī's *al-Muntaẓam* and the *Nights* version was first pointed out by de Goeje (1886, 396 ff., where the reader can find a Dutch translation of the historical report [de Goeje 1886, 397–406]). But de Goeje's view that the Baghdad money-changer story (Q 2:543–51) is derived from the same source (de Goeje 1886, 408; Amedroz 1904, 276 n. 1) tends to confuse matters. As far as I can see, the Baghdad money-changer story is a historical report, or a story that claims to be a historical report, having nothing in common with the historical report transmitted by al-Tanūkhī apart from a few common themes that reveal nothing about which version is the "source" of which. Further, there is no evidence in the Baghdad money-changer story for the kind of transformation we notice in the tale of the King's steward. Finally, the Baghdad money-changer story, which seems to have been composed in Baghdad at about the same time as the historical report transmitted by al-Tanūkhī and to have preserved much of its original form and content, was apparently appended to the *Nights* when the Egyptian branch of the *Nights* was receiving its final shape (see *M* 1:32–36).

3. *M* N 151:33–152:35.

4. See al-Masʿūdī (1965 4:304–5, 308 [secs. 2705–7, 2713]).

5. *M* N 166:14–168:24. See al-Masʿūdī (1965, 4:304–5, 308 [secs. 2705–7, 2713]).

6. See al-Ḥikāyāt (1956, 64–68).

7. Examples where the Nights version transforms literary Arabic expressions found in the historical report into so-called Middle Arabic can be ascertained by comparing *laḥḥaina* (*M* N 121:25) with *aljajnā*, and *yitfassakh* (*M* N 126:10) with *tastaḥīl*, in the historical report. Notice also the absence

of *kayyis*, *ruqʿah*, and *ʿayn* (al-Tanūkhī [1987, 4:365.15, 366.6, 7, 11, 368.15]) from the *Nights*. Examples of tenth-century Iraqi Middle Arabic expressions either omitted or changed into Egyptian-Syrian Mamluk Middle Arabic expressions are the following: the *Nights* version omits *huwa-dhā ajī* (al-Tanūkhī 1987, 4:365.4); *assīʿah* (al-Tanūkhī 1987, 4:365.3; see al-Tanūkhī [1971, 4:184 n. 3 and the note to story no. 8 in vol. 1) is changed to *addī inta tarāh* (*M* N 127:6); *ṭayyār laṭīf* (al-Tanūkhī 1987, 4:363.4, see the explanation in 4:184 n. 3) is changed to *zawraq* (*M* N 125:13); *kūz min māʾ zamzam* (al-Tanūkhī 1987, 4:364.4) is changed to *qārūrah fīhā arbaʿat amnān min māʿ zamzam* (*M* N 126:9). Notice also the omission of the following expressions from the *Nights* version: *abwāb al-ḥurum* (Tanūkhī 1971, 4:363.17), *walīmat al-usbūʿ* (al-Tanūkhī 1987, 4:368.12), *anta wa-huwa* (al-Tanūkhī 1987, 4:364.6), *walak* (al-Tanūkhī 1987, 4:364.11), *hātum* (al-Tanūkhī 1987, 4:368.8), *al-darajah* (al-Tanūkhī 1987, 4:365.6), and *al-shabāb* (al-Tanūkhī 1987, 4:369.10).

8. See nn. 36, 52, 54.

9. In 369 A.H./979 A.D. al-Tanūkhī gave the formal speech at the Caliph's palace on the occasion of the marriage of ʿAḍud al-Dawlah's daughter to the Caliph al-Ṭāʾiʿ, which points to the high position he occupied at the time in the courts of Caliph and King. See al-Ṣābī (1964, 138–39); editor's introduction to al-Tanūkhī (1987, 1:1 ff.).

10. Amedroz (1904) edited a version of the historical report found in a manuscript of Ibn al-Jawzī's *al-Muntaẓam*. (This work was published subsequently; the report titled "The Slave-Girl of Shagab the Mother of al-Muqtadir Billāh" is found in Ibn al-Jawzī 1939, 6:254–61). Ibn al-Jawzī transmitted the report on the authority of Abū Bakr Muḥammad Ibn ʿAbd al-Bāqī al-Bazzāz, known as Ibn Abī Tāhir (442–535 A.H./1011–1139 A.D.), who in turn transmitted it on the authority of Abulqāsim ʿAlī the son of al-Muḥassin al-Tanūkhī, who had transmitted it on the authority of his father al-Muḥassin al-Tanūkhī. Al-Bazzāz was one of Ibn al-Jawzī's teachers; he is cited elsewhere also as Ibn al-Jawzī's authority for reports from ʿAlī al-Tanūkhī. (See Ibn al-Jawzī 1939, 5:80, 6:269, 10:92; Tanūkhī [1971, 4:114, 191. ʿAlī al-Tanūkhī's biography can be found in Yāqūt 1907, 5:301.) Since the son was quite young when the father died, one may assume that he made use of written material left by his father. The son's version, as reported by Ibn al-Jawzī, has been incorporated in the edition of Tanūkhī (1971, 4:177–90), to which we shall refer when citing this version of the report (al-Nuwayrī [1929, 2:165–73] reproduces Ibn al-Jawzī's report).

11. The ingredients of the *dīgparīgah* (al-Tanūkhī [1987, 4:177.11]) are listed in al-Tānukhī (1987, 4:177 n. 2), following Ibn al-Karīm (1964, 15). The *dīgparīgah* is obviously not the same dish as the *zīrbājah*.

12. *M* N 121:22–122:14 = al-Tanūkhī (1987, 4:358.3–59.1).

13. *M* N 122:15–20 = al-Tanūkhī (1987, 4:359.2–6).

14. *M* N 122:20–124:5 = al-Tanūkhī (1987, 4:359.7–60.2).

15. *M* N 124:5–15 = al-Tanūkhī (1987, 4:360.3–17).

16. *M* N 124:15–26 = al-Tanūkhī (1987, 4:360.18–361.16).
17. *M* N 124:26–125:12 = al-Tanūkhī (1987, 4:361.17–363.1).
18. *M* N 125:12–127:15 = al-Tanūkhī (1987, 4:363.12–365.9).
19. *M* N 127:15–22 = al-Tanūkhī (1987, 4:365.10–17).
20. *M* N 127:22–128:8 = [leaves and returns] al-Tanūkhī (1987, 4:365. 17–366.18).
21. *M* N 128:8–12 = al-Tanūkhī (1987, 4:367.1–8).
22. *M* N 128:12–129:12 = al-Tanūkhī (1987, 4:367.9–368.10).
23. *M* N 129:12–23 [not in al-Tanūkhī (1987)].
24. *M* N 130:1–11 = al-Tanūkhī (1987, 4:368.11–369.11).
25. See the editor's introductions to al-Tanūkhī (1971 and 1987); GAL 1:155; Paret (1913, 4:655–56). Amedroz remarks that to question the authority of the transmitters of the historical report "would be in reality to call in doubt a large portion of the history of the period" (Amedroz 1904, 276). He was thinking of the version reported by Ibn al-Jawzī on the authority of al-Tanūkhī's son, a judge and an author well known in his own right. Ibn al-Jawzī (1966, 87 ff.) quotes him a number of times. This does not, however, mean that the historical report may not have been quasi-fictional to begin with.
26. Ibn al-Narsī's family resided in the Syrian Gate quarter of Baghdad. He succeeded another well-known judge, Ibn al-Bahlūl, as judge in the city of Hīt. Al-Tanūkhī knew Ibn al-Narsī well and found him always to be a reliable reporter: *wa-mā ʿalimtuhu illā thiqatan*. As far as I could determine, there is no biography of Ibn al-Narsī in the published portions of Ibn al-Jawzī (1939), or in al-Khaṭīb al-Baghdādī (1931). Ibn al-Bahlūl (ʿAlī Ibn Muḥammad Ibn Aḥmad Ibn Isḥāq Ibn al-Bahlūl al-Tanūkhī, Shawwāl 301–Rabīʿ al Ākhir 354 A.H./914–965 A.D.) succeeded his father as judge in al-Anbār and Hīt. He left the post in 327 A.H./938 A.D. when the Caliph al-Raḍī appointed him as judge in the region called Ṭarīq Khurāsān (usually including the city of Hamadān). In 341 A.H./952 A.D., he was again judge in Hīt and Kufah for a period and then removed. He was also a *ḥadīth* transmitter, and al-Tanūkhī reported *ḥadīth* on his authority (Ibn al-Jawzī [1939, 7:30]). If one assumes that Ibn al-Narsī succeeded Ibn al-Bahlūl as judge of Hīt sometime after 341 A.H./952 A.D., and that he was an older contemporary of al-Tanūkhī, he would indeed have been only a youth shortly after 320 A.H./932 A.D., i.e., shortly after the death of the Caliph al-Muqtadir and of his mother Shaghab, when the story could have been told without the fear of reporting what some may have considered to have been a palace scandal.
27. This is found in the *Nishwār* version (al-Tanūkhī 1971, 4:177, 6–8), where Ibn al-Narsī explains that the merchant's report, addressed to his father, was in response to his father's reciting for his (the son's) benefit "an account of how people are enriched in unusual ways (*ḥadīth wuṣūl al-niʿam ilā al-nās bi'l-alwān al-ṭarīfah*)." The merchant's report was thus meant to be another example of this general theme.
28. According to the *Nishwār* version (al-Tanūkhī 1971, 4:177.9), his wealth was estimated (*yuḥzar*) at 100,000 gold pieces.

29. In the case of the tales told by the barber in "The Hunchback and the King of China," the chain proceeds as follows: (1) the narrator tells the audience, (2) Shahrazad told Shahrayar, (3) the tailor told the king of China, (4) the barber told the company at the banquet, (5) the barber told the Caliph al-Mustanṣir, (6) the barber's brother told *X*. Cf. Todorov (1969, 90).

30. See Gerhardt's (1963, 378 ff.) comments on the relation between the "witnessing system" in medieval Arabic literature and in the *Nights*.

31. Lane and Burton allow the inconsistency to stand in their translations. For Galland, see below n. 36.

32. Burton translates *suʿd/suʿūd* as "galangale" (Burton 1885, 1:279 n. 1) and explains that it is "an Alpinia with pungent rhizome like ginger; here used as a counter-odeur."

33. See *M* N 128:11 ff., 129:20 ff.

34. It is true that the oath he takes ("I will not eat the *zīrbājah* unless I wash my hands" [*M* N 129:20; al-Tanūkhī 1987, 4:368.5; 1971, 4:189.7]) does not specify *when* he is supposed to wash his hands; but in the context of the story, the number of washings makes no sense otherwise. Also, at the beginning of the report in al-Tanūkhī (1987, 4:358.9–12; 1971, 4:177.14–15) it is quite clear that he eats first, and it is when the whole company are washing their hands after the meal that they notice the excessive number of washings he does. It is, of course, to be expected that the whole company would wash their hands before the meal as well, but that washing is sufficiently perfunctory that it is not mentioned in any of the versions of the tale. In the *Nights* version the young cloth merchant performs the necessary washings by himself and then joins the company to begin eating (*M* N 122:4–6).

35. *M* N 129:17 ff.

36. Presumably, the storyteller could have made the cloth merchant eat and thus expose his maimed thumb while eating and tell the company about his other thumb and his great toes, then wash his hands, and then tell his tale. (This is how Galland [1965, 1:384–85] revised the tale.) But that would have pushed the mutilation theme to the background and reduced its relative significance. Apparently, the *Nights* storyteller made his revisions as he went along; when he reached the incident where the story required that the washing be done after eating the *zīrbājah*—a sequence that could not be reversed without destroying the central theme of the tale—he did not, or did not care to, remember his earlier revision; in any case, he did not go over it again to see what he might have done earlier. Amedroz states the fact that in the *Nights* the hand washings "are made to precede his partaking of the dish, and the telling of the story is prompted, not by the washings, but by the loss of the man's thumbs being noticed by those present" (Amedroz 1904, 277), but he was not sufficiently interested in the *Nights* version to see that this was unavoidable if the tale were to be incorporated in the "The Hunchback and the King of China," or to notice that this is not what is supposed to happen in the *Nights* version itself, or to point to the inconsistency in the *Nights* version.

37. "We found this quite amazing and asked him, 'What about this

thumb?' . . . and we became doubly amazed and said, 'We can wait no longer' " (*M* N 122:9, 12–13).

38. Lane (1859, n. 59, cf. n. 70) took the liberty of changing the date to 263 A.H./877 A.D. "in order to avoid a glaring anachronism."

39. The *al-Faraj* and the *Nishwār* versions (al-Tanūkhī 1987; 1971) agree that the youth was twenty years old when the father died. They agree also that the father advised the youth to be the first to enter the marketplace and the last to leave, which explains the fact that the maiden will always find his shop the only one open early in the morning and will have to sit and wait for the other shops to open. In the *Nishwār* version the father is said to have been a merchant dealing in cheap clothes (*khilqānī*) in the Karkh district of Baghdad; and the maiden's first visit occurs a year and some months after the father's death, i.e., when the youth was twenty-one years old. For the rest, the *Nishwār* version seems to elaborate on the historical report found in the *al-Faraj* version, making it difficult to believe that this version of the *Nishwār* (i.e., the version transmitted by Ibn al-Jawzī on the authority of Muḥammad Ibn ʿAbd al-Bāqī al-Bazzāz, on the authority of ʿAlī, on the authority of his father al-Muḥassin al-Tanūkhī) is the source of the version in *al-Faraj.*

40. The name of the maiden was Qamar, according to a marginal note in one of the manuscripts of Ibn al-Jawzī's al-Muntaẓam, which says: "This story was reported by a certain historian, who named this maiden Qamar" (Königliche Bibliothek [Berlin] 1887, MS no. 9436, fol. 49 [Amedroz 1904, 280, 293]). De Goeje, who translated from another manuscript, mentions the name Qamar in the title of the story (de Goeje 1886, 306–7). The *Nights* version elaborates on the maiden's beauty, speaks of her being decked with magnificent ornaments and apparel, surrounds her with two slaves in addition to a servant, and makes the servant attending her speak in a worried tone about her having come out (of the Caliph's palace) without letting anyone know where she planned to go (*M* N 122:21–24).

41. See *Nishwār* 4:179.1 and n. 1, for the attractive Egyptian donkeys preferred by the Abbasid Caliph's households. This particular donkey was covered with a piece of cloth from (the Egyptian town of) Dabīq. She-mules were mounts suitable for commoners like the cloth merchant (al-Tanūkhī 1987, 4:366.13; below, no. 9).

42. The maiden in the historical report embodies the civilized refinement for which the people of Baghdad were famous in medieval times. Even though she is said to be more in love with him than he with her, she is able to engage in pleasant conversation (*muṭāwalah*) and to express her pleasure in laughter (al-Tanūkhī 1987, 4:361.8, 11). See also the scene when the lovers meet in the mosque just before the young merchant is placed in the box (no. 7 and n. 49 below).

43. In al-Tanūkhī (1971, 4:179.1) the maiden arrives at the shop dressed as a *qahramānah*, and later (al-Tanūkhī 1971, 4:183.13–15) the servant explains how the mother of the Caliph al-Muqtadir arranged to promote her to the

position of *qahramānah* in order to enable her to go out of the palace. On the importance of the position of the *qahramānah* at the time of the Caliph al-Muqtadir, see al-Tanūkhī 1971, 4:179 n. 4.

44. See al-Tanūkhī (1987, 4362 n. 14 and the references to Yāqūt 1866, 4:441).

45. The Lady, the mother of the Caliph al-Muqtadir, whose name was Shaghab, was known for having expended her vast wealth in charity and in pious foundations. For her fate after her son's violent death, see Ibn al-Jawzī (1939, 6:253–54); Amedroz (1904, 274–75).

46. See al-Tanūkhī (1987, 4:362 n. 15). Subuktākin died in 363 A.H./974 A.D. His house in al-Mukharrim is mentioned by Ibn al-Jawzī (1939, 7:67–68) along with his position under the Caliph al-Ṭāʾiʿ and the Buyid king ʿIzz al-Dawlah (356–367 A.H./967–978 A.D.); see also Miskawayh (1920, 2:327, 333, 334).

47. In the historical report, the maiden first passes through groups of servants in charge of the doors of the various apartments in the harem. They all demand to inspect the boxes. The maiden yells at some, calls down the wrath of God on others, and cajoles the rest until she reaches the chief servant (al-Tanūkhī 1987, 4:363.17–18; 1971, 4:185.4–6). The *Nights* version skips these details on the way to the chief servant.

48. See the expressions, in n. 7, above, quoted from al-Tanūkhī 1987, and *M*, respectively.

49. Al-Tanūkhī's version (1971, 4:186.9–10) adds here that she kissed him until his spirit was revived and he was made to forget the hardships of the journey.

50. The Commoners' Gate (*bāb al-ʿāmmah*) was on the east side of Dār al-Khulafāʾ, the Caliphs' Residence, close to Masjid al-Khulafāʾ, the Caliphs' Mosque. See al-Tanūkhī (1987, 4:366 n. 24).

51. A detailed description of the ceremonies on the day of the Mawkib can be found in al-Ṣābī (1954, 78 ff., 90 ff.). See also al-Tanūkhī (1987, 4:366 nn. 23, 24).

52. There seems to be yet another inconsistency here resulting from revision. The youth says "I stood up that night/ and they presented me with a meal." Apparently, "I stood up" was to be followed by "and walked about the apartment" in order to get to the kitchen. But the storyteller remembered that in the revised version the youth was fed by the servants in the apartment where he was residing.

53. For the ingredients that went into this dish, see al-Tanūkhī (1987, 4:358 n. 3); Ibn al-Karīm (1964, 16). In the *Nights* version (*M* N 128:10), the storyteller replaces some of the original ingredients. The ingredients are not mentioned in the historical report because the dish was well known. The storyteller calls it a marvelously delicious dish. But while the dish was known to be rather spicy, the storyteller makes it into a sweet dish. Other versions of the *Nights* add other ingredients at will.

54. The expression "why did you not wait for a while" (*M* N 129:14–15) does not make sense in the Nights version where there was no question of his waiting. It is in the historical report (al-Tanūkhī 1987, 4:366.17) that he is made to wait, gets hungry, and goes to the kitchen to fetch some food. It is there also (al-Tanūkhī 1987, 4:368.8–9) that she had a meal waiting to be served after having been conducted to him.

55. *Walīmat al-usbūᶜ* (al-Tanūkhī 1987, 4:368.12 and n. 33); *yawm al-usbūᶜ* (al-Tanūkhī 1971, 4:189.15).

56. When he received the 3,000 gold pieces to spend on equipping himself to be presented before the Caliph, he used only part of the sum for that purpose and kept the rest (al-Tanūkhī 1987, 4:366.11–12). The *Nishwār* version (al-Tanūkhī 1971, 4:187.15–16) is more explicit: "I bought whatever they asked that I buy with a small portion of the sum and retained most of it."

57. See the end of n. 26.

58. The learned audience of the historical report were reminded of the good old times when a Caliph was still powerful and headed a rich household, and when a Caliph's mother was rich enough to endow mosques and religious and charitable foundations. The story was already marvelous at the time of the Buyid kings, when a Caliph no longer ruled or possessed the riches of earlier days; what could have happened two generations earlier now seemed amazing. The audience of the *Nights* version, on the other hand, were ignorant of the time and place of the events. The storyteller had already recreated in their imagination an exotic time and place and filled it with characters who experience all sorts of fantastic things. Nothing seemed impossible at the court of Harun al-Rashid.

59. This is why I found Amedroz's reaction (see above, n. 2) particularly interesting. Amedroz the historian would have been in complete sympathy with the audience of the historical report. He argued the case of the learned audience that might have despised the *Nights*, a case that modern romantics and literary critics do not seem to understand.

References

Editions of the Arabic Text of *The Thousand and One Nights*

C II 1839–42. *Alf Layla wa Layla: The Alif Laila or Book of the Thousand and One Night, commonly known as "The Arabian Nights' Entertainment"; now, for the first time, published complete in the original Arabic, from an Egyptian manuscript brought to India by the late Major Turner Macan*, ed. W. H. Macnaghten, 4 vols. Calcutta.

M 1984–. *The Thousand and One Nights (Alf Layla wa Layla) from the earliest known sources.* Arabic text edited with introduction and notes by Muhsin

Mahdi, vol. I. Leiden. An English translation of this version by Husain Haddawy is published by W. W. Norton in New York.
Q 1835. *Alf Layla wa Layla*, ed. Muḥammad Qiṭṭah al-ʿAdawī, 2 vols. Bulaq. 1251 AH.

Early Arabic Sources

al-Hamadhānī, Abū al-Faḍl Badīʿ al-Zamān Aḥmad Ibn al-Ḥusayn, *Maqāmāt*, ed. Muḥammad ʿAbduh. Beirut, 1889.
al-Ḥikayāt al-ʿAjība, ed. Hans Wehr. Wiesbaden, 1956.
Ibn al-Jawzī, Abū al-Faraj ʿAbd al-Raḥmān Ibn ʿAlī. *Akhbār al-Ḥamqā wa'l-Mughaffalīn*, ed. ʿAlī al-Khāqānī. Baghdad, 1386/1966.
———. *al-Muntaẓam fī Tārīkh al-Mulūk wa'l-Umam* vols. V-X. Hyderabad, 1357/1939.
Ibn al-Karīm al-Baghdādī. *al-Ṭabīkh*, ed. Fakhrī al-Bārūdī. Beirut, 1964.
al-Khaṭīb al-Bahgdādī, Abū Bakr Muḥammad b. ʿAlī. *Tārīkh Baghdād*, 14 vols. Cairo, 1349/1931.
al-Masʿūdī, Abū al-Ḥasan ʿAlī b. al-Ḥusayn. *Murūj al-Dhahab wa Maʿādin al-Jawhar*, ed. C. Barbier de Meynard and Pavet de Courteille, revised and corrected by Charles Pellat, 7 vols. Beirut, 1965–79.
Miskawayh, Abū ʿAlī Aḥmad Ibn Muḥammad. *Tajārib al-Umam. In The Eclipse of the ʿAbbasid Caliphate: Original Chronicles of the Fourth Islamic Century*, ed. trans. and elucidated by H. F. Amedroz and D. S. Margoliouth, 7 vols., vols. I–II (text), IV–V (translation). Oxford, 1920–21. (References are to the volume and page numbers of the Arabic text [vols. V–VI of Miskaway's history], which was printed in Cairo, 1914–15.)
al-Nuwayrī, Abū al-ʿAbbās Aḥmad b. ʿAbd al-Wahāb. *Nihāyat al-Arab fī Funūn al-Adab*, vols. I–. Cairo, 1929–.
al-Ṣābī, Hilāl. *Rusūm Dār al-Khilāfa*, ed. Mikhāʾīl ʿAwwād. Baghdad, 1383/1964.
al-Tanūkhī, Abū ʿAlī al-Muḥassin. *al-Faraj baʿd al-Shidda*, ed. ʿAbbūd al-Shālji, 5 vols. Beirut, 1987.
———. *Nishwār al-Muḥadara wa Akhbār al-Mudhākara*, ed. ʿAbbūd al-Shālji, 8 vols. Beirut, 1971–1973.
Yāqūt, Abū ʿAbdallāh b. ʿAbdallāh al-Ḥamawī. *Muʿjam al-Buldān*, ed. Ferdinand Wüstenfeld, 6 vols. Leipzig, 1866–70.
———. *Muʿjam al-Udabāʾ*, ed. D. S. Margoliouth, 7 vols. Leiden, 1907–31.

Modern Studies and Translations

Amedroz, H. F. 1904. "A Tale of the Arabian Nights Told as History in the "Muntaẓam" of Ibn al-Jawzī." *Journal of the Royal Asiatic Society*, 273–293.

Brockelmann, Carl. 1937–42. *Geschichte der arabischen Litteratur*, 5 vols. Leiden.

Burton, Richard F. 1885–86. *A Plain and Literal Translation of the Arabian Nights Entertainment, Now Entitled the Book of the Thousand Nights and a Night*, 10 vols. Benares (The dates appear under Burton's signatures. I have used the facsimile of this edition published by the Press of Carson-Harper Co., Denver, Colorado, 1900.)

Galland, Antoine. 1704. *Les Mille et Une Nuits, contes arabes*, ed. Gaston Pecard, 2 vols. Paris, 1960.

Gerhardt, Mia I. 1963. *The Art of Story-Telling: A Literary Study of the Thousand and One Nights*. Leiden.

de Goeje, M. J. 1886. De Arabische Nachtvertellingen. *De Gids* 50/3:385–413.

Königliche Bibliothek (Berlin). 1887–99. *Verzeichniss der arabischen Handschriften der Königlichen Bibliothek zu Berlin aus den Gebieten der Poesie, schönen Literatur, Literaturgeschichte und Biographik*, compiled by Theodor Wilhelm Ahlwardt, 10 vols. Berlin.

Lane, Edward William. 1859. *The Thousand and One Nights, Commonly Called, in England, the Arabian Nights' Entertainments*, ed. Edward Stanley Poole, 3 vols. London.

Paret, Rudi. 1913–36. Al-Tanūkhī. *Encyclopaedia of Islam*, 4:655–56.

Todorov, Tzvetan. 1969. *Grammaire du Décaméron*. The Hague/Paris. Appendix, "Les hommes-récits," 85–97. English translation, "Narrative-Men," in *The Poetics of Prose*, trans. from the French by Richard Howard with a new Foreword by Jonathan Culler. Ithaca, 1977.

15 Sinbad the Sailor: A Commentary on the Ethics of Violence

Peter D. Molan

Sinbad the Sailor has come to be regarded as a romantic hero by modern audiences. This article examines the Sinbad tales of the *1001 Nights* from a structuralist point of view and concludes that an ironic disparity exists between the protagonist's actions and his ethical stance. Seen in this light, the Sinbad tales become a parable for the instruction of King Shahriyar in self-deception and injustice thus integrating the episodes of the sailor's voyages within the frame story of Shahrazad. The significance of this interpretation for an understanding of the development of narrative literature is profound. Literary historians generally assign such "protonovelistic" features as first-person narration coupled with a consistent internal development of theme and their integration into the frame story to a much later, and Western, body of literature. The reassessment of the character of Sinbad, however (from romantic hero to self-justifying immoralist, thus linking Sinbad with his analogues in Greek, Latin and, other literatures), is the focus of this essay.

Sinbad the Sailor has become, for his modern audience, a romantic hero. Jabra Ibrahim Jabra, the Palestinian poet and critic, says of him:

> So human in wishes, in reactions, in dreams, and yet, because of his endurance and invention no death or destruction can get at him. His vision

Reprinted from Peter D. Molan, "Sinbad the Sailor: A Commentary on the Ethics of Violence," *Journal of the American Oriental Society* 98 (1987): 237–47. Reprinted by permission of the publisher.

> is all men's dream: his ship is wrecked, his fellow travelers drown, death and horror overtake the world, but Sindbad battles on and survives. The original land-dream was so powerful that the sea has to be conquered, and so have the lands beyond the sea, the islands, the valleys of serpents and jewels.[1]

This view, however, is one based on a popular children's abstraction of the medieval folkloric figure of Sinbad. Even Jabra confesses that his view of Sinbad was formed by the children's stories that he first heard in his own youth and that he, in turn, read to his own children, carefully expurgating the more potent tales of "death and horror."[2] Our view of Sinbad is not based on the reading of the medieval tales of *Dolopathos*, *Syntipas*, or *The Thousand and One Nights.*[3] Instead, our view is formed by the Sinbad the Sailor as portrayed by Douglas Fairbanks Jr., who battled Walter Slezak and Anthony Quinn for the island of gold and the favors of Maureen O'Hara in the RKO-Radio film. As Bosley Crowther has pointed out, the screenplay writers, no Shahrazads at telling an engaging tale, spurred [Fairbanks] to elegant bravado, set him to vaulting oriental walls, and generally playing the bold hero in this gaudy fable.[4] But, it is a spurious fable that Fairbanks's Sinbad undertakes, not one of the so significant *seven* voyages of the traditional tale.[5]

So firmly fixed has this romantic view of Sinbad become that even his most recent and most sophisticated critic, who does examine the *1001 Nights* tales, concludes that "Sindbad is, before all else, a man of action and it is in his action that his characteristic qualities are revealed. In all the terrible situations from which he must extract himself, he, time after time, makes use of [both] boldness and discretion."[6] And that "regarded from this angle, the *Voyages of Sindbad the Sailor* become a veritable glorification of navigation and maritime commerce; and Sindbad, as a model set up for the admiration of a sympathetic public, is the proper symbol of the sailor's profession such as it could appear in that privileged moment in its long history."[7]

In the following pages, we shall present a different analysis of the Sinbad tales, as they occur in the *1001 Nights.*[8] It will reveal a very different appreciation of the character of Sinbad and of the significance of the voyages that, we hope to demonstrate convincingly, is more in keeping with the structure of the medieval tales not only in their Arabic, but also in their Greek and Latin versions.[9]

There are two versions of the Sinbad tales. The best known is that of the editions of Bulaq (1835), of Calcutta (1839–42 [Macnaghten ed.]), and of the later Arab versions in general. The second version is that of the first Calcutta edition (1818) and that of the manuscripts, now lost, upon which Galland based his translation of the entire *1001 Nights* and upon which L. Langles based his *Les voyages de Sind-Bād le Marin et La Ruse des Femmes* (Paris, 1814). The two versions differ in two ways. The second is generally shorter and sparer in its narrative treatment of the various themes. Of considerably more importance, however, is the fact that the end of voyage VI and voyage VII is entirely different in the two versions. It has been the view of most of the translators of the *1001 Nights* that, while the more fully articulated first version is "better" for the bulk of the stories, the conclusion of the second version is more satisfactory to a properly formed tale. Thus Lane follows the first version until the ending of voyage VI. He then shifts to the second version for the translation of the end of voyages VI and VII. Burton simply combines the two, as does Mardrus in his French edition of the *Nights* (Paris, 1900–4). E. Littmann, in his German version (Wiesbaden, 1953), follows the first version to its conclusions and then adds the ending of the second versions as an "important variant."[10]

Littmann's is the appropriate procedure, for the significance of the two versions is precisely that they form two *equally valid* versions of the tale. They offer a marvelous example of the way in which an oral tale may be altered in its presentation and yet remain unaltered as to its significance, its "message," and its "structure." For, though markedly different in narrative detail, the two versions are structurally identical and thus fulfill the same functions in the development of the tale. The analysis that follows, then, will be based on Macnaghten's 1839 Calcutta edition of the *Nights* but will include reference to the second versions of voyage VII for the sake of interest only. Either of the other versions could have been equally well used.

As is so common in the tales of the *1001 Nights*, the fundamental structural elements in the Sinbad stories is a "framing" technique. The stories of the seven voyages made by Sindbad, "the merchant of Baghdad," are first framed within the story of the relationship between that Sinbad, *al-Sindibād al-Baḥrī*, and the poor porter, *al-Sindibād al-Ḥammāl.* This story, in turn, is framed within the continuing story of Shahrazad and the cruel King Shahriyar. This point is essential, for we must always keep in mind that Sinbad the Sailor is only the "putative" narrator of the story of the voyages. In fact, the "real" narrator, as we are constantly reminded, is Shahrazad. Despite the fact that the bulk of the story is made up of Sinbad's *first person* narrative, the figure of Shahrazad narrates the opening and closing of the tales and intrudes some thirty times, never more than three pages apart, reestablishing her role as the narrator by the familiar, formulaic device and once more putting the words in Sinbad's mouth:

> And morning came upon Shahrazad and she fell silent from [this] lawful discourse. Then when it was fully the sixtieth night after the first hundredth, she said, "It has come to my attention, oh happy king, that Sinbad the Sailor, when he had prepared his shipment, stowed it in the ship at the city of Basra, and embarked, said: 'We went on traveling from place to place and from city to city, selling and buying and taking a look at the countries of [various] people.' "[11]

Thus there is inherently an ironic disparity between the point of view of the protagonist, Sinbad, and that of the "narrator," Shahrazad (along with her audience). The knowledge and values of the protagonist are almost inevitably different from those of the narrator; for she, and we, know the characters as they could not possibly know themselves.[12]

Shahrazad then, hoping once more to beguile the King with yet another story (and so stay by yet another day her execution),[13] assures him that the story she has just completed is "not nearly so wonderful as the story of Sinbad." The King replies, "How's that?" and the familiar tale begins.[14] Shahrazad tells that on a burning hot Baghdad afternoon, a poor and lowly porter comes upon the magnificent palace of a rich merchant. Although nominally recognizing God's justice, his true distress at his situation relative to that of the merchant is clear as he recites a short song:

> How many wretched persons are destitute of ease!
> and how many are in luxury, reposing in the shade!

I find myself afflicted by trouble beyond measure;
  and strange is my condition, and heavy is my load!
Others are in prosperity, and from wretchedness are free,
  and never for a single day have borne a load like mine;
Incessantly and amply best, throughout the course of life,
  with happiness and grandeur, as well as drink and meat.
All men whom God hath made are in origin alike;
  and I resemble this man and he resembleth me;
But otherwise, between us is a difference as great as the difference
  that we find between wine and vinegar.
Yet in saying this, I utter no falsehood against Thee,
  [Oh my Lord;] for Thou art wise, and with justice Thou has
    judged.[15]

His feelings are clear to the owner of the palace too, for he calls the porter in, tells him the story of each of seven adventurous voyages and concludes that the porter has been wrong: "These pleasures are a compensation for the toil and humiliation that I have experienced."[16] The porter is convinced and agrees; but are we, the audience to whom Shahrazad tells the tale, convinced? Let us have a closer look at the tales themselves.

Although at first view simply adventure stories, the tales of the seven voyages of Sinbad are in fact subtly structured in a very sophisticated way to bring home a moral through irony. I do not mean to imply by this that the Sinbad tales are a didactic morality play in disguise. The *1001 Nights* are not the conveyance for a moral message. In that sense, they are "amoral," as the term that has so frequently been applied to them would have it. That does not imply, however, the lack of an ethical framework or point of view; and, even more to the point, it in no way precludes an acute and often cynical perception of the relationship to ethical principles of such human foibles and weaknesses as self-righteousness, self-delusion, greed, and hypocrisy. Indeed, these are the fundamental perceptions of the *Nights*.

It may do here, too, to mention that the Sinbad tales find their origin in a universal, oral folk tradition that has analogues everywhere from China to the British Isles.[17] The attempts to trace the "origins" of the *1001 Nights*, as opposed to its "analogues," (through a chain of translations) to Persian and Indian texts is thus dubious at best. The *1001 Nights*' Sinbad, however, has been completely Islamicized and Arabized. A Muslim teller of traditional tales reciting before a Muslim audience will inevitably, even if unconsciously, infuse his tale with a Muslim ethical structure—however the characters, events, and storyline may have entered his tradition. Thus, Sinbad's constant evocation of Allah and his performance of Islamic ritual is not mere window dressing, but reflects the thorough-going infusion of Islamic ideals in the story. The impact of the story is the fact that, in spite of his apparent and self-avowed Muslim piety and righteousness, Sinbad finally contravenes Islamic ideals in the most astounding way during his adventures.

It is the relative number and nature of the adventures and catastrophes that befall Sinbad on his voyages that make up the major structural elements of the tales. These may be schematized here as follows:[18]

Table 1

Voyage	I	II	III	IV	V	VI	VII[1]	VII[2]
	C	C	C	C	C	C	C	M
	Ab	A	Ap	Ap	Ap	A	A	C
		A	Ap	Ab	Ab	Ab		A
				Ap				
	M	M	M		M	M	M	
	R	R	R	R	R	R	R	R

C = Catastrophe
A = Adventure (b = benign; p = perilous)
M = Marvels
R = Return

As may be seen at a glance, in each of his voyages Sinbad suffers a catastrophe, usually a shipwreck or desertion upon the high seas. He then experiences a series of adventures that ebb and flow as the tales proceed. Not only does the number of adventures rise and then symmetrically fall off again, however; so, too, do the violence and horror that characterize the adventures.

In the first story, Sinbad is lost at sea when, having landed on an island, the island sinks! The "island" is, in fact, a huge fish that has been dozing on the surface so long that tress and bushes have sprouted on its back. Upon feeling the cooking fires of the landing party, it dives into the ocean. Sinbad's ship has pulled off to save itself, and Sinbad must save himself by paddling to land in a large wooden bowl. He is taken in by the King of the Sea Horses, becomes the latter's minister, and finally returns home rich.

In the second story, Sinbad is abandoned on a desert island. He manages to escape by tying himself to the leg of the Rukh that flies him off of the island but deposits him in the valley of snakes and diamonds. He again escapes, this time loaded with diamonds, and finally returns home rich.

In the third story, catastrophe overtakes Sinbad when apes attack his ship. He and his companions are cast ashore, where they encounter a huge but manlike monster who eats many of the castaways. They collaborate to put out the monster's eyes; and, though he kills several more of the company by hurling stones at them as they escape in a boat they have made, some finally make good their escape.[19] They fall foul of a man-eating snake, however, and only Sinbad escapes by building a cage in which to hide from the snake. He is soon rescued by a passing ship, fortuitously the very ship from which he had been lost in the preceding voyage, retrieves his goods, and again returns home wealthy.

The fourth story is the keystone of the entire piece. Driven ashore by a storm, the crew and passengers of Sinbad's ship fall into the hands of ghouls who fatten them up and eat them. Sinbad escapes, and happily settles among a nearby people. He becomes rich, initially by introducing the people (especially their King) to saddlery. He marries, but then falls foul of a bizarre custom of the people in which the spouse of a deceased person is buried alive with the corpse in a huge communal tomb. So buried, Sinbad stays alive by killing the newly interred and taking the meager supplies that are initially sent down with each new victim. Sinbad finds a way out of the tomb but returns, amasses the golden jewelry of the corpses, and continues to live by killing those who are sent down until he has enough.[20] He then hails a passing ship and returns home, rich.

In the fifth tale, Rukhs attack Sinbad's ship. He is captured by the Old Man o' the Sea, whom he manages to trick into getting drunk, but then kills him. With the aid of residents of a nearby city, he overcomes imprisonment by apes and makes a fortune out of coconuts that he induces the apes to throw at him by throwing stones at them. Again he returns home rich.

The sixth voyage finds Sinbad battling only the elements and circumstances. Cast ashore on a desert island, his companions die of disease and starvation. Sinbad must raft through an underground river to reach safety, but he does so; and the King of the people whom he finds commissions him as ambassador to the Khalifah Haroun. He makes his way home to wealth and honor.

In the seventh voyage of the fuller version, Sinbad's ship is blown off course and into a distant sea where it is attacked by huge fish and destroyed. Sinbad once again manages to save himself by rafting away from the desert shore upon which he is thrown, through an underground river and to salvation. Salvation comes in the form of an encounter with a wealthy merchant who takes Sinbad in and eventually makes Sinbad his son-in-law and heir. Sinbad relates his encounters with marvels more in the manner of his description than has been the case in the previous voyages. Usually the marvels are simply enumerated. Here, the descriptions of flying men and heavenly beings are more fully articulated. Nonetheless, the scenes appear in the proper relative position and bear no more upon the development of the structure of the tales than do the listed marvels of the previous voyages. Sinbad returns again to Baghdad, wealthy.

The format of the shorter version of the seventh voyage differs materially in its narrative detail, but only marginally in its structure as may be seen from the tabulation of topoi. It carries out the theme of Sinbad's entrance into politics. The impetus of this version of the seventh voyage is the Caliph Haroun al-Rashid's desire to have Sinbad head a return embassy to the king with whom Sinbad had stayed in the previous voyage. Nonetheless, Sinbad suffers the usual catastrophe, this time at the hands of "devil-like" pirates. He then has the one expected fearsome adventure with elephants that leads him to the elephants' graveyard, and makes his fortune yet once more.

Having briefly summarized the catastrophes and adventures that befall Sinbad, let us again tabulate these structural elements of the narrative—but this time, from another point of view: according to the nature of the beings involved in the encounters.

Table 2

Voyage	Catastrophe	Adventure	Adventure	Adventure
I	Fish	Sea-Horse King	X	X
II	(Desertion)	Rukh	Snakes	X
III	Apes	Cyclopsian monster	Snakes	X
IV	(Storm)	Ghouls	Men bury him	Men are murdered & robbed by him
V	Rukhs	Old Man o' the Sea	Apes	X
VI	(Lost at Sea)	Disease	Underground river	X
VII[1]	Fish	Underground river	X	X
VII[2]	Devil-like pirates	Elephants	X	X

It can thus be seen that there is, in addition to the rise, climax, and fall of the *number* of adventures, a concurrent rise, climax, and fall in the "sensibility," or say even "humanity," of the beings whom Sinbad encounters in his adventures. Although not quite as rigidly symmetrical in these terms as in terms of the abstractions, "catastrophe" and "adventure," the same curve of rise and fall operates here. As the tales progress, the nature of those whom Sinbad encounters rises and falls along an almost evolutionary scale: I. sea animals; II. nonmammalian land animals; III. animals (snakes, apes, Cyclops); IV. man; V. animals (Rukhs, sea-man, apes); VI. anomalous; VII. sea-animals.

Let us tabulate Sinbad's adventures from yet one more point of view: the violence involved in his encounters.

Table 3

Voyage	Catastrophe	Adventure	Adventure	Adventure
I	None (Fish)	None (Sea-Horse King)	X	X
II	None (Desertion)	Minor (Rukh flight)	Minor (Snake threat & dangerous rescue)	X
III	Major (Ape attack)	Horrible** (Cyclopsian murders; blinding of Cyclops)	Horrible (Snake attack; defensive cage)	X
IV	Minor (Threat of storm)	Horrible (Threat of Ghouls)	Horrible (Buried alive)	Horrible** (Killing of innocents)
V	Major (Rukh attack)	Horrible** (Old man o' the Sea killed)	Major (Apes imprison him)	X
VI	None (Ship lost)	Minor (Disease kills)	Minor (thread of underground river)	X
VII[1]	Minor (Fish attack ship)	Minor (Thread of underground river)	X	X
VII[2]	Minor/Major (Capture by pirates)	Minor (Carried off by elephants)	X	X

**Sinbad himself commits violent acts in these strategically located instances.

An interesting echo of the basic rise and fall structure of the stories is to be found, too, in Sinbad the Porter's reactions to each of the stories:

Table 4

Voyage	Sinbad the Porter's Reaction
I	"Thinks" about what befalls people.
II	Is "astounded" at what befell the sailor; prays for him.
III	Is "astounded."
IV	Is "astounded" and spends the night in the utmost contentment and pleasure.
V	Is "astounded."
VI	(No reaction recorded.)
VII	(No reaction recorded.)

But why, while the audience reacts with shock and horror, should the porter respond to the most chilling of the tales with "contentment and pleasure?" Perhaps because Sinbad only begins his story after he has lavishly plied his guests, the nameless and faceless "companions" and the porter, with the finest of food and drink:

> When morning dawned, lit [things] up with its light and appeared, Sinbad the porter arose, prayed the morning prayer and came to the house of Sinbad the sailor as [the latter] had ordered him. He entered and said good morning to him. [The sailor] welcomed him and sat with him until the rest of his companions, his group, had arrived and they had eaten, drunk, enjoyed themselves, been pleasured and relaxed. Then Sinbad the sailor began to speak and said: . . . [21]

Perhaps also because the sailor closes each tale with a lavish gift to the porter. He gives a fabulous dinner and then loads the porter with one hundred *mithqāls* of gold. In the final tale, Sinbad the porter takes up permanent residence with the sailor and they live out a happy and contented life:

> They remained in friendship and love with increasing joy and relaxation until [that] destroyer of pleasures, that divider of companions, that destroyer of indolence, that filler of graves—the cup of death—came to them. So praise be to the Living One who does not die.[22]

Sinbad the Sailor, then, tells his tales as an apology. He has been challenged by the porter's song and feels the need to justify his life and actions. But whom is he trying to convince, and how does he proceed to do so? Perhaps he needs to justify his actions to everyone who passes his door. Sinbad the porter receives an impression of the sailor's "companions" at the outset: "He saw, in that abode, a number of noble gentlemen and great lords."[23] But, this is all we know of them. Thereafter, they are merely Sinbad's companions who arrive each day to hear the tales of the sailor's adventures. Perhaps they are fellow merchants whose perceptions and rationalizations are akin to those of Sinbad the Sailor himself. Or, perhaps they too are men who have doubted the justness of Sinbad's wealth and have been rewarded for their acquiescence to his self-justification just as the porter has been rewarded. In any case, the significance of the identity of names between Sinbad the sailor and Sinbad the porter is clear. It can hardly be fortuitous. Sinbad the porter is the sailor's alter ego, the Sinbad who questions the distribution of wealth and the ways in which it has been gained. Finally, the questioning Sinbad is satisfied; but how? If Sinbad's self-justification stands on its own merits, why the need for the lavish presents of gold at the end of each story? Why the need to keep the porter's bought acceptance close at hand for the rest of their lives?

The answers are clear: Sinbad's actions are not finally justifiable. The crescendo and decrescendo of terror and violence that characterize the stories lead the audience from an attitude of readiness to believe, to questioning, doubt, and downright rejection at the climax of the fourth tale. We then trail off into a knowing and cynical skepticism as the stories wind to a close.

Sinbad is plunged into horrible situations to be sure; but they are in large measure of his own making. The fundamental reason for his voyages is greed and his actions are often more violent than those of his antagonists. He himself notes at one point: "I said to myself: 'I deserve all that has happened to me. All this is fated for me by God Most High so that I might turn from the greed by which I am [consumed]. All that I suffer is from my greed.' "[24] Sinbad's wealth and positions are, then, a material reward for a vicious determination to "get on" in the world of commercial wheeling and dealing at the expense of anyone who happens to be in the way. They are clearly not heavenly reward for patience, forbearance, and charity.

The Cyclopsian monster's actions are horrible to be sure; but not apparently malicious. His act is not a moral one, but simply feeding behavior. Sinbad's plot to kill the monster and his blinding of it are, however, gratuitous; for the monster's castle is always open and Sinbad is free to build and provision a boat for his escape. Only after doing so does he return and blind the monster.[25] "So, we carried the wood out of the castle and we built a raft. We tied it at the sea shore and brought a bit of food down to it. Then we returned to the castle."

Such is the situation with the Old Man o' the Sea. The Old Man has used Sinbad harshly to be sure by forcing Sinbad to carry him around under threat of severe punishment:[26] "If I crossed him, he would beat me with his feet more harshly than with a whip." Having gotten him drunk and having escaped, however, Sinbad's murder of the Old Man, regardless of how subhuman and sinister he might have been, is again a gratuitous act of violence.

It is not suggested that either the modern or the medieval audience could not justify Sinbad's actions in the third and fifth stories. Indeed, the shock value of the Old Man of the Sea story arises from the brusque shift from the comical scene of Sinbad making wine in a gourd, arousing the Old Man's curiosity, and getting him drunk, to crushing his skull with a rock. Rather, these two stories serve to raise and then slow the tempo of violence and horror. They shock the audience into an awareness of Sinbad's potential for murder, which culminates horribly in the killing of innocent people in the tomb of the fourth story.

This latter situation is perhaps ambiguous in Muslim law, for the action clearly takes place outside the Dār al-Islām. Thus, the case could never be brought before a *sharīʿah* court. Furthermore, the victims are not even *dhimmī*.[27] Murder of the innocent, however, is abhorrent to Islamic morality under any circumstances: "Hast thou slain an innocent person not guilty of slaying another? Thou hast indeed done a horrible thing!"[28] Whatever justification might have been felt to be attached to Sinbad's being trapped in the tomb is obviated by the fact hat he continues to murder after having found his way out of the tomb and to rob the corpses to make his fortune.[29] "Whomever they buried, I would take his food and water and kill whether man or woman. Then I would go out of the hole and sit on the sea shore." Thus while the first two stories find the audience in sympathy with Sinbad and ready to accept the view he puts forward, our sensibilities begin to be seriously disturbed in the third and we are utterly repulsed by Sinbad's behavior in the fourth tale despite the fact that he has been presented to us as a grave and dignified figure of benign authority: "In the midst of that company was a great, respectable man. Gray had touched his temples and he was fine of stature and handsome of face. He had dignity, sobriety, power and pride."[30]

Three more topoi that occur and reoccur concurrently with the major structural elements of the tale suggest that even Sinbad himself is aware of the indefensibility of the actions for which he is apologizing.[31] In the beginning and ending stories, Sinbad tells the tale of his adventures to all and sundry. But in the middle tales, he does so less and less until, in the fourth—the keystone tale—he not only does not tell his tale but also consciously conceals the story of what has befallen him and what he had done. The captain and crew of the ship that picks him up do ask for his story, but he tells them only of a shipwreck and adds: "I did not inform them of what had happened to me in the city or in the tomb fearing that there might be someone from the city with them aboard the ship."[32] In his own mind, Sinbad represses the memory of his actions. At the end of each story, he tells us that he would forget the hardships of his voyages. But in the middle stories, he increasingly treats the events as if they "had been a dream." In psychological terms, his repression of guilt is clear.

Finally, Sinbad's conscience obviously bothers him, for in the middle stories he returns home not only to enjoy his wealth as he has in the first stories but also to give alms and to clothe widows and orphans. A tabulation of these topoi will make their significance immediately apparent, inversely corresponding as they do to the rise and fall pattern of the story as a whole.

Thus, the structure of the relevant topoi of the story reveals a discrepancy between Sinbad's apology and the ethical principles of his, and the audience's, world. By it, we are led back to the outer frame story of Shahrazad and the king, for the stories are parallel. As Sinbad justifies his unjustifiable murders, so does the king justify the unjustifiable murder of his wives by their potential infidelity. But, as Shahrazad hopes to delay her own murder until the king may see the injustice of his own actions, she spins him a tale of self-justification

Table 5

Voyage	Telling the Tale	Reaction	Charity
I	To horse herder To herder's friend To the king To ship's captain	Forgets	—
II	To merchant To merchant's friends	Forgets	Gives alms and presents
III	(To sailors—mentioned) To ships captain	All seems a dream Forgets	Gives alms, presents; Clothes widows & orphans
IV	(To pepper gatherers and their king—mentioned) REFUSES TO TELL HIS TALE TO SHIP'S COMPANY	Forgets All seems a dream As though his mind is lost	Gives alms, presents; Clothes widows & orphans
V	To ship's company To man from the city (To man from the city—mentioned)	Forgets	Gives alms, presents; Clothes widows & orphans
VI	To Indians and Ethiopians To their king (To the Caliph—mentioned) To the Caliph	Forgets	Gives alms, presents
VII	(To his family—mentioned)	—	—

that can only be had by buying off the conscience. The moral is not stated and the story is not didactic in any overt sense. It is merely one more example of the cunning cleverness of women that is such a common theme of the *1001 Nights*. That cunning is not necessarily condemned, merely noted, and here once again it works for Shahrazad who does finally have her way. As with the king, so for the audience. Not overcome by greed for more material wealth, the audience sees the ironic disparity of an external view of Sinbad's actions and his own unconvincing apology that provides the ethical impact of the story. To be sure, many in any given audience might accept Sinbad's apology. Those who are caught up in the same greed for surplus wealth might need to justify similar actions and so find justification in Sinbad himself. It is that greed that speeds Sinbad on his voyages for, as he points out in introducing each of his tales, he undertakes his voyages not out of need but for the desire for adventure that is subsumed under and intimately related to the desire to buy and sell: the desire for profitable commercial ventures—greed.

Seen in this light, the Sinbad story becomes more coherent in its internal structure and fits nicely into its external frame, the Shahrazad/Shahriyar story. It also comes to tally more closely with its Greek and Latin analogues, for in those stories the protagonist is of questionable moral character at the outset: he is a thief.[33]

The irony is most subtle; it is never stated. Only the audience's own reaction to Sinbad's stories affords an entrance to the teller's ironic intent. Indeed, the second version points out one more irony of the business world. Commercial acuity, however rapacious, piratical, even murderous, can also lead to political preference and power. In the sixth story, the King of Ceylon, impressed by Sinbad's stories of his adventures and by his commercial successes, commissions Sinbad as his Ambassador to Haroun al-Rashid. In the second version of the seventh voyage, Haroun takes Sinbad into the court and, in turn, entrusts him with the return mission to Ceylon. Thus, Sinbad has attained political power and success as well as commercial success and material wealth. But the story has become, not "a veritable glorification of navigation and maritime commerce," but a critique of the disparity between ethics and action. For the audience, including Shahrazad's king, is aware of the cost of Sinbad's successes: the suppression of the merchant's ethical sensibility in his pursuit of material gain.

Notes

1. J. I. Jabra, *Art Dream and Action*, unpublished paper presented at the University of California, Berkeley, May 26, 1976, p. 7.

2. Private communication, May 26, 1976.

3. Cf. Bibliography in note 33.

4. *New York Times*, January 23, 1947, 31:2.

5. So also the more recent *Seventh Voyage of Sinbad*, which bears little or no resemblance to the *1001 Nights* tale. Cf. A. H. Weiler's review, *New York Times*, December 24, 1958.

6. Mia I. Gerhardt, *Les voyages de Sinbad le Marin*, Utrecht, 1957, p. 33.

7. Ibid., p. 39.

8. My thanks to all the students of Intermediate Literary Arabic at the University of California, Berkeley, 1975–76, with whom I read the Sinbad stories and whose perceptive comments and questions have done much to make my own views more clear and concise.

9. Gerhardt ignores one fundamental, and several minor, structural elements in the *1001 Nights* tales that, with a predisposition to see Sinbad as a romantic hero, leads to problems.

10. For a fuller analysis of the variations in the Arabic textual tradition, cf. Gerhardt, pp. 17–27.

11. *Alf Layla wa-Layla*, Calcutta, 1839, Macnaghten, ed., Vol. III, p. 64. It is interesting to note that not only does the Sinbad tale contain this first-person narrative in biographical form, but also that the frame story and episodes form a continuous and integrated whole, no part of which is expendable. Most Western literary historians consider the anonymous, sixteenth-century *Lazarillo de Tormes* and *Don Quixote* as the "progenitors" of the novel precisely because of these features, which distinguish them from the "romance." That they occur here, in an obviously older tale deriving (at least) from an oral tradition, is of rather great significance for our understanding of the narrative art.

12. Cf. Scholes and Kellog, *The Nature of Narrative*, Oxford, 1975, pp. 52–53, for a discussion of this ironic disparity as a constant in fiction. We would suggest a caveat on the Scholes-Kellog point of view, however. They make a sharp distinction between "traditional," i.e., oral, narrative and "written" narrative and confine the sort of irony described above to the written. We would argue that the irony exists in the *1001 Nights*. The *Nights*, however, even in their written form, must represent a transitional stage between oral and written narrative in which elements of the two modes cross-fertilize each other. The terms "narrator" and "protagonist" are, therefore, used to distinguish between the two levels of perception represented by Shahrazad and Sinbad. The potential third level, that of the "narrator" of Shahrazad's story, seems not to be structurally or literally relevant.

13. We will return to this point at some length in our conclusions, but it should be noted here that Gerhardt ignores entirely the relationship of the Shahrazad element in her analysis and thus skews her entire perception of the tale.

14. Macnaghten, Vol. III, p. 4.

15. Ibid., p. 6. The translation is from Lane, Vol. VI, p. 327.

16. From Lane, p. 429. Macnaghten's text is less precise: "So look, Oh Sinbad, Oh landsman, at what has befallen me, and at what has happened to me, and at what my circumstance has been. Then Sinbad the landsman said to Sinbad the sailor, 'By God, you must forgive me for what I felt about your just rewards,' " p. 82. Sinbad's view of his riches is prefigured when he first meets the porter, too: "For verily I have not attained this happiness and this position save after harsh fatigue, great toil and many terrors. How I suffered, at first, from fatigue and hardship." Macnaghten, pp. 7–8. Here, though, the notion of heavenly reward is lacking.

17. I use the term, "analogue" as in Wm. F. Bryan ed., *Sources and Analogues of Chaucer's Canterbury Tales*, Humanities Press, New York, 1958. Analogues are tales having close similarities in plot, characterization, and structure that are not demonstrably derived the one from the other or do not demonstrably form parts of a chain of direct transmission. While a common ancestor may exist for "analogue" tales, said ancestor exists too far removed in time and space to be established by any other means than the comparative method established for the reconstruction of prototypical linguistic forms. Should said reconstruction be made, it must be treated as are such linguistic reconstructions—with a certain circumspection. Furthermore, until a full family tree is made of all of the analogues, great care must be taken about applying the term "source" to any given tale in its relationship to another. While not wanting to exclude the possibility of a direct Greek influence on the Sinbad tales, and particularly the third story, which is an obvious analogue to the Ulysses and Polyphemus story, I find that G. E. von Grunebaum's conclusions as to the Greek origins of much of the Arabian Nights is overly positive in its statement [Cf. *Medieval Islam*, chapter nine, "Creative Borrowing: Greece in the Arabian Nights," esp. III, pp. 298–305 on Sinbad]. As von Grunebaum himself points out, there are discrepancies between the Homeric and *Arabian Nights* versions. These, however, should not be put down merely to corruption by the Arab tellers, for there are discrepancies too between the Greek and the prototypical story as it occurs in so many different versions of the story. To cite but one instance, neither Sinbad nor Ulysses makes reference to the magic ring that figures so prominently in the analogue stories, British and Turkish, to mention but two.

The relationship between the Ulysses and Polyphemus stories and all of their analogues, such as Sinbad's third voyage, is dealt with at length in Appendix XIII to *Apollodorus: The Library*, Loeb Classical Library, New York, 1921, translated by Jas. G. Frazer.

18. This point is apparently missed by all the translators and commentators until Gerhardt. Burton, for instance, feels, "In one point, this world famous tale is badly ordered. The most exciting adventures are the earliest, and the falling off of interest has a somewhat depressing effect. The Rukh, the Ogre and the Old Man o' the Sea should come last." Vol. VI, p. 77, n. Gerhardt, however, has developed a very good analysis of these major structural elements; and we can do no better than to use her categorization. The chart is based on Gerhardt's, p. 30.

19. Cf. note 17.

20. It is interesting to note that the theme of premature burial, salvation from the tomb, and pirating of funerary treasures is a common one in Greek romances. Cf. Moses Hadas, *A History of Greek Literature*, Columbia University Press, 1950, pp. 293–94.

21. This particular version of the scene introduces the third voyage. Cf. Macnaghten, op. cit., p. 27. The topos does not precede the seventh tale.

22. Ibid., p. 83. The suggestion that they actually lived together comes from Lane, p. 429.

23. Ibid., p. 6.

24. Ibid., p. 75.

25. Ibid., pp. 28–32.

26. Ibid., pp. 56–58.

27. Ambiguous is perhaps the wrong term, for the situation is one in contention in Muslim law. Cf., for instance, Muhammad Ibn al-Ḥasan al-Shaybānī, *Kitāb al-Siyar* (The Islamic Law of Nations), translator Majid Khadduri, Baltimore, 1966. Esp. "The Application of Ḥudūd Penalities, "pp. 171–74. Shaybānī holds that any *ḥadd* crime committed by a Muslim in the *Dār al-Ḥarb* would be null and void, as "they were committed [in a territory] where Muslim rulings are not applicable to them," pp. 171–72. Awzāʿī and Shāfiʿī, however, hold the opposing view. Cf. n. 49, p. 172. In any case, Shaybānī would apparently agree that the Muslim would be subject to the local law of such matters. Cf. pp. 173–74.

28. *Al-Qurʾan al-Karīm*, "Sūrat al-Kahf," verse 74.

29. Macnaghten, op. cit., pp. 49–50.

30. Ibid., p. 6.

31. It is interesting to note the topoi used in the development of Sinbad the Sailor that are *not* structurally relevant to the whole of the tale. They occur and reoccur, not regularly as do the themes with which we have been dealing here, but sporadically even where not called for. They suggest another level or element of structure in the technique of oral composition. Oral composition has been well defined for poetry, but not so well defined for the prose tale. Nonetheless, many of the same techniques are found in oral prose tales as in poetry. The "formula" as defined by Parry and Lord is readily apparent in the prose tale, as are the "themes." What we have labeled "topos" seem to be intermediate features. Larger than the formula, though akin to it in form, they are not yet definable as themes. They appear to serve as building blocks for the tale-teller. Each may be formed by a bundle of formulas and be recognizable as a minitheme. They are, in turn, bundled together to form the major themes of the tale. Whereas given themes become structurally significant in the tale, individual topoi, unlike Propp's *functions*, may be, without affecting the tale, left out, added, or interspersed between themes simply to flesh out the story in a familiar way.

We will attempt to pursue this observation in subsequent work.

32. Macnaghten, op. cit., p. 52.

33. We will make no attempt to make a detailed analysis of the Medieval Greek and Latin analogues, but merely make one or two points that may have been obscured in our article and give some bibliography to the materials besides n. 17. It should be noted that *Syntipas* and *Dolopathos* are not analogues to *Sinbad the Sailor* in their entirety, but rather analogues to the *Arabian Nights* tale of the seven wise viziers. In this story, also known as the "Seven Sages of Rome" in other European versions, a young prince is falsely accused by one of his father's (the king's) wives of attempted rape. The details already provide an analogue to the Biblical and Quranic stories of Joseph. Being under a one-week vow of silence, the prince cannot answer the charges; and the king determines to execute him. The boy's tutor calls in a series of wise men, each of whom spins a tale showing that hasty judgments are dangerous and that women are perfidious. Each time the king relents in his judgment, only to have the favorite again incite against the prince. Much to the distress of the favorite, however, they do manage to get through the week, the prince is able to defend himself, she is discomfited, and king and prince live happily ever after. One of the stories told by one of the wise men is of a famous thief who, when called to recite the stories of his most famous exploits, tells of being captured by a Cyclops and of how he managed to escape. This particular tale provides the analogue to the third voyage, in particular, of Sinbad the Sailor. For these tales, cf. the following:

Essai sur les fables indiennes, L. Deslongchamps, Paris, 1838. Which deals with the origin and transmission of many of the analogues and a prose version of the "Seven Sages of Rome" (in Old French) as well as an analysis of the Old French version (thirteenth century) of Dolopathos.

Dolopathos sive de rege et septem sapientibus, H. Oesterley, ed. London, 1873. Edition of the Latin version of Dolopathos.

Li romans de Dolopathos, after Herbers, thirteenth-century poet, ed. C. Brunet and A. Montaiglon, Paris, 1846.

Researches Respecting the Book of Sindibād, D. Comparetti, London, 1882, Publications of the Folk Lore Society, X.

"Syntipas" in *Fabulae Romanenses Graecae Conscriptae ex recensione et cum adnotationibus Alfred Eberhardi*, Lipsiae (Teubner), 1872.

16 Shahrazād Feminist

Fedwa Malti-Douglas

Were the Arabic Shahrazād to awaken, like some fairy tale princess, centuries after she first wove the stories in the *The Thousand and One Nights*, she would undoubtedly be surprised by her numerous literary transformations. Rejuvenated, manipulated, and redefined, she and her cohorts from the frame of the *Nights*, Shahriyār, Shāhzamān, and Dunyāzād, have now transcended their original literary environment to become major players on the world literary scene. And just as Shahrazād found herself caught in a delicate game of sexual politics in the frame of the *Nights*, so does she now find herself the pawn in an equally delicate game of gender and creativity, but this time on a universal scale. Male writers, female writers, Eastern writers, Western writers: neither gender nor geography has kept them from exploiting the dynamics of the frame. Add to this the fact that for many a modern critic, Shahrazād becomes the prototypical woman whose existence permits Arab woman to speak,[1] and one has the perfect locus for a gender analysis. How do contemporary feminists respond to the challenges posed both on the level of sexuality and on that of discourse in the frame? The recasting of one Western feminist, Ethel Johnston Phelps, is lined up, alongside that of one Eastern feminist, the Egyptian physician and writer Dr. Nawal El Saadawi. The first recasting, that of Phelps, is titled "Scheherazade Retold" and is formulated as a folk tale. The second functions as a subtext in a highly complex postmodern novel, *Suqūṭ al-Imām* (The Fall of the Imam).[2]

Reprinted from Fedwa Malti-Douglas, "Shahrazād Feminist," in *The Thousand and One Nights in Arabic Literature and Society*, ed. Richard C. Hovannisian and Georges Sabagh (Cambridge: Cambridge University Press, 1997), 40–55. Reprinted by permission of the publisher.

To isolate these two female authors in their respective enterprises is not meant to downplay the literary ruses of other creative writers. Shahrazād's presence is ubiquitous. She makes an appearance in the middle of Assia Djebar's *Ombre Sultane.*[3] She is transformed by Leila Sebbar into a twentieth-century Beur (a French individual of Arab descent) hitchhiking across France.[4] Examples abound.[5]

But, in a sense, the renditions of Phelps and El Saadawi stand out individually, on the one hand, and form an ideal combination for analysis on the other. Both are self-consciously feminist in their agendas. Yet in one, Shahrazād takes the lead, and in the other, it is Shahriyār. It is when their narratives are compared with those of male writers that unique features appear. Hence, our project is a double one: on the one hand, investigate what constitutes a feminist Shahrazād, and, on the other, where appropriate compare this construct with Shahrazād's literary cousin, the creation of male writers recasting the frame. A word of warning, however, is in order to the bibliographically minded reader: no catalogue and no comprehensive list of rewritings of the frame of the *Nights* are provided here. And this is not to speak of recastings or rewritings of other story cycles, like that of Sindbad, to name but one.[6]

How is it, one might wonder, that we are justified in isolating and comparing the literary creation of a Western feminist with that of an Egyptian feminist? No self-respecting critic would deny that by now *The Thousand and One Nights* can justifiably be said to be as much a part of Western literary and cultural traditions as it is of the Eastern ones. The European language translations, like those of Burton[7] and Galland, to cite but two, helped provide the *Nights* with a permanent position in world literature. It is this that makes possible a project like that of Georges May, whose work on Galland is a questionable attempt to argue for the independence and originality of the translator's text as literary creation.[8] It is the cultural assimilation of the *Nights* into the Western imaginary that can also permit a Warner Brothers animated recasting of it titled *Thousand and One Rabbit Tales.*[9]

Let us allow Ethel Johnston Phelps to be our initial guide on the path toward the feminist Shahrazād, since Nawal El Saadawi's is the more complex of the two contemporary projects. Yet to appreciate the genius of these radical enterprises, a summary of the original medieval Arabic frame story is essential.

Shahriyār, a mythical ruler, longs to see his brother, Shāhzamān. The latter, about to accede to his brother's request, catches his wife frolicking with a loathsome cook. He kills both and proceeds to visit his brother. Once there, he discovers that his brother's wife is also unfaithful, but her perfidy is with a black slave. He eventually reveals this to his older brother and the two set out on a spiritual journey, abandoning the world. On this voyage, they are lured into sexual intercourse by an *ʿifrīt*'s young woman who was locked up by this creature who kidnapped her on her wedding night. After this sexual interlude, Shahriyār returns to his kingdom, has his wife and her black lover disposed of, and begins his one-night stands with virgins, whom he kills after the evening's entertainment. Shahrazād enters the scene at this point and, with her sister's help, she recounts stories that conveniently stretch over the break of day, hence, keeping the king in suspense and herself alive. At the end of the storytelling cycle, we discover that she has given birth to three sons. The monarch lets her live and has her stories engraved for posterity. Her sister weds Shāhzamān and the foursome live happily ever after.[10]

From its title, Phelps's "Scheherazade Retold" reveals its intention. The story forms part of a collection in which strong heroines dominate. Subtitled "A Persian Tale," the recasting stars Shahrazād[11] who lives in Samarkand. The cruel Sultan who rules over the city had his wife put to death because he suspected her of being unfaithful. The young women he then takes on as brides are thrown into a dungeon after "scarcely more than a day or two." Shahrazād sets herself to saving the young women of the kingdom and enlists her sister's aid for that purpose. As with her literary predecessor, this contemporary Western descendant narrates, interrupting the story and keeping the ruler in suspense. This continues for one thousand and one nights. Here, Phelps's tale breaks with the expected structure. A question is posed: "What happened to Scheherazade after the one thousand and one tales were told?"[12] The reader is presented with two traditional variants. The first is that Shahrazād fell in love with the monarch and both lived happily ever after. The second is that she reveals the existence of the three male offspring, at which point she is forgiven and she and the ruler once more live happily ever after.

The narrator of Phelps's story effectively rejects these choices, however, calling them "meek and improbable":

> Rather than force Scheherazade to change her admirable character, I would suggest another ending. Freed at this point by the Sultan's death (for I loyally believe Scheherazade could have produced another thousand tales if necessary), acclaimed by the grateful citizens of Samarkand, she did what any clever storyteller would do: Using her earlier education provided by the best tutors, she of course wrote down for posterity a more polished version of her own thousand and one tales.[13]

What an interesting recasting of the frame! Gone is the problematic relationship of Shahriyār and Shāhzamān,[14] gone is the detailed account of the wife's perfidy. The bare-boned nature of Phelps's succinct yet powerful variant forces to the surface many an issue that might otherwise lie dormant.

For Phelps, Shahrazād is the mistress of the story, a story whose opening words are: "A very long time ago, a young woman named Scheherazade lived in the lovely city of Samarkand."[15] Hence, the female storyteller is the first character to appear on the scene. The city she inhabits is a positive locus, with "fragrant gardens, elegant marble fountains, and heavily laden fruit trees"—until the "cruel Sultan" emerges.[16] From the very beginning of the Phelpsian narrative, the positive female Shahrazād is opposed to the negative male ruler. In this modern tale, the young woman is immune from the fear the Sultan engenders, since her father is one of the ruler's advisers. This immunity makes her self-sacrificing act that much more altruistic.

More is at stake in Phelps's modern rendition. Shahrazād is the only character endowed with a name, singularizing her and setting her apart from even her family members, who, like her sister, are defined through her. The ruler is merely called the Sultan. His namelessness turns him into a quasi-generic monarch and, in a sense, reifies him. He loses part of his identity. And this loss is reinforced when we add to it his solitary nature: he does not form a male couple with a brother, as did his ancestor in the original frame of the *Nights*. This is not the case with Shahrazād, who functions in the Phelpsian variant with her sister much as her medieval namesake did.

What about the Sultan? He is not only cruel, but it also seems "as though the Sultan had in truth gone mad." When Shahrazād's father attempts to dissuade her from her foolish act, he refers to the monarch as "a half-mad old man."[17] The royal wife's infidelity, such a pivotal component of the medieval text, is in this contemporary revival but a figment of the Sultan's imagination. There is no voyeuristic activity to discover the woman's illicit behavior. The entire perfidious adventure that sets the original frame into motion is cast into doubt. The Sultan suspect that his wife has been unfaithful. He is not like his medieval predecessor who had a need to see his wife's perfidious act with his own eyes.[18] Any possible justification for the medieval tyrant's murderous behavior is missing here. Sabry Hafez correctly notes a similar absence in El Saadawi's version.[19] Occulting an explanation of the emotional logic behind Shahriyār's acts is designed to eliminate the possibility of any kind of potential justification of his gynocide. After all, the idea that a male's wronged honor can justify such a murder, or at least serve as an extenuating circumstance, is not yet dead in a number of Christian and Muslim cultures. The feminist perspective of Phelps (and El Saadawi) focuses on the victim, not on the victimizer.

Yet the idea of madness, invoked by Phelps, is not far from the original Shahriyār. After Shāhzamān recounts to his brother what has befallen him with his own wife and the cook, Shahriyār declares that what happened to Shāhzamān was unique and that, were such an adventure to befall him, he would not be satisfied with killing less than a hundred women or even a thousand women. "And I would have gone mad and come out mad."[20] In Phelps's version, Shahriyār's madness has no cause. It is a given, a principle of disorder that begins the chain of disorders. It is no more explained than is the adultery of the royal wives, which was the initial principle of disorder in the medieval text.

Unlike his literary predecessor, Phelps's modern madman is not a gynocidal maniac. He does not kill women in cold blood on a daily basis. He merely throws them into a dungeon. What their fate will ultimately be, however, is not elucidated in Phelps's narrative. The reader can be comfortable in the assumption that this act is tantamount to the elimination of the female.

When Shahrazād's sister begs her to tell her stories, the heroine asks the Sultan for his permission. "He nodded and belched, for he had as usual eaten too heavily."[21] The ruler has been turned into a quasi-buffoon, who overeats. Shahrazād's narration is broken, in Phelps's story, not at the end of the night, but "as the night grew late," and by the narrator's declaration of her own physical exhaustion. She yawns and declares to the ruler that, "too sleepy to remember what happens next," she wishes to continue the tale the next night. He agrees, yet we know that she had purposefully broken the narration "at the most exciting part of the tale."[22]

Striking here are the physical, corporal aspects of the two characters. His overeating is balanced by her yawning. Clearly, his is less excusable, especially when we see that he combines it with belching. Shahrazād's corporality is but a manipulative ruse, designed to trick the old ruler into permitting the continuation of her storytelling. Both activities revolve around the mouth and partake of the oral. But their corporality is antiheroic; both are devalued activities. The physical modes of the original *Nights*, by contrast, were taken far more seriously, involving the genital and the visual gone awry and then repaired by the triumphant oral.[23] True, Shāhzamān, as a result of witnessing his wife's vile act, loses his appetite, something that results in a weakened physical state. But he regains that appetite after he realizes that his brother has been subjected to much the same odious behavior.[24] Yet there is no exaggerated bodily activity on the part of the male; no gluttony. It is only the females whose desires are insatiable.

Phelps's Shahrazād, at the opening of the narrative, is not far from her literary ancestor. When she explains to her father that she must do what she can to save the young women of the city, her justification is: "How can I sit here with my books and do nothing?" Both women are clever and learned.

The two Shahrazāds, that of *The Thousand and One Nights* and her Phelpsian cousin, part ways, however, at the end of the narrative, after Phelps's narrator has exposed the two traditional they-lived-happily-ever-after endings. As the contemporary account would have it, the Sultan dies, Shahrazād is free and "acclaimed by the grateful citizens of Samarkand," and she "wrote down for posterity a more polished version of her one thousand and one tales."[25]

This divergent ending foregrounds several important elements.

The death of the ruler is significant because it is this act that permits Shahrazād to become independent. The opposition of cruel male and clever female with which the story begins has been resolved: the male is eliminated. The popular rejoicing by the citizenry at the heroine's success becomes a collective act that celebrates the demise of the male ruler. In the traditional endings, there is also a collective act of celebration, but it is one of happiness for the heterosexual couple who will live happily ever after. The traditional ending sanctifies male/female relations; Phelps glorifies the solitary woman.[26] The Western writer makes the contrast explicit. Including the traditional endings breaks a pattern. None of Phelps's other changes was compared with the original version. Only the myth of domestic bliss is judged sufficiently contemporary to merit an explicit evocation and rejection.

More radical, however, is how this twentieth-century Shahrazād immortalizes her stories. It is she who sets them down on paper. She has no need of a male to transform her words from the oral to the written. The Phelpsian heroine has simply carried her literary project to its natural conclusion. This is not an insignificant act in the larger literary scheme. Who controls Shahrazād's discourse becomes a tug of war in some modern male narratives, like that of the American John Barth or the Moroccan Négib Bouderbala.[27] And Edgar Allan Poe's solution is the opposite of Phelps's: Shahrazād follows the path of physical destruction that her sisters endured before her. The ruler declares that she has given him "a dreadful headache" with her "lies" and she is strangled at the end of the narrative.[28] Shahrazād is then fortunate that at Phelps's literary hands she can reclaim her own stories and set them down for posterity.

Yet no matter how revolutionary Phelps's recasting of the frame may be, it still shares with the male-generated narratives a centering on the female heroine and storyteller. Nawal El Saadawi's project differs. Her *Suqūṭ al-Imām* occults Shahrazād, choosing instead to foreground the male serial murderer, the ruler Shahriyār. This daring novelistic mythical creation by the Egyptian physician and feminist is by no means a mere rewriting of the frame of *The Thousand and One Nights*. It is a recasting of the patriarchal system that pervades the Islamic and Judeo-Christian religious traditions, as it does the Middle East and the West.

El Saadawi's fictional career has spanned decades. Born in 1931 in the Egyptian Delta and trained at the Faculty of Medicine at the University of Cairo, Nawal El Saadawi practiced in the areas of thoracic medicine and psychiatry, in which field she still takes patients. She was briefly national Public Health Director and was imprisoned under Sadat. She founded and animated the Arab Women's Solidarity Association until the Egyptian government shut it down in 1991.

The life of the pen has, however, had more appeal for the physician than has the life of the scalpel, and her corpus is enormous: medical texts, short stories, novels, plays, prison memoirs, travel texts, critical essays. She, perhaps more than any other Arab woman, has both inspired and infuriated readers all over the world.[29]

Suqūṭ al-Imām is without doubt El Saadawi's most ambitious fictional work. To attempt a summary of its plot would be rash. How does one weave a plot where one does not exist? How does one describe a metafictional postmodern narrative in a coherent manner? Here, first-person narrators live alongside third-person narrators. A single chapter in this highly complex novel can have up to three different voices, weaving their stories in and out. Events repeat; the identity of characters is cast into doubt. *Suqūṭ al-Imām* creates a mythical universe inhabited by a male ruler, the Imam. Surrounded by a coterie of ministers and the standard paraphernalia of male political power, the Imam rules over a land described as "the other world." His wife is a Christian woman, who hails from lands "beyond the sea" and who has converted to Islam. During the Victory Holiday, the Imam is killed. Parallel to the Imam is Bint Allāh, the Daughter of God. She is a student in a nursing school, who lays her paternity at the deity's door. At the same time, she is visited by God and feels Christ moving in her womb. She too is killed, though her demise comes about during a religious holiday. But neither figure dies only once. Each death, that of the Imam and that of Bint Allāh, is repeated obsessively throughout the novel in a complex cyclical pattern. Indeed, the novel combines synchronic discussions and aspects of the Imam's world with an overlay (or is it underlay?) of this mythic, even ritual, cycle of murder. This imaginary earthly kingdom is not a specific place, though it has the uncanny familiarity of a Middle Eastern country. This "other world" is visited by the test-tube man, whose previous love is the Christian wife of the Imam. He himself becomes part of the Imam's entourage, eventually returning to his own land.

The larger onomastic, political, and religious questions that El Saadawi's novel raises are avoided here.[30] My critical task is restricted to an examination of the transformations of *The Thousand and One Nights*. For it is perhaps the *Nights* more than any other work that acts as subtext, that at once governs and directs the entirety of the *Suqūṭ al-Imām*. Thus, I am not in agreement with Sabry Hafez's assessment, when he argues that El Saadawi's "text does not refrain from resorting to generalisations or twisting facts, including universally known ones, such as its twist of the frame story of *The Arabian Nights*," or when he calls it a "deliberate misrepresentation of the frame story."[31] Reinterpreting traditional materials is a staple of postmodern narratives. The changes here are certainly "deliberate," but they are also as political as were those of Phelps.

The *Nights* in the Egyptian feminist's universe comes predominantly through the royal male character, Shahriyār. He is such a powerful patriarchal figure that he can transcend his original locus of *The Thousand and One Nights* and serve as a unifying force for both the Imam's mythical universe and its counterpart, the lands "beyond the sea." The Imam's land is a place without a name. It is an unspecified territory that could obviously stand for any or many a Middle Eastern country. One could comfortably place it in Egypt: there are after all references to water buffaloes. But this would not be intended by the narrative. The text is uncomfortable identifying the "sea" either as the Mediterranean or as the Nile. "They said: the names differ. Time differs. But the place is one. And the sun is one."[32] This society is complete: populated by men, women, and children. The other geographical locus is also unspecified, but for being "beyond the sea." We can conclude that it is the West, the place where the Imam's foreign Christian wife learned political science. It is also the place that creates test-tube babies, and where women give birth to books. This West appears through the narration of the test-tube man, whose beloved ran off to "the other world," that of the Imam, and about which he has heard "fairy tales and the stories of *The Thousand and One Nights*." He himself is an office employee whose male boss makes sexual overtures to him. The woman he marries has "a warm intellect and a cold womb." He warms her in the winter and she keeps him cool in the summer. He will, however, go to the land of the Imam, play the role of philosopher in the ruler's court, and leave with his beloved.[33]

What a grim view, however, of the male hero! The test-tube man confesses to having heard "the stories of *The Thousand and One Nights*."[34] After his psychiatrist recommends travel, the test-tube man tells his wife that he is going to "the other world." After leaving her, he looks in the mirror and sees himself as "King Shahriyār. I will rape a virgin every night and before dawn I will kill her, before she kills me."[35] This last phrase expresses it well: male aggression against the female is reinterpreted as self-protection. I have already redefined the relationship of Shahriyār to his ex-virginal victims: that of fear of the female.

The test-tube man's identification with Shahriyār remains, in a sense, fairly superficial, maintained in the realm of the imaginary. The Imam's identification with Shahriyār is more direct, more violent. In his own first-person narration, the Imam reveals that while in bed, he loved reading books from the *turāth* (the cultural and literary heritage of the Arabs), especially *The Thousand and One Nights*. He would put on his reading glasses and take off the Imam's face. Looking in the mirror, he would watch physical changes that would transform him into Shahriyār: white skin and white teeth. "My heart is white like his heart, loving black slave girls. And my soul is innocent like his, not knowing that a woman can love a man other than her husband." The Imam's body shivers when he sees Shahriyār's wife in bed with the black slave "and in my dreams I see my wife in bed with one of my black slaves." He opens his eyes and instead sees his wife in bed hugging a book. Reassured, he runs to his black slave girl and, on the way, stops under a tree. He enjoys being without his guards, in complete anonymity. But, what does he see? A giant whom he takes to be either a jinni or one of his enemies from the opposition political party. He quickly climbs the tree, as he did when he was a child, and hides in the branches. The giant sits under the tree opening a box with multiple locks. Inside is another box, from which the giant takes out a woman, whose beauty is bewitching, and proceeds to lay his head on her lap and fall asleep. The young woman spots the tree climber, calls out to him to descend, he does, and she proceeds to have sexual intercourse with him. There then follows a conversation recalling those in *The Thousand and One Nights*, about the men's rings this woman has collected from previous similar sexual interludes. She will add the ring of this most recent male to the others. He runs back to the castle, only to find his wife in bed with her lover. He kills the two "just as Shahriyār had done" and adds to this singular gynocide that of his other wives.

Every month, at the new moon, he marries a virgin, deflowers her, and kills her that night. This he does for twenty years, until the people object and the young women flee. So he requests from his Chief of Security a virgin, whose description he reads to the Chief of Security from the *turāth* books. The Chief of Security is flabbergasted at this and begins to believe in reincarnation. He says to himself: "This is King Shahriyār's soul inhabiting the body of the Imam or it is the Imam's soul inhabiting King Shahriyār's body." After a long protracted discussion between the Imam and his Chief of Security during which the Great Writer is also called in to discuss love, the Chief of Security goes out to search for this young girl.[36] The girl turns out to be Bint Allāh, and at this point in the narrative it is no longer Shahriyār whose saga is in question but the Imam's. The bloodthirsty medieval ruler disappears when he has fulfilled his role.[37]

East and West are linked under the sign of Shahriyār. Nawal El Saadawi could not have chosen her male prototype better. This Shahriyār leaps across the ocean, spanning geographical territories, moving from East to West. He is most appropriate as a universal male figure.

Shahriyār has provided an effective and potent model for the Imam's gynocidal instincts. Unlike the test-tube man who only imagined himself to be the medieval Islamic ruler, the Imam becomes that ruler. The book that he is reading is transposed into the reality that he then lives. The Saadawian narrative becomes like a camera lens that is constantly moving from the world of one ruler to that of the other. When the Imam spots the giant whom we know as a character from the frame of *The Thousand and One Nights*, he takes him to be either a jinni or one of his enemies from the opposition political party. By this mere thought, he has brought the two worlds together. When he kills his wife, he does it "as Shahriyār had done."[38]

The differences between the subsequent behaviors of the two

rulers are perhaps as eloquent as the similarities. The sexual interlude between the Imam/Shahriyār and the ʿ*ifrīt*'s mate takes place at an altogether different critical point in the ruler's adventure. He runs into this sexually aggressive woman as he himself is on his way to his black slave girl. When he initially checks on his wife, it is to discover that she is sleeping alone, hugging a book. Only after his own seduction does he discover his wife in bed with her lover. This reshuffling of events shifts attention to the ruler's sexual behavior. It is his setting out to see his black slave girl that unleashes the unfortunate events, and not his wife's illicit behavior, as in the original *Nights.*

When the Saadawian text alludes to the Imam's killing his earlier/older wives,[39] it indirectly makes a commentary on the original Shahriyār's monogamy: the medieval narrator, after all, only speaks of one wife, the unnamed perfidious female. Does this monogamy make the wife's act that much more illicit? It might, since the reader could then assume that she did not share her husband's sexual favors with other wives.[40] Whereas Shahriyār performs his murderous exploits on a daily basis, his modern-day follower transposes the act into a monthly one, performed at the time of the new moon. The Muslim calendar is, of course, a lunar calendar and by turning the killing cycle into a monthly cycle, the deflowering and murder of the virgin by the Imam is turned into a quasi-sacrificial act, opposed to the daily avenging of his medieval predecessor.

The Chief of Security may be correct in reincarnating King Shahriyār and playing musical bodies with the souls of the two governing murderers. But let us not underestimate the constant tension created by the Saadawian recasting of the frame between the past that is Shahriyār and the present that is the Imam.

And what better place for this tension to be embodied than in the woman? Where has Shāhrazād gone in this modern narrative? *Cherchez la femme* becomes a dictum as important for us as it is for the Imam's Chief of Security. The Shahrazād of *The Thousand and One Nights* is occulted, though the name "Shahrazād" does appear once in El Saadawi's *Suqūṭ*. Bint Allāh, in a chapter she narrates, tells of an old grandmother who would tell the children stories. Her stories would merge one into another, her voice never stopping. "As though the cutting off of the story meant the cutting off of her life, like

Shahrazād." To the question, "Who is Shahrazād?" the old grandmother, rather than answering, would simply begin her narration anew.[41] From a major character, the original medieval teller of stories is transformed into a mysterious shadowy figure. Her fortuitous appearance in El Saadawi's text does serve a function. She is a literary herald of sorts who signals to us, the readers, that intricate intertextual games are about to unfold. Then she can comfortably disappear, leaving the frame to her male counterhero, the ruler Shahriyār.

How can this Shahrazād be so passive, so invisible, we might well ask, since we are dealing with a feminist text? Simple. In the frame of the *Nights*, Shahrazād enters the scene as the woman in control. She has read books, she has memorized poetry, she is knowledgeable, intelligent, wise, and an *adība* (a woman learned in the arts of literature and society).[42] She defies her father's advice not to venture into the monarch's bed, and, most of all, she is crafty, saving herself and her female kind. Nawal El Saadawi's novelistic agenda is radically different. It is man who is in control. It is man's murderous acts that chase the women from the kingdom. It is man who orders that the virgin be searched for. It is man who determines characteristics that the virgin will have, guided by the description in his cultural and literary heritage.

More importantly, the Shahrazād of *The Thousand and One Nights* performs a critical role in changing the dynamics of the male/female sexual relations, in redefining sexual politics. When she consciously takes on her shoulders the burden of saving womankind from the royal serial murderer, she had taken on a much more arduous task: educating this ruler in the ways of a nonproblematic heterosexual relationship. The Shahriyār of the *Nights* has, after all, only come in contact with perfidious females. Shahrazād's self-instigated entry into the narrative will change all that.

The Imam's path is different. When he orders his Chief of Security to look for a virgin, it is not to alter his behavior. No single woman will save him from the collective perfidy of the female gender. His Shahrazād is nonexistent. In effect, she has been replaced by Bint Allāh, a very different figure, and one who conforms more closely to the description Fatima Mernissi incorrectly ascribed to Shahrazād, "an innocent young girl whom a fatal destiny has brought into Chahrayar's bed."[43] But the substitution of Bint Allāh for Shahrazād is appropriate to El Saadawi's cyclical vision. The original Shahrazād worked in a linear frame and effected a solution, one that overcame criticism and ultimately sanctioned the patriarchal order. El Saadawi's universe shows no such resolution: the struggle between Bint Allāh and the Imam goes on.

What is true for the Imam is also true for his geographical cousin, the test-tube man. The two are united by a common merger of personality with Shahriyār. Both fuse identities with the medieval serial murderer by looking into a mirror: an instrument of reflection. Both will sacrifice virgins at the altar of their male fear, eloquently expressed by the Western protagonist. Both have also shared the same woman, who is the beloved of the test-tube man and the wife of the Imam. In a sense, these two males are like the two brothers from the Arabic frame who have also shared the same woman, the *ʿifrīt*'s mate. East and West have once again met, this time through male identity and sympathy with the murderous principle of gynocide. Shahriyār survives not only the test of time but also that of place. Politics may vary, places may very, but sexual politics, we learn, do not.

Shahriyār may bring the two patriarchal systems of the East and the West together but, as a model, he still remains more effective in the world of the Imam. His roots are traditionally Arabo-Islamic and will remain so. His adventures are part and parcel of the Arabo-Islamic heritage, affectionately and proudly called the *turāth*. The chapter in which the Imam is metamorphosed into Shahriyār is appropriately titled: "*Iḥyāʾ al-Turāth*" (The Revivification of the Heritage). And when this very same Imam talks about his bedtime reading, it is his passion for the *kutub al-turāth* (the books of the *turāth*) that he singles out.[44]

The literary and cultural traditions of the Arabs are, of course, centuries old and the *turāth* represents a complex and enormous collection of texts ranging from the literary through the historical to the theological and philosophical.

There is an intimate relation between men and this rich textual tradition in the Saadawian fictional universe. They can exploit it, as the Imam does; they can cite it. They are clearly at home with it. More importantly, they use it in a delicate gender game. The search for the virgin described in the *turāth* is perhaps the least ambiguous example. The ideal woman is the object of the *turāth*. She is described in it, but she is not familiar with it. When the Imam asks Bint Allāh whether she has read the *turāth* books, she answers in the negative. What about *The Thousand and One Nights*? The answer is the same.[45] Not surprisingly, the identical situation obtains with the Imam's Christian wife. When he confesses to her that he fears coming back and finding her in bed with the bodyguard, à la Shahriyār, she asks: "Who is Shahriyār?" He responds: "Do you not know Shahriyār?" To which she answers: "No." To the further question of whether she has read the *turāth* books, she again responds in the negative. This is a shortcoming in her culture, she is told, and she must read.[46] In a sense, Bint Allāh is more fortunate than the Imam's wife, if only because she is told who Shahriyār is: "King Shahriyār, whose wife, white like honey, betrayed him with a black slave." This betrayal becomes an obsession in the mind of Imam/Shahriyār and he, unlike Phelps's Sultan, seems to have his wits completely about him. His own parallel betrayal with the black slave girl seems almost irrelevant. This is what the old grandmother meant when she called man's actions a "lawful perfidy."[47] We have come full circle.

But what a far cry this modern Egyptian pseudo-Shahrazād is from her literary predecessor! The twentieth-century Arabic heroine is a player in a literary game in which she ignores the identity of the other players. Unlike her ancestor whose appearance in the text is triumphantly heralded with her in-depth literary and historical knowledge, Bint Allāh is particularly vulnerable. It is not her knowledge that is exposed but her ignorance. And this is also where the Saadawian character departs from her Phelpsian cousin. The English-speaking feminist has created a powerful Shahrazād, one even more able than her medieval Arabic namesake. The twentieth-century Western descendant is associated with "books." Not satisfied to be simply learned, she also herself commits her narratives to posterity: the ultimate liberating act.

Phelps's is the more optimistic of the two revisions of Shahrazād. Yet both El Saadawi's and Phelps's contemporary renditions, no matter what their differences, join forces in their feminist project. Each recasting, in its own way, undercuts the medieval male scribe's agenda. Neither extols the heterosexual couple so dear to the epilogue of the original *Nights*. Both demonstrate that the recasting of the world-famous frame story is not an innocent act.

It would be possible to read into these two texts a different judgment as to the prospects for female liberation seen from these two perspectives, one occidental, the other Middle Eastern. But that would be to forget that Phelps has written the past, while El Saadawi, with her ever-reborn heroine, is rewriting the future.

Notes

1. See, for example, Barbara Harlow, "The Middle East," in *Longman Anthology of World Literature by Women: 1875–1975*, compiled by Marian Arkin and Barbara Shollar (New York: Longman, 1989), p. 1165.

2. Ethel Johnston Phelps, "Scheherazade Retold," in her *The Maid of the North: Feminist Folk Tales from around the World* (New York: Henry Holt, 1981), pp. 167–73; Nawāl Al-Saʿdāwī, *Suqūṭ al-Imām* (Cairo: Dār al-Mustaqbal al-ʿArabī, 1987), trans. Sherif Hetata as *The Fall of the Imam* (London: Methuen, 1988). All translations are my own, unless otherwise noted, and all references are to the Arabic originals.

3. Assia Djebar, *Ombre Sultane* (Paris: Editions Jean-Claude Lattès, 1987).

4. Leïla Sebbar, *Les carnets de Shérazade* (Paris: Stock, 1985).

5. See, for example, Jacqueline Kelen, *Les nuits de Schéhérazade* (Paris: Editions Albin Michel, 1986).

6. For a historical overview and anthology of selected texts, see Hiam Aboul-Hussein and Charles Pellat, *Chéhérazade, personnage littéraire* (Algiers: Société Nationale d'Edition et de Diffusion, 1981). Muhsin Jassim Ali's work, *Sheherazade in England: A Study of Nineteenth-Century English Criticism of the Arabian Nights* (Washington, D.C.: Three Continents Press, 1981), is an excellent source for the period in question.

7. Richard F. Burton, *The Book of the Thousand Nights and a Night* (Burton Club Edition).

8. Georges May, *Les Mille et une nuits d'Antoine Galland* (Paris: Presses Universitaires de France, 1986). On the questionable nature of May's entire enterprise, see Fedwa Malti-Douglas, review of Georges May, *Journal of the American Oriental Society* III (1) (1991): p. 196.

9. Produced by Fritz Freleng, Warner Brothers.

10. *Kitāb Alf Layla wa-Layla*, ed. Muhsin Mahdi (Leiden: E. J. Brill, 1984), I, 56–72. Mahdi's edition does not contain the epilogue of the frame. See also *Alf Layla wa-Layla* (Cairo, Maṭbaʿat Būlāq, 1252/1836), I, 2–6, II, 619;

Burton, *The Thousand Nights*, I, 1–24, X, 54–62. For a gender reading of the frame of the *Nights*, see Fedwa Malti-Douglas, *Woman's Body, Woman's Word: Gender and Discourse in Arabo-Islamic Writing* (Princeton, N.J.: Princeton University Press, 1991), pp. 11–28.

11. For the sake of consistency, I retain, when not quoting, the transcribed form of Shahrazād rather than Phelps's "Scheherazade."

12. Phelps, "Scheherazade," p. 170.

13. Ibid., p. 173.

14. Malti-Douglas, *Woman's Body, Woman's Word*, pp. 11–28.

15. Phelps, "Scheherazade," p. 167.

16. Ibid.

17. Ibid., pp. 167, 168.

18. For the importance of the visual here, see Malti-Douglas, *Woman's Body, Woman's Word*, pp. 11–28.

19. Sabry Hafez, "Intentions and Realisation in the Narratives of Nawal El-Saadawi," *Third World Quarterly* 11 (3) (July 1989): p. 195.

20. *Alf Layla*, ed. Mahdi, I, p. 61.

21. Phelps, "Scheherazade," p. 169.

22. Ibid., pp. 169–70.

23. See Malti-Douglas, *Woman's Body, Woman's Word*, pp. 11–28.

24. *Alf Layla*, ed. Mahdi, I, pp. 58–60.

25. Phelps, "Scheherazade," p. 173.

26. For the larger implications of the traditional ending see Malti-Douglas, *Woman's Body, Woman's Word*, pp. 11–28.

27. See John Barth, *Chimera* (New York: Fawcett Crest Books, 1972), pp. 9–46; Négib Bouderbala, *Les Nouveaux voyages de Sindbad: Chez les Amazones et autres étranges peuplades* (Casablanca: Editions Le Fennec, 1987). This is not really the case, for example, with the modern Arabic versions of Ṭāhā Ḥusayn and Tawfīq al-Ḥakīm. Their texts downplay the issue of sexual politics and concentrate instead on either updating Shahrazād's message or decontextualizing her into a more universal heroine. See Ṭāhā Ḥusayn, *Aḥlām Shahrazād* (Cairo: Dār al-Maʿārif, n.d.); Tawfīq al-Ḥakīm, *Shahrazād* (Cairo: Maktabat al-Ādāb, n.d.). See also, Aboul-Hussein and Pellat, *Chéhérazade*, pp. 33–39.

28. Edgar Allan Poe, "The Thousand and Second Tale of Scheherazade," in his *Short Stories*, Greenwich Unabridged Library Classics (New York: Chatham River Press, 1981), pp. 491–502.

29. See, for example, Hisam Sharabi, *Neopatriarchy: A Theory of Distorted Change in Arab Society* (New York: Oxford University Press, 1988), p. 33. On El Saadawi, see Allen Douglas and Fedwa Malti-Douglas, "Reflections of a Feminist: Conversation with Nawal al-Saadawi," in *Opening the Gates: A Century of Arab Feminist Writing*, ed. Margot Badran and Miriam Cooke (London and Bloomington: Virago and Indiana University Press, 1990), pp. 394–404; and on El Saadawi's fiction, see Malti-Douglas, *Woman's Body, Woman's Word*, pp.

111–43. See also my recent study, *Men, Women and God(s): Nawal El Saadawi and Arab Feminist Poetics* (Berkeley and Los Angeles: University of California Press, 1995).

30. I deal with these issues in *Men, Women and God(s)*, pp. 91–117.

31. Hafez, "Intentions and Realisation," p. 195.

32. Al-Saʿdāwī, *Suqūṭ*, p. 14.

33. Ibid., pp. 83–88.

34. Ibid., p. 83.

35. Ibid., p. 85.

36. Ibid., pp. 93–96.

37. The complex relationship that then develops between the Imam and Bint Allāh does pick up elements of the fantastic that bring it close in spirit to some of the narratives in the Arabic *Nights*. But these components pull us away from Shahrazād herself, hence are not analyzed here.

38. Al-Saʿdāwī, *Suqūṭ*, p. 94.

39. Ibid.

40. In certain medieval anecdotes, it is clear that physically sharing her husband with another wife was not something a woman relished. See, for example, al-Rāghib al-Iṣfahānī, *Muḥāḍarāt al-Udabāʾ wa Muḥāwarāt al-Shuʿarāʾ wal-Bulaghāʾ* (Beirut: Dār Maktabat al-Ḥayāt, n.d.), II, 267; and for a discussion, Malti-Douglas, *Woman's Body, Woman's Word*, pp. 40–41.

41. Al-Saʿdāwī, *Suqūṭ*, p. 53.

42. *Alf Layla*, ed. Mahdi, I, p. 66.

43. Fatima Mernissi, *Chahrazad n'est pas marocaine* (Casablanca: Editions le Fennec, 1988), p. 9.

44. Al-Saʿdāwī, *Suqūṭ*, pp. 93–96.

45. Ibid., p. 99.

46. Ibid., p. 91.

47. Ibid., pp. 53–54.

Index

Note: Italicized page numbers indicate illustrations or tables. *Nights* is used as a general abbreviation for the various titles of the *Arabian Nights*. Stories and tales of the *Nights* are indexed as "tale of . . ." MS and MSS are used in subheadings as abbreviations for manuscript and manuscripts.

narrative world (*continued*)
184–85, 200; in *Suquṭ al-Imām* (El Saadawi), 355; in tale of the King of China's steward, 304–6, 309
narrators, xii, 245–46, 301–3, 330
night stories, 56–57, 69–70
ninth-century fragment of *Nights*, *44–47*; overview of, 21–25; additions to, 31–43; collection represented by, 65–66; decipherment and translation of, 25–31; and early history of *Nights*, 71–73; provenience and date of, 43–54, 60; script of, 52; and Sindbād the Sage, 66–67; textual nature of, 59
Nöldeke, Theodor, 108–9, 166n. 129
Norden, E., 139–40
novels. *See also* romance genre: aretalogical tale and, 154n. 33; Greek, 140–45, 345n. 20; nineteenth-century, compared to *Nights*, 228; tale of Sindbād the Sailor as progenitor of, 343n. 11

Odysseus, character of, 227
Oriental Institute manuscript. *See* ninth-century fragment of *Nights*

paper. *See also* ninth-century fragment of *Nights*: documents, Arabic, 21–22, 48, 54; manufacture and use of, 48, 50–54, 76n. 31, 77n. 33
Parker, Patricia, 177
Payne, John, viii, 4–5, 267–68
Persian *munāẓarāt*, 162–63n. 107
Phelps, Ethel Johnston, 347–53
Poe, Edgar Allen, 7–8, 353
poems, role of in *Nights*, 252–53
Popper, William, 108–9
popularity of *Nights*, 87–88, 106–7, 211
Porter, William S. (O. Henry), 14, 20n. 38
Portor, Laura S., 12
prologue. *See* frame story
prosimetrical form of *Nights* tales, 148
protagonists, in Greek and Arabic stories, 144, 146, 160n. 87, 198–200, 221–22n. 57

Qāʿat Sūdūn ʿAbd al-Raḥmān (Dār Sūdūn Ibn ʿAbd al-Raḥmān), 111–12, 116
Qānsūh al-Ghawrī, monetary policy of, 117–18
Qurʾāns, parchment, 74n. 1

realism, in *Nights*, 178, 184, 206, 224n. 78
recensions, 87–104, 107, 299
Recognitions of Clement, 156n. 57, 157n. 68
regeneration of tales, 259–62
Reinhardt manuscript, 98–100
Robertson, D. W., 174
rogue tales, 208–9
romance genre: comfort in, 210–11; framing technique in, 180, 205–6; French, 219n. 37; Gothic, 225n. 86; idea of, 174–75; motifs in, 142–45, 179, 186–91, 193–96, 200–201, 208–10; narrative and, 181–86, 200–202, 206, 220n. 38; origin of, 5–6; other genres and, 207–11; protagonists in, 198–200; and realism, 224n. 78; scholars on, 176–77; voice in, 197–98, 203–5
Russel, P., 267

Sabbagh, Michel, 126
Ṣabbāgh manuscript, 91–92
Ṣakhr and Solomon legend, 286
Scheherazade: aesthetics of, as storyteller, 12–13; companion of, 79n. 57; and conclusion of *Nights*, 90–100; first tale of, 104n. 32; Grotzfeld on, x; in Habicht's